ALL BAGS

GO TO

CLEVELAND

ALL BAGS

GO TO

CLEVELAND

C.S. Hale

ALL BAGS GO TO CLEVELAND

By C.S. Hale

Copyright @ C.S. Hale

All rights reserved

ISBN: 978-1-948670-04-3

First Edition

Edited by Jody Wallace at www.jodywallace.com
And Jessica Nelson at Indie Books Gone Wild www.ibgw.net
Interior design by Gaynor Smith of Indie Books Gone Wild
www.ibgw.net
Cover design by Melissa Stevens at theillustratedauthor.net

Published in the United States of America

ACKNOWLEDGEMENTS

First of all, thank you to my fabulous beta readers who stuck with me through Cleveland's long journey — Maureen, Megan, and Laurie. You inspired me to keep going.

Holly Ingraham — Your excitement for Cleveland was contagious. Thanks to you, I knew I had something special.

Bethany Adams — You keep me sane. And push me to be a better writer. Thank you for all that you are.

CJ Redwine —You helped bring Angela to life in so many ways. I'm sorry the pie episode is now immortalized.

Marc — Thanks for helping me with the bowling. You were there for so much of Cleveland's beginning. Thank you for believing in me.

Thank you also to Melissa and Gaynor for bringing Cleveland to life in such gorgeous ways.

And thank you readers for going on this journey. May you find lots of love and laughter.

For Maureen

Angela wouldn't be half as fun without you.

Unused magic pressed against Angela's fingers. She flexed her hand, trying to dispel the ache. Much longer and the magic would escape and seek a target of its own. At least Jackson, working at the next counter, wouldn't care what happened. Even if she did.

Even if Alex would.

Angela squeezed her eyes shut. She would *not* think about him.

The next passenger in the queue stepped up to her counter, his phone tucked inside his passport.

"Good evening, sir." Angela raised a smile to hide her distress as she took the items and gave him a onceover. Northwestern sweatshirt. Jeans. Probably tennis shoes, though she couldn't see them from her vantage point. Not your typically dressed first-class passenger, but his luggage proclaimed that he was no frequent-flyer upgrade. The Louis Vuitton garment bag ran around two grand and his Henk rolling briefcase started at twenty. If he could drop that kind of cash on his luggage, then the ten thousand-dollar ticket wouldn't be a problem.

He flashed her a grin of his own. "Evening."

Angela reached out with her magic and probed his mind. Dave had studied the documents Xavier had sent him. It would be a challenge, but he was up for anything.

Why not? Focusing on the sparks of energy skittering along her fingers, she sent her magic into the printer. Angela might look like the cover model she'd once been but no one would guess that Windsor's check-in counter was currently staffed by a pair of gremlins. Dave's day—or rather night and morning—were about to become a little more exciting than he'd imagined. Dave would have a nice, relaxing flight to London while his garment bag went to Cleveland.

All bags went to Cleveland. The majority of the misdirected ones, anyway. A necessity to keep her cousin Wendell busy. Why Wendell had chosen to settle in Cleveland, Angela never understood. Something about the river, he had once said, but it probably had more to do with Cleveland not being a top tourist destination, leaving people to scratch their heads and wonder what could possibly have gone wrong. Besides, Windsor encouraged her to create a little chaos. Why else would a gremlin have founded an airline after World War II? And since her great-uncle had created the company, she couldn't get canned. Unlike that last modeling job in Paris.

Angela looped the routing tag through the strap of Dave's garment bag and tamped down the tendrils of guilt rising in her gut. It needed to be done. It was this bag or some mishap not of her choosing. Besides, who in their right mind would check a Louis Vuitton garment bag? First class contained specially built closets in which to hang them. She searched Dave's thoughts again.

Where have I seen her before?

Angela snapped right back out and jerked her head down. She attached the claim sticker to his boarding pass and handed it to Dave, keeping her focus on the counter. Hopefully, her smile hid the panic now whirring in her chest like the engines that would take Dave across the Atlantic. "Enjoy your flight, Mr. Ford."

"Always do." With a small salute, Dave headed toward the security queue. What were the chances he'd be so cheerful in the morning?

The bolt slid home on her door with a satisfying *thunk*. Angela kicked off her shoes and padded into her tiny kitchen. Just thirty-five seconds and solace would be hers. She placed a frozen brownie into the microwave and watched it do one full spin before slipping off the light blue jacket of her uniform. She hung it up in the hall closet and pulled the pins out of her chignon. Shaking her hair out with a sigh, Angela tossed the pins into a pewter bowl sitting on the hall table. Of course, what passed for a hall in her small apartment in New York's Chelsea neighborhood was really just a bit of wall between the door and the closet, a closet large enough for a mere four coats on the bar and a snug-fitting Game of Life on the top shelf.

Angela ran her fingers through her hair and stepped back into her kitchen nook. She retrieved the brownie and carried it back to the sofa where she curled up and tucked her legs beneath her. Her eyes rolled back as she bit into the warm, gooey deliciousness. Heaven. Those Fat Witch bakers really did do magical things with their creations.

Angela savored the hint of salt in the chocolate, the creaminess as it melted in her mouth, and the perfect balance of goo and fudge. Chocolate was her biggest weakness. Her parents would have said it was her love of humans but Angela considered that a strength. She was more careful about how she used her magic than any gremlin she knew. With chocolate, though, she threw caution to the confectioners.

The wrapper crinkled, echoing in the empty apartment as Angela dabbed her finger against it, collecting every last morsel. She licked the crumbs from her finger and wadded up the plastic. Chocolate hadn't helped. Maybe a shower would ease the sting that had settled into her soul since the night Alex had dumped her.

Until two months ago, Angela had been dating Alex Marriot, a human she had met at a club one night. He had recognized Angela from her famous vodka ad and introduced himself. Angela gave him a little test, making the clasp holding up the halter dress of the woman sitting behind her fail. The woman had been asking for it with her thoughts of "stupid cow" and wondering what she could do to steal Alex away. Alex sat there, eyebrows raised, as the woman squealed and flailed about, gathering up what was left of her dress and her dignity. He'd gotten a good look at what Cow Woman was offering but his attention quickly returned to Angela. Later that evening when he'd asked Angela out, she'd said yes.

Her parents had hated Alex. Of course, they hated Angela's "obsession" with humans. Both successful businesspeople in the human world—as most gremlins are—Angela's parents viewed humans as merely clients, clients who provided opportunities to create mischief, at which they were masters.

However, it wasn't her parents and their barely contained displeasure that had finally driven Alex off after nine months. As much as they disliked Angela's decision to have human friends, her family and the gremlin community left them alone. It was Angela's magic—or rather her lack of control over it—that had incited Alex's exodus. Not that he knew it. Angela needed to use her gremlin magic on a consistent basis or it would back up and spill over, flowing undirected. And overflow it had since childhood.

Her magic was a curse. Something that existed only to cause harm. No matter how she clamped down on it, hiding it away, eventually, like an overstuffed suitcase, it could no longer be contained. It would burst forth, sizzling any nearby electronics or weak metal. Things would go haywire, creating the chaos that had caused Alex to leave.

He had constantly complained about the disasters that surrounded her. Angela bit her lip. Just like nearly everyone she had met while modeling. The harder she tried to keep that part of herself hidden away, the more magic she bottled up. The more magic she bottled up, the bigger the "catastrophe."

You're a magnet for disaster! I'm done with this! Done with you! Your pretty face isn't worth the trouble.

Alex's words still echoed in her ears in the stillness of her apartment. Or on the lonely subway ride home. Words she had to admit were true—she couldn't be trusted.

Pressing her teeth together, Angela leaned into the shower and turned it on high.

A few days later, her best friends Belle and Kate exchanged a nervous glance as she approached their table in the crowded restaurant.

"Uh, oh. What's up?" Angela asked, sliding onto her chair.

Kate shifted her attention to her wine glass. Her long auburn curls created a screen from which Angela heard, "Um…Myles told me that Alex dedicated a song to you today on Facebook." Kate's artist husband, Myles, had kept Alex as one of his "friends" even after the breakup. Alex had been and still was a valuable client.

Angela's heart pressed against her ribs as if the space confining it had somehow shrunk. "Which song?"

Belle and Kate looked at each other again.

Kate swallowed. "Muse's 'Supermassive Black Hole'."

Lovely. According to the lyrics, Alex thought she'd caught him under false pretenses. Sucked him in to his doom. *Jerk.*

"I think you should claim it," Belle announced.

Kate and Angela whipped their heads around to look at her.

Belle shrugged, her perfectly manicured eyebrows mirroring the motion. "It's a powerful song. What woman doesn't want to be powerful?"

Angela did have siren genes—the Lorelei was one of her mother's ancestors—but in this case, Alex had been the one to pursue her and not the other way around, making his accusation sting even more.

Kate frowned. Her head began to bob. "I like it. Alex is just bitter because he had this view of you as the prize for his perfectly ordered world." Kate tried to hide a grin. "But we all know that nothing is ever perfect when you're around."

Angela slumped forward on the table and groaned.

"It's true," Belle added. "But it's one of the things we love about you. Something always happens. Keeps us on our toes."

Magic built, pulsing around Angela's fingers, fueled by the emotions churning away in her. She hated that not only were her friends right but that they soon would have proof. Either she could search for an outlet or the magic would just pick one of its own.

With a weak smile, Angela sat up and scanned the darkly lit restaurant, seeking a target. Candles flickered at every table, bathing the faces of the diners in a yellow glow. A waiter, spotting Angela, headed her direction. *Not him.* A man sat texting a few tables over, focused on his phone, while his girlfriend chatted away. *Possibly.* Then she saw José, the bartender, shaking up a martini while staring at the tits of the woman in front of him. The woman was doing her best to make sure he saw as much of them as possible. José's finger wasn't over the top of the shaker, but the side.

Angela turned her head away and ran her fingers through her hair, trying to look casual. A moment later, the top flew off the shaker, drenching both José and the woman in chocolatini. José stood in open-mouthed horror, clutching the near-empty container.

Heads turned toward the source of the shriek. The woman stood, dripping from head to toe like a well-dressed scarecrow caught in a squall. Belle and Kate returned their attention to Angela, eyebrows rising as they fixed their gazes on her.

"Like that was my fault," Angela said, a blush rising at the lie.

"No." Belle shook her head with a laugh. Her dark brown hair rippled with the motion, making Belle look even more like the Botticelli angel Kate often compared her to. "But I love that it always seems to happen when you're around."

"So fuck him," Kate said, returning to their original topic. "Alex is rich and attractive but the man has a stick up his ass."

The waiter glided up to their table. "What can I get for you, Angela?"

Angela shifted her gaze back to the bar. Nice Tits had recovered enough to toss her glass of wine on José and was now storming towards the door. "I'll have my usual pomegranate martini if you think José can keep the top on." José grabbed the front of his shirt and began to wring it out, showing off his chiseled abs. "On the other hand, maybe I'd be safer with a glass of cabernet."

Angela swung by Whole Foods and picked up a bottle of wine on her way home. Sure, she'd had two glasses at dinner, but maybe a third would finally dull her senses. Kate had Myles waiting for her and Belle had Joe. Her own apartment would be empty. Not even a stupid, silent goldfish waited for her. On the plus side, she had yet to become a crazy cat lady.

Dropping her keys in the dish, Angela kicked off her shoes, and went into the kitchen to open the wine. The rich aroma of pinot noir filled her senses, mirroring the chemical magic of chocolate, and raised a smile. Didn't they both contain poly-something-or-other? Nose in her glass, Angela padded into the living room. She flung herself onto the sofa and turned on the TV.

A sad, blond woman, guzzling wine and singing "All by Myself" into a rolled-up magazine, filled the screen. Angela's eyes flicked to her own glass. Only the fear of wine stains kept it from becoming air-borne. She grabbed the remote and mashed the off button. The screen went dark but the lyrics continued to play in her head. Why did that song have to be so memorable?

Her finger flew as she scrolled through the playlist on her phone. *Lady Gaga.* She could fill the apartment with the sounds of a club. Putting in her ear buds, she turned up the volume until the music drowned out even her thoughts. Angela played the song over and over, losing herself in the hypnotic beat. Belle's words eventually bubbled up to compete with Lady Gaga's lyrics.

Claim it. Be powerful.

Lady Gaga's woman was drunk off her ass but wasn't beating herself up about it. She was convinced she'd be fine and was determined to lose herself in the moment. Angela was a supernatural being able to control elements of the physical world as well as men's hearts, should she choose. Talk about powerful.

Angela hit the pause button. Claim it. Be the woman who led men astray.

Picking up her empty wine glass, she marched with a determined step into the kitchen. But, as her palm smacked the cork into the open wine bottle, the resolve that had filled her moments before dripped away.

Angela's fingers curled around the neck of the bottle. A shower and some sleep. She could claim her heritage tomorrow.

Angela spent the next few days taking Belle's advice to heart and worked on embracing her siren genes. Okay, she *thought* about embracing her inner siren. But she did work much harder at actually using her magic and assuming a more gremlin-like sense of humor. For instance, she sent Barry Carnak's luggage to the Bahamas though Barry himself was going to Cleveland. The poor man had been so stressed out about his job in concrete sales. At least his luggage got the chance to travel somewhere warm and sunny.

She didn't break with tradition when it came to dinner that evening and headed to her parents' as soon as she got off work. Angela inhaled as she opened the door to her parents' apartment. Her mother had made her famous chicken paprikash.

"Hey, sis." Her brother Nicky came in behind her and slung an arm around her shoulders.

Angela slipped an arm around his waist. "Evening, Nicky. What have you been up to lately?"

Nicky's blue eyes twinkled. "No good, as usual. Speaking of which, did you hear that poor Alex had to have his Quattroporte 'round to the mechanics? Seems the engine mysteriously seized up."

"Nicky…"

"Sorry, Ang, but no one insults my sister and gets away with it."

Angela melted a little until Nicky added, "You realize that if he'd been a gremlin none of this would have happened."

"Don't start." Angela glared at him. "Especially here. I don't want Mum to get any ideas." A matchmaking mother was the last thing she wanted.

"Angela, dear!" her mother called as she and Nicky entered the dining room. Knots eased from Angela's shoulders. With its white walls, panels of yellow wallpaper sprinkled with blue birds, and wide windows that looked out on the treetops, this was her favorite room in the house. "You're looking well." Angela's mother drew her into a hug.

"Hi, Mum." Her mother, Evelyn, carried the perfect poise of an English aristocrat, along with the startling blue eyes and blond bombshell looks that she'd passed down to her daughter. Nicky was tall and dark like their father, who could have passed for a Hungarian prince. But where Nicky's eyes were blue like their mother's, their father, Damon, had brown eyes like molten chocolate. Eyes that would have given most wives cause for concern.

"Come and sit and tell me about your day," Evelyn said, leading Angela over to the table which nearly groaned under the weight of the paprikash, mushroom soup, parslied potatoes, and sweet and sour red cabbage. Though she had grown up in England, Evelyn—whose parents had decided on old-fashioned pronunciation of Eve-lyn just for the confusion it would cause—had learned to cook Hungarian after she met Damon at Cambridge. Born and raised in Hungary, Angela's father had missed the flavors of his native land. He often told people that it was Evelyn's pork szelet that had won him over and not her captivating eyes.

The loaf of félbarna—half white, half rye—and a platter of desserts at the other end of the table had come from the Hungarian bakery. Her mother did have a full-time job, after all. Evelyn Events was *the* agency you hired if you wanted your wedding to go off without a hitch. Amazing opportunities dropped into the laps of her brides—strange how Evelyn knew when there'd been a cancelation or computer glitch she could take advantage of—though bridezillas need not apply.

Since her mother worked most weekends, Wednesday night had become family dinner night. Even though she and Nicky had moved out, their parents still expected that they would come to dinner if they were in town. Folklore about gremlins being solitary creatures was a myth they did nothing to correct. Sure, there were some oddballs, like Cousin Wendell, but he was the exception and not the rule. Most gremlins centered their lives around a family core.

Angela threw Nicky a glance, silently asking him if their parents knew about Alex's dedication. His shoulders lifted in a barely perceptible shrug.

"I did my best to keep Wendell busy today," Angela answered. "Though I did send a gentleman to Cleveland and his bags to Nassau."

Her father chuckled. "Hinting he needed a vacation?"

"Of course."

"You've got a lot to live up to," Nicky said as he piled potatoes onto his plate. "No one has yet matched Cousin Harold's feat." Nicky wiped away a tear. "Man, I would have loved to see those guys trying to bat with acrobatic ribbons." Harold had switched Cricket Romania's gear with that of the Chinese National Acrobatic Troupe.

"How about you, Nicky?" her father asked. "What's new in the world of commodities?"

"Chaos as usual. It's been simply wonderful, no thanks to me. I haven't needed to push things along for weeks. Speaking of which, I saw your book is still at the top of the charts."

Even her father found ways to use his magic creatively. A top literary agent, Damon had a knack for picking out authors and stories that would become runaway bestsellers, projects that other agents had written off as hopeless. His slush pile was huge, though it offered authors a dilemma. Damon never asked for manuscripts that excited other agents. If the movers and shakers wanted your story, then he wouldn't touch it. If no one else seemed to want it and Damon did, then the book's success was assured, as his latest find perfectly illustrated.

Pigs Can Fly, a romance about two Iowa pig farmers, had been number one on several lists, including *The New York Times* and *USA Today*, for several weeks. Her father had let it sit in his slush pile until the author had accumulated over a hundred rejection notices. Once his offer of representation had gone public, agents kicked themselves and editors electronically beat down his door. *Pigs* had been given an initial print run of 100,000 copies. Now in its fourth printing, it was a huge success.

"I may have been responsible for influencing twenty or so individuals to create buzz for Oliver but nothing else."

"Do you have the Berman bridesmaids under control?" Angela asked her mother. At least that situation was less depressing. For Angela, anyway. Just four days remained before Ally Berman's wedding at the Mandarin Oriental. While the bride was a delight, her fourteen bridesmaids were proving a challenge, even for Evelyn.

Her mother shuddered. "The magic I've used…I don't know how a *griloss* would have handled that group. Twenty years and nothing like this. Thank God it's over after Saturday."

Her mother had magically vetted Ally before taking her on, but Ally had apparently been oblivious to the true nature of her friends and family, providing Evelyn with quite the surprise.

It was a small dose of comfort. Angela had spent weeks beating herself up about having not discerned Alex's true nature, for having not spent more time digging into his head. She'd worried that she had only seen what she'd wanted to see or, even worse, that his association with *her* had turned him into an ass. But Evelyn had had no clue what she was in for with the Berman wedding so maybe more time inside Alex's mind wouldn't have changed much.

Two hours later, Angela was as stuffed as the bag of leftovers she carried.

Nicky shrugged into his coat. "Share a taxi?"

"Sure. See you next week, Mum." Angela kissed her mother on the cheek and then turned and hugged her father. "Bye, Dad."

"Bye, Angel."

"Think they know?" Angela asked Nicky again as they waited for the elevator.

Nicky huffed and reached out a finger to punch the button again. "Does it matter? It only proves their point."

Angela threw her brother a sideways glance. "And what point would that be?"

"You've got to quit wasting time with humans."

As her mouth dropped open to protest, Nicky cut her off. "Kate and Belle are fine. Great fun to hang out with. And they seem to get you. But dating? No human is going to want to put up with the magic long term. And you're a walking disaster, bottling it up until it explodes out everywhere. Alex proves the point. He's an ass but a perfect illustration."

Angela glowered at Nicky as the elevator dinged and the doors opened.

"Fine. I'll keep that in mind."

"You do that, sis," Nicky said. "I hate to see you waste all of your talent."

"Talent...right," Angela said. *More like a curse.*

With her current work rotation, Friday was the first day of Angela's weekend. Her schedule today consisted of a pedicure in front of the TV, lunch with Kate, and then browsing Chelsea Market before taking in a movie. As she finished off her last pinky toe with Dior #338, her cousin Julia called.

"Hey, cous! What's up?" Angela checked the clock. Julia must have just finished her shift at Heathrow.

Julia chuckled. "I had one of yours go through a little bit ago."

"How do you know it was one of mine?" Angela screwed the cap back on the polish. Tendrils of guilt snaked into her stomach

"Said his bag had gone to Cleveland."

"Ah." The guilt hardened into a lump.

Julia's voice gathered all the calm of a racehorse at the starting gate. "But here's the best part, he asked me to ticket his luggage not for New York but, wait for it…Cleveland!"

Angela gasped. "What!"

"Yes. Said he figured that since his luggage had gone to Cleveland instead of London on his way over, maybe it would make it to New York if I tried to send it to Cleveland instead."

"Where is his luggage going?" Angela asked.

"New York."

Angela tsked. "Poor Wendell. Fewer bags for him to reroute." Wendell surely would have been happier in London or Atlanta where there were more bags to cause mischief with.

"No," Julia said. "Poor Mr. Ford. He was really hoping I'd do it. I checked."

Angela opened her mouth to reply but it stuck in her throat. *Mr. Ford? The guy in the sweatshirt with the Louis Vuitton?* Her words squeaked when they finally came out. "What was he thinking?"

"It was like he was playing the lottery," Julia said. "He truly wanted to see if it would work and was disappointed that I wouldn't go along with it."

"Strange man."

"Speaking of men." Concern filled Julia's voice. "Nicky texted me that your ex had gone totally gonzo. Did he attack you or something?"

Angela sighed. "I guess you could say he attacked me electronically. Dedication on Facebook linked to a YouTube video."

"Uh oh. Which one?"

Angela ground her teeth. "Supermassive Black Hole."

"Ouch! That was cold. Though…" Angela could practically hear the gears turning in Julia's head. "You *are* descended from sirens. Leading men to their doom. You could just say that he was tapping into your true nature."

"Julia!"

"No one escapes the pull of our Angela." Julia giggled. "You should just turn on the charm and have all of New York salivating after you. Claim your heritage. Be the powerful woman."

Angela began to sense a theme. "Belle said something similar."

"See! And she doesn't even know your true nature. Or does she?"

"No, I haven't told them. They know that things happen when I'm around but what human would guess what we truly are?"

"Even Kate? After all these years?"

That was a sobering thought. What if Kate figured it out? "No, she just thinks that I'm a magnet for disaster."

"And she loves you anyway."

"Yes, she does," Angela said with a sigh.

"So you just need to find a man that thinks the same way. There are lots of hot gremlins out there. They don't all look like Wendell."

Angela shivered. Wendell could have been hired as a goblin for the *Harry Potter* movies.

"I know," Angela said. "I'm related to one. And don't you go giving my mother any ideas. Last thing I need is a parade of potential husbands at Wednesday night dinners. I need a break from men for a while."

"A break in London, perhaps?" Julia asked hopefully.

"That would be wonderful," Angela said. "But no. I'm staying put. It would be too much like running away. Not to mention it would all be waiting here for me when I got back."

"I can dream. No one's as fun to take to high tea as you are."

A gentle laugh filled Angela's belly. "I miss you, too."

Angela rung off. She fanned her toes, shivering as a sense of déjà vu curled in her stomach. A break in London. Definitely, the last thing she needed.

"You owe me."

Angela glanced up from her computer screen. Dave Ford stood in front of her. The blood drained from her face. "Do I?" She raised her "helpful" smile.

"Yes." Dave handed over his passport and put the Louis Vuitton garment bag on the scale. "Last time, you sent my bag to Cleveland."

"The system isn't perfect," Angela said, punching Dave's information into the computer. "Things do happen sometimes."

"You control the system. I think you owe me a glass of wine for having to find a tailor at six a.m. I had a nine o'clock business meeting and just my jeans and sweatshirt."

"Hmm. By that reckoning, I think I'd owe the tailor for having to get you a functional suit so quickly at that early hour."

"I tipped him £100. Least you can do is buy me a glass of wine in return."

Angela lifted her gaze. Dave—all six feet of him with his fabulous hair—had a hopeful expression on his face.

"I'm not in the habit of buying strange men alcohol."

Dave stuck his hand out. "Hi. Dave Ford. Business traveler." Angela laughed. "All I'm asking for is a glass of Malbec. Or maybe pinot noir. Small price to pay in comparison to my having to fight off jet lag via acupuncture."

"Acupuncture?"

Dave shrugged. "It was early for the tailor. His aim wasn't quite what it could have been."

Angela dipped into Dave's mind. The tailor *had* stabbed him a couple of times. And Dave was playing with her. He wanted to see what she'd do.

She sent her magic into the right wheel of a suitcase passing outside the queue. It froze up, stopping the bag's forward momentum. A startled squawk came from the suitcase's owner as her feet continued forward while her arm remained behind, bending her dangerously backward and creating a jam in the almost orchestrated flow of travelers.

"A blood offense," Angela said, her attention on the resulting commotion. "Hmm. I guess as a representative of Windsor Airlines, I could apologize for your pain and inconvenience with a glass of wine. What did you have in mind?"

"I get back from Chicago on Wednesday. How about Wednesday night?"

"I'm already booked Wednesday. How about Thursday?"

"Boyfriend?" Dave asked.

"How about Thursday?" Angela repeated.

"A woman of mystery," Dave said. "Okay, Thursday. The wine bar on Eighth in the Village…about seven?"

"See you then. Enjoy your flight to Chicago, Mr. Ford." Angela handed him the baggage claim tag.

"Is my bag going to Chicago or Cleveland?" Dave asked, slipping it into his pocket.

Angela offered him a mysterious smile as she put his garment bag on the conveyor behind her. "You'll just have to find out when you get there."

"Good," Dave called out, already moving toward the stream of passengers snaking toward the security line. "I love surprises."

"Hey, Ang," said Belle. "Joe's just been assigned this big audit thing that's due on Monday. He's having to sneak in sleep and bathroom breaks so there's no way he can even think about dinner Thursday night and I made reservations at Le Bernardin for dinner before Kate's opening. Well, I guess it's really John Consuelos's opening and—"

"Crap!" Angela cried, interrupting Belle's monologue.

"You forgot, didn't you?"

"Yes! Crap. Shit!"

"What did you do?" Belle asked with a sigh.

Angela took her phone in both hands and beat it against her forehead. Not only had she totally forgotten the show that Kate had spent the last three months slaving over for the art gallery she worked for but Angela realized she had made a "date" for the same night. She couldn't even call to reschedule. Dave hadn't thought to give her his phone number and she hadn't asked. She could have probably had a peek at his information in the Windsor client database, but with all the safeguards Windsor had installed as a result of some identity theft at one of their competitors, someone was sure to find out she'd looked. Ask questions as to why she was checking up on their customers on days when they weren't actually flying. Angela tried to suppress a shiver.

"You made other plans," she heard Belle say as she brought the phone back to her ear.

"Yes!"

"And those plans consist of…?"

"A date," Angela mumbled. Making plans to meet someone for a glass of wine was a date, right? What had she been thinking?

"You're late?" Belle asked. Then she gasped. "Oh, my God! Did Alex get you pregnant?"

"No!" Angela shouted. She pressed her teeth together and inhaled deeply. "I have a *date*. What did you think? I made plans to go to some late-night obstetrician's appointment?"

"That would be weird," Belle said. "I don't know what I thought. But what else could be so horrible you'd react like that? A date, huh? What's so awful about that?"

"I don't want a date," Angela moaned.

"Angela, Angela, Angela. Why do you have a date if you don't want one?" Angela could tell Belle was trying desperately to keep the giggles at bay.

"It just kind of happened."

Belle erupted in laughter. When she was finally able to catch her breath, she took on the tone of a concerned therapist. "You poor thing. You want to share?"

Angela sighed. "It's a passenger. His bag got sent to Cleveland the last time he flew out of JFK."

"That town has some strange pull," Belle said. "Why do bags always go to Cleveland? Why can't they go to Paris…and then you have to go there to retrieve them?" Belle fell silent.

"Anyway," Angela said, sweeping away Belle's dreams of Paris. "He flew out again yesterday and told me that I owed him for the trouble the misdirection caused."

"Oh! So he talked you into taking him out. Just how expensive was one misdirected bag?"

"A glass of wine."

"That's not so bad," Belle said. "Unless you intend on making a night of it."

"No! One glass and then I'm out of there."

"So what's the problem? The opening's from six to nine. You'll miss out on dinner at Le Bernardin but…Dang! Now I don't have a dinner date."

"You could borrow Nicky," Angela offered. "He was already planning to swing by the opening. Plus, I've never known him to turn down an opportunity to dine at some swanky restaurant."

"I love that I can borrow your brother." Belle sighed. "If Joe ever let me have a one-off, forget Chris Hemsworth or Orlando Bloom, it would be Nicky."

Her brother did seem to have that effect on women. "Yes, well, I'd better double check that he's actually available." *Damn.* She'd have to tell him why she wasn't available. "And you do know that one-off thing works both ways. Do you know who Joe's is?"

"Charlize Theron. It's that perfume commercial where she walks along tossing away everything she's wearing. Heck, I get all hot watching that one too."

"TMI, Belle. TMI."

"Hey, that's what I thought walking through Times Square when your vodka ad was plastered there. I've seen you naked plenty of times, dressing you for all those photo shoots, but that was just embarrassing. I didn't know where to look."

"Fair enough." There had been more of herself on display than even Angela was comfortable with. It had to be the camera angle. "So, I'll have

Nicky give you a call and work out the details if he's available."

"How did you get talked into buying this guy a glass of wine?" Belle asked.

"It was the acupuncture."

"Huh?"

"He'd lost his clothes and the tailor who altered his replacement suit stabbed him with several pins."

Belle sighed heavily. "I love you but you really are one of the most gullible people I've ever met. That was a pick-up line. A good one, but a line nonetheless. So what does this guy look like? Is he eye candy, worth a glass of wine to view?"

"Um." Angela chewed on her lip. "No, not really. Brown hair, brown eyes. Cute, I guess in a kind of rugby player way. Kind of normal."

"Wait…some average guy off the street just talks you into buying him a glass of wine?"

"He may have been average looking—great hair, though. Nice curl to it—but he didn't have an average attitude." Being able to explain her dip into Dave's brain would have made this so much easier. "The bag that got misdirected was a Louis Vuitton. He could have housed it in the first class hanging rack but he didn't. It was almost like it was a roulette ball and he was trying to see where it would end up."

"And he wasn't an ass about it?"

"Actually, no," Angela said.

Belle blew out a low whistle. "Wow. That is strange. Maybe he is worth a glass of wine. I'd like to meet a guy that didn't take life so seriously."

Uh, oh. "Problems with Joe?"

"No. No! I'm in love but I'm not dead. Joe's great but an accountant takes life so seriously. And look at Myles—an amazing artist but so focused." Belle stopped, and Angela could practically hear the gears turning in her head. "Louis Vuitton, huh? You must have been working the first class counter. Maybe he's so rich he doesn't care if he loses them." Angela knew where this was going and wished she could just tell Belle that Dave had been thinking it was all just a game. "Be careful, Ang. You liked Alex's attitude and look where that got you."

Angela had learned her lesson. She had done her best to stay out of Alex's head and had missed so much by doing so. From now on she was going to use her "insider information."

"Point taken. But it's only wine. If he's awful, I can slam it and be out of there in five minutes. I don't have his number. He doesn't have mine. He can only track me down at work and—" Angela's fingers wiggled as she added in an evil tone, "I do have power over his luggage."

"Fine," said Belle. "Go on your date. Just don't be a modern-day Cinderella and stay too long at the ball. If you miss the opening, Kate will kill you." Angela and Belle both knew their friend would unleash her red-headed fury, and it certainly wouldn't be pretty.

"That gives me an emergency out." Angela mentally gave herself a little pep talk. She still wasn't quite sure how she'd gotten herself into this.

"Yes. And you'll call Nicky? I'm going even if I have to eat alone. And I'm not eating alone!"

Angela tossed two brownies into the microwave. One would definitely not be enough. After the chocolate worked its wonder, she finally gathered enough courage to call her brother. Once again, he was going to have to come to her rescue because she was "wasting time" with a human. Angela punched Nicky's phone number before the sugar rush wore off.

"Hey, Angela. What's up?"

"What do you have going on Thursday night?'

"Nothing I can't move around. What do you need?"

"Belle made reservations for dinner at Le Bernardin before that show Kate's coordinating. Joe got pulled into some big audit and can't go."

A heavy silence filled the air.

"Why…can't…you…go?" Nicky asked in a voice of complete steel. Magic crackled in the background. Something in Nicky's vicinity was going to break.

"Um. I have a date," Angela squeaked.

"A date." The word seemed to hang in the air. "I assume this would be with a human."

"It's not exactly a date. More like an appointment to buy someone a glass of wine." Angela winced and waited for the verbal axe to fall.

"With a human."

"Yes."

Angela held her breath as Nicky huffed, breathing deep, struggling with his anger.

"You never learn, do you?" he asked. "Alex burns you big time, totally humiliates you only last week, and yet here you go again."

"It's not a real date!" Angela said.

"Then cancel and go with Belle!"

"I don't actually know how to get ahold of him." Okay, she could if she really wanted to but Angela wasn't going to tell Nicky that.

"You are unbelievable," he said. "Yeah, I'll go. Lucky for you I like Belle and I love Le Bernardin. I'd been thinking about popping round the opening anyway. Are you going to blow that off, as well?"

"I'm not blowing off Belle. This came up only minutes ago and—"

"Whatever. You need to stop this, Ang. Either start loving them and leaving them or leave them completely alone. If you don't, you won't need to worry about Mum setting you up. I'll help her marry you off for your own good."

His was no idle threat. Arranged marriages were common in the magical community. Nicky had always worried about her, and Alex was proving to have been his final straw.

"One glass of wine and I'm out of there," she promised.

"How did you get yourself into this? No, wait. I don't want to know. Just…tell Belle I'll call her. And I don't want to talk to you until Wednesday when I suppose I'll have to explain to Mum and Dad that you've done it yet again!"

The line went dead. Nicky had hung up.

Angela chewed on her lip as she surveyed her wardrobe. What did one wear to a pseudo-date one wasn't sure one wanted, followed by hobnobbing with a bunch of art critics and collectors? Whatever she wore would need to withstand the highly critical eyes that would be present at the opening. No need for her to be judged as well as the art.

But Dave thinking that she was dressing to impress him? Bad idea.

Her hand finally closed around a soft gray dress made up of rows of fabric cut to resemble feathers. Belle had saved it for her when it went on sale in the Barneys boutique at Saks where Belle currently worked as a personal shopper. It skimmed Angela's curves and accentuated her long legs in a way that was sultry yet classy. She added a darker gray leather jacket and gray suede high-heeled gladiator sandals to complete the ensemble. Most people would have frozen in the cold night air of New York City in mid-March but gremlins never got hypothermia. A simple thought would change her body temperature. She'd barely notice the cold.

Angela hadn't seen or heard from Dave since Sunday even though she'd been working Wednesday when his flight arrived from Chicago. He'd left the airport without stopping by her counter.

Which was a good thing for him. Had he checked in, she would have canceled. Besides Kate's opening, the shocked response she'd received from Nicky and her friends had made her think meeting him for drinks wasn't such a good idea. At least Nicky had kept mum about her plans at the family dinner, choosing instead to glare at her whenever their parents weren't watching. Sure, she'd been childish, sticking her tongue out at him in return, but he'd been asking for it.

Kate had called Tuesday to ask Angela to come early to the gallery to hold her hand. When Angela confessed she had a date, Kate had been speechless.

"You forgot the opening?"

"Yes. No," Angela said. "I mean he'd wanted Wednesday and I'm never available on Wednesdays so I just automatically suggested the next day."

"And it never occurred to you to just say 'no'?"

"His first words were, 'You owe me'."

"No!" Kate breathed in horror.

"And I told him I don't buy strange men alcohol. And then he introduced himself as if I didn't already know what his name was what with his record there on the screen and in my hand. He was just so good natured about it and the lost luggage and the tailor stabbing him with pins—"

"Now you've lost me," Kate said.

"There was a bunch of stuff that went wrong for him and he was so cheerful about it."

"Ah. Quite the opposite of Alex."

Maybe that's what it was.

"So of course, you decide you need to make it up to him by buying him a glass of wine. All thoughts of me and my future in the art world pushed completely aside," Kate said.

"Um, yes, momentarily. But Myles will be there the whole time. And how can anything go wrong? It will be amazing and the whole show will be sold out before I get there at eight."

"Eight! Your date is smack in the middle of my opening?"

"Yes, but it's just one glass of wine, and then I'll be there before the food's been gobbled up by all the critics."

"I can't believe it," Kate said. "I can't believe you forgot I'm exhibiting my very first artist. And I can't believe you have a date. Did he blind you with his gorgeousness?"

"No," Angela said. "He's kind of average looking. But confident. Maybe it was the outrageousness of the whole thing. And I'm not really considering it a date. I'm buying the man one glass of wine, and then I'm out of there."

Kate sighed. "Just…bring him along if it gets to be more than that. You can both eat for free and maybe I'll talk him into buying something."

Angela zipped up her dress. *No way that's going to happen.*

She slid on the jacket and double checked the contents of her little silver purse—driver's license, credit card, keys, lipstick, compact, some emergency chocolate—and slipped the strap over her wrist. Squaring her shoulders, she went out to face her doom.

4

Angela put a hand against the stone wall and forced her feet down each step to the wine bar's basement entrance. Instinct tugged, telling her to flee to the gallery opening. But she couldn't. She would never stand someone up. Not on purpose, anyway.

At the bottom of the stairs, Angela wrapped her fingers around the handle, sucked in a breath, and opened the door. Patches of flickering light illuminated the darkness that greeted her. A tangle of voices filled the air along with the earthy scent of candles and wine.

A shape rose from the banquette side of a row of tables for two. Dave. Despite the suit coat he wore, his striped shirt was open at the neck. Dark-washed jeans toned his look down to dressy casual.

"You made it," he said as she came over. An awkward smile lifted the corners of his mouth.

"Yeah, well," Angela answered a little breathlessly. "I'm actually supposed to be somewhere else." Her shoulders lifted. "I guess I've got a bad memory."

"Yet you remembered this." Dave motioned to the chair across from him. "I'd pull it out for you but I'm kind of hemmed in here."

Angela sat down. The glass of wine in front of Dave contained a scant inch of liquid.

"I wasn't sure you'd show," Dave said in response to her glance. He took his seat and pulled the glass toward him. His gaze dropped to the ruby liquid. "Where should you be?"

Angela slipped the purse off her wrist and placed it on the table. "A gallery opening. One my best friend has spent the last three months putting together."

Dave's face fell. "Oh." He knocked back his glass and drained the rest of the wine. "There," he said, placing it back on the table. "One glass of wine."

His hand rose, flagging down the waiter.

"I hope you're calling him over to take our order," Angela said.

"I'm giving you an out. If I'd done it earlier, you wouldn't be here."

She had certainly wanted it, just moments ago, outside the door. But now, sitting across from him, curiosity pulled at her. "Maybe I don't want one."

Dave's eyes widened. "Why? Wouldn't that just get you more trouble?"

Angela shrugged again. "I'm good at trouble. It follows me wherever I go."

The waiter arrived at their table. "What can I get you?"

"A glass of pinot grigio," Angela told him.

"And for you, sir?" the waiter asked, turning to Dave. "Another glass of the same?"

"Sure," Dave said, staring at Angela. As the waiter left, he asked, "How does trouble follow you?"

Angela considered how to answer that. "You know how your bag went to Cleveland—and let me say that anyone who'd check a Louis Vuitton garment bag is just insane—stuff like that happens around me all the time. Things get lost, malfunction…people get pissed off."

"I didn't," said Dave.

"No, you didn't." Angela debated whether she should tell him how much she knew about his reaction to the lost bag. Her mouth curled as she remembered her conversation with Julia.

"What?" Dave asked.

"Instead you decided to try and outwit the system, Mr. Tag-My-Bag-For-Cleveland."

"You heard about that, did you?" Dave asked. A sheepish grin spread across his face.

"The girl at the counter in London was my cousin. You made her day."

"Yeah, well…I like to make a game out of trouble. But that's different from blowing off something my best friend has been working on for three months."

"Oh, I'm not blowing it off. Delaying my appearance, yes. But I'll be there before the hors d'oeuvres are gone."

"Then I should just drink my glass of wine and let you be on your way."

"You tried that already," Angela said. "I'm going to drink *my* glass of wine and then be on my way."

Dave stared at her with a mixture of disbelief and awe. Angela's gaze fell to the table. She racked her brain for something to fill the silence with.

"So Dave Ford, business traveler, what kind of business do you travel for?"

"Oh, um…" Dave turned his attention to his empty wine glass. "I'm a management consultant."

"Which means you…"

"Companies hire me to review their management practices and determine how to help them improve their productivity or morale or relationships within the community."

"Ah, trouble is your business," Angela said with a smile.

Dave chuckled. "In a way. More like creating order out of chaos. Though that sounds much more uptight than my approach."

His comment was so un-Alex-like that Angela found herself in Dave's brain before she realized what she was doing. He loved teaching. The ins and outs of what he did reminded Angela of a dance. She pulled back and quickly searched for an outlet for the developing magic. There wasn't anything mechanical behind the bar. She didn't feel like breaking anything.

The magic grew, pushing against her constraints.

"Any insight there?" Dave asked, his head cocked to the side, staring at Angela.

Out of the corner of her eye, Angela saw a man seated at a table not far from them take out his phone. Focusing her intent, Angela sent out her magic. A cacophony of jangled ringtones erupted, erasing the calm. Dave jumped as his phone vibrated in his front pocket and then burst out laughing as people looked around in bewilderment and scrambled to silence theirs.

He reached into his jacket to stop the buzzing. "You?" he asked Angela.

Heat rushed to her face. "I-I…" How had he guessed?

Dave laughed. "Don't be so serious. You said that trouble follows you. Is this what you were talking about?"

"Things like this do seem to happen frequently whenever I'm around," she said weakly.

"That should keep you on your toes."

Angela resisted another foray into Dave's brain. While she would have loved to know what he was thinking, she would then have to find an outlet for the magic another dip would raise. Stupid gremlin powers—find the human's intent then act.

"It does," she answered. "Though some find it annoying. I've lost friends, been sacked, and practically become a pariah because people don't like having to deal with it."

Dave gave his head a shake. "People. No sense of adventure."

"It doesn't bother you?"

"Look at the life of the average person—." Their waiter appeared, placed their wine, and removed Dave's empty glass before departing. "Take the guy sitting behind you, as an example," Dave continued. "Got up, probably at his own place, showered, shaved, ate breakfast. Caught a cab or bus to work. Sat at some desk talking to customers or doing data entry. Had lunch in the cafeteria. Spent the afternoon doing the same thing he did this morning. His excitement today was coming here. He's sitting there with his buddies, eating gourmet pigs in a blanket, and hoping he'll get laid this weekend. He just needs to survive tomorrow, and then life will have the possibility of excitement for a whopping forty-eight hours before it's back to another week of the same old same old.

"*I* spent the day doing the same old same old but had the suspense of finding out if some stranger I'd tried to convince to buy me a glass of wine would actually show up. Not only did she, but strange things are happening around us. My options tonight were this or take out in front of the TV. I'd rather have this any day of the week."

"So what were your expectations for tonight?" Angela asked.

"If you showed, I was hoping for wine and dinner."

"That doesn't seem very adventurous."

Color crept across Dave's cheeks. "I spend a lot of time traveling but I'm not into casual relationships. Wine and dinner is adventurous enough the first time."

"That's all that would have happened anyway," Angela said. "You asked Sunday if there's a boyfriend. I didn't answer then but the truth is

I just got out of a bad relationship. I'm not interested in dating anyone anytime soon."

"So why come?"

Angela shrugged. "You made me laugh. I figured you'd keep passing through my station…I guess that sense of adventure you keep talking about got to me."

"See, you're not the only one with a contagious condition."

Angela laughed. She'd certainly felt contagious over the years. Dave might not be a gremlin but she got the sense that things happened around him, too. That would be a welcome change. Something worth exploring. "You got wine tonight but no dinner," she said. "I'm buying the wine but next time you're buying dinner."

A hopeful expression lit Dave's face. "There's going to be a next time?"

"How about Saturday?"

"That works. How about meeting me at the fifties diner on Broadway?"

"Okay." Angela polished off her wine, dug fifty dollars out of her purse, and placed it on the table. "I'll see you at seven on Saturday." Angela rose.

"Wait a minute! Don't I get your number?" Dave asked as she turned from the table.

Angela glanced back over her shoulder. "No. You're just going to have to live adventurously and hope I'll be there."

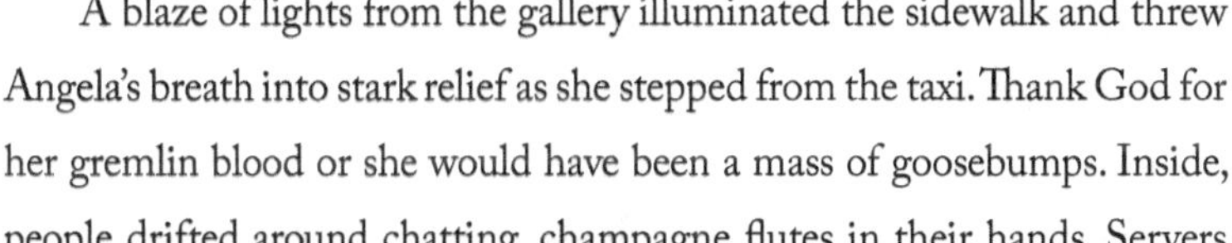

A blaze of lights from the gallery illuminated the sidewalk and threw Angela's breath into stark relief as she stepped from the taxi. Thank God for her gremlin blood or she would have been a mass of goosebumps. Inside, people drifted around chatting, champagne flutes in their hands. Servers still circled with trays of hors d'oeuvres, so they hadn't run out of food.

Angela snagged an ahi carpaccio on a rice cracker and a glass of champagne as she searched for Kate, weaving her way in between throngs of people dressed to impress. Hopefully, the crowd had translated into buyers. Angela drifted over to the first wall of pastel portraits. Tiny red "sold" dots adorned each of the cards that displayed the title and medium, their presence proof of a successful event. A win for both Kate and the artist she was championing.

A win she really should have been here for. Angela stepped away and continued her quest. She finally spotted Kate across the room, chatting with a tall, thin man who looked to be—with his impeccable suit and bored expression—a critic.

Kate caught Angela's eye and, as she responded to something the man had said, motioned her over. Why did Kate have to be talking to him instead of a potential buyer? The last thing Angela wanted was a critique of her own.

She did need to eat, though.

Angela headed in the direction of a server and plucked a miniature buckwheat pancake topped with braised duck from the tray. Her eyes rolled back as she stifled a moan. The duck was so tender it practically melted in her mouth, filling it with flavor. How had there been any of those left? The tray had disappeared into the crowd when she opened her eyes. Dang. She would have liked a few more of those.

Glancing around the room, Angela didn't spy Belle, Joe, Myles, or Nicky anywhere, though they could easily be hidden by one of the tall white dividers that crisscrossed the space. With no excuses left, she made her way over to Kate.

Kate opened her arm as Angela approached and brought her into a sidelong hug without a break in her conversation.

"I'm expecting great things from you, Louis. I'll be very disappointed if you've been telling me one thing tonight and then I find you've written something different."

Louis adjusted his glasses, his bald head glinting under the lights. "How could I contradict the public? The gallery is awash in red dots," he said to Kate in a somewhat affronted tone, though they both knew that wasn't the truth. He would be more than willing to trash the public's endorsement of Consuelos's skill if he believed otherwise.

Louis nodded his farewell to Kate and raked an appreciative eye over Angela.

"You made it," Kate said to Angela and leaned her head against her.

"I told you I'd be here. And it looks like I only missed watching your success unfold. The evidence is everywhere."

"It has gone well," Kate said, nodding in agreement. "Of course, John has such an amazing eye and brings such depth to his subjects. They really do sell themselves. I'm glad I could help him get the attention he deserves. But what about your evening? You're here so early you must really have had just one glass of wine. Was it that bad?"

"No." Angela paused. "He wanted to rush me out when I told him I'd double booked. But I sat, had a glass of wine…we talked."

"And?"

"He'd been hoping for wine and dinner so we're meeting again on Saturday."

Kate pulled back and searched Angela's face long and hard. "You do know what you're doing?" she asked.

"He's funny," Angela said. "I could do with some funny."

Kate hugged her closer. "Yes. You certainly could."

Angela stared into her open closet once again. What did one wear to whatever this was at a fifties diner?

Pseudo-date? Dinner with a friend?

Angela's attention drifted. Her hands pulled hanger after hanger along the rod, stuck on the task of sorting through her clothing options, while her mind tried to settle on a definition of the event.

Test run?

An Armani shirt with French cuffs caught her eye and offered inspiration. It would be perfect with a black pencil skirt. She pulled them out and tossed them onto her bed with a sigh. At least she knew what she was wearing, even if she wasn't quite sure what she was doing.

Angela hung her robe on its hook and slipped on the skirt. She put on the blouse and tried it both tucked in and un-tucked before settling on tucked in. After sorting through her stocking drawer, she pulled out a pair of seam-up-the-back hose. Once her seams were perfectly straight, Angela added a pair of black pumps.

She checked her reflection in her old-fashioned full-length mirror. She looked ready even if she didn't feel it. Angela sighed, grabbed her purse and coat, and headed out the door.

The only insight she found during the cab ride was that it was nice to be doing something with someone new. Someone she didn't need to explain her actions to.

Dave waited on a bench covered in sparkly red vinyl when Angela opened the door. He stood, bathed in the glow of the neon lights that ran along every wall, a smile lighting his face. Her fingers slipped from the handle. She had gone fifties chic but Dave was dressed in jeans and a lightweight, dark red sweater pushed up to his elbows. Angela swallowed hard, her smile aching as she held it in place.

"Hi." She braced herself for his comments on her over-the-top outfit.

"No double booking tonight? No need to go rushing off?" Dave asked.

Heat crept up Angela's cheeks. "No."

"Good." A mischievous grin crinkled Dave's eyes. "I've got some fun planned this evening."

It took every drop of her self-control not to dip into Dave's brain and read what the plans were. Alex had done this to her too many times— create situations in which she was expected to perform, and perform to his standards, with no warning or input. She beat down her panic. Dave was not Alex. And she did want to be surprised. And not raise magic that would then need an outlet. The phone thing at the wine bar had been embarrassing enough.

"Hmm…" Angela hummed.

The hostess collected a couple of menus and called Dave's name. She ushered them over to a booth for two.

"Melanie will be your server tonight. Enjoy!"

Angela glanced around at the neon lights, gleaming chrome, and vintage advertising posters before she flipped open her menu. While the atmosphere was steeped in the 1950s, the menu reflected a more hybrid fare—lobster mac and cheese, beef brisket, chicken pot pie with spring vegetables, veal parmigiana with homemade whole wheat pasta.

"I like your outfit, by the way," Dave said as he picked up his menu. "Very Janet Leigh."

Her cheeks burned. He had noticed. At least she was hidden by the menu. "Thank you," she said, brushing away the compliment.

You just have to be the center of attention, don't you?

Angela tightened her grip on the menu, trying to keep it steady. Alex may as well have been stalking her. Before she had time to recover, a waitress wearing a classic pink and white uniform appeared at their table.

"Good evening. I'm Melanie. Our blue plate special tonight is turkey with garlic mashed potatoes and cranberry chutney. Can I answer any questions for you or start you out with anything?"

"Try their Electric Pink Lemonade," Dave said to Angela.

"I'll have one of those," Angela told their waitress, still trying to shove the memory away.

"Same for me," Dave said.

"I'll give you a moment more and be right back with your drinks."

"I take it you've been here before," Angela said once their waitress had walked away.

"It's fun. They've got good food. And…" Dave gave her a saucy smile. "The lemonade will change your life."

"Are you saying my life needs to change?" Angela asked. It did, actually. But still…

Dave held up his hands. "No, no. Just one of those things that you find and wonder how you ever lived without."

"I see." Angela scanned the menu. "Anything you'd suggest, other than the lemonade?"

"Their burgers are good. So is the lobster mac and cheese. But tonight, I think I'm going to go for the special."

Angela's heart still danced like a nervous colt. And things had a tendency to "happen" if she wasn't paying attention. It would be a shame to stain her blouse. Dave's cranberries were probably safe on the other side of the table, but definitely not the red sauce of the veal parmigiana.

She'd decided on the chicken pot pie by the time the waitress returned with their drinks. Once Melanie had taken their order and left with the menus, an awkward silence fell across the table.

Angela sipped her drink. Sweet and tangy, the lemonade gave no hint to the alcohol that was lurking in it. It would be way too easy to down a pitcher of these and regret it in the morning. "Tasty," she said and smiled. Maybe they would change her life.

"You know," Dave said, stirring the ice cubes in his drink. "Not only do I not have your number, I don't even know your last name."

"Oh…it's Grimalke."

"What nationality is that?" Dave asked.

"Hungarian. My father grew up in Hungary."

"Now that is one place I haven't visited, though I hear Budapest is beautiful. How did he end up in New York?"

"Publishing. Went to Cambridge for college, where he met my mother. They moved here after they finished. He's a literary agent…I don't suppose you're writing the great American novel?" Angela asked.

"No," Dave said with a chuckle. "I'm not creative. I've got a great sense of adventure but I can't imagine sitting and typing on something for months. Don't get me wrong, I love to read and do a lot of it with all the travel I do, but writing…" Dave shuddered. "Is your father like Jimmy Stewart in *Arsenic and Old Lace*, people pitching to him wherever he goes?"

"He's had people follow him into the men's room and stand there while he's…standing there. Or worse."

Dave laughed. "So mother, father. Any siblings?"

"I have a brother who's a commodities broker. I guess we're the typical American family, though we don't have a dog or cat." The irony of it hit her. "And how about you, Dave Ford? What's your family like?"

"Well, we help make that point one percent in the statistics. I've got a brother in Florida and a sister in Michigan. My parents live in St. Louis where I grew up. My dad's been with Boeing there since it was McDonnell Douglas. I tell him I'm not really a management consultant, that I'm actually doing market research for him with all the travel I do."

"How did you end up doing what you do?" Angela asked.

"I've always been curious about how things work. Played a lot of soccer growing up and was struck by how the coaching seemed to make more of a difference in how we did than the talents of the players on our team. Had some great bosses and some bad bosses working after-school jobs. Decided I wanted to help increase the number of good bosses out there. How did you end up at Windsor?" Dave asked. "Love travel?"

"Ah, no." Angela's fingers tightened on her glass. "My last job didn't work out so well. They got tired of me being a jinx."

"A jinx?"

"Things always seemed to go wrong when I was around," Angela said.

"Right, trouble follows you. And that's a path to aviation?"

"Family business," Angela said. "My mother's uncle founded Windsor."

"Ah, nepotism."

"Yes, which was good for me. There's so much chaos in travel that I fit right in. And I'm good at smoothing things over when they've gone awry."

Dave stopped mid-sip, a calculating expression spreading across his face. "You're good at dealing with chaos, are you?"

"Y-e-e-s," Angela said cautiously, her brow wrinkling.

"Good." A devilish grin rose on Dave's face. Then he set his drink to the side and changed the subject as the waitress arrived with their dinner, leaving Angela to wonder what he could be planning.

Angela looked down at her feet and cringed. How had he talked her into this? Here she stood, dressed in Armani and hideous rented shoes, hoisting a huge ball, and facing a bunch of pins that looked to be a mile away. She might as well have a flashing neon sign over her that said, "Out of place."

"I can't believe you took me bowling."

"You said you were willing to continue the fifties theme," Dave said from behind her.

"Yes, well, I was thinking more jazz nightclub," Angela said, wrinkling her nose against the smell of the disinfectant wafting up from her shoes.

"Hmm. I hadn't thought of that. Maybe next time."

If there is a next time. "So I just throw the ball?" she asked.

Dave came up behind her and put one hand on her shoulder. He leaned in, his breath warm in her ear.

"Hold the ball in front of you with both hands, thumb up."

Angela held up the ball, hefting its weight. Dave reached over her and adjusted her hand.

"Now focus on the front pin. Your hand will follow your eyes. Take a step forward with your left leg, bending your knees as you go."

Angela let out a breath and reached out with a foot. Dave's warm fingers closed around her wrist and pulled it back. Her hand jerked at his touch and her concentration broke. *Thunk!*

Shit. At least she hadn't dropped it on her foot.

"Sorry." Dave scooped up her ball. "I should have warned you. There's a rhythm where your arm and leg coordinate to provide the momentum to send the ball down the lane. I'll just adjust your movements…if that's okay?"

Angela gulped and took the ball from him. "Not a problem. I had no idea I could be so inept at bowling."

"You're not," Dave said. "It only feels that way at first."

She set up again and then lowered the ball. "What if it goes flying?"

Dave's breathy chuckle warmed the back of her neck. "Don't worry. Someone always seems to do that." The guy in the lane next to them rolled his eyes so strongly that his head followed. "Now focus…step forward…bring your arm back…step forward again."

The hair on the back of her neck rose at the way Dave bent around her, speaking softly in her ear. She clamped down, fighting back a shiver.

"Bend your knees…then swing your arm forward."

Angela swung. The lights and commotion surrounding her faded away. Only Dave's presence filled her senses. And his voice.

"Normally you'd let the ball slide off right about here," he said.

Mortification washed through her, heating her face. "Right. Um, maybe I'd better watch you do it one more time."

"Sure." Dave retrieved his ball. "Set up, focusing on the pin you want. Put your weight on your front foot as you swing forward, another step to align your arm…and release."

Dave's ball flew down the lane and smacked into the front pin with a *crash*, scattering them everywhere. Two remained in the left corner. One wobbled before deciding to stay upright.

"Now if I get those two on my next ball," Dave said as the mechanism came down and lifted the vertical pins while an arm swept the others away. "It's called a spare." Dave's ball rose up through the apparatus in the floor. "Focusing on the pins you want is even more important this time."

He picked it up and talked Angela through his movements. The ball flew down the lane and knocked over the last two pins.

"Your turn."

Angela hoisted her ball and walked toward the lane. Holding the ball in front of her, she focused on the pins. And not the man sitting behind her.

She gave her head a shake. Following Dave's instructions, Angela swung back and released the ball on the forward motion. It flew off her fingers, thumped down the lane in smaller and smaller bounces, and managed to connect with three pins before being swallowed by the black nothingness beyond.

Dave cheered from the bench but the eye-rolling guy in the next lane threw her a look of pure disgust.

What a stupid bitch. I can't believe they let her in here.

Angela's heart crashed against her ribs. Mind reading was such a great ability to have. *Yeah, right.* Why had she listened in? It had to be the stress of the odd situation.

As Angela turned, Dave wrapped her in a congratulatory hug. She squeezed back tears as she held onto him. The gremlin in her rose up and took over. Magic swelled.

Mr. Grumpy in the next lane set up for his next shot, oozing superiority. Angela's magic leapt out and slid across the floor. As Mr. Grumpy stepped toward the release line, his toe connected.

He tripped. The ball flew wildly from his hand. It bounced once in his lane, and then once in the lane to the left, before sliding across a third and into the gutter, touching off a powder keg of testosterone.

"What the fuck?! What the hell do you think you're doing?!" a male voice shouted from Angela's left.

As New York attitude erupted around them, Dave whispered in Angela's ear, "See, I told you it happens to everyone. At least yours went down your own lane."

He spun Angela around and, right on cue, her ball was spit out of the return. "Try to release the ball a little closer to the ground this time."

Angela picked up her ball and took a moment to compose herself. Chaos. The whole point of bowling was to create chaos. She could do that.

Be the ball. Be the ball. It slid smoothly from her fingers upon her release, rolled down the lane, and actually hit the pins, knocking down all but three. Not bad for her second attempt.

"Way to go!" Dave cheered and gave her a high-ten as she came over.

A satisfied smile lifted the corners of her mouth. She had a feeling she was actually going to like this game.

"I have to say, I'm pleasantly surprised," Dave said as Angela stirred cream into her coffee.

"What? That I'm not afraid of a fat-filled dairy product?"

"No. Though now that you mention it, it is surprising you're adding cream. And you had dessert."

Angela sighed. The warm, gooey Valhrona chocolate pudding cake the bowling alley had on offer had been a pleasant surprise. "As you could probably tell, I'm addicted to chocolate."

"That's not the surprising part," Dave said. "You look—wow—and yet you're not afraid of cream or dessert. Or bowling."

"Did you expect to scare me off?" Angela asked.

"Umm…in a way."

Angela's head jerked up. "Excuse me?"

"I took you bowling yet you're still here. Most women would have run for the hills, or at least the nearest cab."

"I do have to say," Angela told him. "I thought you were trying to get rid of me. But you were right, it's fun. Nice to be able to create some chaos and have it not matter. Count even."

"Well, I'm glad to find out that you don't mind a challenge, that you're not afraid to try new things. I'd like there to be a next time."

Angela squirmed. What they were doing could be considered a date. "I don't know. Like I told you last time, I just got out of a bad relationship. I'm not looking for another one right now."

"I'm not looking for a bad relationship either," Dave said. Angela smiled. "Look, girlfriends don't like how much time I spend out of town. They say they don't care but then it gets old and the nagging and whining starts."

"So why ask me out?"

"I want someone to do things with who's not a guy. I can only take so much racquetball and golf, and cigars just aren't my thing. And you'd only have to put up with me a few days a month. I'm out of town, usually out of the country, two weeks a month. As a matter of fact, I'm leaving Monday for a week in Zurich. But maybe, when I get back, we could do that jazz club you expected."

Angela hesitated. She picked up the empty little cartons of creamer and stacked them. "If I say 'yes,' what does that make us?"

"Friends?"

Angela slowly nodded her head. "And you don't think I'll whine?"

Dave laughed. "You wore rented shoes and risked breaking a nail. I think I'm safe for a couple more adventures."

"Where you'll see if you can scare me off?"

Dave held up his hands. "I'm just being myself here. Can I help it if some people find my life scary?"

There was something ridiculous about Dave that she found intriguing, alluring even. Part of her wanted to say "no" but—

Angela threw a glance toward the heavens, praying she wouldn't regret the decision. "212-555-1678. That's my cell. Give me a call when you get back from Zurich."

Dave clinked his cup against hers. "I'll be looking forward to it, Miss Grimalke."

Angela met Belle and Kate for brunch the next morning at the Belgian restaurant not far from her apartment.

"So what did you do?" Kate asked as soon as they'd sent their waiter off with their order.

"Dinner…and bowling."

Her friends froze in the middle of what they were doing and slowly looked over at her.

Belle's eyebrows met her hairline. "You…went…bowling?"

Angela nodded. "In Armani and those ugly shoes they make you wear."

"He…took…you…bowling," Belle repeated. "The klutziest woman alive."

"It was actually kind of fun," Angela said. "Things are supposed to go flying. You're supposed to knock things over."

"I guess that would be right up your alley," Kate said with a quirky grin. "Pun intended."

"Are you seeing him again?" Belle asked.

"I gave him my number."

"Wow," Kate said. "I hadn't expected you to jump back in the dating pool so quickly."

"Oh, we're not dating. He's just looking for a friend who isn't a guy."

"Men say that," Belle said. "But it's really just a way to date without strings attached. Remember what Harry told Sally in that movie."

"Harry and Sally became friends," Angela said.

Belle rolled her eyes. "They ended up in bed!"

Angela shrugged. "I like his sense of humor. He makes me laugh. And Dave isn't looking for a girlfriend 'cause he travels so much. Seems like the best of both worlds to me."

"Minus the sex," Belle said over the top of her coffee.

"I can do without sex for a while," Angela said. "Alex was amazing in bed and look what that got me."

"We did wonder how you ended up as arm candy," Kate said. "We were kind of worried about you, you know, trying so hard to be what Alex wanted. We didn't think it was his money that you were after, though you'd make a great addition to 'ladies who lunch'."

"So amazing, huh?" Belle asked, a naughty twinkle in her eye.

"You know Alex—always has to be the best at everything he does," Angela said.

"Including being a jerk," said Belle.

"When did you figure out he was a jerk?" Had she been the only one blind to Alex's true nature?

"He is one smooth operator," Kate said. "You don't realize what he's really like until something doesn't meet his expectations. I think you guys had been going out about six months before I saw the first red flag—the charity dinner where he didn't like your dress."

"And then began providing you with proper—" Belle put quote marks around the word with her fingers. "—clothes."

Alex had seemed like the perfect boyfriend for quite a while, though he had been far from amused by the chaos her magic inevitably caused. Then there'd been that dinner. Alex had not been happy about what she'd worn to the event, which still mystified Angela. There hadn't been any wardrobe malfunctions and the dress had been a beautiful designer gown. When a box containing a dress, shoes, and accessories arrived for their next outing, she had been touched and done her best to please Alex. Wasn't he treating her like a princess?

"I just thought he was spoiling me," Angela said.

"Men who shower you with presents expect something in return," Belle said. "And Alex expected you to be perfect."

Kate laughed. "He certainly didn't know you very well."

The girls spied the waiter with their plates and made room on the blue and white checkered table cloth for them.

"It always amazes me that you can eat like that," Belle said as the waiter put Angela's waffle topped with ice cream, chocolate syrup, and whipped cream in front of her.

Angela picked up her fork and scooped up some of the ice cream. "Good genes."

"Your mother still looks so amazing," Kate said as she gazed wistfully at the egg white omelet the waiter placed in front of her.

"Yeah, some of us have to work at it." Belle stabbed her fork at the tuna in her salad Niçoise.

"I'm sure I'll have to one of these days," Angela said, and crossed her fingers under the table.

Angela hugged Belle and Kate goodbye and headed back to her apartment. She hadn't thought about the gala episode in months.

She had met Alex there as he'd had a business meeting that had run late. Belle had helped her pick out a stunning dress, its sheer lace overlay shot with pewter and gold threads. Angela had loved it, but Alex froze when he saw her, and not in a good way. The smile he'd forced on his face had been angry. Tension had rolled off him in waves, but he didn't comment, didn't tell her what was wrong.

Magic had built as she fought her confusion, fought the temptation to peek inside Alex's thoughts; fought the urge to be gremlin when she so desperately wanted to be human. Eventually, it burst out, striking a table leg, collapsing the table and sending the contents crashing to the floor.

Alex's jaw had clenched, and he'd stared hard at her face. Then he raked his eyes over her dress.

Back at his place that night, he'd ripped the dress from her, the beautiful lace tearing in his hands. She'd considered his actions passion at the time, though she had mourned the loss of the dress. Alex had sent over a new one the next day with a note of apology, but now Angela wondered if it hadn't been something else.

What would she have found if she'd read his mind? Had she been simply a possession? One more thing to add to his collection?

She continued to debate, even after she'd returned home and stood in front of her open closet.

You tried so hard to be what Alex wanted…You don't realize what he's really like until something doesn't meet his expectations…

Angela hadn't met his expectations that night. The dress hadn't met his expectations. So he'd destroyed it and made sure that Angela's clothes at least wouldn't disappoint him again.

Air rushed into her lungs, spasming as she fought for control. She had found the gifts thoughtful. But they hadn't been. They had been a way to control her.

His efforts still hung there, sprinkled throughout her closet. Each one a reminder that she couldn't be trusted. She was a supermassive black hole who needed to be managed.

Angela grabbed a hanger and ripped it out of her closet, tossing it on the floor behind her. Another followed. Then another. A fit of frenzy took over. Garment after garment flew from the closet, a pile growing behind her. Shoe boxes soon followed…and then jewelry.

Her chest heaved as she stared at the resulting pile. Even from the floor, they mocked her. Angela turned on her heel, marching into the kitchen. She grabbed the box of garbage bags, a sharp *crack* filling the air as she flicked one open. She shoved the pile—hangers, boxes, and all— into bag after bag, trembling with the deluge of emotion.

Once the last one had been tied closed, she hauled them out of her apartment, down the elevator, and out to the curb.

It's time to take out the trash.

Back in the elevator, Angela punched the button for her floor and slumped against the side. She should have known. She, more than anyone else, should have realized Alex's true intentions. She should have read his mind. She should have been a gremlin.

She was not going to make that mistake again.

Dave rolled into line the next afternoon as Angela was working with another customer. A playful grin lit up his face. Taking the routing tags from the printer, she secured them to the bags.

"Where are they going?" Dave mouthed from behind the guy, pointing at the luggage, as Angela straightened up.

She rolled her eyes. "Here are your boarding passes for the London and Amsterdam flights." Angela slid the documents into the man's passport and handed it back. "The flight for London will begin boarding at six. Feel free to wait in our club lounge or at the gate."

The customer thanked her and moved off.

"Good afternoon," Dave said. He slipped his garment bag from his shoulder and placed it on the scale.

"Good afternoon."

"Do you always work afternoons?" Dave asked her as he handed over his papers.

"Yes." Angela threw him a questioning look. "Why do you ask?"

Dave fought a losing battle to look nonchalant. "No reason. Just curious."

Her eyebrow hooked. "Are you asking for my schedule?"

"No, no. Don't need to know." Dave rocked on his feet while Angela punched his information into the computer. "So…you work the late shift on Mondays."

Angela looked up from her typing. "I thought you didn't need to know."

"Just an observation. Here it is, early Monday evening…And you must work the same shift on Sunday."

She pulled up Dave's flight information—a Sunday return.

"Yes, Sherlock. I did check you in for London and Chicago on a Sunday."

Dave chuckled. "Well, my mad skills do include a keen sense of observation."

"And my mad skills include the ability to sense that you're up to something."

A look of mock indignation stole over Dave's face. "Me? Up to something? Why Miss Grimalke, you do have a suspicious nature."

Angela had had enough of surprises. Remembering her promise to herself, she dipped into Dave's brain. *I hope she'll be there Sunday. I'll have to pick her up something.*

Angela's heart sank. Her previous presents should have been picked up by the garbage collectors this morning. Unless someone had scrounged the bags of designer clothes, which in New York City was a real possibility.

She dug deeper into Dave's brain. No Swiss watches. No thoughts of jewelers. Dave didn't have clothing in mind. It was something simpler.

Angela pulled out before she found out exactly what he intended. She could handle something small. And she did want to be surprised.

Now there was just the problem of where to send the magic. Her deeper foray into Dave's brain meant it was more powerful than usual. It pushed against her control as she searched for an outlet.

Her fingers twitched, grasping for it, as the magic broke free and slipped into the closest mechanical device running—the luggage conveyor belt. The belt shuddered and groaned to a halt, an echo repeated by her coworkers. At least it hadn't been the computers.

"My bag's still going to make my flight, right?" the man at the next counter demanded of her coworker.

"We will make sure all the bags get loaded," Jackson replied, throwing Angela a look.

"Hmm," Dave said, a smile lighting up his face. "Another trip with a fifty-fifty chance of getting my bags. I love flying."

"How do you manage to maintain such a good attitude about it?" Angela asked as she printed out the routing tag for Dave's bag.

"Keep a spare pair of underwear and a toothbrush in my carry-on. I can live without the rest. Besides, I get to meet all kinds of fascinating people when I go in search of replacements."

"Who may or may not perform acupuncture," Angela said, hanging Dave's papers to him.

He broke out in a hearty laugh. "That was a first. But you've got to love tailors. They're immensely fascinating with their chalk and their pins." He gave his documents a sharp tap on the counter. "I am off. Have a good week. Maybe, if I'm lucky, I'll see you on Sunday. Otherwise, I will give you a call."

"Have a good week…Dave," Angela said. Papers in hand, he offered her a salute as he strode off. Angela watched him go with a wistful smile. It was a good thing she was working Sunday. She was now too curious about her present to wait much longer.

"Want a ride?" Nicky asked when Angela picked up the phone Wednesday evening.

"Sure. How soon 'til you pick me up?"

"I'm downstairs."

Angela's heart skipped a beat. That didn't bode well.

"Okay, I'll be down in a minute," she forced out, trying to keep her voice positive.

There was only one reason why Nicky would pull such a stunt—he wanted to talk to her before dinner, before there were any parents around to witness. He wanted to use any information gleaned on the way over *at* dinner. Or at least have it as collateral.

"Meter's running," Nicky said and hung up.

Yes, it *was* running. And it could run a bit longer.

Angela moseyed over to the hall closet and slipped on her coat. She wandered into the kitchen to check that the burners were off on the stove. They were, of course. She rarely used it.

Next, she traipsed into the bathroom to make sure her curling iron was unplugged. While there, she checked her make up. She added another layer of mascara to her lashes and touched up her blush. She decided to change her shoes and went to her closet where she tried on five different pairs before keeping the ones she started out with.

The pulsing beats of "The Devil Inside" blared from her phone. Nicky's ringtone.

"I'm in the hall," she answered, and hung up. Sighing, she put her phone in her purse and went out to face the music.

"Took you long enough," Nicky said, huffing, when Angela got in the cab.

"I'm a girl. These things take time."

Nicky shook his head and groaned as the cab pulled away from the curb. Newscasters bantered back and forth on the TV mounted on the seat in front of them, commenting on a storm front predicted to hit New York early the next morning. High winds, hail, and lightning expected.

Angela's mouth thinned. They were a bit off in their forecasting. Based on the tension in the cab, a storm was much closer than that.

"I didn't have a chance to ask you last week," Nicky said, breaking their silence. "How did your date go Thursday?"

Yep, definitely a storm ahead.

"It wasn't a date," Angela said.

"So how did it go? Are you seeing him again?"

"It was one glass of wine. Then I left."

"And?"

"And what?" Hopefully, playing dumb would discourage her brother's current line of investigation.

"Are you seeing him again?" Nicky asked.

"Of course. He flies Windsor. I checked him in just two days ago."

"You know that's not what I meant," Nicky said. Irritation laced his voice.

"I'm not dating him."

Nicky turned and looked hard at her through narrowed eyes. Magic pricked against her skin.

"Careful, Nicky. You know that won't work. We'll only end up needing to change cabs."

Nicky's eyes narrowed further. "You're lying."

Their cabbie's focus shifted to his phone, though he continued to weave in and out of traffic. Cyrillic lettering flashed across the now glitchy screen, along with the picture of an angry young man covered in tattoos. After a giving it a shake, he whacked the device a couple of times against the dash.

"I am not," Angela replied as their cabbie continued to shake his phone, glancing back and forth between the road and the screen. "Nice going," she added. "Were you wanting us to get in an accident?"

"You're the accident waiting to happen. You're seeing this guy, aren't you?"

Angela sighed. "I told you, I can't help but see him. He's a customer."

"But you're seeing him outside the airport as well, aren't you?" Angela stalled for time. This was why Nicky wanted to grill her before dinner, checking to see if he needed to make good on his "marry her off" threat.

"He's not interested in dating."

"But you are."

"Look—" Angela turned in her seat. "We're not dating. He's funny. He's fun to be around. But he doesn't want a girlfriend and I certainly don't want a boyfriend."

"So you are seeing him. Outside of work."

"As I am sure you are seeing plenty of women. You don't see me all up in arms about them."

"Well, I'm not going to be marrying any of them."

"Oh, so you *are* thinking of marriage." Angela latched onto the thread that took the focus off her. "Remember, Dad was married and had both of us by the time he was your age. Which I will be only too willing to point out if you breathe a word of this to either of our parents. I can just picture the line of candidates they'll parade through."

"I've already got someone picked out," Nicky said. "She's a gremlin, so I don't need to worry about that."

"Really?" Angela asked, deflating like a pricked balloon. "You're getting married?"

"No!" Nicky gave Angela a horrified look. "Not any time soon. There are too many women I haven't sampled. I'm just saying that when the time comes, I know what I'll be doing."

"Too many women you haven't sampled," Angela repeated.

"I'm a gremlin. I'm supposed to be out there charming the opposite sex."

"And I'm not allowed to?"

"Of course, you are. But you don't. You want to love them."

A heavy sigh heaved her chest. "Yeah, and that's worked out so well for me."

"So go out. Sample the men. Be a siren," Nicky said. "Laugh with Whatshisname. Just keep love off the menu."

The cab pulled up in front of their parents' building. Nicky took out his credit card and swiped it, declining a receipt.

"So what are you going to do?" Angela asked as they got out of the car.

"With you?" Nicky rolled his eyes heavenward. "God only knows."

"I meant tonight."

Nicky stared at Angela and finally shook his head. "Don't make me regret this. Don't make me regret not telling them. Go have your fun."

"Thanks."

"But I swear, Angela, if I get any sense that you're getting attached to this guy, the parade will begin."

Angela opened the door to the building. "So who's your future wife? Does she know?"

"You haven't met her. She works for Guinness in Dublin."

Nicky crashed into her as Angela stopped short. She whirled around to face him. "Dublin? Where did you meet her?"

"An event they threw in New York."

He hadn't been simply trying to get her thinking of marriage. He was serious!

"Does she know your intentions? What does she think about your continuing to 'sample' other women?"

Nicky spun Angela back around and gave her a little push toward the elevator.

"No, we have no firm understanding. And she's busy leading men astray in Ireland."

"What are you going to do if some other gremlin sweeps her off her feet?"

"I will deal with that when and if the situation arises."

The elevator doors slid open. Nicky got in first and punched the button for their parents' floor. "You don't seem to have much confidence in my magnetism."

Maybe all the time she spent surrounded by humans and their fears had rubbed off on her. Nicky had definitely inherited the siren genes as opposed to the more homely ones that had produced Cousin Wendell. Belle's lust for her brother was proof of that. There probably wasn't a woman on the planet who wouldn't come running if he crooked his little finger at her.

"Well, you're here, she's there. You know what they say about out of sight, out of mind," Angela added.

"Hmm. I hadn't thought of that. Certainly don't want to start over from scratch." Nicky shuddered. "God, I couldn't stand a parade."

"Yet you're willing to put me through one."

Nicky gave his sister a playful shove. "Yeah, but you're hopeless."

"Well, thanks," Angela said, not bothering to keep the sarcasm from her voice.

"That's what big brothers are for."

The rest of the week passed as routine. Angela sent more bags to Cleveland and other destinations their owners weren't actually traveling to. Barry Carnak came through, flying to Nassau, this time looking definitely more relaxed, even with all the delays caused by the big thunderstorm. Angela spent a still very rainy Friday morning at the Metropolitan and then had lunch with Belle, who was excited that Joe had finished his big project and was taking her to One If By Land on Saturday night to celebrate.

Rain continued to cover the city in darkness on Saturday. Angela curled up on the sofa and binged on the latest season of the period drama on PBS that had everyone glued to their sets, breaking only to call out for Chinese and go to the bathroom.

By Sunday, the downpour finally subsided. As the sun came out, spring exploded all over the city. Vases of tulips decorated every table at the restaurant Angela, Belle, and Kate met at for an early brunch.

"You're lucky I'm even here," Belle said as she sat down. She picked up her menu and nearly blinded Kate and Angela with the sunlight that glinted off a giant diamond on her left hand.

"Oh, my God!" Kate grabbed Belle's hand and brought the ring in for a closer look.

"Joe proposed last night," Belle told them unnecessarily. "He wanted to continue celebrating this morning but I told him, 'Honey, you know you will always take a backseat to Kate and Angela'."

"Have you set a date yet?" Angela asked. She gripped the edge of her chair as her heart did strange flips inside her chest.

"No, I wanted to talk to your mother first. But probably sometime next spring. And, of course, you'll both be bridesmaids."

Kate's face soured. "Only for you. And I'm counting on you putting us into something fabulous."

"Of course. I do have a reputation to maintain," Belle said.

A waiter appeared at their table. "Can I get you ladies anything to start with?"

"I think we can all use a glass of champagne," Belle said.

"Special occasion?" their waiter asked with a grin.

"Oh, I don't know." Belle brought her fingers to her lips, bringing the diamond front and center.

"Congratulations," he said, grinning more broadly. "I'll be right back with those."

"How did he ask you?" Kate asked as their waiter walked away.

"We'd finished dinner and they'd brought out the dessert menus and I asked Joe what he wanted for dessert and he said, 'How about a lifetime with you?' and I looked up and he had a Harry Winston box in his hand. I nearly fainted dead away. Then he opened it and, as I sat there gasping, said, 'Belle Pearson, will you marry me?'"

Kate chuckled. "I'm guessing you said 'yes.' Did you get dessert? One you could actually eat?"

"We did the *prix fixe* dinner, so dessert came with it."

"I'm so happy for you," Angela said, pushing a smile onto her face. Kate had Myles. Belle was now engaged. Even Nicky had someone. She was alone. And would likely stay that way, being such a terrible judge of men.

The parade of suitable, single male gremlins that Nicky threatened to unleash on her might have to do. Though, with her luck, it was sure to rival the ordeal she had witnessed in that movie about the Greek wedding. A shudder ran through her. Gremlin males had such an odd way of looking at things. Not to mention their inflated sense of self-importance. Nicky being the perfect example. Gorgeous, but really! Sample the women? There were too few like her father who, as far as she knew, had always been devoted to her mother.

That was what Angela wanted. She just didn't see many gremlin men like that. Players, the lot of them.

Angela suppressed a sigh. "Give my mother a call today," she told Belle. "She won't mind it being Sunday since it's you. She'll be excited to plan a wedding for family."

Belle's face fell. "I'm sorry, Angela. This has got to bother you."

"Of course not." Angela pushed her pangs of jealousy away. "You deserve it. He's going to make you very happy."

Kate picked up and brandished her knife. "He better." She waved it around in emphasis. "Or he's going to have to deal with us!" Belle rolled her eyes.

The waiter came back with their champagne. "Here you go," he said, setting down the glasses. He untwisted the wire basket holding the cork in place and eased it out of the bottle with more hiss than *pop*. After filling their glasses, he gave them a little nod. "Enjoy. And congratulations again."

Kate picked up her flute and held it high. "To Belle and Joe…and what promises to be a fabulous wedding."

Angela clinked her glass against the other two. "To finding your other half."

The rhythmic clatter of the train did nothing to dispel the misery that settled into Angela's soul. A lifetime of not fitting in had left scars that ached. She didn't want to be alone. *Did humans ever marry only for companionship?* As much as she despised the notion, she could save herself a lot of heartache if she'd let her parents matchmake.

By the time Angela got to work, she had worn through her ability to give a fuck. The universe, however, mocked her, giving her Brock Jameson as her first passenger. If he'd been able to read Angela's mind, he would have known to keep his mouth shut. But he couldn't, so his tongue just kept wagging.

After listening to his stream of bitching and complaining for a steady five minutes, the forced smile on Angela's face transformed into a real one. The routing tag she attached to Mr. Jameson's luggage was completely unreadable. Who knew where it would end up? Someday, Mr. Jameson would be reunited with his bag. Someday, after being shuffled around from place to place, sometime in the far distant future, someone would finally think to read the ID tag.

Angela had finished checking in passengers for the London flight and had leaned against the counter, relaxing in the lull, when she saw Dave approaching down the concourse, his familiar briefcase rolling along behind him. It had completely slipped her mind he'd be returning today.

His hand curled around a small package wrapped in brightly colored paper and tied with a ribbon in a poisonous shade of green.

"Good afternoon, Mr. Ford. This is a surprise," Angela said as Dave wheeled up.

"Didn't want anything to happen to this." With a little flourish, he handed her the gift.

"Quite the ribbon," she said as she stared at the strip of green, so bright it nearly glowed.

"It's a clue."

Angela cocked an eyebrow. "Really?"

"You have no idea." Dave flashed her an evil grin.

"Hmm."

"Well, I'm off. You're busy, I'm tired. I had them enclose my business card under the wrapping paper. Give me a call tomorrow when you get a chance. Let me know what you think. Maybe we can make plans for Friday."

Angela eyed the ribbon again. "Am I going to survive that long?"

Dave laughed and turned away. "Depends on who you ask," he called over his shoulder.

Angela's eyes narrowed though the corners of her mouth crept into a smile. She fought back the urge to peek into Dave's mind.

Angela watched Dave's retreating form and placed the package under the counter. Sometimes a little mystery was a good thing.

Angela set Dave's gift on her coffee table. After washing her face and slipping on her pajamas, she padded back into the living room and crossed her legs on the sofa. She stared at the ribbon. How could the color be a clue? *Green? Intense chartreuse green?* Her nose crinkled in thought.

With a tug, the ribbon came loose. Angela pulled back the paper. Dave's business card sat on top of six bars of dark chocolate filled with absinthe. A favorite beverage in France in the late 1800s, the bright green alcohol had gained a reputation for causing madness and been outlawed. It had been said that to drink absinthe was to court insanity.

Her mouth curled. The ribbon was definitely apropos. He'd bought her "poisoned" chocolate.

She opened one bar and broke off a piece. The absinthe had crystalized inside the chocolate, lending it a geode-like appearance. Just a trace of syrup oozed from the cavities.

Angela popped the piece in her mouth. It melted and crunched, releasing a flavor that was magical—chocolate and something else she couldn't quite put her finger on. Not anise, though that's what absinthe was supposed to taste like.

Covering the bar back in its foil, Angela made herself walk away. And not consume the entire bar. For that would leave her only five. Unless she had Dave bring her more.

No, better to walk away from temptation.

She called Dave the next morning. "Just what was your evil plan?"

A hearty laugh rang through the phone. "Chocolate is evil?"

"You know what I mean—laced with absinthe."

"Old wives tale created by winemakers when the French took to drinking absinthe instead of wine."

"Really?" Angela said. "An old wives tale got it banned in multiple countries?"

"A very successful bad PR campaign. But you don't have to eat it. I remembered you'd said you were addicted to chocolate and thought I'd bring you something a little different."

"Different, yes. And madness inducing. I've already tried it, and it's completely seductive. I ate an entire bar for breakfast. I had to get out a chair and put the rest up on the top shelf of my cupboard behind a bunch of glasses I never use."

Dave chuckled again. "I'm sorry. It was just meant to be fun. Do you want me to relieve you of the rest?" With a jerk, her body shifted, willing to rush to the kitchen to protect her stash.

"No!"

"I'll make it up to you. Where would you like to go on Friday? We could do that jazz club you were hoping for last time."

Angela shifted in her seat. She wasn't really into jazz. It had just seemed to go with the fifties theme. "Wherever you like."

"Where do you usually go?"

"Uh…I don't, but that's not to say I can't have my horizons expanded. Look at the absinthe, never tried it before and now I seem to be addicted."

"Abilene," Dave said.

"I haven't heard of it. Is it new?" Angela asked.

"No, no. We were about to go to Abilene."

Angela's brow wrinkled. "I think you've lost me."

"Twenty years ago my father's group at Boeing watched this movie called *The Road to Abilene*. It was about this family who ended up driving to Abilene for dinner, something no one wanted to do but everyone thought everyone else wanted to. Since then, my family has always checked to see if we all really want to do something or if we're 'going to Abilene'."

"So you were suggesting a jazz club because you thought that's what I wanted to do and I was saying 'yes' because I thought that's what you wanted to do."

"Exactly."

"Wow," Angela said. "I wonder how often that happens."

"All the time. Which is why Boeing showed the film. It's one of those weird things with human behavior. People go along with things they don't want to do just because they don't want to rock the boat."

"And if you don't speak up, you could end up in Abilene," Angela said.

"Yup. So where would you like to go?" Dave asked.

"I don't know. I'm still so amazed by the absinthe that I'm open for suggestion. Who knows what else I'm missing?"

"Maybe we could continue with the absinthe. There's a little French place near Times Square that has good food as well as a number of different absinthes and absinthe cocktails," Dave suggested.

"If I didn't know better," Angela said. "I'd swear you were trying to lead me astray."

He chuckled. "No, no. Just allowing you to expand your horizons. So what do you say? Do you want to risk the madness of *la fee verte*?"

Yes, she must be mad indeed. "What time?"

"About seven? I could meet you there."

A mixture of relief and something else coiled inside her. It would have felt more like a date if Dave had picked her up.

"I'll meet you there at seven," Angela echoed.

"Have a good week," Dave said. "And try not to lose too many bags."

"Hardy har har," Angela said, and hung up. And yet…A compulsion began to creep over her. Losing luggage sounded like fun.

Angela sighed and got up to get ready for work.

Maybe it would pass.

By the time Nicky picked her up for dinner on Wednesday evening, Angela was well on her way to a record-breaking week. Sunday, she'd only magicked the ticket for Brock Jameson's bag. Monday had produced a personal high of five in a single day. There'd been three on Tuesday and then another two today. Hopefully, she would be able to exert better control over herself tomorrow and do none.

She wasn't quite sure what had caused the increase. It could be simply a spike in the number of worthy passengers. Grumpy people were always deserving of a little chaos. Though that wouldn't explain why she had dipped into passengers' minds more often than she usually did, checking intentions and attitudes.

Angela sent Elmer Thistle's bag to Cleveland when she'd caught his wife Ethel's wish that his Boca Raton wardrobe—bought without her—would just disappear. Nothing would have been able to control the shudder that ran through her when she picked up Ethel's vision of Elmer in his golf outfit. Some things deserved to be burned. She had even texted Wendell about it, asking him to have the bag disappear permanently.

Then there'd been Snakeskin Coat Man with the slip-on shoes sans socks traveling to Vegas with a suitcase full of pimp-like clothes and condoms. Anyone looking for that much tail deserved to be slowed down.

"Hey, sis. Have a good week?" Nicky asked when Angela opened her door. Tonight, he'd come upstairs to hurry her along.

"Belle got engaged."

"To that accountant?"

"Yes. Joe." Angela picked up her purse and took her keys from the dish.

"I assume Mum's doing the wedding."

"I don't have that confirmed but I would be surprised if she hadn't taken Belle on."

Angela locked the door and followed Nicky down the hall.

"Hmm," Nicky said as he punched the elevator button.

"What?"

"Oh…uh…I was just trying to picture you in a bridesmaid's dress," he said.

His rushed tone gave Angela the impression that her brother was lying. She decided, however, to play along. "Why? Because she's got such great taste?"

"There is that," Nicky conceded. "She's going to go for something more runway, don't you think?"

Angela did a double take. She was talking wedding clothes with her brother?

"Probably. Is there any particular reason you're interested?"

"Just all those years of living with a bridal consultant."

"Uh huh." Nicky had shown no interest at all in Kate's wedding plans two years earlier.

"You sound like you don't believe me," Nicky retorted.

"I'm just saying…" Angela drifted off. Best not to call her brother a liar out loud.

Dave was already waiting at the restaurant when Angela arrived. As a nod to the absinthe, she'd decided to wear a silk wrap-dress sporting a green print.

Dave stood up as she approached, a smile lighting his face.

"*La fee verte*, I see."

"Something like that." Angela grinned. A gremlin in a green dress was kind of like a green fairy.

"Now I do have to warn you," Dave said as they both sat down. "The anise flavor has a tendency to overwhelm most foods, so if you're going to try it before dinner you might want to choose things that go well with fennel."

Angela's brow crinkled. "Not something I usually order." She picked up her menu. "Do you even know what goes well with fennel?"

"Seafood, citrus, anything with a bright herbaceous taste."

Angela slowly raised her eyes from her menu. "You're a foodie?"

Dave shrugged. "Not really. I like to cook but—" He shuddered. "I once made the mistake of ordering the fois gras after having absinthe. You do not want to do that."

"So what would you suggest?"

"You could have the mussels or the arugula salad. The scallops are probably safe. Or you could save the absinthe for dessert."

"No, that's what chocolate is for." Angela put her menu down. "How about I live on the dangerous side and let you order my dinner."

"I think that would be more dangerous for me," Dave said.

"How so?"

"You might hate it all and then I'd end up eating two dinners."

Angela flashed Dave a wicked grin. "Are you willing to risk it?"

"And here I was going to have the duck and red wine," he said mournfully.

"No absinthe for you?" Angela asked.

Dave held up his hands in apology. "I have experienced the magic. It's your turn to try it. In something other than chocolate."

The waiter, dressed all in black except for a white towel at his waist, glided up to their table. "Good evening. Can I get you anything to start?"

"I'll have the *le fee verte*," Angela said.

"Very good. And for you, sir?"

"A glass of the Malbec," Dave said.

"I'll be right back with your drinks and take your order in a just a moment."

"You cook," Angela said after the waiter walked away.

"When I get the chance. No matter where you go in the world, restaurant food all starts to taste the same after a while."

"I suppose that's true," Angela said. "Though I'm one of those

New Yorkers who never uses their kitchen. My mother makes the most amazing food, but I've never learned."

"Do you miss her cooking?" Dave asked.

"At times. But then I am over at my parents' every Wednesday for dinner."

"So that was the mystery date!" Dave exclaimed.

Angela laughed. "I suppose you could say that. I never schedule anything else on Wednesdays. If we're in town, it's expected that we will be there for dinner."

"Does she have a specialty?"

"Hungarian. My father missed his favorite foods, so my mother learned to make them. How about you? Anything you're famous for?"

"A little of this and a little of that," Dave said. "I like to wander Union Square Market when I'm home and see what inspires me."

"So you *are* creative. Didn't you tell me last time that you weren't?"

"We were talking about writing," Dave said. "There, I wouldn't know where to begin. But food, it speaks to me."

"And what does it say?" Angela asked.

Dave waggled his eyebrows. "The siren's song, 'Try me, try me.'"

"Oh, you listen to sirens, do you?"

"I certainly do." Dave moved his silverware to the side as the waiter approached with their drinks.

Angela's face fell when he placed a glass filled with ice and a cloudy, white liquid in front of her. Surely, this wasn't what she'd ordered?

"Have you decided on dinner?" the waiter asked.

Angela picked up her menu and peered at it. "Go ahead," she said to Dave.

"I'll have the mesclun greens and the duck confit."

Angela scanned the list but nothing jumped out at her. She sighed. "I'm going to have to ask you to choose for me," she said to Dave.

"She'll have the mesclun and the mussels," he told the waiter. Dave leaned toward Angela and whispered, "That way you'll have room for dessert."

Angela thanked their waiter and handed back her menu. As he walked away, she stared at her drink. "Are you sure there's absinthe in this?" Frowning, Angela gave it a stir with the strange, silver spoon. "It's not even green."

Dave's face twisted into a mischievous smile, and he leaned in again. "It's magic. Green in the bottle but pour it in a glass, mix it with water, and *voila*! It becomes a harmless looking white."

"And madness inducing."

Dave laughed. "No more so than tequila in a green margarita. It's the high alcohol content. A few rounds with Jose Cuervo and you're off to Margaritaville wondering where your new tattoo came from. A few rounds with absinthe and you're seeing lots of pretty colors."

Angela gave Dave a hard look before she picked up her glass and took a sip. Very sweet and *very* licorice.

"Wow! I see now why you said I could have this for dessert."

"Are you sorry?"

"No, no. It's good to experiment. But you were right about the taste. It could overwhelm everything else."

"Well you don't have to finish it. We could always get you a glass of wine instead."

Angela stirred the silver spoon and listened to the ice cubes tinkle in the glass. Wine would be the safe choice. "Let's see how it goes. I did want to try something new."

"Just make sure you're not going to Abilene."

"That story certainly made an impression on you."

"It did," Dave said. "I was already in FBLA—"

"What?"

"Future Business Leaders of America. It's a high school business club," Dave said. "My dad came home with the story and not only did it become our family double check, but it got me thinking about and looking at how people work in groups, make decisions. I got on the Management Decision Making Team, and we went all the way to take first place at Nationals."

"They hold competitions for management practices? At the high school level?" Angela asked incredulously.

"Sure. There's about fifty different categories you can compete in."

"And you, or your team, won the management one."

Dave flushed a bit. "Yup."

He was hiding something from her. Angela lifted her glass, tilted her head to take a sip, and peeked into his mind. He'd been on the team that took first place in the Global Business event as well. Two first place wins at National. Something he wasn't mentioning because he was afraid she'd see him as a nerd.

Angela sent the magic she'd raised into the reader board flashing in the adult DVD store across the street, freezing it on *LATEX GOODIES!!!*

"That's really something," Angela said as she put her glass down.

"Thanks," Dave said a little sheepishly. "So, yeah, the whole management psychology and group psychology thing, or rather my interest in it, got started 'cause of Abilene."

"And you've built a career on it."

"Amazing, isn't it? I've known what I've wanted to do since I was sixteen years old."

"That's a rare gift," Angela said, thinking of her own lack of direction. Working at Windsor was not something she could picture doing long term.

The waiter appeared with their salads and departed as soon as he'd placed them.

"So you spend half your time on the road?" Angela asked after she'd swallowed her first bite.

"Some place or other. Usually a week at a time."

"Do you enjoy it or does it get old?"

Dave speared another forkful of salad, chewed slowly, and swallowed before he answered. "There's always new places to see, new people to meet—as well as having clients I've worked with for years, who've become friends. I like traveling. I like coming home. But I'm gone so much that when I do come home it feels like I'm playing catch up. People, friends have moved on in a lot of ways. I miss a lot. But I'd miss the road, the people I'd help, if I didn't travel."

"So it's what you're meant to do."

"It is," Dave said, a smile creeping onto his face. "Not many people get that. How about you? You're working for your uncle."

Angela laughed. "The family, yes. But they're in London. I'm working for Windsor…because they picked me up and dusted me off when I was low."

Dave looked up as Angela stared at her salad. "Well I'm glad you're there. Your smiling face has certainly brightened up my travel."

"Even if you've needed acupuncture?"

"Especially as I've needed acupuncture."

7

"We're doing the Boathouse," Belle told Kate and Angela Sunday morning at brunch. "We talked to your mother and came up with a nature theme. The wedding's set for the third Saturday in May next year. Joe and I had originally talked about doing it the second weekend but then your mother pointed out that's Mother's Day weekend and every year after that I'd be having to choose between celebrating my anniversary in some cute little hotel or with my mother."

"Your mother lives in Baltimore," Kate said.

"Yes, but it's the *idea* that I'd be making myself unavailable."

"So my mother is getting you organized?" Angela asked, cutting into her waffle.

"Yep. We've the location and the theme…Oh, and we've got an appointment at Kleinfeld's on Saturday."

Angela groaned inwardly. Spending the day in a wedding store with her mother might give the woman ideas. Especially if Nicky had said anything to her.

"Wow! Evelyn's free on a Saturday?" Kate asked.

"No," Belle said. "It's just us."

Angela's eyebrows hit her hairline. "My mother is letting you run wild alone in a bridal salon?"

"She's booked with the Crimini wedding and she figured I do sell clothes for a living."

"Yes, you do. And you have fabulous taste. You're lucky, though. She doesn't usually let her brides do anything on their own."

Belle leaned across the table and whispered, "I didn't think you'd want to be in a bridal salon with her."

"Thank you. You have no idea," Angela said. "After the Alex fiasco, I've been afraid they'd go all old-world on me."

"What about Dave?" Kate asked.

"What about Dave?"

"Well, he sounds normal. Other than all that travel. And the bowling. That should help."

"Nicky's not too happy about him, even if he is only friend material. Doesn't trust my judgment."

Kate and Belle shared a look.

"Alex fooled all of us for a while," Belle said. "But we can check out this Dave for you if you want. When are you seeing him next?"

"Probably Saturday. He's in Seattle all this week. What time is your appointment?"

"Nine-thirty. As soon as they open. I want them fresh and not worn down by some entourage or cranky mother."

"Is your mother coming?" Kate asked Belle.

"No!" Belle said, her eyes wide. "God, no! She still thinks Laura Ashley was the height of fashion. I want to be me on my wedding day."

"Which, of course, is fabulous."

"Of course."

"Do you have any ideas yet for your dress?" Kate asked.

"I have a couple in mind but you're just going to have to wait to see them." Belle looked heavenward and zipped her lip.

"Good afternoon, Mr. Ford," Angela said as Dave walked up. "Have your umbrella all packed?"

"Never." Dave handed over his ticket and garment bag. "Believe it or not, people in Seattle only carry umbrellas if it's a total downpour. Usually they just walk bare-headed through the mist."

"And you're always up for some adventure."

"Yes, I am. How about you? Are you willing to risk having me cook for you on Saturday?"

Angela took Dave's boarding pass from the printer. "What time?"

"Around two? You can help me pick out dinner at Union Square."

Angela handed the documents to Dave. "That should be fine. I'm going with a friend to look at wedding dresses in the morning, but we should be done by then."

"Not double booking again, are you?"

Angela laughed. "No, Belle has us opening the shop. I'm sure they'd kick us out long before two."

"Great! I'll see you then at two on the 17th Street corner."

Angela found herself smiling as Dave walked away, and there was not a grumpy passenger the rest of the day.

Kate speared a banana from Angela's plate as it passed. "Umm," she said, closing her eyes and moaning. "I love bananas with maple syrup."

"You don't have to be afraid of food, you know." Angela poured more maple syrup over her pancakes. "Carbs won't kill you. And just think about all the potassium the bananas contain. They're good for you."

"I like being a size four. At some point I'll be all poochie but until then, I'm just going to watch what I eat. You're just lucky you have your mother's metabolism."

Angela took a bite. The fluffy pancakes, salty butter, tangy maple syrup, and tropical sweetness of the bananas hit her taste buds and her eyes rolled back into her head. "I am," she said around the mouthful, trying to control her drool.

"Your mother is your best advertising." Belle picked up the pepper and shook it over her egg white omelet. "Men like to check out mothers," she said, fixing Angela with an intense look of purpose. "Get an idea of what you'll look like in twenty, thirty years."

"What does Joe think of your mother?" If men really did think you'd turn into your mother, Belle might be in trouble.

"She's a decent size 12, even if she is still stuck in 1985. And she is in Baltimore. She's fine for family gatherings and stuff. And she really likes Joe. She won't be a monster-in-law. It is a little nerve-wracking," Belle continued. "Knowing that you're not just getting a spouse, you're getting a whole other family as well. But Kate seems to have survived. And I did like Joe's folks the one time I met them."

"Yes, I did get lucky in the in-law department," Kate said. "Especially as they're here in the city. It's a weird balancing act at first—creating your own life, keeping part of the past, finding a way to fit someone else's family into your own. It won't be such a change for you, though, since it's just the two of you here. There'll just be the holiday and vacation divisions to deal with."

"Divisions." Belle moaned and covered her eyes. "That is the one thing I'm not looking forward to. How do you manage it?"

"It's not too tricky," Kate said. "But then, I don't have kids. It's one thing to miss out on Christmas. It's another to keep the grandparents from the grandkids."

Angela and Belle slowly raised their eyes to her.

"No!" Kate said, stopping their question before it was asked. "But my mother never really complained about my sister Noelle moving New Hampshire until she had kids."

Belle shook her head, a new weight slowing down its movement. "I guess kids really do change things."

"I do have to say, this is a first—an Evelyn bride without Evelyn," their consultant, Cari, said, taking Belle's hand.

"I'm sure she only let me come on my own as I've got her daughter with me," Belle replied.

"You must be Angela!" Cari gushed and turned to clasp Angela's hand. "I've been dying to meet you for years!"

"Thank you," Angela said, throwing the girls a pleading look. She tried to slip her hand out of the grasp. At least the woman hadn't hugged her. "I'm just here today as a friend of the bride."

"Of course." Cari let Angela's hand go. "Well, come with me!" She led the way to a set of dressing rooms centered around a more private lounge than the one in the main salon.

"Do you have anything in mind?" she asked Belle.

"Yes, but I'll show you after we get in the dressing room. I want them to be surprised."

Kate and Angela settled themselves in seats outside the room.

"Avant-garde?" Kate asked, staring at the door Belle and Cari had disappeared behind.

"I would have said yes if it wasn't a nature theme. See-through? Pnina has some see-through ones. Skin's natural, right?"

Kate met Angela's glance, her lips held in her teeth. They erupted into giggles.

"Maybe," Kate said, trying to catch her breath. "But I can't see Belle doing Lady Godiva. In all honesty, 'nature' is the last thing I expected Belle to pick. Fashion forward and edgy would have been more like it.

This must be your mother's doing."

Which was more true than Kate knew. Evelyn usually picked out what the bride wanted right from her head and then tailored things to create a tasteful fantasy that fit.

"Belle must be a nature girl at heart if that's what they're going with," Angela said to her friend. "She nailed your Gaelic wedding."

Kate had wanted her wedding to be a nod to her and Myles's Irish roots without taking on the air of a Renaissance fair. Evelyn had added touches that made it distinctly Gaelic but classy enough that they'd never look back at their photos and cringe.

It wasn't long before Cari was back with three garment bags. Angela thought she spied ruffles before Cari scolded, "Uh uhn uhn," and whisked them away.

A few minutes later Belle emerged. Those hadn't been ruffles, they were blossoms. On this dress, at least. The bodice was tightly fitted and ruched. The sweetheart neckline gave Belle an hourglass figure while the skirt was a perfect proportion of flair and froth.

"Oh, Belle!" the girls said in unison as she stepped onto the platform.

It was perfect.

"I love what the designer has done with the flowers," Belle said, running her hands over them. "It's an edgy interpretation of roses and yet it doesn't scream, *Roses!*"

"It's perfect," Kate and Angela said, still speaking as one.

Belle swished back and forth in it. "I'm thinking no veil."

"So is this your dress?" Cari asked, hovering at Belle's shoulder, a hopeful expression on her face.

"Umm…"

"Try on the other two," Cari said. "That way you'll know for sure."

Belle hiked up her skirts and returned to the dressing room. A few minutes later she emerged in a Lazaro they deemed too frothy. Next was a Pnina that was more what Angela would have put Belle in—a form-fitting mermaid with cascades of roses down the skirt's cut-out.

"Wow!" Kate and Angela said as Belle stepped onto the platform.

"I know. It's me." Belle scrunched up her face. "But it's not the park. Joe and I just want a day at the park with our friends and family."

"Yep. Too formal," Kate said. "Put the first back on."

"Who would have thought our fashionista is really a laid-back girl at heart?" Kate said to Angela when the dressing room door closed. "I was thinking they'd have it someplace like the Waldorf. Even the Boathouse can be fancy."

"I can kind of see it," Angela said. "Both their jobs are pretty structured. And it's stressful putting a wedding together, even if my mother is coordinating it. Who knows? Maybe they'd been thinking formal and she suggested a day in the park as a way of taking some of the pressure off."

"I love your mother," Kate said. "She always seems to know what's best."

Angela groaned. "Please don't say that."

Kate gave her a sideways look. "Why?" Her eyebrows shot up. "Have they done it? Gone old-world on you?"

"Well, I can't read their minds, but I'm beginning to wish they lived in Baltimore. The last couple of Wednesdays have been a little uncomfortable. I get the feeling that one of these days there'll be someone new at dinner."

Kate offered Angela a sympathetic smile. "Maybe you could start working Wednesday nights."

"Family business. You know that will never happen. I could arrange it but as soon as I said anything, my mother would make one phone call and it would all be undone."

The door opened and Belle came out in the first dress again.

"Perfect," Kate said.

"It is, isn't it?"

They spent another hour trying the dress with and without veils before finding a small one that clipped on via a comb in the back, as well as the perfect necklace. They left and grabbed a quick lunch and a celebratory glass of wine at a nearby café before Angela announced that she needed to dash.

"Dave's cooking for me," she informed her friends.

Kate looked up, her fork frozen in mid-air. "You've found a man who cooks for you?"

"He said he gets tired of restaurant food so he likes to cook."

"What's he making?" Belle asked.

"Whatever he finds at Union Square Market."

"We could stalk her," Belle said to Kate. "Run into them accidentally-on-purpose. Then he could cook for us, too."

Angela was half-afraid they would.

Dave waited for her by the street sign, two canvas bags rolled under his arm.

"Did they have to kick you out?" he asked, a grin on his face.

"No, it was actually the first dress she tried on, though we made her try two more just to be sure."

Dave tsked. "And here I was hoping you'd have worked up an appetite."

"Sorry, we finished early enough for lunch. But I'm sure I'll be hungry again in a few hours."

Dave lifted a devilish grin. "Then let's see what we can find to whet it."

They spent the next hour wandering the stalls of the farmer's market that lined the square's pathways. Dave selected lamb chops at one, heirloom tomatoes and zucchini from another. Lemons, lavender, and olives were added to the sacks. Cream and whole milk soon followed. Bunches of fresh herbs. Finally, two bottles of pinot noir.

They strolled back to Dave's apartment, the spring sun warming their shoulders.

Angela stopped in surprise at the space that greeted her when Dave pushed open his door. A true chef's kitchen gave way to a dining room. A spacious living room with large windows lay off to the left.

"I took out the bedroom on this floor," Dave said, following her gaze. He placed the bags on the granite island.

"This floor," Angela repeated. Holy cow. Most New Yorkers had tiny apartments. Even hers was large by New York standards. She actually had rooms.

"There's a loft above with my office. Downstairs, I took most of the former media room and added a master suite, though I left enough space for a couch and TV. There's a guest bathroom and bedroom down there, too."

Angela wandered into the living room. "So you have three levels?"

"Two really. Plus the loft," Dave said as he unpacked the bags.

Dave's view faced into the courtyard. Chairs and a small table sat on the patio below. Angela glanced up at the loft. Situated above the kitchen, it lowered the ceiling and then disappeared, opening up the dining room and giving it a nice sense of height.

Dave selected a dish and placed the lamb chops in it. He drizzled them with olive oil and began chopping herbs. Angela slipped onto a stool across from him.

"Anything I can do to help?"

Dave's mouth curled into a smile but he kept his eyes on his chopping. "I do have something in mind, but you'll have to wait just a bit. I'll get set that up for you once the lamb is marinating."

Once the chops were chilling in the fridge, Dave poured milk, cream, and sugar into a pan and set it on the flame. He dug in a drawer and added a candy thermometer.

"Quite the stove," Angela said, eyeing the six burners, grill, and griddle.

"As I said," he told her over his shoulder, dumping lemon peel into the mixture. "I like to cook."

"So what's that? Lemon pudding? Lemon-lavender pudding?" Angela amended as Dave added a scoop of lavender blossoms.

"You'll see."

He took a spoon and stirred the mixture. Once it had reached whatever temperature he'd been watching for, he pulled it off the flame and set it aside.

"We'll just let that cool a bit before phase two."

"Phase two?"

"You'll love phase two," Dave said with a gleam in his eye.

"What else do we need to do?" Angela asked.

"Nothing for a while. So I was thinking we could play Scrabble."

Angela's brow wrinkled. "Scrabble?"

"You draw letters and come up with—"

"I know what Scrabble is," she said. "I'm just surprised you're suggesting it."

"I find it's kind of like baseball."

Angela didn't say anything to Dave but the look on her face spoke volumes.

"Why do the British love cricket?" Dave asked.

"No idea."

"It combines their two favorite things, sport and tea."

"And baseball…?" she prompted.

"Let's people talk and eat with bouts of action thrown in for excitement."

"So Scrabble—"

"Let's us think and talk and still mind the minor things going on in the kitchen."

Dave stepped over to the hall closet…to the strains of "The Devil Inside."

"Sorry," Angela said. "I should get that."

She pulled her phone from her purse and walked over to the window in the living room. "What's up?"

"Hello to you, too," Nicky said. "I figured since you'd spent the morning immersed in bridal goings-on that you could use an escape. Claire's in town. A bunch of us are going clubbing. You should come along."

"Who's Claire?"

"My future intended. You can meet her and dance away the morning's drama."

"Thanks, Nicky," Angela said. "But I already have plans."

"Ditch the girls. You've spent all day with them."

Angela braced herself. "I'm not with the girls. A friend is cooking me dinner."

Angela could practically hear Nicky's eyes narrow. "A friend. You mean Whatshisname."

"Yes."

Huffing sounds filled the receiver and then silence. It took Angela a moment to realize that Nicky had hung up on her. That wasn't good. Though she wasn't sure she would have wanted to hear his thoughts on the matter.

"Everything okay?" Dave asked as she came back and put her phone away.

"Just my brother. His girlfriend, who I haven't met, is in town. Wanted to see if I'd go clubbing with them."

"Double booked again," Dave said, shaking his head.

"Only in Nicky's eyes." Angela attempted to work a smile onto her face. No need for Dave to notice her concern.

He gave her a hard look before it was replaced with one of sudden remembrance. With a click, he snapped his fingers. "I almost forgot. I picked you up a little something in Seattle. Where did I put it?" His hand tapped in the air as he thought. Then he pointed his finger at Angela and jogged for the stairs to the loft.

"You don't need to be bringing me anything," Angela called after him.

"I know," Dave's voice floated down. "That's what makes it fun."

He trotted back down the stairs with a square package. "Here you go." With a shove, it skidded across the counter and slid to a stop by her arm.

Angela ignored the renewed banging of cupboards and eyed the black ribbon. "Is the ribbon a clue?"

Dave laughed. "Not this time."

She untied it and pulled back the paper to reveal a brown candy box. Angela lifted the lid. "Salted caramels."

"The reason we currently have a salted caramel craze in this country," Dave said. "Even the President orders them."

"Am I meant to try them now or will they spoil my appetite?"

"Um…go ahead and have one or two. You might need the energy."

Angela glanced up. Dave had placed a white container of some sort on the counter. He pulled the towel from the oven door and opened the freezer. Using the towel with both hands, he removed a frosty steel cylinder and plopped it into the white container.

"Why would I need the energy?" Angela asked.

Dave stuck a finger in the lemon-lavender mixture and then into his mouth.

"You're making the ice cream."

It took Angela a minute to get over the shock. "*I'm* making the ice cream?"

"You can stir, can't you?"

"Yes."

"Then you can make ice cream."

Dave poured the mixture through a strainer and into the cylinder. He stuck in a paddle, attached a lid and handle, and carried it over to the table.

"Every so often just give it a couple of cranks this way then that way." Dave demonstrated the technique. "In the meantime, Scrabble!"

They set up the board. Angela picked the highest value tile from the bag and ended up going first.

It was indeed like baseball, she decided after a couple of turns. You needed time to think and plan but could carry on a conversation or—

"Stir!" Dave commanded, breaking into her thoughts

"You're just trying to distract me." Angela gave the handle a couple of cranks and peeked through the lid. "How will I know when it's done?"

The mixture was still pretty soupy but chunks of more frozen stuff had begun to stick to the paddle.

"You'll know. It just won't want to seem to freeze anymore."

Angela brought her attention back to the tiles. "Haven," she said, using the H from Dave's CHARM.

Dave wrote down her score. "What's your haven?"

Angela pulled four tiles out of the bag and placed them on her bar. "Probably my friends."

"Not a place, then?"

"No."

"Well, that's a good answer. Your haven is wherever your friends are. But…never mind." Dave peered at his tiles.

"But what?"

"No, probably one of those questions best left unasked."

Angela thought about it a minute.

"You might as well ask it. Otherwise I'll just keep thinking of what the question could be."

Dave squirmed a little. "I was going to ask, 'But what about your family?' You seem close. But your haven is your friends."

"My family adores me but in some ways I'm a misfit. They don't always get my choices."

"But your friends do."

"Yes. My family is also very overprotective."

Dave added tiles to Angela's V, spelling out QUIVER. "Thirty-six points. So your brother is overprotective?"

"Got that, did you?"

"You seemed a little upset after his call."

It was Angela's turn to squirm. "He didn't like hearing that I had plans with a man."

"Ah. The bad-breakup thing."

"Yep." Angela tried to figure out if she could use Dave's Q. "How about you? What's your haven?"

"Well, these days it's this apartment. But, I guess in many ways, it's the house I grew up in in Kirkwood. My childhood was truly a slice of Americana. Big old house with a big old yard, a neighborhood that decorates for every holiday and every season. Life was simple and easy."

"Do your parents still live there?"

"Yes, even though the house is now much too big for them, all their children living in different states."

"That must be hard."

"Yeah. They'd like to be closer to us, but Mom loves the neighborhood and Dad still has a few more years before he can retire."

"I guess I'm spoiled," Angela said. "Living in the same town as my parents."

"No, they're spoiled," Dave said. "They haven't had to live without you."

"Oh, they did," Angela said, trying to decide if she wanted to use her blank tile. "I used to travel a lot with my old job."

"What was your old job?"

Heat rushed to Angela's face. She really would like to sweep all those years under the rug. Except for Belle. And the income that had allowed her to buy her apartment.

"I modeled." She slapped down her tiles, hoping to distract Dave. "Quince."

Dave studied her for a moment. "I can see that. How does it compare with your new job—other than the being home for Wednesday night dinners and losing people's luggage?"

"Well, as I told you, I'm a klutz so that didn't help."

"I bet you take great pictures," Dave said, rearranging the tiles on his bar.

Angela stared hard at him. It sounded like an off-handed comment. But after Alex…

She dipped into his brain. Dave was trying to figure out how to use his Z, no thoughts at all of her vodka ad. Now she just needed to figure out what to do with the magic. After a fleeting second, she sent it to her phone.

Nicky's ringtone sounded from Angela's purse. "Checking up on you again?" Dave asked. "He really must not trust me."

"Sorry." Angela pulled out her phone. "Hmm. Not there. He must have misdialed."

"Or have a sister who's trying to avoid him. Stir!"

Angela turned the handle a few times and gave an inward sigh. "No, really. He wasn't there. Must have been a pocket dial."

"Uh huh," Dave said with a smile.

"Why? Did you want me to dash off?"

"Not until after dinner, too much for me to eat on my own. And you're not done with the ice cream."

Angela peered through the clear top. Was it finished yet?

"Elegizing," Dave said and started to count his points aloud.

"I don't think it's freezing anymore," Angela told him. She drew her eyes away from the contents of the ice cream maker and groaned. Not only had Dave managed to squeeze ELEGIZING in between two other words, he'd used all seven of his tiles. "Is that even a word?"

Dave pointed a pencil at the dictionary on the table. "Yep. Look it up. It's the process of writing an elegy, a mournful poem. Have you seen the movie *Elegy* with Penélope Cruz and Ben Kingsley?"

"Can't say as I have." Angela gave the handle of the ice cream maker a few more cranks.

Dave wrote down his score. He pulled the ice cream over and peered through the lid. "Yep, time to put it in the freezer." He took the ice cream maker over to the kitchen counter, dug a plastic container out of a drawer, and scraped the ice cream into it. Once it was tucked away in the bottom freezer drawer, Dave returned to the table and picked up the bag of Scrabble tiles.

"Hmm, guess we're getting down to the last ones," he said, staring into the depths of the bag.

"No fair peeking," Angela said.

"There's only five. They're all mine." Dave reached in and scooped up the tiles.

Angela's lips twitched as she studied the board. "How long have you been playing this game?" There had to be some place on the board she could use her B and H and bunch of vowels. Book? Nope, no K.

"Off and on over the years." Dave glanced at the board and began rearranging his tiles. "It was one of our family game night games. I've been playing it more since I added it to my phone."

"Your phone!" Angela choked. "You didn't warn me!"

"Got your little gray cells working, didn't it? It was this or Mexican Train. What have you got in your cupboard?"

"The Game of Life."

Dave smirked.

"What?"

"Nothing." Dave unsuccessfully attempted to arrange his features into a blank expression.

"And you wow clients with that kind of acting job?"

"Okay, Miss Smarty-pants. I was thinking it was the perfect game for someone still searching for their calling." The muscles in Dave's face worked desperately to hold back a smirk.

Angela's eyes narrowed. "Are you trying to insult me?"

"No, no. Just the management consultant in me. I get the feeling that you both like and dislike your job. Your choice of games tells me you wonder how other careers would fit you."

His observation was so close to home that Angela's heart sank. But only for a moment. It hit her belly and surged back up. "And you seem to surround yourself with things you know you'll be successful at. Do you have anything here that could possibly challenge you?"

"Hmm." Dave thought for a moment. "I haven't really touched the sports package that came with my gaming system. I bought it mainly for the exercise program. Though—" Dave's eyes narrowed. "Were you some jock in high school? Basketball? Archery?"

"Archery!" Angela laughed. "Get real. I'm a New York City girl. The only sharp thing I own is a pair of scissors. I have used a steak knife but don't actually own one."

"That's right. You said you don't cook."

"Well, brownies. From a box. But that's it."

"Chocolate!" Dave chuckled. "Of course. But you must have done some kind of sport in high school."

Angela shuddered. "Only in PE. No, I went to high school with Kate, and she was so into art that we spent the afternoons wandering art galleries."

"She was the one into art? What was your thing?"

Angela thought back. "I don't know that I really had a *thing*."

"How did you end up modeling?"

"Discovered at an art gallery shortly after high school graduation." Which had brought relief to a small, terror-filled part of Angela. Kate was headed off to study art history at Brown, and Angela had had no clue what she was going to do with herself.

"A beauty among the beauties," Dave said.

"Something like that. I'd thought it was the worst pick-up line ever when he approached me, but he turned out to be legit." She'd dipped into the guy's head to make sure. Not that she'd mention that to Dave.

Dave fell silent. A thoughtful expression settled onto his face. Just when Angela was going to throw a tile at him to break him out of his reverie, he gave his head a little shake and said, "So how about something neither of us would have done growing up. Cow racing."

"Cow racing?" No way had she heard him right.

"Yep. You ride a cow and jump fences. Knock over scarecrows."

Angela laughed. "You really are ridiculous sometimes."

Dave waggled his eyebrows. "I certainly try."

"I'll have a coffee," Angela told Henri the next morning at her favorite restaurant.

Her waiter's eyebrows shot up in surprise but he wrote it down. *Really!* She'd ordered coffee before. And so what if she was actually reading the menu?

Angela watched Henri go and then brought her attention back to the laminated card. Maybe the salad Niçoise. There was something about meeting Nicky's Claire that made her usual waffle seem like too much.

In the cab ride home from Dave's, Angela had texted Nicky, hoping to meet for brunch. She could have gone clubbing but what with shopping, lunch, more shopping, cooking, and everything else, she'd been ready to put her feet up and watch an old movie.

Nicky had texted back, **BELGIAN PLACE 11AM.**

Angela was still trying to decide on breakfast when Nicky and Claire walked in. Nicky's chosen definitely had some siren genes. With her perfect skin and hair that somehow managed to shimmer between red and gold, even Angela wondered what she'd look like naked.

Angela blinked and looked back at her menu, swallowing down the blush that warmed her cheeks as her brother and his girlfriend wound their way through the crowded restaurant. Thankfully, she managed to compose herself by the time they pulled out their chairs.

"Morning, sis. Claire, this is Angela. Angela—Claire."

"So sorry you weren't able to join us last night," Claire said in a lilting voice so beautiful that Angela found herself somewhat mesmerized.

Join them…last night…

Angela's spoon thunked on the table. Startled, she looked down and found she'd been leaning across the table toward Claire. Nicky chuckled and held a hand over his mouth.

Ew!

"I'd already had a full day," Angela said, rearranging her silverware. "And I have to work this afternoon."

"How was your dinner?" Nicky asked.

"Good." Angela left it at that. He didn't need any more details.

"Oh, come now," Claire said. "I hear the man cooked for you."

"Yes," Angela said. "He gets tired of eating out."

"What did you have?" Claire purred. "I love a man who knows his way around a kitchen."

"Lamb, a couscous salad. Grilled zucchini. Homemade lemon-lavender ice cream."

"Yum. And Nicky tells me he's just a friend?"

"Yes."

"Umm," Claire purred again. Nicky's eyes narrowed. "I would have skipped the club, too."

Henri appeared with Angela's coffee. "Can I start you off with anything this morning?" he asked.

"Why don't you bring us a half-pitcher of Bellini," Claire said.

Henri looked at Claire and gulped. "Sure."

He stayed frozen, staring at Claire, until Nicky cleared his throat. Henri startled, then flashed them a flustered smile and moved off.

"You wicked thing," Nicky said to Claire.

"I know. I just can't help myself," she said with a smile. Claire leaned in closer and whispered to Angela, "And really, why shouldn't I?" She sat back and took a moment to look around. What would Claire make of the quaint restaurant with its bentwood chairs and checkered tablecloths? Angela loved it for its homey atmosphere—and decadent breakfasts—but Claire gave off the air of someone used to more sophisticated surroundings. "I haven't been here before," Claire continued. "Is the food good?"

"Very," Nicky said, wrapping a possessive arm around her.

"What do you usually order?" Claire asked Angela, ignoring Nicky's arm.

Nicky answered for her. "The waffle with ice cream and chocolate sauce and an order of strawberries on the side."

"Sounds tasty! Aren't you glad we don't have to follow those ridiculous diets that the…others have to? It's so nice to be able to order whatever you want."

Henri arrived back at their table as if on wings with the pitcher of Bellini and three glasses.

"No, thanks," Angela said as he started to place one in front of her. "I'm working today."

"That's right," Claire said. "Nicky told me you work at Windsor."

"Keeping Cousin Wendell busy."

"And you met your…friend there?"

"Yes, he accused me of misdirecting his luggage and told me I owed him."

Nicky and Claire shared the same wide-eyed expression.

"How did he know?" Nicky asked. A scowl pulled down his eyebrows.

"He didn't. He loves chaos. He tried to get Julia to purposely tag his bag for Cleveland on the return trip, telling her that way it would end up in New York."

"And he's human?" Claire asked.

"Yes."

"He cooks. He loves chaos. Does he dance?"

"Hey!" Nicky said.

"I don't know," Angela told her.

Claire gave Nicky a smoldering look. "I'm only asking for your sister's sake. So the next time I'm in town, we can double date. He can cook. We can go to a club. See what else develops..."

The look on Nicky's face said there was no way that was going to happen. Then his eyes met Angela's and lingered.

If she hadn't been in trouble before, she was now.

"What is with you today?" Jackson hissed in Angela's ear.

Angela pulled herself away from where she'd been, lost in her thoughts. Nicky had been too quiet during breakfast. While it had been nice to watch him struggle to keep up with a female version of himself, Claire's interest in Dave had not been good. Nicky had to be planning something. Angela was more focused on figuring out what that was than the line of passengers before her.

"Can you at least try to put some of their bags on this flight?"

"What?"

"You've misdirected the last five!"

Angela looked at the tag in her hands. Vegas. Not Miami, which was where Doris Wasserstein was actually headed.

"Leave that one, just don't do any others."

Jackson gave her a hard look and then smiled widely at Doris, who blushed.

Angela forced a smile onto her face. "Off to enjoy the sun?" she asked Doris.

"My son and his family are picking me up at the airport and then we're driving to Disney World. Never too old to enjoy the rides! The kids will get some Grandma time and my son and his wife will get to spend evenings alone."

Angela couldn't ruin a Disney vacation with Grandma! They'd be worried about Grandma's luggage. Maybe even miss a day, waiting for it.

"Who's more excited," Angela asked. "You, the grandkids, or your son and his wife?"

"Definitely me!" Doris chortled. "Sprinkle me with fairy dust and I could fly there myself."

Angela smiled and then made a show of catching something that didn't look right when she went to attach the routing tag to Doris's bag.

"Wait a sec." Angela held it close, supposedly to get a good look at it. Out of the corner of her eye, she caught Jackson rolling his. "Let's just reprint this."

"Don't want my bag to end up somewhere else," Doris said.

"No, that would be a disaster," Angela agreed, reprinting the label. "Can't have Grandma late for the magic."

"Enjoy your trip," she told Doris as she handed over the claim ticket.

Doris waved it at her as she walked away. "Thanks. Enjoy your day!"

"Is Claire still here or has she returned to Dublin?" Angela asked Nicky as they walked through their parents' front door Wednesday evening.

As they rounded the corner to the dining room, Angela stopped short. There at the dining room table, in her favorite room in the house, sat her worst nightmare.

"She's—oomph!" Nicky gasped, crashing into Angela from behind.

The man rose. "Hello, Angela."

"Warrick. What are you doing here?" Angela shoved her brother with her shoulder as he tried to steady himself. Why should she be his salvation when he was her ruin?

"Your mother invited me for dinner. And it's just Rick now."

Angela pressed her teeth together, praying for patience, and took a deep breath through her nose. Swiveling her head back over her shoulder, she beseeched the gods for the ability to shoot laser beams from her eyes.

No luck. But at least Nicky had the grace to look abashed.

Silencing an angry huff, Angela marched through to the kitchen, forcing a smile onto her face as she passed by Warrick—Rick. It wasn't his fault her family was impossible.

The rich aroma of spices hung in the kitchen.

"There you are." Evelyn opened a cupboard door. "You can put the potatoes in this and I'll slice up the bread."

"What is Warrick doing here?" Angela asked, obediently taking the bowl despite her anger.

"It's time you stopped denying who you are. Time to stop messing around with humans and be what you're supposed to be."

"Really? You want me to just ditch Kate and Belle? Won't that be kind of awkward since you're doing Belle's wedding?"

"Don't be ridiculous," Evelyn said. "I mean that man you're currently with. I thought you would have learned after Alex."

"I'm not involved with anyone right now."

Evelyn looked up from the bread she was slicing. "Then the man you blew off your brother for."

She was really going to do it this time. She was going to kill her brother. Angela just needed to figure out how. *Should it be painful? Or in secret?*

"I didn't blow off Nicky. He called me at the last minute and I'd already had a full day."

"Dresses and then dinner, I hear."

"Belle found a dress." Angela tucked a spoon into the potatoes.

"Yes, I've seen the pictures." Evelyn transferred the bread onto a plate. "It's the dinner I'm more concerned about."

"He's just a friend."

Evelyn pinched the bridge of her nose and closed her eyes. "Angela…

your father and I have been very indulgent because we love you. But enough is enough." Her hand dropped away and she gave her daughter a hard look. "I know there's more about Alex than we've heard. You don't seem able to look out for yourself so it's our responsibility to do that for you. You need another gremlin in your life. Someone you don't have to hide your powers from."

"Warrick?" Angela asked in utter disbelief. "He's part of the reason I begged to go to Hewitt. Always pushing the line, seeing what he could get away with."

"They're all like that at that age, dear. Give him a chance. He's teaching computer science at MIT now."

"What? You want me to move to Boston?"

Evelyn pulled the gravy boat from its place on the shelf. "If that's what it takes to make sure you're happy, I'd send you anywhere."

Angela snorted. "Really? And you don't think I'm happy here?"

Evelyn gave her daughter a sad smile. "No. No, I don't."

Angela took a large swig of her wine as she and Kate sat at lunch two days later. "Ever have a nightmare where your parents marry you off to that geeky guy you couldn't stand in middle school?"

"You're getting married?" Kate spluttered, choking on her drink.

"No. But only because I do have a choice."

"Well, since there weren't any guys at Hewitt, I have to use my imagination, but I take it they finally went all old-world on you."

"Yup." Angela stared gloomily into the depths of her wine glass.

"So your family dinner was a nightmare?"

"I actually thought my life couldn't get any more depressing but it has."

"How about dinner with Dave? Was that a bomb?"

Angela shook her head, the wine buzz making the motion somewhat floppy. "It went well. I actually helped cook."

Kate blinked at the glass in her hand and slowly put it down. "I guess I shouldn't drink at lunch. I thought I heard you say you cooked."

Angela polished off her wine and set the glass on the table. "I did. I made the ice cream and grilled the zucchini."

Kate stared at Angela. "You…made…ice cream?"

"Okay, Dave made the ice cream stuff but I stirred it in the thing until it froze."

Kate remained wide-eyed so long that Angela finally waved her hand in Kate's face.

"That's the man you need to marry," Kate said.

Angela rolled her eyes. "We're just friends."

"Yeah, yeah. So you've told me. But instead of inviting Dave over and pushing him your direction, Evelyn asked some geek from your past?"

Angela cradled the empty glass between her hands and slumped over. "Yep. And he won't be the last."

Kate's eyes grew large. "Why?"

"Alex. Stupid, fucking Alex."

"What's he done now?"

Angela squeezed her eyes closed and bent further until her hair fell like a screen. "Fooled me," she whispered. "Proved I can't be trusted to make decisions for myself."

Kate gave a gentle sigh. "He's fooled lots of people. He's a master liar and manipulator. How were you to know?"

But I should have known. I, of all people, had the ability to know what he was, yet I chose not to.

"Maybe my mother was right," Angela muttered.

"Right about what?"

Angela gave her head a shake. "Never mind. Think there's any way I can avoid Wednesday night dinners for…oh, the next six or seven years?"

"Only if you're willing to move. Any openings in London or Paris?"

"Wouldn't matter," Angela said. "I still have relatives in those towns. They'd just pick up the matchmaking."

"Hmm," Kate mused. A wicked grin spread across her face. "Does Dave need an assistant?" she asked, waggling her eyebrows. "He travels all the time, doesn't he? You could claim to be out of the country even when you're not. And think of all those late nights together. Sounds perfect."

"Sounds perfect on the work front, but Dave doesn't travel with an assistant. Not that my parents would know…" Angela shook her head to clear it. "No, it would probably make things worse. If I went to work for Dave, my parents would become all the more anxious to marry me off."

Kate sighed. "I got nothing else."

Angela's phone rang. *Dave Ford* illuminated the display.

"Who is it?" Kate asked.

"Dave," Angela said, and then answered the call.

"Hey!" Dave said, launching in as soon as Angela said *hello*. "I know this is kind of last minute so feel free to say 'no.' Actually, feel free to say 'no' if this isn't your thing, but I've just found out that *Lawrence of Arabia* is playing at the Film Forum. You know, big screen. And I've always wanted to see it, on the big screen. Supposed to be one of those 'must see' movies. Um, so I was wondering if you'd want to see it, too? Unless you've already seen it and hated it or something. Or already have plans. It is kind of last minute—"

"I'd love to," Angela said, breaking in. "I could certainly do with an oasis."

"Well, great! The movie starts at six-thirty. Can you meet me there? My afternoon is pretty full. I'll probably need to go in and finish up on Saturday. But when something comes along you've always wanted to do, you just need to go for it."

"No, that's fine. What time would you like to meet?"

"Six-fifteen? Is that cutting it too close? I could meet you in the lobby. Give you more time to get popcorn before the movie, if you want."

"That's fine," Angela said. "I'll see you at six-fifteen."

Angela put her phone back into her purse. An expression of pure satisfaction had blossomed across Kate's face. "Did you catch a canary I wasn't aware of?" Angela asked. She'd seen similar grins on felines in cartoons. Kate was only missing the yellow feathers.

"Did you just make a date?" The corners of Kate's smile curled even higher.

"I'm meeting Dave at the movies this evening. It's Dave, so it's not a date."

"Hmm." Kate picked up her wine. "Yet it is an oasis."

"We're seeing *Lawrence of Arabia*. I was using a metaphor."

"Weren't you just," Kate said. A triumphant grin spread across her face.

Angela groaned and looked to flag down the waitress. Kate obviously needed some food to soak up that wine.

"I'm so sorry," Dave said again as they sat at a restaurant after the show. "I had no idea the movie was so depressing."

"That does seem to be the part people leave out when they talk about it," Angela said. The spoon clinked against her cup as she stirred whipped cream from the tray of condiments into her coffee.

"The scenery was beautiful though. And I'm glad I saw it on the big screen. You felt like you were there, other than the heat."

"I didn't miss that." Angela frowned as misery washed over her anew. Switch out Arabia for NYC and the movie could almost have been the story of her life. "This was the desert without all the sweating."

Dave seemed to crumple before her eyes. "You've been?"

"Morocco—photo shoot. It was hot. The glare was terrible. And sand has a way of creeping into places you'd rather it didn't. This desert was much better."

"Even with all the death?"

"The death didn't bother me. It was…I don't know. The way he seemed to be made for Arabia but the place was slowly killing him on the inside."

"Yes, two halves that didn't quite seem to fit together."

"What would my management consultant make of that?"

"Idealism is great but it needs to mesh with the real world."

"So he got in trouble for not being who he was supposed to be," Angela said.

"I guess you could say that."

Angela played with a packet of raw sugar. "What about the parts of himself he didn't like? What was he supposed to do about that?"

"If someone had found a way for him to stay in Arabia, some place where he could just live, do you think Lawrence would have died?"

Angela bowed her head and slowly shook it. "I don't know."

"He kept trying to deny the part of him that was truly Arab. He didn't fit back in England and it caused him to become reckless. Denying who he was cost him his life."

The packet tore in her hands, spilling sugar on the table. "Sorry," she said and brushed it away.

"No, I'm sorry. God!" Dave ran his hands through his hair. "You wanted an oasis and not only did I take you to a depressing movie, I let it follow us home."

Angela pulled the sugar container toward her and began to arrange the tubes of sweetener by color. "It was already at my home," she said, sighing. "Have you seen *My Big, Fat Greek Wedding?*"

"Yes, but I thought you were Hungarian. And English."

"I am. But you know how her dad starts bringing home guys for her to meet?"

Dave's face broke out in a grin he tried to hide. "Yup."

"That was my life this week."

"So you identify with Lawrence because you're trying to deny the, what? Hungarian side?" Angela nodded. "Ah. And how was it?"

"Just like the big, fat movie," she said.

"Comb over and all?"

"No. Ew. Just a guy I couldn't stand growing up. I begged my parents to send me to Hewitt to get away from these guys."

"And now they'll be paraded at your family dinners until you pick one of them."

"Yep…You don't need an assistant to travel with you, do you?"

"No, sorry. I think you're perfect for the job you have any way."

"You do?"

"You're kind. You're helpful. Have a good sense of humor. I've never seen you grouchy. You certainly make my travel more enjoyable."

Angela managed a weak smile. "Thanks. I just can't help feeling that it's a dead-end job."

"Modeling was what you really wanted to do?"

"No, a lucky accident. At the time."

"So what's been your dream?"

"I guess I've never really had one," Angela said. *Other than being human*. And that wasn't going to happen.

"What are you good at?"

"Trouble."

"Hmm. I'll have to think about where that particular skill comes in handy. Bail bondsman, maybe," Dave said with a twinkle in his eye. "Causing trouble for the criminal. You're certainly not afraid to break a nail."

"Yes, perfect job for the total klutz."

"Works in literature."

"Which means it won't work in real life."

"You could become a flight attendant. Travel the world. You do have an in at the airline."

"Right," Angela said. "Let's put the klutz inside the tiny tube with turbulence and hot coffee."

"Ouch! Maybe not. Acupuncture's bad enough."

"See," Angela said. "I'm just hard to employ."

"Or you're already exactly where you should be and you just don't know it yet."

Riiight, Angela thought, but she just smiled at Dave over the rim of her cup.

9

Sunday, Angela sent Valerie Manheim's makeup bag to L.A. rather than Paris. Valerie's boyfriend had been a little too suave with Angela. Normally she would have sent his bag somewhere, but when Angela picked up the "blond viper" that Valerie had broadcast, Angela had been more inclined to leave Valerie without her face, at least temporarily, in Paris.

Then there was Max Jurgenson. She ended up not sending his bags, all five of them, anywhere.

His shouting about the extra-baggage fees he should have known about—they were clearly posted on the website—but was refusing to pay only increased when Angela politely asked him to lower his voice and not disturb the passengers around him. He made such a ruckus she wouldn't have been surprised if they could hear him down at the British Air and Air France counters.

Max then made the mistake of asking for Angela's supervisor. Actually, Max slapped his hand on the counter and *demanded* to speak to her supervisor.

Angela couldn't blame the people who took a step away, creating a greater space for Max's hostility bubble. That was a lot of negative energy he was throwing off.

"Certainly, sir," Angela said, unable to rein in the grin that spread from ear to ear. "Let me get him for you."

One didn't cause a disturbance on Windsor, especially in first class. The airline was known for its serene luxury cabin. Even business and coach made more of an effort. Where other airlines had cut back their services along with their prices, Windsor had instituted an a la carte structure. Sure, some passengers were perfectly fine eating whatever the standard dinner and lunch and breakfast were in their class. Others were more than willing to pay an extra fifty dollars and more to select meals from an award-winning menu tailored for each route. Additional amenities included a sliding scale for buying your seat selection, instituted long before British Airways introduced their program, and a structured baggage program where no package was too strange or too big.

The result was happy customers. Happy customers willing to pay, and they expected fabulous service and some tranquility. If you were over the age of five, you needed to be quiet and polite.

Max turned puce when Angela's supervisor informed him that Windsor would be refunding his ticket and he was now free to seek travel on another airline. As he stood there spitting incoherently, the other passengers broke into applause.

Maybe Dave had a point, Angela thought as she basked in the glow of the happy people around her. Working at Windsor did have its rewards.

Angela wasn't certain what the reward of her family dinners was. Who could it be this week? Gregory Bakó who'd liked letting the air out of the tires of the more aggressive taxi drivers as they'd whizzed by? Or Roland Rothschild who'd always stuck his foot out to trip the bike couriers that ventured onto the sidewalks, saving his magic for truly spectacular events. Angela was certain there had to be someone.

An odd sensation in her finger interrupted her thoughts. Looking down, she found her index finger had turned purple, the chain of her purse wrapped so tightly around that it had cut off the circulation. Angela unwound the strap and flexed her hand to get the blood moving again.

No way were her parents going to stop the parade with Warrick. But there had to be some way to make it end.

Without actually marrying one of them. Angela shuddered. Her hand shook as she knocked on the door of her parents' apartment.

"Did you forget your key?" Evelyn asked when she let Angela in.

"Um? Yes?"

Evelyn rolled her eyes and bustled Angela in. "You can finish setting the table."

Four place settings sat stacked in the center. Angela let go of the breath she'd been holding. Just Nicky.

Though that wasn't Nicky's voice coming from her father's office.

Did she really want to know?

Yes. It could be just a client of her father's or something. No sense worrying if it was nothing.

Angela left the table untouched and snuck down the hall to peek into her father's office.

Young and nerdy. Not a client.

"Ah! Angela," her father called out, spying her in the doorway. "Come in and meet Reggie Knowles. Works at Microsoft."

"Programming," Reggie said. "Have you used Cloud?"

"Didn't Amazon develop that?" Angela asked, hovering in the doorway.

Reggie nodded. "Yep. Moved over from Amazon to help Microsoft develop and launch their version. Help keep it up to date."

"So you really just work with hot air." Angela inched her way backward.

"Not air, the fifth dimension. Or at least one of the seven that aren't time or spatial."

There were others? Angela squeezed her eyes shut. She didn't really want to know. "Actually, I was looking for Nicky."

"He had a client dinner tonight," her father said.

Of course, he did.

Angela pasted a smile on her face. "That's too bad," she said between her clenched teeth. "I'll just go set the table like Mum asked."

"You have to save me!" Angela pleaded into the phone from her perch on the toilet. Her hushed voice bounced around the tiled room.

"Are you okay?" Dave asked, his voice sharp with concern. "What's that strange echo…? Oh, my God! Are you at a hospital?"

"No," Angela moaned.

She heard Dave exhale. "Wait." Angela could practically hear the thoughts bouncing around in his brain. "It's Wednesday…You're at your parents'."

"Yep," Angela said, popping the P at the end of the word.

Dave's gentle laughter drifted through the phone. "I take it you're hiding from the parade."

"I've been dropped into an episode of *The Big Bang Theory*. He's been talking about other dimensions since we were introduced."

"Is he a physicist?" Dave asked.

"Programmer for Microsoft. Works on the Cloud."

"I love that application," Dave said. "Very handy."

"You're not helping."

"Are you looking for someone on a white horse?" Dave asked. "How would your parents take to me showing up?"

Angela pictured their reaction and groaned. She slapped her free hand across her eyes, catching its downward motion just before she smeared her makeup. "It would just make things worse."

"Then I guess I can't ride to your rescue."

"I guess not," Angela said, slumping further.

"What would you like me to do to save you?"

"I don't know." Angela sighed, considering. "I could really use another glass of wine but I have to work in the morning."

"Why don't you tell your mother you have a Belle emergency and I'll buy you dessert at that patisserie in the Village that stays open until the wee hours. She could be freaking out about some wedding detail."

"You're a genius!" Angela said, hopping up. "I'll see you there in twenty!"

Angela closed her eyes and licked her spoon. "Chocolate really does make everything better."

"So you keep telling me," Dave said with a gentle laugh.

Angela focused on her spoon and fought the urge to pick up her plate and lick remains of the molten center of her lava cake from it. It would be a waste of good chocolate, but she was in public. Manners and all that.

"Don't forget to fill Belle in in case your mother checks up on her," Dave said. "She's coordinating Belle's wedding, right?"

Angela's eyes snapped open. "Thanks. I'd be sunk if she figured out the reason I'd run off wasn't real."

Dave took a sip of his beer. "How long will you need to put up with this?"

"Every Wednesday until I'm engaged. To someone they approve of."

"That's a lot of chocolate cake."

"Thanks again," Angela said. "For the cake and the excuse."

"My pleasure," Dave said. "So, you don't think their plan will work?"

Misery marched across Angela's face, etching it into a mournful mask. "Even Nicky skipped out tonight."

The sympathetic shake of Dave's head warmed her heart until Dave added, "Well, you're on your own the next two weeks. I'm off to Strasbourg on Saturday."

"Doing something for the Council of Europe?" Angela asked.

"For a client who does something for the Council of Europe."

"Fancy."

"No, that would be Gregor's weekend house on the Neckar in Heidelberg."

Angela wistfully shook her head. "What an exciting life you lead."

Dave laughed. "Sounds like I've got a lot to do to catch up with you, Ms. Former Fashion Model. Photo shoots in the Moroccan desert. I bet you've been lots of places I've never been."

"At least we share a common theme, lots of travel for work instead of pleasure. Speaking of which," Angela said, checking her watch. "I really should head home. Early alarm."

Dave gulped down the rest of his beer and flagged down the waiter. "Well, I'm glad I could ride to your rescue this time."

"Yes, you've been a prince. Any special upgrade I can stick in the system for you?"

"I'm already flying first class," Dave said, digging out his wallet. "You can make it up to me in the kitchen."

An unladylike snort erupted from her. Good thing she wasn't the one with a beer. It probably would have come out her nose. "Certainly, Rumpelstiltskin. I'm great at turning straw into gold."

Dave chuckled. "You're getting better, you know. Haven't had any more fires. You already do brownies. Maybe we'll move on to cookies. My sister Jenny has this great mocha cookie recipe that looks like scoops of ice cream. You'd only need to mix and scoop."

Angela ran a finger over her plate, gathering the chocolate her fork hadn't managed to scrape up. "Deal."

"God! What time is it?" Nicky's sleep-laden voice demanded the next morning.

"Six!" Angela sang cheerfully into her phone. "No rest for the wicked!"

"I had dinner with a client." Angela was pleased to hear him wrestling with his sheets.

"That you purposefully scheduled so you wouldn't have to meet 'Reg'."

"Are you going to do this every morning?" Nicky asked.

"Yep. Every time you leave me alone with the results of your having opened your big, fat mouth, I'm going to make sure you suffer as well."

"Reg, huh? Sounds like one from Mom's side."

"He was a total geek! Spent the whole time talking about the eleven dimensions of reality. It was like having dinner with the guys from *Big Bang Theory*."

Nicky chuckled. "Could have been worse. Could have ended up with someone from Wendell's side."

Angela shuddered. "You're going to have to be there, Nicky. Every dinner. Every week. Until this goes away. You will be the buffer between me and…them. Unless you can find a way to keep me out of it, too. Or make it stop."

Nicky sighed. "I knew I should have put my phone on silent when I went to bed."

"Suffer, Nicky! I will find a way to make you suffer!"

Angela pressed the button and disconnected the call before she could hear Nicky's reply.

The savory aroma of lamb porkolt greeted Angela and Nicky before they opened the door to the apartment. Angela ignored the dark-haired man talking to her father in the living room and drifted into the kitchen.

"Ummm." Angela inhaled the steam rising from a pot bubbling away on the stove.

"There's palacsinta for dessert tonight," her mother said, slicing a loaf of bread.

"Palacsinta!" Angela's mouth watered. Creamy pancakes filled with almonds and drizzled with chocolate. She could taste them already.

"I know they're your favorite," Evelyn said. She added noodles to a boiling pot of water and stirred them with a spoon.

"Bribing me now, are we?"

"It never hurts to see what's out there." Evelyn placed the bread on a plate and handed it to Angela.

"Who is it this week?"

"Zoli Gaspar."

Zoli Gaspar? The Shrimp? The man talking to her father must have finally grown. She hadn't noticed any difference in height between them. The Zoli she remembered had vaguely reminded her of Napoleon.

"What's he doing these days?" Angela asked.

Her mother gave her a push toward the door. "Why don't you go ask him yourself?"

Angela wandered back down the hall. Zoli stood with Nicky and her father, deep in conversation, glasses of wine in their hands. Angela placed the bread on the table and went over to join them.

Zoli still looked a bit like Napoleon. Same lightly curved nose, same dark hair, and piercing blue-gray eyes. He stood at ease, chatting with her father and brother, and flashed Angela a warm smile as she approached.

"Nice to see you again," he said.

"Been a long time," Angela acknowledged.

"Thirteen? Fourteen years? Ever since you transferred schools."

"Probably," Angela said. "How have you been?"

"Good," Zoli said, a slight quirk to his lips.

"Zoli's a news photographer now," Angela's father informed her.

"Really?"

"Staff photographer at the *Daily News*," Zoli said with a hint of pride.

"That seems like an odd profession for a gremlin."

"Nah," Zoli said with a smile. "Puts me out there with all the action." He threw a glance at Damon. "Lets me use my magic in different ways." Angela got the feeling he wanted to say something more, but Zoli tossed another glance Damon's direction and simply smiled.

"Angela!" Evelyn called from the kitchen. "Can you come here? I need your help."

Angela pushed her chair back from the dinner table and excused herself.

"I forgot to get whipping cream," her mother said as Angela came through the door. "Can you run down to the corner and get some?"

"Carton or can?" Angela asked.

"Can. It will keep longer."

"Sorry, gentlemen," Angela said as she walked past the table and picked up her purse. "Mother forgot the whipping cream."

"Can't have that," Damon said, his eyes twinkling, which Angela found odd. Until Zoli pushed back his chair.

"Mind if I join you?"

Angela hid a small sigh of exasperation. So that's why her mother had "forgotten" the whipping cream. "No. Fine. Come along then."

Zoli followed her out to the elevator. They were silent as they waited for it, silent after the doors opened, silent as Angela pushed the button for the lobby.

Zoli finally spoke about two floors down. "I get it now."

Angela shot him a sidelong look. "Get what?"

"This thing you have with humans, their vulnerability. I see it every day with what I do."

"Yes," Angela said. "Hard to play around with that."

Zoli fell silent again.

"What do you do about it?" Angela asked.

The elevator doors opened. Zoli put his arm against the door to keep it from closing again and made an "after you" gesture with the other.

"Help when I can," Zoli said as he followed her out. "The fire fighters and police officers I cover, their fears are easy to read, their concern." He was quiet for a moment, and his seriousness transformed. A laugh brightened his face. "Never thought I'd turn into you, but they've become friends. I probably have more human friends now than…other friends.

"So anyway, these days I generally use my magic to help them out, make sure things go more smoothly. Bolts on hydrants come right off. I adjust the traffic lights so they get where they're needed quicker. Make sure cellphone batteries don't go dead. Things like that. I get it."

Angela opened the door to Paulsen's Corner Market and made her way back to the dairy case. "Well, it's nice to hear you say that."

"I think most of us have grown up, Angela. We were young. The temptation to do parlor tricks was just too great. Don't you think most of us grow out of that?"

Angela opened the refrigerator door, grabbed a can, and shut it. Her fingers tightened around the handle. "Not from what I've seen. My father creates success from unlikely stories. Not life changing ones, just stories that no one else seems to want. And my mother manipulates the system for her brides. Someone else's arrangements fall through because of her.

"And then there's me." Angela headed toward the front of the store. "I finally figured out I have to use…mine…every once and a while or things happen that I definitely don't want. Because of me, someone's trip is ruined."

"But are you choosing or do you leave it to chance?"

Angela put the can on the counter by the register.

"Anything else for you?" the clerk asked. His gaze shifted from the can of whipped cream over to the rack of condoms on the wall.

Heat rushed to her face. "No, just this." *Please don't notice. Please don't notice.*

The clerk ran the can over the scanner.

Zoli bent close to her ear. "Are you going to let him get away with that?" he whispered.

"$3.97," the clerk said. Angela handed over a five. He counted out her change and slid the can into a narrow paper bag. Magic brushed past Angela as the clerk handed Angela the bag.

She waited until they'd left the store before she whirled around and demanded, "Okay, Mr. I-Only-Use-My-Magic-For-Good, what did you do?"

"Really!" Zoli said. "Can't a man and woman buy a can of whipped cream without people thinking it's for sex? The man needs to get his mind out of the gutter."

"What did you do?" Angela repeated.

"His next five transactions will all ring up as condoms."

Her laugh bent her double. Angela tried to stand, but humor had wrapped itself around her middle, seizing her muscles. She inched her way over to the wall, gasping for breath, tears leaking from her eyes.

"You want me to hold that for you?" Zoli asked, his face twisted into an amused expression.

Angela shook her head. She put a hand on her side and straightened up, finally drawing a breath. It was still a moment before she could say anything.

"And here you'd told me you'd become Mother Theresa," she said, wiping at the tears, and nearly poked herself in the eye with the can.

"Okay, give that to me." Zoli eased the can from her grip. "You're endangering your well-being with that."

"See, that's my problem. With or without my magic, I'm a total klutz."

A chuckled rippled, shaking Zoli's chest, but he didn't say anything.

"What?"

He slowly shook his head, a smile radiating across his face. "You haven't grown out of that?"

Angela gave him her best disapproving look. "No," she said, and started down the sidewalk.

"I've always thought it was cute. You always seemed so bewildered when things happened."

"Almost poking myself in the eye had nothing to do with magic."

"That's what's so cute about it—a powerful magical being who's a klutz. Though I bet it would happen less if you used your magic more."

Angela glared at Zoli as the doorman held the door open for them.

"What I'm trying to say," he continued, "is that I like you, just as you are. Always have, though I was too shy in my teens to say anything. I was short. You were tall and beautiful. The klutz thing made you less intimidating, but you didn't hide the fact you couldn't stand gremlins. That and how I didn't even come up to your chin kept me from asking you out then. But I'd like to do that now. Ask you out."

The elevator doors opened. Angela sighed as she got on. "I'm not in a good place right now, Zoli. My last relationship ended badly. I'm not looking to start a new one right now."

The elevator cables rumbled like thunder in the silence that followed.

Zoli opened his mouth but then shut it. The muscles in his jaw worked for a moment. "You sure I can't buy you coffee sometime?"

The elevator dinged at their floor.

"I don't think that would be fair to you."

Zoli held the elevator door open for her. "Well the offer still stands. If you'd like to join a gremlin who likes you, idiosyncrasies and all…"

"Then I'll give you a call at the Daily News," Angela promised.

Kate's text alert chimed as Angela rode in the cab back home. **How was this one?**

Not bad. Definitely an improvement.

So?

Nothing. I'm not dating.

Angela's phone rang. "So tell me about him," Kate said.

"I knew him in school, the one before Hewitt."

"So your parents really are working their way through your middle school yearbook?"

Angela sighed. "Seems like it."

"But this one wasn't so bad?"

"No." *He really wasn't.* She might even have gone out with him all those years ago, if he'd asked. If he'd been as sweet as he'd been tonight. She'd been sorry to see him go halfway through dessert when he'd dashed off to cover a fire in the East Village. Maybe she'd give him a call one day. One day when she didn't feel like such a failure.

Angela had received two voice mails while she'd been at work. The first one was from Dave.

"Just calling to see if you survived the parade this week. Hate the six-hour time difference. Text me back so I know you're not lying in a coma in some hospital due to an aneurism brought on by the stress of keeping a smile on your face. Or leave a voice mail if you need to unload all the gory details. Feel free to take your time. I've got unlimited international minutes. Though I'm not sure what the capacity of my mailbox is. Anyway, here's hoping you survived."

Angela smiled and saved Dave's message then pulled up the next one. It was from Belle.

"Meet me for breakfast before we meet with your mother tomorrow? In the coffee place next door to her office? We could do the Belgian place if you'd rather. Just let me know."

Evelyn was turning them loose again without her, this time for the bridesmaid dresses. She was having Belle and Angela come in and see if they couldn't add to Belle's storyboard before the shopping trip. Evelyn had all her brides put one together—a poster that ended up being a collage of all the elements of the wedding. She found it kept the more "odd" elements from sneaking into the plans, such as the bride and groom who'd loved Chinese food so much they wanted to have their wedding at Jing Fong, not just the reception. Evelyn had opened her huge collection of binders and showed the couple the Banquet Suite at the Asia Society and the entire planning process shifted. Ben and Tracie's wedding still had the Chinese influences they wanted but without having to share space at a busy restaurant.

Coco's is fine, Angela texted back. **What time?**

9?

See you then

Belle took a big bite of her breakfast sandwich—egg white omelet, avocado, and tomato on toast. She chewed carefully, swallowed, and sighed. "Just what I needed to calm my nerves."

"You're not scared of my mother, are you?"

"No. God, no! It's all those details. My mother sent up one of those books for brides. The check list was three pages long!"

"You've got a whole year to get it all done."

Belle chewed and swallowed another bite. "Yeah, but I have a feeling it's going to fly by like nothing. And some of the lead times can be horrendous." A look of terror crossed her face. "What if I forget something!"

Angela chuckled. "Do you really think my mother would allow that to happen?"

"No, no. You're right. Evelyn's too well organized. I'm fine. Perfectly fine." Belle bit into her sandwich again, though she still looked as if she expected something to jump out at her.

Angela shook her head. Her mother would smooth Belle over.

Evelyn's office was located on the second floor of a converted house in the Village and reflected her British upbringing. The walls had been painted a deep lavender, a color which made any white—the antique molding, the oversized plate rail, and bridal dresses—seem to glow from within. Couches covered in a luxurious nickel-colored velvet invited one to sink into them, yet they were firm enough that one didn't get too comfortable and could attend to the business at hand. Evelyn's desk was mahogany, as were the racks of bookcases that housed leather binders sporting tidy labels. A refreshment center housed a Nespresso machine, a plug-in tea kettle, and a jar of lavender shortbread. A collection of tea pots and various cups for tea and coffee ran along the plate rail, just begging to be taken down and used.

Ginny, Evelyn's assistant, was nowhere to be seen when Belle and Angela arrived.

"Morning, girls!" Evelyn called out when they arrived. "Can I get you anything?"

"Thank you, but we just came from Coco's."

Evelyn gestured toward the sofas. She laid Belle's storyboard on the poufy ottoman between them.

"Today we're going to try and add in some more elements to your theme so you have a better idea of what you're looking for when you're out tomorrow." She handed Belle a binder with her name on it. "I've collected some ideas for you of various elements, all separated by tab. Go ahead and flip through and see if anything speaks to you."

Belle opened the binder and gulped. She shot Angela a look of terror.

"Why don't you start with something fun?" Angela suggested. "How about the 'Favors' tab?"

Belle's hands shook as she turned to it. The first page showed a nest with three speckled eggs in it.

"Those are truffles," Evelyn said, pointing to the eggs, and then flipped to the next page. "The chef has favor boxes we can use as well."

"Ooh!" Belle ran her fingers over the picture. Clear boxes had been filled with iced cookies and an assortment of sweets in pale pastel shades of blue and green. "This is perfect!"

Evelyn pulled the pages out and set them on the board. "If you like the nest idea, there's a designer who does the most wonderful handcrafted fabric birds you could use for the cake topper." She slipped her finger under the tab marking the section and found the page.

"Those are cute," Belle said, but her face didn't reflect her words.

"She does custom sets, as well. She's always getting new fabrics in." Evelyn pointed to a pair of particularly smart dressed birds. "These were made out of the satin and lace of an Edwardian wedding dress that was beyond repair."

Belle's eyes took on a shine. "I wonder what other fabrics she has."

Evelyn popped that page out as well and added it to the stack. "So, you have the dress, location, party favors, and cake topper. Do you like the blue and green?"

"I do. And I like the pale yellow of the hydrangeas on that table," Belle said, pointing at the favor box photo. "The whole setting just says spring."

"Have you thought about the fabric choice for your bridesmaid dresses?"

"Chiffon? Something floaty?"

"And how about color?"

"Hmm."

Evelyn hopped up and pulled down one of the binders. "I know you work in fashion but it often helps to get an idea of what's out there before you go. This is the color palette for Badgley Mischka's current spring collection."

"I like this dusty violet," Belle said, fingering a swatch. She tucked the favor box photograph next to it. "The other colors play off it so well."

"Let me give Gail, the baker, a call and have her put together a collection of your color choices for the items in the favor boxes. You can take those with you and see how everything's going to work together. Provide you with a little snack to keep your energy up, as well."

Belle looked much more relieved.

"Thank you so much, Mrs. Grimalke."

Angela could see the reason for Belle's long looks before the reason walked through the door to the salon. Not only had Belle's sister Piper joined them, but so had Belle's mother, dressed in her usual skirt and twin set accessorized with a single string of pearls.

"She just showed up!" Belle hissed in Angela's ear as she hugged her hello.

Piper looked around her and sniffed. "Am I going to be able to afford this?"

"Don't worry, dear. I'm sure I'll be the one paying for the dress," Belle's mother, Janice, said.

"Mom, we've talked about this," Belle said. "You bought my dress. Joe and I are paying for the rest of the wedding. And yes, Piper, that means I'm paying for your dress." She threw Angela and Kate a *Help me!* look.

"The dress I didn't get to help you pick out. Do I even get to see it before you walk down the aisle?"

"I'm sure Belle can make an appointment for you to see her in the sample," Angela said.

"But I'm only here for the day."

"If you'd warned me, Mother, I could have made an appointment."

"But you didn't want to include me in the activities. You would have invited me, if you had. I wouldn't have needed to tag along with Piper."

The clerk came along at that point.

"Hi!" Belle said. "Appointment for Pearson."

"Ah, yes. One of Evelyn's brides. Right this way."

"What kind of wedding planner have you hired?" Janice asked. "I suppose I should be glad that if I wasn't there for your dress neither was she. But really! Is she going to make you do everything on your own?"

"I haven't hired her, Mother. As I told you before, Angela's mother is doing this as a gift. And I just met with her yesterday. She was great in helping me narrow down my ideas for today."

"So we won't be here all day?" Piper drawled. "I don't want to spend my entire day looking at clothes."

"And they wonder why Belle didn't invite them for the wedding dress," Kate whispered to Angela.

"Think I should try to get them into Kleinfeld's? I could text my mother."

Piper pulled out a dress. "I'm not wearing yellow. Or satin. Yellow makes me look like a Martian and satin adds ten pounds."

"I'm going with something in the purple family," Belle said. "In chiffon."

"You think chocolate will put them in a better mood?" Angela asked Belle. She pulled out a white paper bag and passed it to her. "I swung by and picked up those samples for you."

The clerk ushered them into a large dressing room that already contained three racks of dresses. "Evelyn said you were leaning toward cocktail length chiffon and would probably go with something purple. I've pulled some to get you started but feel free to wander out and browse. And let me know if you have any questions."

She threw Belle a sympathetic smile and shut the door behind her.

"Nothing will put them in a better mood," Belle muttered and peeked in the bag. She rummaged around, pulled out what looked like a bird's egg, and popped it into her mouth. "Umm," Belle said as she chewed. "Definitely having those, tho-ough—" She swallowed and gave Angela a significant look. "I'm surprised there are any left."

"What's that? What are you eating?" demanded Piper.

"Party favor samples." Belle pulled out two clear boxes.

"Pastels? Eggs?" Piper said, wrinkling her nose.

"Joe and I are having a nature theme. Mrs. Grimalke sent samples to help me coordinate my colors."

"I'm not wearing pastel. It will wash me out." Piper crossed her arms.

"Nature? You're a city girl. Why would you want nature?" Janice asked.

"It's relaxing. It's fun. We're getting married in the park. It's perfect."

"I thought you were getting married in a restaurant."

Belle started to tear up. "The Lake Room looks out over the park and the lake. My dress is covered in flowers."

A furrow formed on Piper's brow. "Flowers?" She shuddered.

"Maybe you should see the dress. Have dinner at the restaurant," Kate said.

Angela texted her mother. **911! Belle's mom a nightmare. Appt possible today at K's? Dinner at Boathouse?**

Belle's phone began to ring.

"Hi, Mrs. Grimalke," Belle said. "Yes, we just got here…Yes, they're being very helpful…Oh! You can do that?…No. Joe's working tonight."

"What's going on?" Janice hissed.

Belle put her hand over the phone. "We can show you the dress this evening. At five."

"We?"

"Well, I can."

"Angela and I can come, too!" Kate said.

Janice narrowed her eyes at Kate. "I'd been looking forward to a quiet evening with my daughter."

"But this way you could see the dress. Evelyn—Mrs. Grimalke—can get us a table for the Boathouse, too," Belle said.

"For five?"

"More like six-thirty, I think, since our other appointment's at five."

"I meant people," her mother said.

Belle gave Kate a desperate look.

"We need to celebrate that you're in town. And you'll love the venue," Kate said.

"I want you to spend some time with my friends, too," Belle added. "Let us welcome you to New York."

"I don't like the shoulder on this one," Piper said, holding up a dress. "No one-shoulder things…Ugh! Especially with flowers." She held up another.

Belle's mother closed her eyes. "Fine. Do whatever you want, Belle. You always do."

"Sorry, Mrs. Grimalke—Evelyn. Yes, both should be fine. And reservations for five people if you can." *Thank you*, Belle mouthed to Angela.

Kate walked over to the other end of the rack. Piper glared at her then turned her frown back to the dresses. The hangers began to protest as she scraped them across the rod.

"Ooh! Belle, come look at this!" Kate said, pulling one from the rack and holding it up in front of her. "What do you think? It's floaty. The flower detail is just a hint of your dress."

Piper huffed and flicked the dresses quicker.

"I like that one," Belle said.

Piper held up one. "How about this one? It's plain."

"I thought you didn't want satin," Belle said. "The sash and underskirt are satin."

"Better than the fabric corsage. This would provide a blank canvas for your bouquets."

Kate held the dress out again. "Huh. Hadn't thought of that."

"Of course you didn't," Piper muttered under her breath.

"Maybe we should just narrow it down today to your top three or four," Angela said. "It's still a year away. You might change your mind in six months."

Belle chewed on her lip. "That's true."

Piper spun and looked at them in horror. "So, I've come out here for nothing!"

"You've already given us lots of feedback," Kate said. "No yellow. No satin. No flowers. How would Belle know what not to pick without you?"

Piper glared at Kate and walked over to another rack.

"Are you sure you don't want long? This is kind of pretty." Piper held up a long, flowing chiffon number with beading on the bodice. Angela frowned, trying to place where she'd seen it before. Oh, yeah. Kate Winslet's evening dresses in *Titanic*.

"I thought it would be hard to get in and out of the gondolas in a long dress," Belle said.

"Gondolas!" Piper and Janice exclaimed.

"You can hire them to row people on the lake. They look so pretty in some of the photographer portfolios Joe and I have seen online."

Piper's hand dropped, creating a puddle of lavender-gray silk at her feet. Then in one smooth motion, she turned her back on Belle and slammed the dress onto the rack.

"Good idea," Angela said. "The weather should be nice and people are always out rowing on the lake. Reminds me of all those Edwardian stories where he's dressed in white with a straw boater and she's carrying a parasol."

The hangers in Piper's direction stopped moving.

"Well, let's get this show on the road," Angela said. "Things always look different on the hanger than the person." She pulled the plain dress that Piper had suggested from the rack. "Belle, you take a seat, enjoy the delicacies in the bag, and Kate and I will model these for you."

"Hey! That's not fair!" Kate exclaimed. "You're a professional! I'm eight inches shorter than you and I've never done a catwalk."

"That may be true," Angela said, her eyes twinkling. "But you've got attitude."

"It's the red hair," Kate said with a grin, and took the corsage dress with her.

Two hours later Belle had narrowed her choices down to four, the top pick being, oddly enough, the more plain dress Piper had suggested.

They flagged down two taxis—one for Belle's family and one for Angela and Kate—and gave the address of a wine and chocolate bar in Chelsea.

"Oh, my God!" Kate said as she sank onto the seat of their taxi. "If we weren't on our way to fortification, I'd have you just shoot me now. We've still got five hours of them!"

"What do you think Belle will do if her mother hates her dress?" Angela asked.

"I'm sure that's why she went without her. And can you imagine what it would have been like with Piper there, too?"

A shudder rocked Angela's frame. One that Kate joined in with.

"Well, it's on order and we both know it's perfect. We'll just have to gush loud enough to drown them out," Angela said.

"Can't you—" Kate began and then stopped.

"What?"

"Never mind."

"Can't I what?" Angela asked.

"Get enough wine into Belle that she's too oblivious to really notice any comments those two might make?" Kate said, though Angela got the feeling that wasn't what she'd originally been going to say.

She let it pass. "That's just what I need, Piper and Janice thinking I like to get Belle drunk."

"At least they're going back to Baltimore. Thank God they live in Baltimore."

"Yes," Angela said. "With luck we'll only have to see them a couple of more times before the wedding."

"Makes you realize how fortunate we are to have families that aren't like that. Though your parents are putting you through that parade."

"I don't know that they'll keep that up," Angela said.

Kate looked sideways at her. "Really? Why is that?"

"Zoli was kind of perfect."

"I see," Kate said. Her face looked suspiciously like she was holding back a smirk. "Perfect, huh? So they know that, do they?"

Angela blushed. "Well, I didn't say anything to them, but…"

"You didn't fight them on this one," Kate finished for her, no longer attempting to hold back the smile.

"No. Not really."

"Any idea—"

"No!"

"Okay. Just wondering. You're friends with Dave. You could be friends with Zoli…in the meantime."

"Zoli would like to date me. Dave does not."

"He asked you out? Zoli, I mean."

"Yep."

"Hmm. Well, at least you have one waiting in the wings. For whenever you're ready."

Kleinfeld's had the dress already pulled and waiting for Belle in the dressing room. Once again, Angela's breath stole away when Belle came out in it. Kate uttered a similar gasp.

Piper flicked her gaze up and down Belle. "It's definitely…you," she drawled and pointedly turned her attention to a display.

Janice said nothing.

"Mom?" Belle asked.

Janice squeezed her eyes shut. "My baby's getting married," she choked out and covered her eyes with a hand.

"Oh, Mom," Belle said as her mother began to sob.

"You just look so beautiful," Janice said and reached for Belle, drawing her into a hug.

Piper rolled her eyes and jiggled her foot. "What time is dinner?" she asked, crossing her arms and looking away again.

"Not soon enough, apparently," Kate whispered to Angela.

"Well, at least Janice likes it," Angela whispered back. "I was really worried there."

"So was I," Kate said, watching Belle and her mother laugh and blot their eyes with tissues. "Now we just need to survive dinner."

Angela still hadn't recovered from it the next day. Janice had complained all through dinner that if Belle "wanted to get married in a restaurant" that there were "plenty in Baltimore" that she could have chosen. And her blood still ran cold from all the chilly glances Piper had shot at her and Kate. They had been so worried about the browbeating Belle's mother and sister were dishing out that Kate had texted Joe during a trip to the ladies room.

At least they'd taken an early flight back to Baltimore. She'd had been half afraid they'd track her down at work to confront her about something.

Still half lost in her thoughts, Angela didn't notice the next customer until he set his passport down on the counter.

"Hello, doll."

Giving herself a shake, Angela looked up. Tall. Blond. Nordic. His hair curled down to the ends of his collar in soft waves. He reminded her of someone. Had they worked together? Or was it that Swedish coffee commercial that made him look so familiar?

"Good afternoon, Mr. Stenberg," Angela replied, looking at his passport.

"It is indeed," he said and ran his gaze over her, undressing her with his eyes. A sensation she could feel all too well.

Angela suppressed a shudder, pulling up magic to add as a buffer. She typed his information into the computer. "So…we have you booked first class from here to Paris, with a change in London."

"Umm," the man purred and leaned in closer.

Heat blossomed across Angela's face. Her fingers slipped on the keys. She clamped down so hard on her magic she had to blink to read the screen.

"Do you get flying perks with this job?" he asked.

Angela braced herself. "Yes."

"So you could join me on my next trip. Travel with me…" And before she could stop it, Angela was in his mind. Squished in the airplane lavatory, actively participating in the mile-high club. "I always stay at the George V…" Wrapped in the white sheets, the green damask bedspread a puddle on the floor. "Paris at your fingertips…" Angela's fingers around—

"Not a good idea. Sorry," Angela said with a gasp, trying to block out the image.

She couldn't misdirect his luggage now. And how had she ended up in his head? Magic continued to build, but her mind was too muddled to focus.

"Oh, come on. A girl like you should be up for a little fun."

More of his ideas of fun flashed before her. Then, like a needle across a record, his words screeched through the din.

A girl like me?

"There can't be any rules against it," he continued, leaning across the counter toward her.

Raising a sweet smile, she sent the magic out to fry his phone. That should slow him down some. "Only my own, Mr. Stenberg."

"Erik."

Angela took the luggage tags from the printer and wrapped them around the handles of his suitcases.

"My, you're strong," he said appreciatively as she hoisted them onto the conveyor belt behind her.

Angela printed out his boarding passes. "The club lounge is located in Concourse A," she said, handing the documents to him.

He drank in Angela a moment more and then reached inside his jacket. With a perfectly manicured finger, he slid a business card across the counter to her. "Call me. You won't regret it."

Angela waited until…Erik…had turned the corner before she tossed his card in the trash.

"You're not going to call him?" Jackson exclaimed next to her.

"Ew! No!"

"I'd have gone if he'd asked me. His plans looked quite…pleasurable," Jackson said.

Angela gagged. "You got that? Great! Just great! So you saw us…?"

"Angela, half the men who walk up here broadcast stuff like that. It's nothing new to me." Jackson gave her an apologetic smile and then turned his full charm on for the next passenger.

Angela searched the back recesses of the cupboard, her hand high above her head. Somewhere back there was the last bar of absinthe chocolate. She'd already had two brownies and a glass of wine, but they hadn't worked.

Her fingers brushed the paper and she drew it out. Her last one. The bright green cocktail printed on the front called to her, a little oblivion to dull the cacophony of the last few days. Her head buzzed, overloaded from the shopping, the dinners, the complaining, and the unwanted images Mr. Paris had provided her with.

Angela slit the paper open with her finger and broke off a piece. She shoved it in her mouth as she sat back down on the sofa and stared at the blank screen of her TV. She'd been looking forward to a little peace and quiet, but her apartment wasn't peaceful. It was lonely. She broke off another piece and tried to think positive. Life could be worse. Her family could be like Belle's. She couldn't imagine dealing with Janice and Piper on a consistent basis.

Angela shuddered and shoveled in more chocolate. At least she only had to deal with the parade. Her family only wanted her to be happy. Maybe she would be, if she were more like them. She could have taken Mr. Paris up on his offer, shown him she was even more a siren than he thought she was.

But she wasn't a siren. She wasn't even much of a gremlin.

The paper crinkled in Angela's hand. Empty. Angela closed her eyes. She had wanted a moment of bliss and now it was gone. It was gone, and she was still miserable.

Tears swelled in her eyes, but she would not let them fall. Crying wouldn't make it better. Nothing would make it better.

Unless…

Angela allowed the spark of hope to grow. Maybe she could have Dave bring her more of the bewitching chocolate. Sure, he was in France, but that was close to Switzerland. It might be possible to get it there.

Angela got out her phone and took a picture of the empty wrapper.

Help! Mice have eaten last of absinthe. Can you get more? she added to the picture message. Her thumb hovered over the "send" button. What time was it in France?

She glanced at the time on her phone. 12:35 a.m. London was five hours ahead so Strasbourg was six. Maybe he was up. At least he wouldn't be getting a text from her at 3 a.m., beeping, waking him up in the middle of the night, all for chocolate.

She pressed the send arrow before she could change her mind. Her lips curled around her teeth, and she bit down, creating a pain to drive away the regret swirling in her gut. She was officially addicted.

At least Dave would understand. Heck, he was the one who got her addicted in the first place. To the absinthe, anyway.

Angela picked up the wrapper and inhaled the last of the aroma that clung to the foil. Maybe one more glass of wine and then she'd try to sleep.

A moan rose from Angela's throat as the sound of a text alert pierced her slumber. She raised heavy lids and peered at her phone, squinting against the harsh light of the display. It was already eight. And she had a text from Dave. Her mouth quirked into a smile. He'd waited to reply, waited until he thought she'd be up.

Angela swiped her finger and brought up the message.

Mice, huh? Gray or blond?

Blond, she texted back.

I'll see what I can do.

Angela set her phone back on the nightstand and rolled onto her pillow, staring at the ceiling. She had three hours before she needed to move. Three hours before anyone needed her.

The melancholy of the previous night gained strength in the utter silence of her apartment. She'd never wanted pets, and yet, now she wished she had something. Someone to greet her, someone to be glad she was there.

Last night's tears welled up again. *No crying.*

She tamped down on the water rising in her eyes, willing the tears back to wherever they came from, and flung herself out of bed. The heat of her shower should wash them away for good.

12

"Here's your fix." Dave pulled a ribbon-wrapped stack of chocolate from the picnic basket.

"That would make you my dealer," Angela said as she took the parcel and put it in her purse.

"Yes, it would," Dave confirmed with a grin. He pulled a second package from the basket, this one wrapped in red paper and tied with a black ribbon.

"What's that?"

"Trouble," Dave said with a wag of his eyebrows.

"Another brand of heroin?"

"I don't know how addictive it is," Dave said. "But it has a long history of causing trouble."

Angela threw him a sidelong glance and peeled back the paper. "Heidelberger Studentenkuß—student kisses?"

"Invented by a Heidelberg chocolatier so that students and young ladies could have a way to circumvent the watchful eyes of the ladies' chaperones. Who could object to the bestowing of a simple chocolate?"

"Is that what they are? Only simple chocolates?" She threw as much "come hither" into her voice as possible. He'd asked for it.

Dave choked on his wine. "A souvenir. An addition to your collection. No kissing intended."

Angela tucked both packages into her purse. "Your bags were certainly full of sweets this trip."

"You have no idea. I also brought back two kilos of prosecco gummi bears."

"Two kilos!" That was more than four pounds of gummi bears.

"I can only find them in Europe so I stock up when I'm there."

A boy walked past them, a boat cradled in both hands. Dave smiled and rested his arms on his knees. "This is the first place I came when I moved to New York."

"Central Park?" It wouldn't have been her first stop.

"The boat pond."

"Really? Not the Empire State building?"

"I wanted to see the place where *Stuart Little* raced. Even at twenty-five, part of me was still there with Stuart as he stood on the bow and captained the *Wasp*."

"Ah." Angela back a grin, warmth filling her heart. "Gummi bears. *Stuart Little*. Here we are at the boat pond."

"I thought you'd already figured that out."

"What? That you're a big kid? It's kind of hidden behind the world traveling, gourmet cooking management consultant."

Dave dug into the basket and drew out a bag filled with pink and white gummi bears. He popped a couple in his mouth and then held it out to Angela. "These may not be chocolate, but they might just change your life."

"Are you sure you want to risk it?" Angela asked. "You only have two kilos, and you've already got me addicted to absinthe chocolate."

Dave snapped the bag back and clasped it to his chest. "True." He gave Angela a suspicious glare before breaking into a grin. "Eh, you're worth the risk. And if you do eat them all, you'll just owe me."

"Owe you what?"

Dave thought. "First class upgrade?"

"You already fly first class."

"Real champagne, then. A bottle of Cristal."

Angela winced. "Ouch!"

"Well, if you add up the price of the first class round-trip ticket to Paris, and then the train to and from Strasbourg. Gregor drove the Heidelberg leg, so we'll throw that in for free—"

"Cristal it is, then!" Angela said, stopping Dave with a playful shove of her shoulder.

"Come on." Dave jiggled the bag as Angela hesitated. "Worst case scenario, it costs you a two hundred-dollar bottle of champagne."

Angela cautiously picked a few. "Do the pink ones taste different from the white?"

"I did separate them out once but could never tell the difference."

"Not bad," Angela said, chewing. They didn't really scream "champagne" but she'd tasted worse. Definitely, not something she'd give up chocolate for. Or bring back four pounds of. Unless it was for Dave.

He flashed her a grin and turned his attention to the boat pond. The boy had set his boat in the water. His father helped him straighten it, pointing it away from the edge and toward the open expanse, full of reflected clouds, before handing over the RC controller.

"Did you sail? On that first visit?" Angela asked. A wistful expression had filled Dave's face. Even without her magic she could feel his longing.

Dave nodded. "Not quite the same as Stuart's wind driven model, but I pictured Stuart on the bow. It was amazing, doing something I'd dreamed of doing for so long. Not exactly like I'd pictured it, but I held onto the fact I was doing it. That I'd actually made it here. That it no longer needed to be a dream. That I could be Stuart, the most amazing person I'd ever encountered."

Angela's brow furrowed. "I thought Stuart was a mouse."

"Exactly!" Dave said. "He should have been just like the other members of his family, but he wasn't. They brought home a mouse, and they loved him anyway. And Stuart didn't let his being different or only three inches tall stop him. He followed his heart and just went out and did things. So the boat pond and being here in New York…I'd done it. I was on my way to being Stuart."

Angela's hand twitched, wanting to cup Dave's face and smooth away the raw emotion that flowed from him. She shifted her gaze back to the pond. The boy's father had his arms around his son, helping him with the controller. Total joy radiated from the boy's entire being. His father's expression held quiet contentment.

As the boat headed out into the open water of the pond, Angela could imagine Stuart on the bow, hands on his hips as the wind blew back his whiskers. "It does put the saying 'Man or mouse?' in a whole new light."

"Mouse," Dave replied, still staring at the pond, a look of longing on his face. "Definitely mouse."

"When do your old friends get to meet your new friend?" Belle asked, stabbing a strawberry at breakfast the next morning.

"The one with whom you're having picnics in the park," Kate added.

"We've picnicked in the park," Angela said.

"Yes. We have," Kate said. "Which just proves that if you're picnicking with someone else, we should meet him. Or her."

"It's only fair," Belle said.

"Dave's out of town a lot." Angela swirled the bite of waffle on her fork in a figure-eight pattern through the chocolate sauce and whipped cream on her plate. "Even when he is in town, I don't often see him. Or talk to him."

Belle's eyebrows rose to her hairline. She attacked her egg white omelet with new gusto. "Good thing he's not your boyfriend."

"See," Angela said, jabbing her fork in Belle's direction. "That attitude right there is why Dave doesn't have or want a girlfriend."

"Well, then it's a good thing you're just friends," Belle said. "I don't see how a real relationship can last when there's so little time actually spent together."

Shock froze Angela. Her eyebrows rose. "A real relationship?" Had Belle really just said that?

"What Belle means," Kate said, jumping in. "Is that you'd find it frustrating, having your best friend out of town all the time. Or putting work before you."

"Exactly," Belle said. "Look at all the Hollywood couples who claim they really loved each other but their careers kept them apart so they split up. Love died because they didn't spend enough time together."

"If that was actually true," Angela interjected. "Wouldn't I be eating alone? Or with other friends? I used to travel a lot and you two are still here."

"But you are actually in town these days. And you are actually available," Kate said.

"But my point is that I wasn't always, and you two are still part of my life."

Belle put her fork down. "Okay, I'm going to make a point here and it's going to sting." She drew a breath. "If Alex hadn't at least appeared to put you first, would you have stayed?" Belle's words rubbed against the open wound that Angela could ignore but never seem to heal.

But Belle had a point. Angela closed her eyes, trying to block out the pain and focus on her answer. "I don't know. And it doesn't matter with Dave because we're only friends. That's all I want. That's all he wants."

"Okay! Okay!" Kate held up her hands. "But we still want to meet him."

Angela cut up more of her waffle. Her knife squeaked on the plate with the force she was using. "Fine! What did you have in mind?"

"Huh. We hadn't thought that far," Kate said.

"Brunch?" Belle suggested.

"So the two of you can grill him? I don't think so."

"The gallery has a reception Thursday night," Kate said. "A series of landscapes by this artist that manages to combine the feel of Monet's *Water Lilies* with the surrealism of Salvador Dali. It's more casual than brunch. More escape routes. But should you want to linger and chat…"

Angela stared first at Kate and then Belle, slowly chewing a bite of her waffle.

"Fine. I'll see if he's available."

Angela called during her dinner break.

"Hey, gorgeous! What's up?" Dave answered.

"They're asking to meet you."

"Who? Your parents?"

"God, no!" Angela said, blanching at the thought. "Kate and Belle."

"Ah." Angela could hear Dave's attempt to suppress a laugh.

"Ha ha ha. Keep up that attitude and I'll let them go with their evil Plan A."

"I take it you made them come up with Plan B. What's Plan B?"

"Gallery opening," Angela said. "Reception Thursday night. If you're available."

"Seems fair. I did make you late to the last one."

"Oh, Kate's not in charge of this one. But it will be more relaxed than the brunch they first suggested. 'More escape routes,' I believe Kate said."

"I like her already."

"So any time between six and nine. I don't know what time you usually knock off."

"Pardon?"

Heat rushed to Angela's face. How had she missed the double entendre of that? "Get through with work."

"It varies. What's the attire for this soirée?"

"Oh, the sort of thing you'd wear out in the evening. A suit if you wish, though you needn't be that formal."

"Date wear, huh?" Dave said.

A knot formed in Angela's stomach, wisting her insides. "You know this isn't a date."

"Sure it is," Dave said. "It's a date with Kate and Belle." Relief flooded her system, washing away the knot, though the prick of adrenaline still flowed through her veins. "And their significant others?"

Angela grabbed onto Dave's calm and used it to steady her voice. "I didn't think to ask. Is it important?"

"Well, it's one thing to meet your girlfriends. It's another to get checked out by the men in their lives."

Angela stifled a snort. "Like that made a difference in *New York Ladies*. They never cared what the guys thought of their guy friends."

"You do realize the 'guy friends' were all gay."

Except for Mr. Handsome. But Angela didn't like to think about how that had ended up. "You're my friend. They don't care about your sexual orientation."

Dave laughed. "Fine! Let's see…looks like I've blocked out the afternoon to review some organizational material for my trip to Chicago next week. I should be able to do six. We could go to dinner after. Did you want me to pick you up or meet you there?"

Showing up together would give the impression that they were a couple. Having Dave meet her there, he'd be walking into an already established group. "Why don't you meet me there? That way, if something comes up, you don't need to worry about making me late."

"Sounds like a plan," Dave said. "I will see you and your posse on Thursday."

"Hey, Angela!" Myles said, handing her a flute of champagne as she caught up to him in the gallery Thursday evening.

"Myles." Angela took the glass from him and kissed his cheek. "Where's our girl?"

"Off coordinating the caterers. Jovan wasn't happy with something and Kate's back there trying to sort it out."

"What's wrong with the food?" She snagged an ahi carpaccio from a passing tray.

"Apparently it's supposed to reflect the hidden surrealism of his paintings. For instance, the black sesame seeds in that were supposed to be in the form of a face and not just mixed in."

Angela stopped mid-swallow and choked.

Myles pounded on her back. "Exactly. Not for the squeamish. I hope Kate convinces him these are just fine."

Myles's ministrations managed to dislodge the tuna enough for it to continue its trek down. "Thanks," Angela gasped as tears streamed down her face.

"So where's this new guy of yours?" Myles asked, looking around.

Angela carefully brushed away the tears. "He's not 'my guy.' He's just a friend. He's meeting us here."

"He's a customer, Kate said?"

"Yes, he flies a lot for business. That's how we met."

"And what does he do?"

"Management consultant."

"Hey, Ang!" she heard Belle's voice shout. Belle came around a corner and gave her a hug. "Where's he at?"

"He's not here yet," Angela said, returning the embrace. "Hey, Joe!" she said over Belle's shoulder. "Congratulations!"

Joe raised an embarrassed smile. A flush crept onto his cheeks. "Thanks."

"You're not all going to lie in wait for him, are you?" Angela asked, meeting the eyes of each in turn with a hard stare.

"Oh, um…" They shuffled their feet.

"So you see, it's probably best to have everyone's attention focused on your work and not the work of the caterer." Kate's voice drifted closer.

"It's just such a disappointment," a foreign-sounding voice replied. Angela turned toward the sound. Waving his arms in emphasis, a shortish man with dark hair wound his way toward them with Kate. "I wanted theme!"

"Theme is all nice and good," Kate soothed. "But what you really want are sold stickers. Trust me. Your art will be much more center stage if people aren't distracted by the food. Hello, everyone," Kate said, stopping by them. "This is Jovan Hickson, the creator of these amazing works."

Introductions were made. Kate looked around surreptitiously and threw Angela a questioning glance.

Not yet, Angela communicated with a little shake of her head.

"Well now that you've met my contingent, let's get you introduced to some of those journalists," Kate said brightly and escorted Jovan away.

Belle glanced at the door, sighed, and grabbed Joe's arm. "Come on. Don't want to be waiting in a scrum and frighten off Angela's new friend. I think there's a few we haven't checked out over here," she said, pulling him away.

"You should take a look around," Myles told her. "They're quite interesting."

"How's your latest series coming?" Myles's work generally reflected a combination of pop culture and cubism, done in oil on canvas.

Myles blushed. "Oh, um…fine. Kate gave me an idea that I've, um…been running with." The flush spread to his ears.

Crap! Pulling up a tune to keep from accidentally dipping into Myles's brain, Angela began to hum. She did *not* want to know what he was working on. At least until the subject had been more obscured by Myles's paintbrush.

"Sounds interesting," she said, and hid behind a sip of her champagne.

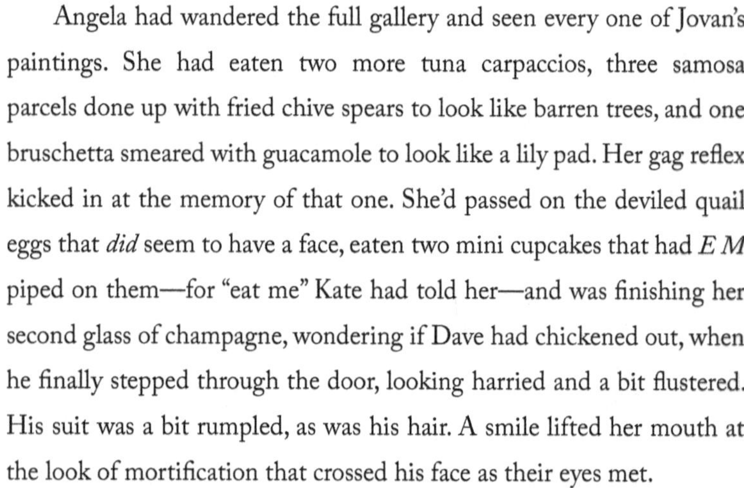

Angela had wandered the full gallery and seen every one of Jovan's paintings. She had eaten two more tuna carpaccios, three samosa parcels done up with fried chive spears to look like barren trees, and one bruschetta smeared with guacamole to look like a lily pad. Her gag reflex kicked in at the memory of that one. She'd passed on the deviled quail eggs that *did* seem to have a face, eaten two mini cupcakes that had *E M* piped on them—for "eat me" Kate had told her—and was finishing her second glass of champagne, wondering if Dave had chickened out, when he finally stepped through the door, looking harried and a bit flustered. His suit was a bit rumpled, as was his hair. A smile lifted her mouth at the look of mortification that crossed his face as their eyes met.

"I am so sorry," he said, a little breathlessly, sliding between the other guests and coming to her side. "I got a call from a Seattle client just as I was getting ready to leave. They do tend to forget about the three-hour time difference. Big crisis! I ended up having to juggle my Chicago client around so I could spend Monday in Seattle instead of with them all next week and—" He stopped abruptly and stared at Angela. "I'm rambling, aren't I?" Dave's hands rose toward his mouth.

Angela suppressed a giggle. "Just a bit. It's rather charming."

His hands bypassed his mouth and clutched his hair. "Sorry! This is so what my life is like—all nice and ordered and then one little thing sends it all tumbling down. Sure you're not angry?"

"No," Angela said with a laugh and hooked her arm through Dave's. "Let's see if we can't rustle you up something that will help you forget Seattle and Chicago for at least tonight."

Dave melted against her. His hand covered hers. "Thanks. I'm glad you're so understanding."

"I have spent the last hour surrounded by food, champagne, and art." She snagged a flute from a passing waiter and handed it to Dave. "By the way, don't look too closely at the deviled eggs."

Dave's eyebrows knit together. "Why?"

"Well," Angela lowered her voice in a conspiratorial whisper. "They look a little like this."

She parked Dave in front of a painting that, at first glance, appeared to be a close-up view of water lily blossoms. Upon further inspection, however, faces came into view, and the golden center of one flower revealed a tethered embryo.

"Huh. Pretty creative," Dave said and drifted over to the next—a stand of trees on the edge of a meadow; old, wrinkled faces in the bark; flowers actually the upturned heads of young girls, their eyes closed in rapture. "Reminds me of a CD cover my parents had."

"Really?"

"Yup. At first, it appeared to be just swirls of color, but when you examined it closer there were all kinds of things going on."

Dave drifted down to the next one.

"Hey! Now this one I like!"

The painting resembled one of Monet's *Water Lilies*. Only the koi had human faces and disembodied eyes peered from behind the lily pads.

"You do?" Those eyes were creepy.

"There's so much depth to it. And it's quite the conversation piece." Dave looked around. "Which one's Kate? I want to get this one."

Kate stood not far off, chatting to a couple who were wearing a rather exorbitant amount of gold and diamonds, all the while keeping an eye on Angela and Dave as they moved through the gallery. Angela raised a hand to get her attention.

Kate excused herself and came over.

"Dave Ford—Kate Hannigan. Kate, this is Dave."

"Nice to meet you," Kate said, extending her hand.

"Likewise." Dave shook her hand and turned back to the painting. "I'd like to get this one."

"Ah—great!" Kate said, and threw Angela a surprised look.

Angela shrugged.

"*What Lies Beneath*," Dave said, peering at the card. "Title certainly fits."

"I'm glad you're enjoying the show," Kate said, an odd smile on her face. "Ah…what drew you to this one in particular?"

Dave held his chin. "I guess it's the layers of imagery. I've always been a Monet fan and this could almost pass as one of his. But when you get close and look deeper—there we are, surrounded by nature."

"Yes, we've come out of the dark to bask in the sun," said a voice behind them.

"Jovan!" Kate said. "Dave, this is the artist, Jovan Hickson. Jovan, Mr. Ford has decided to purchase this one."

Jovan inclined his head. "Obviously a man of great taste."

Dave acknowledged the compliment with a smile. "So what's the theme?" he asked, taking in the expanse of the gallery with a gesture.

"It's a response to the preoccupation today's society has with dystopian art and literature. As Hemingway put it so well during another time of disillusionment and angst, 'The sun may set but the sun also rises.' Humanity is strong and resilient. Returning to nature, we find ourselves. We will go forward, better than before."

Dave nodded. "That's what I like about this, the hope. There are still those hiding in the dark, but emerging into the sun brings out our color and we can shine."

Angela exchanged a shocked look with Kate. Kate lifted one shoulder in a "*whatever*" gesture, but she dealt with artists daily so the talk was nothing new.

"Great!" Kate said. "Shall we walk back to the office then and we'll get you written up?" Dave excused himself.

Jovan drifted off to talk with another group, but Angela stayed where she was. They didn't need her watching while Dave filled out the papers. Her eyes traced the painting again. Where would he hang it? Having heard Dave and Jovan's insight, it didn't seem as creepy before, but she wouldn't want it in her bedroom. Those eyes would probably glow in lower light.

Belle and Joe joined her.

"He's dropping $2,600 on this!" Belle exclaimed, peering at the tag.

"Art's a good investment," Joe said. "And you get to enjoy it while it appreciates."

"We are not taking any of this home," Belle stated flatly. "I'm not having things watch me. Other than you, of course."

"Our cash is tied up in this little thing called a wedding. And the honeymoon in Paris."

"Umm, Paris!" Belle's eyes closed. A smile lit her face. "I'd rather have memories than art any day."

"Or shoes," Joe added with a snort.

Belle's eyes snapped back open. "Some things just go without saying. And shoes are art. They're in museums and everything."

"So that's why you have so many," Joe said. "You're opening your own museum."

Belle blushed. "Maybe one day," she said. "You never know!"

"Have you found shoes for the wedding yet?" Angela asked.

Belle started to make slashing motions and then stopped and smiled sweetly when Joe looked at her. "Still looking," she said in a funny voice, her smile a little too wide.

Joe gave her a suspicious look.

"So, um, Paris," Angela said, redirecting the subject. "Not sun and bikinis?"

"Joe was afraid of sunburn," Belle said.

"Too much time spent indoors," he explained. "Hank in my office went to Belize on his honeymoon, got fried the second day, and then was in too much pain to…ah, do much of anything. Stuck inside for all the wrong reasons. So—" He threw Belle a roguish smile. "I thought, why not be romantic instead?"

"Won't hear me complain." Belle placed a kiss on his cheek.

Angela spied Kate and Dave returning through the crowd.

"We'll give you a call after the show ends and make arrangements to have it delivered."

"Ah! More of the gang," Dave said, extending his hand.

"Belle Pearson, Joe Lambert—Dave Ford," Angela said, making the introductions.

"Pleasure." Dave shook the offered hands.

"So you're the man who demanded Angela buy him a drink," Belle said. Her eyes flashed with glee.

"Guilty as charged," Dave said, a little sheepishly.

"Yes, you've certainly brought about a change in her. Bowling, cooking. But I have to ask, do you really think it's wise to expand her chocolate habit?"

Angela's cheeks flamed. *Really!* She didn't eat much more chocolate than the next person.

"Chocolate's good for you," Dave said. "And isn't it better than wine? At least I'm not bringing a bottle back every time and getting her drunk."

"Very true," Kate said. "You certainly don't want to see what Angela's like when she's drunk."

"So!" Angela said, raising her voice and breaking in. "Great nibbles here but I could do with some actual dinner. How about we move this party down the street?"

Kate glanced at her watch. "I've still got an hour but I can catch up with you. Where are you thinking of going?"

"The Pickling Shed?" Dave said, suggesting the farm-to-table restaurant a couple of blocks down.

Belle snorted. "Sure. Let's see if we can't get Angela pickled."

"Just keep her from dancing on the tables until after I get there," Kate said with a smile and waved them off.

Dave's eyebrows lifted nearly to his hairline. He cocked his head and gave Angela a questioning look.

"It was Barbados and I'd had several glasses of rum punch," she explained. "There is no way I'll end up on a table tonight."

"More fun on it than under it," Dave said, biting back a smile. He held the door open as they tramped noisily out of the gallery and down the street.

Angela got Dave off to Seattle without incident, on his part. "Where do you want me to tag your bag for?" she teased as she punched in his information.

"Surprise me," he said with a twinkle, and wagged his eyebrows. Angela lifted a mysterious smile as she passed over the papers.

He gave her a merry wave and headed toward the security queue.

"Really!" her next passenger said, slapping his ticket down on the counter. "How unprofessional!"

Jackson's eyes bugged and he threw Angela a meaningful look.

Angela forced a smile onto her face. "You sure you don't want to play luggage roulette? Everybody's doing it. I could send your bags to Cleveland. Or Las Vegas."

"Or just have Wendell lose it," she heard Jackson mutter.

The man fixed Angela with an frosty glare. "Do I need to speak to your supervisor?"

Jackson burst out in a laugh he attempted to cover as a sneeze.

"I take it this is your first flight with us…Mr. Hollingsworth," Angela said, pulling the man's information toward her and checking his name.

"Yes." He puffed out his chest and looked imperiously down his nose at her. "And I expected more professionalism from an airline with a reputation such as yours."

"We do have a reputation of being a joy to fly," Angela said. "One, I should tell you, earned by being rather selective as to our passengers. Our 'do not fly' list is probably longer than the U.S. government's." She smiled sweetly at him and waited for the penny to drop.

But the information didn't change Harlan Hollingsworth's demeanor. It made it worse.

"Are you threatening me?" he demanded, his tone icy, his words clipped.

"No, not at all. Let me get that supervisor for you," Angela said and pushed a button under the counter while Jackson choked so badly on his laughter that his passenger asked him if he was okay.

Angela's supervisor changed Mr. Hollingsworth's flight to Virgin Atlantic. He apologized profusely but explained that they did, after all, have a reputation to uphold.

Angela swung by Whole Foods on Friday, picked up a selection of containers for a picnic, and met Belle for lunch in Central Park. The park was crowded with people lounging around, their pants rolled up, their shoulders bare, trying to catch a bit of sun on their lunch break.

"I can't believe I have to be back inside in twenty minutes," Belle said, sighing as she put the lid back on the now-empty strawberry container. "You have all afternoon. And a fluffy book to read. I want fluffy."

Angela grinned. "I thought feathers were all the rage this season."

"Har har. Though there are these delicious pumps with white feathers that just came in. Like a swan princess in a fairy tale. I'd been thinking the blue Manolo Blahniks I've got hidden away, but maybe those..." Belle said dreamily.

"Swans and flowers?" Angela asked.

Belle's bliss vanished. "Okay, maybe not. Though we are going with those handmade birds for the cake topper. I picked out some beautiful Edwardian lace for the bride bird, and the designer is going to do a miniature flower for its headpiece to match the ones on my dress."

"What do you have left to plan?" Angela asked.

"Food, flowers...guest list." Belle shuddered. "Joe and I already have the cake tasting set up. Um, what else? Invitations. I have no clue what I want to do with those. I've always liked homemade paper but then I saw one on Pintrest that had a really cute photo of the couple." Belle frowned. "But then we'd have to hire a photographer to get that done before we even designed the invitations. It's a nightmare, I tell you. I'm just glad I have a year and your mother. I can see why so many girls go all bridezilla."

"They go all bridezilla because they're overgrown two-year-olds who think the world revolves around them. Yes, it's their day, but show more restraint and consideration than a toddler."

"They are rather like toddlers, aren't they?" Belle said. "Stomping their feet, shouting orders, turning red when they don't get their way."

Ripples of revulsion shook Angela's body. A reaction that carried Belle away, as well.

"Any way," Belle continued once the shiver had passed. "Every time I get one thing checked off the list, I feel like I need a vacation for somehow it's grown even longer."

Angela bit her lip and hid a snort with a sneeze. *Do not go there. Do not go there.*

Belle threw her a suspicious glance. "Hmm. Made any vacation plans yet this year?"

"Nope," Angela said.

"You could always travel with Dave. Sounds like he's always off to somewhere exciting."

"No." Angela snapped the lid on the last of the potato salad with more force than was necessary. "It would be too weird. Too much like a girlfriend."

"Well, if this wedding pushes me over the edge and I need to detox at a spa, you can always come with me. There's one an hour and a half away in Pennsylvania that was rated among the world's best."

"I might need detoxing if my mother starts up the parade again," Angela offered.

"She's halted the parade for now?"

"I think Zoli must have had a word with her," she said a little wistfully.

"Do I detect a note of regret?" Belle asked.

"No. Well, maybe." Angela twisted the napkin in her hands. "It would be nice to have someone. And Zoli wasn't as bad as I'd remembered. He was nice. And funny." She sighed and continued more firmly, "But I'm not ready."

"And you have Dave," Belle said.

"Yes, I do," Angela agreed, and offered Belle the strawberry meringue cookies.

Angela met Dave at their usual corner, his grocery bags rolled up under his arm.

"It's so nice of you to have everyone over for dinner," she said as they headed off toward Dave's favorite produce stand. After Dave had complained that the potato and parsnip gratin accompanying his lamb rump that night at The Pickling Shed had needed more cheese, Angela's friends begged him to have them over for dinner. Dave had arranged to cook for them tonight, even though he had just returned from his trip and it was the Saturday of Memorial Day Weekend. It had been the only day their schedules all aligned.

"I like to entertain. I did take out a bedroom so I'd have the space to do so. I'm just not in town often enough."

"What about your other friends?" Angela asked as Dave picked out some potatoes. "Surely you had other friends before I came along."

"I do. They're all men and married." Dave added a purple onion to his pile and started looking through tomatoes. "I see them for squash and golf. Anything else and their wives feel the necessity to invite someone to pair me up with. Can't have an odd number!" he said in mock horror.

"Wow! At least Belle and Kate don't try to fix me up," Angela said.

"Just your mother," Dave replied with a guffaw.

"Yes, well, that's tapered off now."

"What? She's giving up that easily?"

"That will be $13.65," the man at the stand said, counting up Dave's purchases.

Dave handed over a twenty and pocketed his change as Angela put the heavier items into the canvas bag.

"I don't think so, but I told the last one I wasn't ready to date. I think he may have said something to my mother." Angela leaned in as they made their way toward the dairy stand. "Turns out, he had a crush on me years ago but was too chicken to ask me out."

"Well, you are kind of intimidating," Dave said.

"What!" Angela exclaimed.

Dave lifted a shoulder. "Blond bombshell. How was he to know you have a gooey center?"

"Oh, he knew. Loves the fact that I'm a klutz. But he was short and by the time he'd gotten up his confidence I was off to Hewitt."

Dave chuckled. "So you think he told your mother he'd take you as soon as you were ready."

Angela rolled her eyes and ignored the double entendre. "Something like that."

"How about you? Are you keeping him in the wings?"

"I don't need to," Angela said. "My family is more than willing to do it for me."

Dave gave a hearty laugh and led Angela off to get the remainder of their grocery list.

"It's so nice to see the men cooking," Belle said as she watched Dave show Joe how to check the burgers grilling on his stove.

Dave had put Myles and Joe to work while the girls sat around the table, a pitcher of some watermelon-blueberry-tequila cocktail Dave had whipped up sitting between them.

"You know," Kate said. "In my family, 'He who cooks does not do the dishes.' We could be stuck with the clean-up."

"Give me another pitcher of these and I won't care," Belle said merrily, waving her glass around. Her face fell, and she sighed. "I can't believe you have a man who cooks. Why would his old girlfriends let him get away?"

"Because he's a workaholic who's out of town half the time," Angela reminded her.

"True. There is that. But I'm marrying a workaholic. Joe's long hours leave me more time and more cash for shopping."

"Belle!" Angela exclaimed.

"It's all trade-offs," Belle said. "Joe works really hard, I get to spend his money, and he gets a very grateful me in Agent Provocateur undies when he gets home. Makes it all worthwhile to him." Belle flashed her bedroom eyes at Joe who happened to look over.

Angela willed the flush from her face. "Well, I'm not complaining. We wouldn't be here now if one of his girlfriends had decided to stick around. I'm sure they wouldn't share."

"What was his last girlfriend like?" Kate asked. "Have you talked about her?"

"A little." Angela stirred the pitcher and topped off her glass. "She dumped him in Paris after having begged to go with him. Complained he was always too busy to do anything with her."

"Have you talked about Alex?" Kate asked.

"Nope. He hasn't come up since I first told Dave I wasn't interested in dating anyone."

Dave started pulling the burgers off the grill and set Myles and Joe to work giving the warm potato salad another stir and tossing the mixed greens.

"Kind of an international meal," Dave said as the men placed the offerings on the table. "American burgers, German potato salad, Mexican-style cocktails, and English trifle for dessert."

"A true reflection of the chef," Kate said as she helped herself to a large serving of the potatoes. "Things you picked up from your travels?"

"Food Network," Dave said and passed the platter of burgers to Joe. "Except for the potato salad recipe. That I got from the head chef of the Spatenhaus in Munich." Dave gave a small head shake of pleasure.

"Wonderful food there. And the ambience can't be beat, either."

"Can you suggest some restaurants Belle and I should try when we're in Paris?" Joe asked.

"Certainly. Do you know where you're staying yet?"

"Ahh." Joe flushed and looked nervously in Belle's direction.

"Well, if you don't," Dave hurried on. "I have one or two you might want to check out. A real Paris experience without breaking the bank."

Kate fixed Angela with a pointed look.

"Well, um, you see," Joe said, decidedly not looking at Belle, who was now giving their conversation her undivided attention.

Dave glanced back and forth between them and then broke into a smile. "Oh, you want it to be a surprise!"

"Yes!" Joe said with a rush of relief. Belle frowned.

"I'll just give you a call at work next week," Dave said with a conspiratorial grin. "Give Belle less of a chance to be tempted to look through your notes."

"I like surprises," Belle said. "But I like dreaming about something even more," she added under her breath.

It was only a matter of time before Belle began searching the internet for hotel rooms—if she hadn't started already—the better to imagine what her trip would be like. Angela debated whether to pick the list from Dave's brain so she could check them out herself., having a better understanding of Belle's taste than Joe or Dave. Joe went more for the sleek modern look. He'd once had a furious debate with Kate on whether the pyramid at the Louvre was a complement to or detractor from the classic architecture. Joe had won the argument when he'd pointed out that the pyramid was a classic shape and, being constructed of glass, less obstructive than the undulating steel of Seattle's Museum of Pop Culture or L.A.'s Disney Concert Hall, at which point Kate had shuddered visibly and conceded the point.

Yes, Angela could picture Joe wanting some place funky and modern, not at all what Belle would choose. Then Belle's comment about the slinky underwear reward swam to the surface, and Angela spent the next several minutes desperately trying to scrub the image of Belle in nipple tassels from her mind. Best to stay out of Dave's. She could have a word with him later.

The cocktails had turned to coffee, the trifle devoured, the dishes mostly done, and dusk had darkened the windows before Angela got a chance to have her word with Dave. The others were in the kitchen, rinsing out their coffee cups and gathering up their things.

"How about brunch tomorrow?" Dave asked as he collected Angela's cup. "I brought you something from Chicago but if I gave it to you now, you'd have to share."

"You don't have to bring me anything," Angela said, following him into the kitchen.

"I know," Dave said over his shoulder, a smile brightening his face. "But it's kind of become tradition. Besides, hunting down chocolate gives me a break from my meetings and gets me out to try new things. This time I discovered chocolate with bacon."

"Chocolate and bacon?" Angela's face twisted in disgust.

"Not bad, actually. Though," he added, catching her grimace. "I did bring you something else."

"I wish I had unlimited supplies of chocolate," Kate said, whimpering.

"I thought you preferred tequila." Myles whipped the dish towel at her with a playful grin.

"You did do magical things with it," Kate told Dave. "I'd gladly hand over chocolate for a pitcher of what you whipped up today."

"Where are you guys going for brunch?" Belle asked, trying to look innocent.

"Don't know yet," Dave said, throwing her a puzzled look.

"You should try the Belgian place," Kate said. Her mischievous tone matched the evil glint in her eye.

"Oh, yeah," Myles said. "Breakfast with Angela is a whole new experience."

A ngela followed Dave's progress through the crowded restaurant, a café au lait nestled between her hands.

"Ordered already, I see." Dave slipped a bright purple box onto the table and took his seat.

"Just a coffee." She set it down and picked up the package. Silver lettering adorned the top. "Exotic truffles," she said, reading the label.

"A trip around the world in chocolate. A showcase of ingredients from all over the globe."

"Interesting. The video game *Chocolatier* brought to life. Thank you," Angela said and set them on the seat beside her.

"Chocolate video games. Why am I not surprised?" Dave gave a small shake of his head and picked up his menu. "What's good here?"

"They're famous for their waffles," Angela said from over the rim of her cup, leaving her menu untouched.

His brow furrowed as Dave glanced from her menu to her. "You've got it memorized? Or do you already know what you want?"

"Both," Angela answered with a smug grin.

Dave growled and looked back at his menu. The crease on his

forehead deepened. His lips twitched from side to side as he thought.

Angela snorted back a giggle and then quickly put her cup down. With her luck she'd give her nasal passages a coffee purge.

Dave was still debating when the waiter came over.

"Usual for you, Angela?" he asked, writing it down before she answered.

"Yes, please, Francois."

"And for you, sir?"

Dave frowned at his menu again. "Are you getting waffles? I have to have protein in the morning, but if their waffles are really that good…"

"He'll have a liege waffle," Angela told the waiter. "And…" She inclined her head and encouraged Dave to finish.

"The omelet with goat cheese, tomato, and asparagus," he said, and handed his menu to the waiter.

Angela picked her cup back up as Dave added a macchiato to his order.

"What are you up to the rest of the weekend?" Angela asked as the waiter left their table.

"Golfing with my friend Bruce," Dave answered.

"Any place I'd know?"

Dave looked a little shifty. "Long Island."

"Oh. You're going to be golfing the whole island. Won't that probably take you more than a day and a half?"

Dave sighed. "Bruce belongs to Maidstone," he said with an air of defeat.

"I'm guessing from your reaction, that's someplace exclusive. The Hamptons, maybe?"

Dave nodded.

"Do you have an evening tee time? It's going to take you ages to get out there on a holiday weekend."

"He's—" Dave began but the rest was lost in a mumble as Dave slipped his hand over his mouth.

"Sorry. Didn't catch that."

Dave hung his head and enunciated clearly. "His helicopter's picking me up at one-thirty."

Angela sat in stunned surprise for a moment. "Wow! Okay. I had no idea that was the crowd you run with. I'm surprised you're not spending the whole weekend there."

"He invited me, but I already had plans."

Angela was stunned again as she did the calculations. Dave had given up half his weekend to hang out with—no, to host—her and her friends.

Their waiter set Dave's coffee down and vanished without a word. Steam curled from his cup as Angela tried to recover and Dave waited for her response.

"Well thank you," Angela said, still reeling. "It was nice of you to stay and cook for my friends."

"My pleasure. I like your friends. Last night was fun. We'll have to do it again sometime."

Angela picked her coffee up. "Says the man who's always out of town."

"True," Dave said. "But we'll just have to get it on the calendar. Speaking of which, a client gave me two tickets to the new Peter Pan play. Interested in joining me?"

"Peter Pan, huh," Angela said with a growing smile. "Your client must know you well," she added and hid behind her coffee.

"What do you say? Want to check it out and see why it was nominated for nine Tonys?"

"Love to."

Angela had just finished adding it to her calendar when the waiter returned with their order.

"My God!" Dave said as Angela's plate was placed in front of her.

"Anything else I can get you?"

Angela turned her smile up to Francois. "Not right now. Thank you."

Dave's mouth hung open as he stared at the pile of ice cream on Angela's waffle. Little rivulets ran into the cavities. A generous amount of whipped cream and chocolate sauce added to the illusion of a dessert volcano erupting on her plate.

Angela raised her shoulders in a small shrug and picked up her fork. Dave stared a moment longer and then gave a loud guffaw.

"Only you," he choked out, trying to hold back his laughter. "Only you would have dessert for breakfast. Of course, it is covered in Belgian chocolate," he said and wiped his eyes.

Angela chewed and swallowed then licked her lips.

"It's creamy and crispy, warm and cool, sweet and salty, and covered in chocolate. Why not start the day out with a bit of heaven?"

"I suppose you're going to tell me that it has nutritional value, as well," he said with a shake of his head.

"Of course." Angela spread the ice cream like butter. She picked up the small pitcher and poured additional chocolate over it. "It has wheat and dairy. And chocolate is full of antioxidants. Besides, farmers often eat pie for breakfast."

"And how would you know that?"

"*Pigs Can Fly*. My father's the agent."

Dave shook his head again and started in on his own breakfast. "My grandfather actually farmed in Iowa. Soy beans, though," he said, looking up from his cutting. "Not pigs. And he did say that they'd sometimes have apple pie with a slice of cheddar melted on top for breakfast, but I always thought he was pulling my leg."

"You're certainly eating the farmer's breakfast today," Angela remarked.

"Eggs, potatoes. And don't forget my waffle." Dave picked it up with his fingers and took a bite. "Um hum, um hum," he hummed, nodding as he chewed. "Just like the ones in Brussels."

"Why am I not surprised?" Angela said with a little sigh of disappointment. "Is there any place you haven't been?"

Dave finished chewing and swallowed before he answered. "Asia… most of South America. How about you? Where did modeling take you other than Morocco?"

"France, Germany, Italy, Greece…Kenya. Did a shoot in the Maasai Mara that was truly amazing…Australia…Norway."

"You gave up modeling because you were a klutz?"

Angela stabbed at her waffle. "Things tended to happen when I was around. Digital files disappeared, cameras went wonky, lighting went out. Photographers got great pictures, when they got great pictures, but I developed a reputation and…they let me go."

"Jeez," Dave said. "That was harsh. It's not like you were actually messing with the stuff." He caught sight of Angela's crestfallen face and nudged her under the table. "Hey! Their loss is my gain. I'm glad you're a klutz. Probably never would have met you if you were still some supermodel, and you brighten up my life immeasurably."

Dave held up his coffee in toast. "Here's to the klutzes in life and the joy they bring to the rest of us."

"Come on," he prompted when Angela didn't join him right away. "You know you love it when someone knocks something over or sticks their hand in their pie."

"I have not stuck my hand in my pie," Angela said.

"Not yet, you haven't. But it's an event waiting to happen. Just think of all that banana cream out there waiting to be turned into a facial."

"I thought you said my hand, not my face."

"Yes, but it's a short trip from your hand to your face. Come on, coffee cup up." Angela rolled her eyes and picked up her cup. "To the klutzes," Dave said.

He gave her such an encouraging smile that she knocked her cup against his and echoed his words.

Angela didn't see Dave again before he left for London. He was too busy packing and wrapping things up on her Friday off to meet. Instead, she swung by the bookstore and picked up *Stuart Little* before heading off to Alice's for tea. There had to be some advantage to a Friday off. Especially alone. As her Fridays generally were.

Kate and Belle still had to work. They managed to meet her for lunch occasionally. But even if they did, she had the morning and afternoon to fill. Once her laundry was done, she was nearly always by herself.

The table next to hers contained two polished mothers and their sparkly, butterfly-winged daughters. The women exchanged silent looks of disapproval as they spied Angela's reading material. At least, that was what she guessed their wide eyes meant. Their botoxed foreheads didn't move.

Her book was met with more interest by the girls.

"That's Stuart!" the blue-winged butterfly exclaimed, pointing at Angela's book. "You're reading *Stuart Little*!"

"Yes," Angela said. "A friend of mine wants to be Stuart when he grows up."

"He wants to be a mouse when he grows up?" the butterfly said, her eyes growing wide.

"He wants to have adventures like Stuart," Angela explained.

"Stuart has lots of those…but he needs to be careful of cats," the little girl said, nodding her head sagely.

"I'll make sure to tell my friend," Angela replied, and then hid behind her book as the butterfly's mother glared at her.

When Angela's tea tray came, she positioned it as a screen between them, though she was unable to block out their complaints about "what one has to go through to get on the lists of the best schools in New York."

She didn't linger like she'd planned. As soon as she'd eaten, Angela paid the bill and walked over to the park, settling herself on the same knoll overlooking the boat pond where she and Dave had picnicked. Somewhere in the city, he was busy at his office and she was the one at the pond.

Angela lost track of the time, curled up on the grass, preoccupied with her thoughts, until her phone rang.

"Come out clubbing tonight," Nicky begged when she answered.

"Why? Are you picking up where Mum left off?"

"No," Nicky said, though his voice sounded strange, shifty. "A bunch of us are going out and I want a girl to dance with."

Angela squinched her eyes closed. "You're never without a girl to dance with, and if you need 'a girl' that can only mean you're going out with the guys. So why me?"

"Hector Martinez wants to meet you," Nicky said in defeat.

"Clumsy Hector?" The only gremlin Angela knew growing up who was as klutzy as she. Hector never remembered to tie his shoelaces and was, hence, always tripping over them.

"You're one to talk," Nicky said.

"I'm not spending an evening with Hector Martinez."

"We don't do anything together anymore," Nicky wheedled.

Dancing did sound like fun, but not with a bunch of other gremlins.

"Only if it's just you and me. Ditch the guys—and no accidentally running into them—and I'll go."

Noises of irritation drifted through the phone.

"Fine! But I get to choose the club."

"Okay," Angela said. "But you'll need to tell me how to dress. I'm not doing sparkly if we're going to a salsa club."

"You know how to salsa?" Nicky asked.

"No, but I can fake it. So, sparkly or flowy?"

"Sparkly. And shoes you can actually dance in. I'll pick you up at ten."

A harsh buzzing filled the apartment just as Angela stepped into her turquoise Mui Mui pumps. She hit the door release without bothering to respond and then slipped her credit card, driver's license, and keys into a little wristlet purse.

She met Nicky halfway down the hall.

"Wow!" he exclaimed, coming to a sudden standstill. He lurched into the wall and braced himself with a supporting hand. "Good thing Hector's not coming. You dressed like that would have given him heart failure."

"Thank you," Angela replied primly. "Had to do something to scare off your usual flock. Didn't want to be sitting there all by myself."

Nicky shook his head and muttered something that sounded suspiciously like, "Only you."

The cab dropped them off at the entrance to one of the trendier clubs. Angela started for the line but Nicky walked right up to the guy manning the ropes who whisked it open before Nicky even got there. "Good evening, Mr. Grimalke," the attendant said with a little bow.

Angela stared at the spectacle. Nicky turned and gave her a "What-are-you-doing?" look, complete with open arms. She broke into a trot when Nicky started the arm flapping most often seen in goose herders.

"I take it you've been here before," she said as she trailed after him through the open door.

A dark, skinny girl dressed in opaque tights, a tube top masquerading as a skirt, two tank tops that left a good six inches of her highly toned stomach exposed, layers of long necklaces, and enough arm bangles to put an Indian bride to shame lounged against the hostess stand. A hungry smile transformed her face as Nicky approached.

"Good evening, Mr. Grimalke," the hostess said, rising. Her gaze flicked over Angela as if determining how much competition she would prove to be. "Your table's right this way."

The door attendant was good at his job. There were enough people in the club to prove it was popular but not so many that there was a crush. The hostess led them to a smaller table in the back, hugged by a semi-circular banquette dotted with bright purple cushions. A waitress in a tight black dress shimmied up as soon as they sat down.

"Hi, Nicky," she said, throwing back her shoulders. She placed a hand on the table and leaned in, the better to show off her cleavage. "The usual for you?"

Angela fought back a gag, though at least Nicky's smoldering glance stayed on the woman's face.

"Thanks, Nanette."

"I'll have a pomegranate martini," Angela said, as Nicky and the waitress continued to stare at each other.

Nanette smirked and slowly turned, giving Nicky a long, backward glance as she sauntered off, her hips swaying.

"Ugh!" Angela grimaced. "I'll give you half an hour and then I'm done."

"You'll be fine," Nicky said. "Have a drink, we'll hit the dance floor, and she'll leave us alone."

"Yeah, right."

"Come on," Nicky said. "You won't care when you're out there dancing. The music here is great."

Her brother was not the only one who thought so. The club was full of young, hip professionals, as well as a few others who looked vaguely familiar. And that was definitely the young actress who not only had a popular sitcom but several commercials pitching everything from phones to juice to fabric.

Angela startled when the actress looked their direction and squealed.

"Nicky!" the woman shouted, waving to be seen through the crowd. Then she grabbed her male companion by the hand and pulled him toward their seats.

"Nicky!" she gushed again when she reached their table and exchanged air kisses with Angela's brother. "I had no idea you were going to be here tonight!"

"Good to see you, Chloe. This is my sister, Angela."

Chloe cocked her head to the side and gazed intently at Angela. "You look familiar. Have we met before?"

"I don't think so." Hopefully, Chloe wouldn't be able to place her.

"Angela used to model," Nicky said. Angela kicked him under the table, connecting with his ankle. Nicky winced and tapped a fist against his thigh. "You probably saw her in *Vogue*."

Chloe gave a little sigh. "That must be it. Oh! This is Greg," she said, finally introducing her companion. "Greg plays the bass in this totally great band."

"Nice to meet you," Angela said, giving Greg a smile.

The song changed and Chloe grabbed Nicky by the wrist.

"You have to come dance with me to this one," she said, pulling Nicky toward the dance floor.

Nicky shrugged his shoulders and threw Angela a bemused look before he was swallowed up by the crowd.

Greg stood beside the table, staring after his departing companion, a look of dumb disbelief on his face. "What just happened?"

"We've been momentarily dumped. Want to have a seat?"

"Think they'll be back?" Greg asked, sinking onto the cushions. His brow furrowed as he scanned the crowd for Nicky and Chloe.

"They'll be back," Angela assured him.

Greg turned a somewhat frightened face to Angela. "You're sure about that?"

"Yes." She gave him a little shoulder nudge. "My brother dragged me here tonight. He knows better than to do that and then abandon me."

"Well…if you're sure."

Nanette soon appeared with their drinks. "Here you go," she said, placing them on the table. "Can I get you something?" she asked Greg.

Greg gave her half a glance before returning to his task. "Um…no thanks."

Nanette lifted her eyes heavenward and, with a small shake of her head, walked off without the wiggle she'd given Nicky.

Greg's attention remained on the gyrating crowd. Angela sighed and picked up her martini. If Nicky wasn't back by the time she finished it, she was out of there.

"How do you know Chloe?" Angela asked.

"Um…we met at a club," he said, his eyes still scanning the crowd.

Had she become part of the furniture? She might as well for the amount of attention Greg was paying her. Angela threw back her martini, swallowing half before putting it down. One more gulp and Nicky would be out of time.

Greg remained perched on the edge of his seat, a spaniel ready to return to his mistress's side as soon as she appeared.

Angela swiped the olive out of Nicky's drink and chewed it dejectedly. Was this his way of getting her back for not letting the guys join them?

As she swallowed the last of her martini, Greg sprang from his seat. He met Chloe and Nicky before they were halfway back to the table. The three of them exchanged a few words, Chloe did the double air kiss again, and Greg dragged her off.

"Hey!" Nicky exclaimed, sitting down. He picked up his drink. "You ate my olive!"

"You abandoned me," Angela said. "After you dragged me here for whatever reason."

Nicky took a couple of long gulps and then took Angela by the wrist. "Let's dance."

The pulsing beat worked its way under her skin, pushing at her irritation, massaging it away. Her feet began to move, and she let the music take over. As Nicky smiled at her, her face returned his contented glow.

They'd polished off a second set of drinks and were back on the dance floor when Nicky bent over and shouted in her ear, his voice competing with Dua Lipa's blasting lyrics, "I'm thinking of moving to Dublin."

"What?" There was no way she'd heard him right.

"I'm thinking of moving to Dublin," Nicky repeated.

Angela's arms sank to her side as she stared at her brother.

Nicky grimaced. "Come on. Don't look like that."

An elbow dug into her back as she was jostled from behind, but her eyes remained frozen on her brother.

Nicky swore. What, Angela couldn't say for it was drowned out by the music. His fingers wrapped around her arm. Nicky marched her back to their table, pushing her onto the seat when she just stood there. He scooted in next to her.

"Not now!" he spat as Nanette shimmied up again. Nanette blanched and took a couple of steps back, wobbling as she turned around. "Not for sure," he said, leaning close to Angela's ear. "But you got me thinking."

"Me?"

"What you said about 'out of sight, out of mind'."

"Wow," Angela said softly.

"So, I was thinking, maybe I should move there." Nicky bowed his head and fixed his attention on the drink in front of him.

Her own glass was empty, other than the remains of the sugar around the rim. She could use another. Anything to cut through the shock.

"Well, yeah. If you think she's the one." Knots formed in her stomach. Knots that were now migrating north, working their way into her throat.

"I think so. But only seeing each other once and a while…Claire living in another city…" He raised half a smile. *Shit.* Her brother was leaving.

"Besides, you've gotten to travel the world. My turn to expand my horizons," he said, giving her a nudge.

The table swam in and out of focus. "When are you going?"

"I've got to find a job first."

"You know that won't be that difficult."

"Well, yeah, but I've gotten used to my current standard of living. I don't want just any old job—Oh! Sorry," he added as Angela flinched. "Do you really hate working at Windsor?"

Angela closed her eyes and wobbled her head in a half-hearted shake. "No. It's just…I guess I don't really know what I'm supposed to do. Where I fit."

Nicky put an arm around her shoulders and drew her close. "Your purpose is to be a mirror—reflect back the best and the worst. You can do that at Windsor or anywhere else you choose. But if you don't choose…" He reached over to wipe away a tear that slid down her cheek. "If you don't choose, you'll never be truly happy."

Her limbs became too heavy to hold her. Angela tipped her head against her brother. How could she choose when it was her purpose that didn't make her happy? She didn't want to be a mirror.

Nicky rested his head against Angela's. "Want to dance some more?"

Angela shook her head. How could she dance when her body wouldn't move? A fresh wave of misery washed over her, a knife to her heart when she realized why.

Last chance to dance with him.

Nicky patted her shoulder. "Come on. Up you get. Either you dance with me or I'm calling Hector. He'll step on your toes and give you something to really cry about." Nicky pulled her to her feet. "What am I going to do with you?" he asked, leaning in until his nose touched hers.

Lady Gaga blasted from the speakers, filling the club with an *I don't care* attitude that Angela wanted for her own.

"How about you buy me a couple of Jell-O shooters and spin me around the dance floor?" Those would work way quicker than a martini. Topped with a little whipped cream.

A naughty twinkle entered Nicky's eyes. "Only if you promise to unleash the siren."

Angela gasped. "You're my brother!"

"Exactly. What harm is there? You can drive them all wild and know that you're going home with me."

"That seems almost cruel."

"Not cruel." An evil smile lit Nicky's face. "Fun."

Angela sighed. It would be easier to just give in. "Fine. But I want the blue ones."

Nicky pulled her close and planted a kiss on her forehead. Then he took her hand and hauled her off in the direction of the glow-necklaced waitress circulating with the tray of Jell-O shooters.

Angela lifted her head off the pillow, squinting at the utter brightness of her room. A sour taste filled her mouth and her tongue felt furry. She fought her way through her foggy brain, trying to figure out why.

As she turned her head, hundreds of tiny suns seared her retinas, the silver spangles on the dress draped over her chair working like mirrors with the light streaming in through the cracks in her blinds.

Nicky. She'd been out with Nicky last night. Angela groaned.

But if her dress was on her chair, what did she have on? Gingerly, Angela lifted the covers. Her bra and underwear. But who had undressed her? Angela squinched her eyes closed and searched her memory.

The last thing she remembered was downing her fourth—was it her fourth?—Jell-O shooter and yelling that the music needed to be louder.

Angela opened her eyes and squinted at the beams of light dancing on her ceiling. Thank heavens it was Saturday. There was nowhere she needed to be while the alcohol fog clogging her brain wore off. Maybe coffee would help.

Angela threw back the sheets and winced as her feet hit the floor.

They had swollen up like sausages. She snagged her robe and limped out to the kitchen.

Her new Nespresso maker stood on the counter. Angela popped a capsule in and pushed the button. Dave was strangely rubbing off on her. She now owned a coffee maker and even had milk in her fridge, which she pulled out and poured into the foamer.

Angela cringed as the steam whistled through the milk. It was worth it though—not having to leave her house to get a latte.

She poured the coffee and hot milk into one of the new glass mugs she'd picked up at Williams Sonoma and shuffled into the living room.

She was halfway through her drink when her brain revealed something she'd buried. Nicky was moving.

Belle is getting married and Nicky is moving.

Angela finished her drink in two large gulps and hobbled back toward bed.

Belle is getting married, Nicky is moving, and Dave is leaving today for London. Kate—

Her brain couldn't pull up anything about Kate.

Angela flopped onto the bed and pulled the covers over her head. It was Saturday. She had no plans.

There was no reason to get out of bed.

Angela wore her most comfortable pair of shoes to work the next day. Even though the swelling in her feet had gone down and she was no longer limping, a dull ache had settled in, almost as if her feet remembered their misuse and were sending her a warning.

She smiled as she chatted, smiled as she typed, and smiled as she tagged and moved luggage. As the day wore on, she noticed Jackson's increasing glances her way. Was there something in her teeth? Something in her hair?

As Milton Harvey stepped away from the counter, Angela ran her tongue over her teeth and felt at her chignon.

She jumped a little as Jackson's voice murmured in her ear, "Are you okay?"

"Fine," she said a little breathlessly.

"No, you're not fine," Jackson said, his eyes narrowed in concern. "You're like some robotic, Stepford ticketing agent and you're so empty of magic there's no way you could misdirect even one bag today."

Angela stared back at him. Empty of magic?

"Eh hem!" The passenger at Jackson's station loudly cleared his throat and tapped the spine of his e-ticket on the counter.

Jackson ignored him and searched Angela's face. Looking for what, Angela couldn't guess.

"I went out with Nicky Friday night," she said.

Jackson's gray eyes narrowed further. A look of puzzlement washed over him. "Nicky?"

Jackson's passenger cleared his throat again, louder than before. Angela's let out a timid, "Hello?"

"We went to a club," Angela said. "I guess I'm still feeling the effects."

"What did you do?" Jackson asked as his passenger said, in a loud voice, "What does someone need to do to get some service around here?"

Jackson huffed and cast one last look at Angela before hoisting a smile on his face and graciously saying, "So sorry to keep you waiting."

"Hello?" Angela's passenger gently called out.

Angela pasted a smile on her face and went back to work. But her mind stayed elsewhere, stuck on Jackson's question.

What had she done?

Angela dragged through the week. Dinner with Nicky and her

parents felt even more like a chore. On the plus side, there was no one new at dinner. On the minus side, Nicky didn't do much talking. There was no conversation about his potential departure, their having been out Friday night, or what Angela could have done that used up all her magic.

Dave's imminent return and a night at the fun-filled play was the only thing getting her through the day. And then Dave left a voice mail canceling.

"Hey, Angela! You're not going to be very happy with me. Got a referral for a big insurance company in Edinburgh. They'd like me to come up right away so…I won't be back tomorrow." At least he sounded regretful. "But use the tickets. I'll give Maria, my housekeeper, a call and she can let you in. They're pinned on the board by my desk in the loft. Take the tickets and go with Kate or Belle.

"I'm sorry I won't be going with you, but this is how my business is. It's all based on referral and I need to take advantage when someone new is interested. But I'll make it up to you. I'll bring you back something great!

"Text me in the morning and I'll give you a call when I can, apologize in person and make sure you get coordinated with Maria."

Angela listened, deflating with Dave's every word. The one thing she'd been looking forward to all week—gone. She managed to scrape up enough emotion to realize Dave probably did this all the time, something that provided her with a little insight into why Dave's girlfriends ended up so disgruntled with him.

Not that she had any reason to be upset. One—she was not his girlfriend. And two—she knew from the stack of unhappy people in her wake that she was even more difficult to live with.

Angela called Belle when she got home, as Kate was out of town for a long anniversary weekend.

"What are you up to Saturday night?"

"Recovering," Belle said. "Joe and I are spending the morning looking at wedding invitations and then the afternoon cake tasting. You want to come? To the cake tasting, that is. Joe likes anything sweet and I don't want to eat a bunch of cake. Whereas, you're not afraid of extra calories and I need an honest opinion as to the flavors."

"I can do that with you if Joe doesn't mind," Angela said. "But how about the evening?"

"I'm free. What's up?"

"Dave has tickets for that new Peter Pan play, but he's stuck in the UK for another week. Told me to go anyway and take you or Kate—"

"And since Kate is away at some romantic inn—"

"You get the chance."

"Sure! I'll go," Belle said. "How good do you think these seats are?"

"Um? They were a gift from a client," Angela said, wondering herself. Balcony? Orchestra? Box seats?

"Ooh! Probably pretty good then. I'm in! And let's have dinner after. We probably won't be hungry until then anyway."

Angela hung up after agreeing to let Belle pick the restaurant. There seemed to be a heaviness in her chest again. She hoped she wasn't coming down with something.

Angela texted Dave the next morning while she waited for the milk for her espresso to steam. He didn't call back until around noon.

"Thanks for being so understanding," he said, speaking over the sounds of traffic.

"Where are you?" Angela asked.

"In a cab, on my way back to the hotel to pack. I've got an eight o'clock flight to Edinburgh. So, Maria is expecting your call. She can meet you at my apartment this evening, as long as it's not too late." Angela had the feeling Dave was running a hand through his hair, just like he'd done when he'd been late to the gallery. "I hope you won't have to shuffle any plans."

"Nope. Quiet night in," Angela said, suppressing a sigh. Just her and Netflix.

Angela could hear the cabbie's muffled voice and then Dave answering. The street noises got louder.

"I'll text Maria's number to you. And thanks again for being so understanding. I'll make it up to you." Angela's stomach rumbled as she thought about how he'd do that. "And I want you to know that I'm jealous. I'd been looking forward to an evening of Peter Pan."

Angela arranged to meet Maria at Dave's apartment at five. Maria eyed Angela suspiciously as she unlocked the door for her and turned off the alarm. Angela couldn't think of what'd she'd done to upset the woman, who stood in the dining room, arms crossed, a scowl on her face, as she watched Angela climb the stairs to the loft.

The lily pad and koi painting hung at the top of the stairs. Eyes peered out at her from the darkness under the lily pads. Angela suppressed a shiver as she walked by.

She found the tickets pinned to the cork board next to Dave's desk, just as he'd told her. She shoved them into her purse and headed back down the stairs as a tapping noise started. Maria's foot, she noticed as she cleared the last step.

"Thanks," Angela said.

Maria replied with a non-committal, "Hmm," and showed Angela out.

Saturday afternoon, Angela met Belle and Joe at the baker. By three o'clock they were in agreement on all three tiers. The first represented the fresh, new season—a lemon scented cake filled with a tart and creamy lemon curd. The second played homage to Joe's favorite way to start and end the day—a cake dark with espresso and filled with chocolate cream. The last layer was a nod to Joe and Belle's first date at Barbetta—toasted almond cake filled with a cannoli cream that had made Angela swoon.

As Belle had predicted, Joe loved every one of the twelve cake flavors and twenty-two different fillings. Belle had offered suggestions on combinations but had made Angela voice her approval first, like some royal food taster weeding out poison, before Belle would allow the dessert to pass her lips.

"Are you even going to eat any of these at your reception?" Angela asked her.

Belle's eyes flew open. "God, yes!" she replied, and resumed licking microscopic traces off her fork, a look of rapture on her face. "I may have all three. I can't decide which one's my favorite."

At seven twenty-eight, a taxi deposited Belle next to Angela in the ticket holders line.

"So," Belle asked, adjusting her bright blue cashmere shawl around her shoulders. "Where are these seats located?"

Angela pulled them out and squinted at them. "Center orchestra, row D, seats 107 and 108."

The house doors opened and the line began to move.

"Did you want to get a drink before?" Belle asked.

"Maybe at intermission. I've still got somewhat of a sugar high." The udon bowl she'd had on the way home from the cake tasting had helped, but now her insides felt sloshy.

Inside the theater, they climbed the stairs and an usher showed them to their seats. Belle slipped the shawl from her shoulders and arranged it about her.

"Oh, here you go." Angela handed Belle a ticket and tucked the other into her purse.

Belle studied hers for a moment. Her eyes flew wide.

"What?" Angela asked.

Belle turned her ticket toward Angela and pointed at the script at the bottom. "Two hundred fifty dollars!" she said in a choked whisper. "These seats were two hundred fifty dollars. Each!"

Angela's eyes grew as wide as Belle's. She'd known that orchestra seats were more expensive than the mezzanine where she usually sat, but this was five hundred dollars for two people.

"Good thing they were a gift," she said. A flare of mixed emotions shot through her, disappointment and a bit of regret. They were a gift Dave probably wouldn't replace.

After lunch the following Friday, Angela dropped Belle back at work and stopped by the Dior counter on her way out. One bottle of bright red polish later, she headed home for a pedicure. Dave rang before she could add a second coat.

"I have a little something for you for being so understanding last week," he said when she answered.

Angela screwed the top back on the bottle and fanned her toes. "Yes, you would need to offer me an apology for forcing me to go to a play you would have loved, with seats to die for, with one of my best friends instead of you."

"It was that good?" Dave asked wistfully.

"It was. But you can always buy tickets for it."

"But you've already seen it."

Angela stopped fanning as her heart constricted a little. "Was it worth it? How's your new client working out?"

"Great. Nice people. Edinburgh's a great city and I've discovered... Well, you'll find out soon enough. I know I usually cook, but I'm tired. Do you want to meet me for dinner? Some restaurant where we can sit outside and enjoy the summer air?"

After arranging a time and place, Dave rang off. Angela swung her feet, toes still spread by her purple spacers, and shuffled off to look through her closet.

A large red box tied with a gold ribbon completely obscured the plate at Angela's place setting.

"I see you brought me a coordinating accessory," she said as she took her seat. Her newly painted toenails were highlighted by red high-heeled sandals and matched the poppies on her sundress. "Though it's rather larger than a clutch."

"Biggest one they had," Dave said.

"My addiction isn't that bad," Angela said.

"But my guilt is. It wasn't fair of me to cancel on you at the last minute."

"You're the one who lost out," Angela said. "I still got my evening."

"You're really not mad?"

"No," Angela insisted.

"Well, thanks. I'm told those are really something special," he said as Angela tucked the box under her chair. "Have you been to Scotland?"

Angela shook her head. "I've never made it that far north."

"You should," Dave said. "Those are made in a little town about an hour north of Edinburgh. They have a chocolate museum and everything."

"A chocolate museum? You got to go to a chocolate museum?" Angela asked wistfully.

Dave's eyes twinkled. "No, I didn't have time this trip. Picked those up at Harvey Nichols."

The waiter came over and took their drink order.

"What are you up to this summer?" Dave asked.

"Work. Weekends in the park. How about you? What are you doing this summer?"

"I'm off to Paris in two weeks. And I'm hosting a dinner party right before. A little birdie informed me that someone's having a birthday a couple of days before I go."

Angela flushed. "Really? Someone's having a birthday?"

"Says the guilty party," Dave said with a laugh. "Kate let it slip, hoping for a repeat of Memorial Weekend. But it's up to you. Want me to cook for you? Or, as Kate put it, 'Make up for the horror of a birthday parade'?"

"Thanks," Angela said, not bothering to hide her sarcasm. "Hadn't realized my birthday fell on a Wednesday."

"Sorry."

Memorial Weekend had been wonderful. And if her parents did put someone else at the table, it would be nice to follow it up with an evening she'd actually enjoy.

"Sure," she said. "Sounds wonderful."

"Have any favorites you'd like me to fix?"

Her mother would prepare her Hungarian favorites. "Whatever you'd like to make," Angela said. She'd never been disappointed with what had come out of Dave's kitchen. "As long as there's—"

"Chocolate for dessert," Dave finished with a grin.

Dave gave Angela a picnic at the beach for her birthday, only it was inside his apartment. The six of them shared a bucket of clams steamed on his stove, a roasted corn salad mixed with grilled zucchini, a crusty loaf of bread, and more than one pitcher of tangy white sangria.

The windows had been thrown wide, capturing the summer breeze.

"Thanks for doing this," Kate called from her place on the living room rug.

"My pleasure," Dave replied, sliding a tray of baking dishes into the oven.

"What's that?" Belle asked.

"Dur! Something chocolate," Joe told her. "I can't believe you're doing all of this and then leaving for Paris tomorrow," he said to Dave.

Dave set the timer by the stove. "Practice. I spend half my life living out of a suitcase. And tonight's dinner was easy." He picked up his glass of wine and joined them in the living room.

"Right. Easy," Belle said. "You do know most people don't cook like you do."

"Probably not," Dave admitted. "But it's not that much of an effort. Though I guess I might feel different if I had to do it every day."

There had been no one new at dinner Wednesday night. It had even been pleasant. But for Angela, this was the evening that had made her birthday—all her friends sitting around, talking, enjoying a meal, sharing a pitcher of wine.

Angela lifted her glass. "I'd like to make a toast, to all of you. Thank you for being here, not just tonight, but being in my life. This is the way life is supposed to be lived, surrounded by food and friendship."

"Your version of wine, women, and song?" Myles asked.

"Uh, no," Belle said. "You do not want to hear Joe sing."

Angela laughed and continued, "So thank you, all of you. Especially Dave for cooking and hosting. It's been a perfect birthday."

Dave's week in Paris was followed by another foray through Union Square Market. Though he'd left Paris only that morning, he didn't look jet lagged.

"What's on the menu tonight?" she asked, hooking her arm through his.

"Raspberry chicken. I want fresh and fruity."

"Something to help you stay awake?" Raspberries always provided her with some energy.

"No, a week of seeing summer's bounty on every Paris street corner. I might be back in New York, but I can capture a little bit of Paris."

Chicken and the raspberries for the marinade found their way into the bags. Haricot verts, heirloom tomatoes, lemons, and a bottle of white zinfandel soon followed. It was easy for Angela to imagine they were wandering the open air markets of the City of Light. Striped umbrellas providing shade over the stiff paper baskets overflowing with produce. Bottles of milk and wine and honey lined up on the tables. Stacks of bread, dusty with flour. Only the architecture gave away their location.

All too soon, they arrived back at Dave's apartment. While he unpacked the bags, he put Angela to work slicing up the tomatoes for the salad. The door to the coat closet door clicked as Dave hung up the shopping bags. A scraping noise soon followed, and a box covered in brightly colored café scenes skidded to a stop next to the cutting board.

Angela swallowed down her drool. Visions of sugarplums might dance in some people's dreams, according to that Christmas poem. She dreamed of the creations that came from that store. Their chocolate olives her favorite—roasted almonds covered in dark chocolate then enrobed in white chocolate and colored to look like the savory fruit.

"I walked up to Montmartre on Sunday afternoon," Dave said. "I passed by this shop and it whispered your name."

"You know you don't need to bring me anything," Angela said, wiping off her hands.

"Consider it a late birthday present."

"You already gave me one. You cooked dinner. For six."

Angela lifted the lid. Instead of the olives, pink-tinged bars of nougat mixed with almonds sat nestled in the paper. Lifting one to her nose, Angela inhaled. *Roses.*

"They reminded me of you," Dave said, pulling out a dish. "Strong, sweet." A lopsided grin lit up his face. "In this case, kind of nutty."

Angela gave him a playful shove and inhaled the scent again. "No chocolate from Paris?"

"Not this time. In Paris you were roses. Roses and something more unusual."

Unusual. She was certainly that.

"Miss Grimalke, would you do me the honor of accompanying me to this year's Light Up the World gala?"

Angela shivered as she stared into her closet. She could do this. *Just reach out an arm and take an item.* But her arm hung as heavy as lead at her side.

Whipping around, she marched over to her dresser and pulled out a t-shirt and jeans. She had to wear something. She couldn't meet Dave on their usual corner in her pjs. There were many unusual sights in New York but her shopping at Union Square in her pajamas would not be one of them.

Angela squeezed her eyes shut. *Fuck.* How had she gotten herself into this mess? Why had she said yes to Dave's invitation?

Because he'd had no clue. And she wasn't about to tell him. No need to bring up Alex and the horror of last year's event. Dave couldn't have known that his request would fill her with such terror that her stomach kept voting to empty its contents. At least she now had that under control. Sort of.

Angela shoved her feet into the shoes she'd kicked off yesterday. The yellow espadrilles didn't really go with her shirt but there was no way she was walking back into that closet. Maybe she would have to hold an exorcism. Perhaps magic would finally remove Alex from her life.

Angela sent out a burst toward the closet before grabbing the sweater off the floor where she'd dropped it the night before. Once she got back from Dave's, she'd have to deal with the closet more fully.

Union Square Market was even more festive in September. A rich harvest overflowed the tables, a multitude of offerings that had taken advantage of the summer to fill out and mature. Angela's heart eased with the familiar task of picking out produce, filling the bags, learning about the latest ingredients they'd be working with.

But the enormous box obscuring Dave's table stopped her heart. Her grocery bag hit the floor with a *thunk* as she stood in the doorway, unable to move. Unable to breathe.

"Okay, it's a little bigger than chocolate this time," Dave said as he rescued Angela's bag and put it on the counter. All summer he'd continued to find exquisite chocolates for her on his travels. "But you were so nice to say you'd go with me to the gala and I didn't want you to have to go to any expense."

Dave's words managed to propel Angela two steps closer. *Jenny Packham* scrolled across the box. Closing her eyes, Angela drew a breath.

"Take a look," Dave said, oblivious to her distress. "I had to guess at your size. I told the gal you'd modeled and she said you were probably a six."

Dave's excitement pushed Angela forward the last few steps. "How did you get it back on the plane?" she asked, stalling for time. *Not Alex. Not Alex. Not Alex.* Perhaps if she repeated it enough, it would sink in.

"I told your cousin Julia it was for you and it kind of snowballed from there. I was surprised they didn't give the box its own seat, the way they fussed over it."

Her hands still refused to reach for it. Dave's joy began to evaporate. Drawing a deep breath, Angela pulled off the ribbon and lifted the lid. There, under the tissue, was a gown of rose silk, the same color as the candy he'd bought in Paris. Crystal embellishments traced a scrollwork pattern across the bodice down to the waist. It was beautiful.

"I guess you were roses in London, too," Dave said.

Angela reached out a hand to touch the silk but her fingers curled into her palm.

Pain filled Dave's voice. "I get the feeling I've done something wrong."

Angela cringed. Guilt swirled in her gut. She wanted to slam the lid shut and never see the dress again, but this was Dave's gift. Dave's, not Alex's.

"I'm sorry, it's just…" Angela drew in breath and braced herself. "That last relationship that ended badly, he used to buy me clothes. But not because he was being nice. Because he wanted to make sure that I looked acceptable. That I reflected well on him. That…that…" The words which had rushed out so easily now failed.

A cold horror swept over Dave's face. "I'm so sorry," he whispered. "I had no idea! It's just the gala's kind of formal and the women at Martin's table will all be in designer gowns. I didn't want you to feel out of place or have to go to huge expense because of me."

That was probably why Alex had been so upset. Her dress hadn't been a top-drawer label.

"It's fine," Dave said. "I'm used to doing these things by myself. I'll take the dress back."

But it was beautiful. And it was from Dave, who'd bought it because he was thinking of her, not himself. Who was willing to go alone rather than make her uncomfortable.

Angela pressed her hand against her lips and stared down at the dress, blinked back tears that escaped anyway.

"It's lovely," she said from behind her fingers.

"I thought it would go well with your hair."

She would look amazing in it. Her hair in a soft chignon with escaping curls. And she'd be with Dave.

If she went with Dave, she'd be strong enough to stare down the ghosts that would prowl the event, waiting to remind her of her foolish blindness. She had removed Alex from her closet. It was time to erase the last of his influence over her.

"I'd be honored to go with you. If you'll still have me," she said.

Dave made a movement toward her but stopped and gripped the table instead. "Still have you?" he asked. "How can you ask that? Are you sure you want to go?"

"You weren't to know."

"Well…" Dave cleared his throat. "If that's settled, there are tomatoes that need to be sliced and lettuce that needs to be torn." He went back to the chores in the kitchen.

Angela wiped her eyes, put the lid back on the box, retied the ribbon, and stepped over to the cutting board. Dave gave her a small, encouraging smile, handed her the tomato knife, and they settled into fixing dinner as if nothing had happened.

Belle helped Angela find a small, silver, beaded bag and the palest pink high-heeled sandals to go with the gown, which fitted perfectly. She felt like a princess when she stepped into the town car three weeks later. Stepping out of it made her feel a bit like a rock star, of which there were plenty, milling about and posing for the paparazzi.

One of the photographers nudged his neighbor and pointed at Angela. She shifted, presenting them a view of her back as she moved through the doors with Dave.

Most of the women were in cocktail dresses, just as she had been last year. Though that dress was a Marchesa. And that one was definitely Carolina Herrera. On Renée Zellweger, Angela noticed, as the woman turned around.

Angela stuck to Dave's shoulder as they wove through the crowd. Her hand snuck out for Dave's. She caught it just in time, curling her fingers back. It would be weird. They were just friends.

Dave maneuvered through the crush of people, finally stopping by a tall, gray-haired man with a luxurious salt-and-pepper beard.

"David!" Joy filled the man's greeting. He took Dave's extended hand and clapped him on the shoulder. "I'm so glad you were able to make it. And who is your charming companion?"

"Martin Wolfe, this is my friend Angela Grimalke." Martin's eyes widened at Angela's name. "Angela, our host for this event—Martin Wolfe."

"Very nice to meet you, Mr. Wolfe," Angela said, taking his offered hand.

"Grimalke? Is your family from Hungary?" he asked.

Swallowing a gulp, Angela made sure there was a smile on her face. "My father grew up there."

"Was his father Agoston Grimalke by any chance?"

Angela started in surprise. "Yes, actually."

"Agoston was a good friend of my father's," Martin said, lighting up. "It's nice to meet his granddaughter."

"You don't happen to know my father, do you?" Angela asked.

"No, I've never had the pleasure. Is he here, in New York?"

"Yes, he's a literary agent. Damon Grimalke."

"I'll have to get his information from you," Martin said. "I'd like a chat about Agoston. Great man. Great man."

"I'll do that." What a small world it was. Their host actually knew her grandfather!

"Martin!" a man called out in greeting.

"Dmitry! Just the man I was looking for. I've been wanting to introduce you to my good friend, David Ford. David is an utter genius when it comes to management."

Angela took a step back to give them room and helped herself to a glass of champagne from a passing tray. The men's talk turned to business. She shifted farther away, sipping the champagne, and cast her eyes about the ballroom. The myriad of glasses and tall, lit vases adorning the tables acted as mirrors, reflecting the white and gold splendor of the room.

Her champagne sloshed as a strong hand grabbed her upper arm and spun her around.

"What the hell are you doing here?" Angela's heart stopped beating. Alex's livid face peered into her own.

Magic and adrenaline coursed through her, restarting her heart. "A friend brought me." Angela twisted her arm, attempting to free it from Alex's painful grip.

"A friend?" Alex practically spat the words. His eyes raked over her, taking in her dress. "I thought they called it something else when you're paid for."

"She's with me." Angela heard Dave's voice from behind her.

Alex's face twisted into a sneer. His fingers tightened around Angela's arm, pressing to the bone. "Who the hell are you?"

"My guest," Martin said. Alex paled as he came into view over Angela's shoulder.

"M—Mr. Wolfe," Alex stammered, releasing Angela.

"I'm afraid I can't have you manhandling my guests." Martin raised his hand and motioned for someone. Two men in dark suits quickly appeared. They gestured for Alex to follow them.

"But I've paid to be here!" Alex shouted, attempting to shrug off the guiding hands.

"And I thank you for your donation. Good night," Martin said with a nod and turned away.

"Get your hands off me!" Alex snapped as security began a more determined effort to show him out, his voice vicious and low. He threw Angela a withering look. "You'll pay for this. I will find a way to make you pay for this."

Angela glanced down at the angry red marks Alex's fingers had left on her arm and covered them with her hand. The paleness of her dress seemed to illuminate them. Why hadn't she brought a wrap? Now she had no way to hide the evidence of just how stupid she was.

Dave leaned in and whispered, "Are you okay?"

Alex's escort parted the crowd, moving him swiftly toward the doors. A woman in a long purple dress gave them a startled look and then hurried to catch up.

Angela nodded and prayed Dave wouldn't notice the tears she was struggling to contain.

"I'm not a mind reader, but I'm guessing that's the ex."

Turning her face up to Dave, Angela managed a small nod of confirmation. With a sad smile, he reached out, grasping her hand, and held it until they took their seats for dinner.

"Don't go home," Dave said as their car pulled away from the curb. Angela whipped her head around. The muscles in her neck seized up, pinching the nerves and sending rivers of pain shooting down her spine. "I don't think it's safe. He was angry. He threatened you. Does he have a key?"

Angela shook her head, mentally pushing at the painful bands binding her neck, willing them to loosen.

"Still…" Dave looked at his hands. "Martin told me he tried to get back in. I don't know if you noticed the man Martin had follow us to the car."

Her heart slammed into her ribs. Angela pressed her teeth together to keep them from chattering and shook her head again. Alex was a fool but he wouldn't actually harm her. Would he? Her upper arm chose that moment to remind her that he already had. Her fingers slipped up to cover the mark he'd left.

"No? Well, I didn't want to alarm you. Martin feared your...ex... might be waiting for you."

"Alex." Somehow, she'd managed to push the word past the emotion knotting her throat.

"So don't go home. Stay at my place tonight. You can use the guest room. Kate or Belle can bring you some clothes in the morning."

Her arm throbbed as she considered. Alex wouldn't actually lie in wait for her, would he? He'd been rough with her before but had never actually harmed her. Humiliation was more his style. But actually harm her? No, he wouldn't risk it.

However, Dave's concern was so real, his eyes so pleading, she relented.

"Fine. If that's what you want."

"Thank you." Dave squeezed her hand. "I couldn't forgive myself if something happened to you."

He let go of her hand. It felt strangely empty. Maybe because her heart felt so empty as well. Alex had ruined their night.

Dave's night, she corrected. The night had been about Dave and, once again, she'd refused to connect the dots, refused to see what was right in front of her. Had gone after what *she* wanted, not what was best. She should have realized Alex would be there tonight. She had ruined Dave's night. It was best she did what Dave wanted, best that Dave not worry about her any more tonight. *His* night.

The first welling tear spilled down her cheek. Angela closed her eyes and willed the others to stay put.

"I'm so sorry I insisted you come." Dave's voice cut through her thoughts. "I should have realized…your reaction to the dress."

"But I told you I wanted to go," Angela answered miserably. "I should have told you I'd gone last year with him. That was the first night he—"

She stopped before the full humiliation slipped out. "He disapproved of what I was wearing. He started buying me clothes after that and, foolish me!" Her voice rose higher, rushing to beat the anguished sobs that coursed out of the deep place she had hidden them. "I thought he was being KIND!"

Pulling in deep breaths, she turned her head to stare out the car window. Tears clung to her lashes, threatening to follow the first. At least Dave wasn't her boyfriend. It wouldn't hurt so bad when he wanted nothing more to do with her. No one would want anyone as foolish as her.

Dave's warm, strong fingers closed over hers. "I am so sorry."

Angela pressed her teeth together. This time she was going to know, to be prepared. She reached in, grabbing at his thoughts.

A tangle of concern and self-recrimination greeted her. *He was the one to blame. He should have known better, should have read what was going on with the dress. Wasn't that his job, to read people and situations? He'd been selfish and had hurt the best thing to happen to him in a long time and the only way he could even begin to make it better was to just keep his mouth SHUT!*

Angela's sobs ended in a startled hiccup. Best thing to happen to him?

With a sudden squealing of brakes, Angela flew forward. The seatbelt cut into her hips and chest as it jerked her back against the seat. "Sorry, Mr. Ford," their driver said with absolute mortification. "Light went straight to red."

So that's where the magic had gone. Angela bit her lips to hold back her giggle. She hadn't even realized she'd released it. The stoplight. *Great!* Now she was one of *those* gremlins.

"These things happen, Manuel," Dave said, his voice choked. He caught Angela's eye and they both erupted in laughter. The stress of the evening melted away.

Until a few minutes later when Dave unlocked the door to his apartment. Angela followed him in. Just when she thought the evening couldn't get any worse, she stood outside Dave's bedroom, clutching a pair of his sweatpants and a T-shirt. She might not be sleeping *with* him, but she'd be wearing him to bed, sleeping between his sheets.

Okay, so technically not the sheets on his bed, but they were still his sheets.

"I'd loan you a robe." Dave's ears turned pink. "But I've only the one. Jenny, my sister, might have left one in the guest closet. She likes to pretend I'm a four-star hotel. She's even stocked the bathroom with products from the various makeup counters at Macy's."

Angela must have looked puzzled because Dave added, "She works in…I forget which department, at the Macy's in Grand Rapids. So you should find anything you need in there."

Angela nodded.

"Well, goodnight," Dave said with a tight smile. Then, with a quick nod that echoed his words, he walked past her and up the stairs…

To dig out the bottle of fifty-year-old Scotch he'd brought back from Edinburgh. See if that wouldn't drown out the voice of accusation he couldn't get out of his head.

The force of his anger sent Angela scurrying out of his head. She hadn't meant to peek but she must have. Those were his thoughts, not his words. And now magic pulsed in her fingers.

Angela sent it to the clock in her room. Unplugging it and plugging it back in might clear it.

Pressing the clothes to her chest, Angela padded into her room and checked the closet. No robe. As promised, though, Jenny had stocked the bathroom with samples—shampoo, body wash, face cleanser, moisturizer, and even deodorant.

Turning the shower as hot as it would go, Angela stood under the stream, washing off the effects of the evening, though not the bruises that were growing ever darker on her upper arm. Alex had left his mark on her body now, as well as her heart. She curled her hand over the bruises, blocking them from view.

Upstairs, Dave had finished his…third…shot of whiskey and sat, elbows on knees, his hand running through his hair, still cursing his stupidity.

Angela forcibly shut out the image and then burned out the bathroom nightlight.

She had curled under the covers when Dave finally clomped back down the stairs, his anguish numbed but still present. The soft whisper of his feet on the carpet passed by her door, then a click and a *thunk* as Dave's door opened and closed.

Angela reached out to touch the wall between them. She and Dave would not be the same because of this night, and her heart ached at the thought of it.

Angela texted Kate the next morning.

AM AT DAVE'S. NEED YOU TO BRING SOME CLOTHES.

Her phone rang almost immediately.

"You slept over!" Kate exclaimed, as if Angela had announced she was going skydiving.

"No, there was an incident at the gala and Dave insisted it wasn't safe for me to go home."

"What!"

Angela quickly explained about Alex, grumbling when she got to the part about Martin's warning to Dave and his over-reaction of sending a man with them to the car.

"So you see, he freaked Dave out to the point that Dave insisted I spend the night."

"Martin Wolfe. *The* Martin Wolfe of Wolfe Global Industries feared for your safety," Kate repeated, a little awed.

"He apparently knew my grandfather. Or rather his father did. Anyway, I'm here with only an evening gown. Can you swing by my place and bring me something?"

"And when would you like these clothes?" Kate asked suggestively. Probably complete with eyebrow wag.

"As soon as you can bring them."

"Am I going to get fed out of this?" Myles added something that Angela didn't catch. "Oh, excuse me! 'Are *we* going to get fed out of this?' I am bidden to say."

Angela could hear Dave moving around in the kitchen. "Sure. Just get those clothes! And hurry. I'm currently wearing his and it's really rather awkward!"

Angela hung up and reluctantly marched up the stairs…to find Dave pouring waffles.

"Morning!" he called. His gaze traveled over her.

As red crept toward his ears, Dave spun around to the freezer and pulled out a canister of his homemade ice cream. After a moment's hesitation, his grip tightened around the frosty cylinder and he turned back around.

"I can't quite duplicate your usual Belgian waffle, but I do have ice cream." He presented the canister with a little flourish. "Himalayan pink sea salt. And with some macerated strawberries and a drizzle of this fabulous dark chocolate sauce I picked up in Seattle, I think I may be able to give the Belgians a run for their money."

A shy smile tugged up the corners of Angela's mouth. "Oh, you do, do you?" She slid onto a stool at the counter.

"Worth a try."

"Are you going to put me to work? Do I have to, what did you say? Matterate the strawberries?"

"Macerate—let them soak up a liquid, infuse a flavor. In this case, their own juice and a sprinkle of sugar. No, I've already sliced them. Coffee?"

"Yes, please."

"So," Dave said as he pulled a cup from the cupboard and set it under the coffee-maker. "How many am I fixing breakfast for?"

"Four."

Dave broke into a grin. "Thought as much. What do they eat for breakfast?"

"You're not just going to pick one thing and serve it to them?" Angela asked.

"I don't see Kate eating what you eat." Dave took out a frying pan and gave it a twirl before setting it on the flame. "And I need some protein."

"Ice cream has protein in it," Angela said, striking a pose of innocence most often seen on Renaissance cherubs.

Dave laughed. "Not enough for me! I'll have a waffle but I need eggs as well."

They were lingering over coffee when Myles and Kate buzzed. Kate had a garment bag for Angela's dress as well as jeans and whatever else was in the tote she had slung over her arm.

She inhaled deeply. "Is that waffles I smell?"

"Yup," Dave said. "Wanted to see if I could out do the Belgians."

Kate handed the bags to Angela. "Do you do half orders? Angela's already finished and you really should have more than one judge."

"Three," Myles said. "I'll take the other half. Less tricky for you to do a whole waffle rather than try for a half."

Angela gave Dave an amused grin and slipped off her stool.

"Back in a jiffy."

Angela quickly headed down the stairs and threw on the jeans and shirt Kate had brought. She carefully zipped the rose-colored dress into the garment bag, pausing to take one last look at the scrollwork of crystals on the bodice before sealing it away. She shoved her shoes and purse into the tote then, with a little breath of determination, threw the garment bag over her arm and trotted back up the stairs.

Kate and Myles sat at the counter, plates of eggs and waffles in front of them.

"Oh my God!" Kate said, her eyes closed. "I can't believe you don't have your own restaurant."

"I do." Dave grinned. "It's just a very exclusive one with very restricted opening times. Prices are great, though." He tossed Angela a wink.

"What are your plans for the day?" he asked Angela.

"Don't know. I took today off. Wasn't sure how late we'd be."

"You guys could come with us," Kate said. "Myles and I are headed out to a winery in the Hudson valley." A sly smile slid up her face as she turned her gaze on Dave. "Life's always more interesting with Angela around."

"Very true," he said, suppressing a grin.

Angela glanced back and forth between them. They had to have been talking about her while she was changing. A conversation that wasn't going to stay private.

She turned her back under the guise of putting her things on the sofa and dipped into their heads.

Dave was still upset about last night. He was sure Angela wasn't going to want anything more to do with him. Kate had assured him that Alex was an ass and that, more than ever now, Angela needed him.

She set her things down. The living room slipped out of focus as her mind reeled and her eyes filled. This was not the change she'd expected. Dave wasn't running. He expected her to.

And Kate thought she needed him.

The frother on the Nespresso sprang to life, whirring away, empty.

"What the…?"

"Life's never dull," Kate's sing-song voice called from behind her.

"Hardee-har," Angela said. She pulled herself together and went to join them in the kitchen.

"So what about it?" Kate asked. "Wine…apples…lunch. The glory that is the Hudson valley in autumn."

"Apples, huh?" Dave said. "It *is* pie season. I'm in."

"Ang?" Kate asked gently.

Myles caught her eye. "Won't be the same without you."

"Fine," Angela said, somewhat defeated. No going home to lick her wounds. "Might as well take full advantage of my day off."

They piled into Myles's battered green Subaru station wagon, which always smelled faintly of paint and canvas, and followed the Hudson northbound until they crossed it on the George Washington Bridge. A short while later, they picked up 17 and drove north and west, leaving the New Jersey suburbs behind, traveling on smaller roads bordered by houses with white rail fences.

Dave, Kate, and Myles talked cooking as they drove. Angela sat in the back, marveling at Dave's easy manner—stretched out, taking up his full space next to her, chatting away with her friends.

The full messiness of her life had blown over the two of them and, instead of running for the hills, Dave blamed himself for not protecting her. He was unlike any man she'd met before. Or at least any man who'd wanted her, even as a friend.

Her jet-setting-model life had brought her men who had been interested in her for her looks and the prestige of dating a model. Men not interested in the reality of the accident-prone woman she actually was.

Her looks had brought her Alex, and he'd tried to reshape her, abandoning her when it became clear his efforts were futile.

Dave laughed, and a strange pain blossomed in her chest, something so rare it took a while for her to recognize it.

Hope.

Had she finally found a man who valued her? Even as a friend?

Myles's Subaru became the stuff of fairy tales, transporting Angela to a world she'd only dreamt of before; where the ordinary, because of its rarity, became extraordinary. For her, it was a road trip in the company of friends; wine drunk outside in warm, apple-scented air; easy laughter; and a sleepy drive back to the city, the paint smell now overpowered by the boxes of apples Dave had purchased.

They dropped Angela off, a bag of Dave's prized Macoun apples clutched in her hand. Certain she moved in a dream, Angela rode the elevator to her floor, dumped the apples in the blown glass bowl she'd bought in Venice, and went to bed, wondering when she'd wake up.

The alarm on her clock went off at eight. Angela rolled over and silenced it. She was in her own bed, underneath her own sheets. The day on the clock said "Monday." She'd either slept through the weekend, or parts of it had been real.

Angela closed her eyes, took a deep breath, and then surveyed her upper arm. The ugly bruises proved that part had happened.

Slipping out of bed, she grabbed her robe and padded into the living room. The green glass bowl on her coffee table was indeed full of purple-red apples.

Angela sank down onto the sofa and stared hard at the orbs in the bowl. What she wouldn't give to be able pick one up and have it reveal the future, like some strange crystal ball. Things between her and Dave had changed Saturday night. But to what? He wasn't her boyfriend. But he was more than the simple friend he had been.

As much as she wished and stared, the apples stayed as they were, kept the secrets of the future to themselves. Finding no answers, Angela got up and went to get ready for the day.

Dave flew out to Chicago Tuesday morning, missing Angela, but still having time to courier a pie to Kate at the gallery, a note of thanks enclosed. Angela received a brief text from him, that Martin had spoken to Alex and made it clear there would be consequences if he contacted or harmed Angela in any way. Dave could have called, but he didn't.

Her family acted odd at dinner on Wednesday. She had the feeling they'd heard about the gala. There were too many shared glances when they thought she wasn't looking.

Nicky especially acted strange. Had he given her parents a list for the parade? At one point he had started what sounded like an apology, but a quick look from their mother had shut him down mid-sentence.

The oddness continued, putting her on edge. On Thursday, when Aaron Waitfield had come through, traveling to London on "business" with both his wife and his mistress, she misdirected all of their bags rather than choosing. She also made sure the flight attendants knew about his plan to "occupy" some of the time in the darkness at forty thousand feet.

Angela approached her Friday off with dread. It would leave her with too much time on her hands. Time she would, no doubt, just spend trying to figure out what the hell was going on in her life.

Perhaps she simply needed a vacation. Time spent somewhere warm and sunny, away from all that New York seemed to be right now. She could give Julia a call. Julia had been raving about a small town on the French Riviera rumored to have the most amazing beach. And it was wine season. There were worse ways Angela could spend a week. She'd have her favorite cousin, warm waves, and wine.

But Angela didn't call. She spent lunch on Friday with Kate and listened to her gush about Dave's apple pie. Drowned her sorrows in cupcakes from Billy's Bakery on the way home. The evening she spent surfing Netflix and calling out for Chinese, saving the excitement of doing her laundry for Saturday.

She had just walked back through the door, her basket still warm from the dryer, when her phone rang.

Dave.

Drawing in a deep breath, she answered

"Are you busy this evening?" Dave asked.

Lie or the truth? She could never come up with good fibs when she needed to, so—"No plans."

"Want to have dinner with me? I can promise a drama-free evening, even if the devil is on the menu?"

"What?" Okay, he'd lost her.

"El Diablo. An amazingly sinful chocolate dessert that's laced with cayenne for some heat, topped with spicy almonds and a tequila caramel sauce, all resting on a bed of burnt meringue."

Angela swallowed her drool before replying. "That sounds good."

Dave's next words were drowned out by a boarding call.

"Sorry?" Angela said.

"Sorry about that. I'm at O'Hare. Is it okay if I pick you up at seven? I don't feel like cooking tonight and I don't want to eat alone. And I didn't get a chance to find you any chocolate so I thought I could take you to some."

Her heart warmed. "You don't need to get me anything, you know."

"Yeah, I know. But it's kind of become tradition. Hate to break a tradition." The gate attendant in the background called for rows 22 through 31.

"I'll see you at seven."

Angela's insides lurched as she came down the steps. Dave had kept the town car that had picked him up from JFK, so for the second Saturday in a row, Manuel whisked her and Dave off for an evening out. This time through the Lincoln Tunnel to Jersey and a Spanish restaurant nestled right along the Hudson. They skipped the restaurant's famous paella and ordered several of the smaller dishes.

"How was your week?" Dave asked, spreading jam onto his Croquetas de Papas with his fork.

Angela swirled the port wine reduction through her miniature cheese soufflé, watched the fluffy white insides turn lavender. "Fine. Though Wednesday dinner was a little weird. I think Martin must have called my father. There was definitely an undercurrent of something there."

A lopsided grin lifted Dave's mouth. "Does that mean the parade's back?"

"Probably." Angela stabbed at her soufflé.

Dave's face fell. "Sorry. It's all my stupid, *stupid* fault!"

"It's Alex's fault for being such an ass. Or mine, for not telling you about him."

The muscles in Dave's jaw stood out as he clenched his teeth. "I'm the one who made you go."

Angela reared back. "You didn't make me do anything. You were just being sweet. A little like the fairy godmother in Cinderella." She stabbed viciously at her soufflé. "It's my disaster of a life that seems to mess everything up."

"If I was really a fairy god-*father*, I'd have known better. Or had magic to wave my hand and make it all better."

Heaven help her. "That's not how magic works."

"Sure it is," Dave said. "Don't you read fairy tales? And your life is not a disaster."

"Uh, it was *my* ex that made the scene. Didn't see any of yours lurking around." Dave colored and carefully cut up another croquette with his fork. "That is the story of my life. My family knows it, hence the parade. And it's a constant source of amusement for Kate and Myles and Belle and Joe."

Her fingers tightened. Angela bowed her head and stared at her plate. "So I'm giving you fair warning. Last Saturday…that's what you can expect to happen on a fairly regular basis." She swallowed hard, forced her jaw to work. "Might want to get out now."

"That's not funny."

No, it wasn't. Her fork fell from her hand with a clatter. Twisting them together, she placed her hands in her lap.

Dave cocked his head to the side. "Are you trying to tell me you've got more angry exes lurking around?"

Angela's head snapped up. "No!"

"Kate's still around, you haven't warned her off or—" Dave's eyes bugged. "Are you trying to tell me you don't want to see me anymore? I know we're not dating but…" He swallowed hard, unable to finish.

Angela looked away. How could she ask him to stay when he was just going to leave anyway? It was only a matter of time. With supreme effort, she pulled the napkin from her lap and pushed back her chair.

"Where are you going?"

"Thanks for dinner. But I can't do this."

A shocked expression filled Dave's face, almost as if Angela had reached across the table and punched him. "I know I messed up with the dress but—"

Dave stopped and studied her. "But that's not the problem. You're bailing because you think this is inevitable. This is what usually happens to you, so you're going to end it on your terms." Dave leaned back and crossed his arms. "Well, not this time, Miss Grimalke. It is not inevitable that your messed up life is going to make me run for the hills. Messed up lives are my business. I laugh in the face of messed up lives. They're merely a challenge. So you sit down, put that napkin back in your lap, and pick up your fork. You're not going anywhere!"

Angela scowled daggers at him. "Fine!" She snatched her napkin off the table. "Are you always such a bossy boots?"

"When it really matters, absolutely."

A lump formed in her throat. "Why does it matter?"

Air rushed from Dave's lungs in a huff. "Wow! You don't think much of yourself, do you?"

Gasping, Angela pushed her chair back. The table swam out of focus as she tried to rise, unable to see through the tears filling eyes.

Dave was there before she'd taken a step. "No you don't." He gently pushed her into her chair. "I'm not letting you leave. It's about time someone convinced you of your value. I don't know what Alex or the others have said to you over the years, but apparently they don't see in you what Kate sees. What I see. You, Angela Grimalke, are one of the kindest, funniest people I've ever met."

Dave squatted down and took her hand. "I can only image the voices you must have running in your head, telling you you're not good enough. But you are. You've made my life immeasurably more enjoyable. So I'm not going to let you walk out that door and deprive me of that. You are just going to have to accept that I want you around. Accidents and all," he added with a twinkle.

Angela raised her head. Every eye in the restaurant had turned toward them. "Can you get up now?" she hissed. "People are starting to think you're in the middle of a proposal."

Dave laughed and patted her hand. "Wouldn't be the worst thing."

"Yes, it would!"

"No," Dave said, returning to his seat. "The worst thing would be you missing dessert. They say the devil is in the details, but I say the devil is in the chocolate."

Angela picked up her fork and glared daggers at him. "You're impossible, you know."

He flashed her a wicked grin. "That's what makes me so successful."

And a perfect match for you, she heard in his head before she stopped his watch.

They parted that evening, Dave even more attentive, as if to prove to her he couldn't be scared off. Angela's contemplation of their relationship left her unable to focus at work, resulting in a new record of misdirected bags.

Jackson left her alone, though. She could feel his piercing gray eyes following her movements, noting what she was doing, but he didn't correct her, didn't ask what was wrong.

At home, she filled her apartment with Katherine Jenkins's operatic tones. Her life had begun to feel like it was some grand soap opera, and it made it easier to pretend it was the music making her feel the way she did. She had turned the volume up Wednesday night, in no mood to deal with the drama her family dinners had become and determined to skip at least one, when Nicky showed up at her apartment.

"*Con Te Partiro?*" he said, frowning as he shut the door.

Angela hit the remote button, stopping the music. Why had she ever given her brother a key? "I've been in an opera phase lately."

"Dave take you?" Nicky asked, scowling.

"No. What do you want?" she asked, glaring back.

"Duh. I'm here to escort you to dinner."

"And what if I don't want to go tonight?"

Nicky blanched. "But you have to."

"Why? Who've you got coming this time that I have to meet? Julian Grimes?"

"No, though Dad did hear about what happened at the gala."

"Well then, I'm staying home, thank you very much."

Nicky swallowed hard. "But you have to go."

"Oh no, I don't." Angela crossed her arms. She placed one foot and then the other on the coffee table, crossing her ankles as well.

"Angela…Angela, I'm leaving Saturday."

Her arms slipped to her side. Angela lowered her feet back to the floor. "Leaving? Like in 'checking out Dublin' leaving?"

"As in 'moving to Dublin' leaving. Leaving leaving."

The lamentation of the last song echoed in her soul. It would be the perfect soundtrack with which to play this scene. A little too perfect.

Angela swallowed down the lump filling her throat. "Leaving leaving," she said softly. "And you just spring this on me?"

Nicky sat down next to her. "I wanted to tell you last week, but Mum and Dad thought you'd had enough surprises…after the gala."

Angela crossed her arms again and looked away. "So that's what you were trying to tell me when Mum shut you down."

Nicky nudged her shoulder. "Come on. You're the one who told me I shouldn't be out of sight. I'm doing this because of you. Who knew you could give such great advice?"

"Oh, gee. Thanks, Nicky."

"Besides, you had your turn. You left home, traveled the world. I had seven years of family dinners where you only deigned to grace us with your presence on the rarest of occasions. My turn to spread my wings."

Angela turned her gaze to the window. Why wasn't there a rewind or pause button for life? Why did things seem to gain speed just when you wanted them to slow down, to have time to find the ground beneath your feet?

Nicky shifted next to her. *Crunch.*

"Oh, my God!" he moaned. "Where did you get these apples?"

"Hey! Those are mine!"

"No, seriously," Nicky said, a dreamy look on his face. "Where did you get these?"

Angela wrestled the urge to rip it out of Nicky's hand and put it back in the bowl. "A winery I went to last week."

"You went to a winery?"

"With Kate and Myles." Angela scowled at her brother. "Do you always take things without asking?"

"Frequently," Nicky said with a smile, and took another bite.

"Oh, so you're trying to make me glad you're leaving town."

"Maybe." He took another bite, slurped the juice that was threatening to run down his chin.

"Fine. Great. Let's get you out of here." Angela gave his knee a shove.

"Can I have another for the road?" Nicky asked, grinning.

"No! Move it!"

Nicky looked from the apples back to Angela, a calculating smile growing on his face.

"With Kate and Myles, huh?"

"Yes! Now let's get going."

With a last loud crunch, Nicky rose and followed Angela.

Dinner was a celebration. Evelyn had made all of Nicky's favorites. They toasted to his new life in Dublin. Angela even managed to give him a hug and wish him good luck when she left.

But she cried the entire cab ride home.

She drifted through work the next day, dismissed an offer from a concerned Jackson to get a drink after work, and somehow found herself outside Dave's apartment building without any clear memory of how she'd gotten there.

She dug out her phone.

"Are you home?" she asked when Dave answered.

"I am. What are you up to?"

"Can I come up for some ice cream?"

"Up? Where are you?" Dave asked.

"The door in front of your building."

The lock buzzed. "Sure. Come on up."

A tub of ice cream and a spoon sat on the island counter when Dave let Angela in.

"You came straight from work?" Dave asked, looking at her uniform.

"I guess." Angela sat down on a stool. "No bowl?"

"I wasn't sure if you wanted one. In my experience, when a woman asks for ice cream, she's usually stress eating. And I haven't seen one use a bowl yet. Did you want one?"

Angela pulled the carton toward her. "No. Not really." She stabbed at the contents with her spoon. "Nicky's moving to Dublin."

Dave slid onto a stool across from her. "I see. When's he moving?"

"Saturday," Angela said around a mouthful.

Dave's eyebrows shot up. "Sa-Saturday?"

"Um hmm," Angela said, shoving in another spoonful.

Silence fell as Dave sat in shocked silence and Angela shoveled in more mouthfuls of ice cream.

"Wow! I take it he kind of sprung this on you."

Angela gave Dave an angry glare of confirmation and kept eating.

"So the weird dinner last week…"

Angela swallowed the latest mouthful before answering. "They knew. They just didn't want to tell me after what had happened at the gala."

"So they decided to spring it on you at the last minute instead?" Dave retorted.

Angela twisted her face into an angry smile.

"Jeez." Dave groaned, hanging his head. "That was just the gift from hell that keeps on giving."

Angela extended the carton toward Dave. He reached around, pulled out a drawer, and grabbed a spoon.

"You good with ice cream or do you want to open a bottle of something stronger?" he asked, digging in.

"I don't know. What goes good with chocolate peanut butter?"

"I brought a bottle of Banyuls back from Strasbourg. Had it with dessert one evening. Did amazing things to the chocolate madeleines. Does have a kick to it, though."

"Open away," Angela said with a wave of her spoon.

Dave disappeared down the stairs and soon returned, carrying a bottle. He took two glasses from the cupboard and uncorked it.

"Now the alcohol content of this is about thirteen percent," he said, pouring the garnet-colored liquid. "So it's two for the price of one."

Angela licked off her spoon and laid it on the counter. "I'll drink to that," she said, and clinked her glass against Dave's.

"Want to talk about it?" Dave asked as Angela guzzled half her glass before coming up for air.

Angela shook her head and stared into the depths of her wine. "I'm an ungrateful bitch," she said with a hiccup.

Dave gave a small laugh. "What makes you say that?"

"I ran off...I ran off at eighteen...became a model...traveled the world." She took a choking breath and blinked back tears. Then turned her bleary eyes upon Dave. "I left them, but when my stupid brother takes my stupid advice—'Out of sight, out of mind' I told him. And now he's going...and Belle's getting married...and I'm...I'm..."

"Feeling rather alone," Dave said.

"Yep," Angela said, popping the P. "I'm a bitch."

"And I'm a 'stinking bastard.' At least according to my last two girlfriends. My work always comes first. I just don't care."

Angela clinked her glass against his. "Then we belong together. The bitch and the bastard."

Dave chuckled lightly. "I'm not really a bastard and you're not really a bitch. I've just had the misfortune to link up with people who want more than I can give. You…I get the feeling you've gone a long time without life feeling solid beneath your feet. Wanting that doesn't make you a bitch."

Angela heaved a sigh and slumped forward onto the counter, laying her cheek against the cool granite. "You don't think I'm a bitch?"

"Hmm. I tell you that you're one of the kindest and funniest people I've met—" Angela shot him a look of disbelief from her position on the counter. Dave laughed softly and shook his head. "Have you seen how you look right now? Yes, funny! And somehow, you think I'd find these the qualities of a bitch? Well, Miss Grimalke, that's not my definition of a bitch. Far from it."

"I heard it a lot when I was modeling."

"Women do seem to do an excellent job tearing each other apart."

"Between that…and my screw ups…getting fired…"

"Having a hard time landing on your feet," Dave continued for her. "And your family certainly hasn't helped."

"They only started that after Alex. And it is rather traditional."

"Traditional? Your mother's English and your father's Hungarian."

Angela blanched. "Old Hungarian custom that hasn't died out yet," she stammered. "Kind of like *My Big, Fat Greek Wedding* or even India."

"But your parents' marriage wasn't arranged, was it?"

"No, they met at Cambridge."

"So why—" Dave suddenly broke off. "You know what, never mind. Nicky's off on his big Irish adventure. We just need to find some way for you to stretch your wings. If you can't feel grounded, you may as well soar."

Angela sat up and blinked at him.

"What?" Dave asked.

"Is this the you that everyone pays a bajillion dollars for?"

Dave flushed. "Maybe."

"'Cause I've never really been into the whole corporate thing. I've always preferred actions to words."

"Words are pretty powerful things," Dave said. "But they do need to be followed up by actions. Unfortunately, you're only going to be getting words from me for a while. Martin called and wants me in Munich the week after next."

"After Edinburgh?"

"Right after. And then I'm supposed to be in Zurich the week after that, so I'll be gone for three whole weeks."

"Bastard," Angela said with a grin.

"You keep trying to warn me about you but my life is just as messy. Just in a different way."

"So Nicky's leaving. You're leaving."

"I'm just a text away."

"Maybe," Angela said. "But five to six time zones away. And with my weird schedule…"

"There's always voice mail."

"Yeah. I suppose," she said with a sigh.

Dave lifted a devilish smile. "Now you know why I'm single. And a bastard."

17

It was odd, heading to her parents' on Wednesday, knowing Nicky wouldn't be there. But Angela's depression quickly turned to irritation when she saw the table had been set for four instead of three.

"Really? Again?" she said to her mother, tracking her down in the kitchen. Evelyn simply gave her a sharp look and handed her the bread basket.

"Could you get that?" Evelyn asked a moment later when the doorbell rang.

"Oh, for crying out loud!" Angela muttered before spinning on her heel and marching out of the kitchen. She slammed the bread basket on the table on her way to the door.

The bell rang again as she reached it.

"For heaven's sake!" Angela said as she wrenched the door open—

Air rushed into Angela's lungs. Standing in front of her was a god of a man. Her body tingled, begging her to knock him down and have her way with him right there in the hall.

"Hi. I'm Carlos. Carlos Pelli. Your mother invited me to dinner."

Angela attempted to make her jaw move as she stared at his

outstretched hand. "C-c-ome in," she managed, opening the door further. She curled her fingers into it for support as he stepped past her.

"You must be Angela." Carlos tucked his hands into the pockets of his jeans.

Jeans that fitted perfectly. Everywhere.

Angela hauled her eyes back up. "That's me," she said, turning her back on him to close the door. After a steadying breath, she turned around. "Dinner's right this way."

Leading the way, she attempted to still her hammering heart. Hopefully, her face didn't have the deer-in-the-headlights look she feared it did. *Holy cow!*

Evelyn was placing the stuffed peppers on the table when they walked in.

"Carlos," she said, extending her hand. "I'm so glad you were able to join us."

Damon emerged from his study. "Ah, Mr. Pelli. Glad to see you were able to find us."

"Go ahead and sit down," Angela's mother said, taking her seat and shaking out her napkin.

"Wine?" Damon asked.

"Yes, please!" Angela thrust her glass forward.

Damon shot her a disapproving look. "I was asking our guest."

Carlos threw Angela a bemused smile. "Ladies first, I always say." Her toes curled.

Her father followed Carlos's command and filled her glass first. Her hand shook as she retrieved it. What the hell was this man sitting across from her? Some kind of siren? Never had she met a gremlin who affected her like this.

"How are you finding New York, Mr. Pelli?" Evelyn asked as she passed him the platter of Damon's favorite Hungarian sausages.

"I just got in last night," he said, helping himself to some before passing the plate to Angela's father. "And please call me Carlos."

"Your first time in the city?" Damon asked.

"Yes."

"Where is it you're from?" Angela asked as she took the platter from her father.

"New Mexico. Just outside of Taos."

"And what do you do there?"

"I'm a travel guide. River rafting, fishing, hiking. That sort of thing." He offered her a smile, and Angela thanked the heavens for the padding in her bra.

"Did you do any sightseeing today?" Evelyn asked.

"Went to Central Park. Grabbed lunch at Gray's Papaya. It's a bit overwhelming, all the people."

"Yes, completely different energy," her father said.

"Angela can show you some of the more out of the way places," Evelyn said.

Angela nearly dropped her fork. "I'm working tomorrow."

"Yes, dear, but tomorrow is one of your early days. You could take Carlos out to dinner or clubbing. And then you're off Friday. You have the whole day to show him around. Angela works as a ticketing agent for Windsor Airlines and has a crazy work schedule," her mother said to Carlos.

"I'd love to have the company, if she's willing." Carlos turned his gaze to Angela. The depths of his eyes twinkled with what seemed like all the stars in the sky.

Between the air of determination emanating from her parents and the hopeful look Carlos was giving her, she didn't really have the option to say "no."

"I'll collect you from your hotel tomorrow evening," she said, not bothering to fight them, and her heart did an almighty fist pump in triumph.

Angela Googled him when she got home. According to the spotlight page on his employer's website, Carlos had majored in foreign language at the University of New Mexico and spoke Spanish, French, Italian, Japanese, and Tiwa. She popped up a new screen and Googled Tiwa—a language spoken by Pueblo people in New Mexico and Texas—and then went back to his bio. Carlos had been working as a guide for the last twelve years and had been given five stars by all the reviewers on the site.

About half an hour into her search, Angela smacked her hand to her forehead. *Carlos Pelli.* Of course. The magical community just couldn't resist a joke, even when it came to names. After all, she was an "angel" and her father was a "demon." What were the chances he was actually what he was named for? She'd be way out of her league if he was.

Now there was just the problem of what to actually do with him. The thought consumed her, even at work the next day. Should she take him to dinner or a club?

Dinner, she finally decided. No way did she want to watch a club full of women throwing themselves at him. Or risk his full magnetism unleashed on the dance floor. Angela shuddered, a delicious shiver that nearly took leave of her senses. Yes, better to be somewhere safe like a restaurant.

She made reservations at a quaint little Italian place in the Village known for their seafood dishes and picked him up at seven.

Walking out of the hotel instead of pushing him into the elevator and taking him back upstairs required every ounce of her self-control. Even standing on the sidewalk, her gaze wanted nothing more than to linger on the bronze curve of his neck. Or his sinewy wrists, framed by the cuffs of his red shirt, rolled up, exposing even more of his delicious skin.

Angela tamped down her lust and focused on Carlos's lack of jacket. "I thought you were from the desert."

"High desert. Taos is at seven thousand feet. It was thirty-four degrees when I left Tuesday morning."

Which was a good ten degrees colder than the current temperature outside. Who would have guessed? "So you left the southwest in search of warmth."

"In more ways than one."

Angela's heart voted to help him out with that. Wrap her arms around him and run her fingers through the dark, shimmery hair curling irresistibly around his face.

"What do you have planned for this evening?" Carlos asked.

Angela's brain lingered on her earlier desires before giving her a swift kick. Right. Restaurant. "A couple of typical New York things— Italian food and Greenwich Village. Give you more of a small town feel. A crowded small town," she admitted. Anything New York had to offer would be teeming with people compared to New Mexico. Their largest city was what? Albuquerque?

"So just like home," Carlos said. "Taos is a tourist mecca, you know."

"You'll have to let me know if the streets are as congested." Angela led the way to a cab. "Not bothered by the crazy driving?" she asked as the cab lurched away and quickly wove its way through traffic.

Carlos chuckled. "I ride white water for a living. Doesn't bother me at all. But tell me—" He bent his head, his breath warming Angela's neck. "Ever fiddle with the motor? Just for fun?"

"No!"

"Oh, come on. Isn't that a gremlin specialty? Motors?"

Rearing back, Angela shot him her best disbelieving look. "Yes. And no, I don't. Not for fun." She took a moment to study him. "I take it you're not one."

"Something more ancient," Carlos said.

"Really? As obvious as your name?"

A deep, musical sound, like the ringing of bells, filled the air as Carlos laughed. "My parents' idea of a joke."

"I have an affinity for all things mechanical, and you—music, tricks, and…" Angela trailed off, unable to breathe under the focus of Carlos's smoldering gaze.

"Fertility is what the anthropologists call it," he finished for her.

"Yes."

"But I can tell you're part siren," Carlos said. "Which nature has the greatest pull for you?"

"Neither." She considered Carlos for a moment. "They brought you out here to meet me, but they didn't warn you about me?"

"Do I need warning?"

"Uh, yeah. I'm not normal," Angela said, putting quote marks around the last word with her fingers. "Just so you know."

"In what way?" Carlos asked with a bemused grin.

With a glance to confirm the cabbie was otherwise occupied and she wouldn't be overheard, she leaned in. "I don't like to use my magic."

"Why is that?"

"I didn't like how I saw it being used when I was growing up. Mainly to play practical jokes. Caused too much chaos."

"So you're a gremlin with a heart."

"Now you're just making fun of me," Angela said.

"Not at all. My ancestors had two reputations, one positive and one more along the lines of 'lock up your daughters.' I choose to use my abilities to ignite the emotions of people around me. Make them feel the magic around them. Hopefully bring some joy."

"Is that what they're calling it these days?"

A laugh rumbled in his chest. "The…fertility…attribute *was* last on the list, after—"

"Music and tricks."

"And you don't like tricks?"

"No. I don't."

"What about music?"

"Gremlins aren't in to music." Angela tore her eyes away from him and gazed out the window.

"No, but sirens are. It's one of their weapons." Carlos leaned closer. "And what do you think of music?" he whispered.

A song rose up inside her, fluttered in her heart, begging to be set free. For one brief moment, the gremlin melted away, and she became a creature that belonged to the sea.

"I think it's something to get lost in," Angela said, tamping down the feeling. "Which is why a siren is so successful."

"My, my. You are one perceptive person." His mouth curved into a smile.

Angela curled her fingers into the leather of her purse, filling her hands with it, instead of the soft fabric of his shirt. She would not reach out, take hold of the deep red cloth, and pull him close for a kiss.

Her lips tingled at the thought. *Damn.* It was going to be a long night.

"What do you have planned for us for tomorrow?" Carlos asked when the cab pulled up to his hotel. "Your mother is expecting you to show me around."

While the night had gone better than she'd anticipated—he hadn't tried to seduce her, and she had managed avoid accidents of either the magical or the klutz kind. Or act on the impulses being around him created—there was the very real fact that her parents had called him here and pushed him her way. They were expecting that she and Carlos would be a good match.

But then they'd thought Rick and Reg were good matches, too. Ugh. Her life was just fine, thank you.

However, it would be easier to do what her mother wanted, show him around.

And then she'd send him back to New Mexico and never see him again.

Angela pressed her teeth together and lifted a smile, "What would you like to do?"

"I hear the view of the city is amazing on a dinner cruise."

"No!" Angela drew a breath before continuing more softly, "I'm not doing anything where there's dancing."

Carlos tsked. "Am I to miss New York's famous clubs?"

"With me, yes. I'm not going anywhere where you'll unleash the full force of…you," she said with a vague wave of her hand.

Bells filled the cab again as Carlos laughed. "Where then?"

"I'll think of something. You think of something…tonight." Her breath rushed out. He'd have to take those clothes off to go to bed.

Carlos stepped out. "Until then." He pressed a kiss to his fingers.

Carlos shut the door and blew her another kiss. His hand still reached for her as the cab re-entered traffic. Before they had traveled halfway down the block, Angela gave up and fanned herself with her purse.

The skies opened up overnight, a deluge that continued past what should have been sunrise but merely became a lightening of black to dark steel-gray. Silver, marble-sized raindrops pounded against Angela's window.

She pulled the covers up to her chin and sighed. What could she do with Carlos now that her plan of a nice, safe walking tour had been washed away? Without the obligation, she probably would have spent the day at the Metropolitan.

Angela sat bolt upright. *Why not?* They could spend the day looking at art.

"Not what would have been on the top of my list," Carlos told Angela as they wandered the medieval art gallery.

"Music, but not art?"

Carlos lifted a shoulder. "There's just a…presence that I find missing from European art. Georgia O'Keefe—that, I like. R.C. Gorman. There's a vibrancy, a life, to those works that you don't find elsewhere."

A sly smile curled Angela's face. "I think I may know one or two portraits that will change your mind." She motioned with her head for him to follow.

"How did you learn so much about art?" Carlos asked a few minutes later when they stood in front of Ingres's *The Princesse de Broglie*.

"My best friend studied art history. Works in a gallery. Something was bound to rub off."

"Human?" Carlos asked.

"Yes. I don't have gremlin friends, other than a cousin in London."

"And do you have many human friends?"

"A few."

"So, no gremlin friends and only a few human ones. Sounds lonely."

Angela scowled at him and shifted down the gallery to the next painting.

"Are you lonely?" he asked, coming alongside her again.

"I'm fine." She fixed her gaze on the portrait in front of her.

"Are you?"

Turning her back on him, Angela stepped two paintings farther. Still he followed and pressed her. "If your life is so happy, so full, why are your parents trying to set you up?"

Angela attempted to walk away again but her feet refused to budge. Why did her parents have to find the one magical being that seemed to have an effect on her? Why couldn't they just leave her life alone? She didn't want a life filled with magic.

"They don't trust my judgment." Perhaps an answer would break the bond she felt rooting her to the spot.

"And do you? Trust yours?"

Heat flamed her face. A wash of emotions rose in her throat. Angela swallowed heavily. "It's fine."

His eyes stayed on the portrait but Carlos leaned his head toward hers. "You keep saying that, but I don't quite believe you."

Her heart constricted. Pain radiated in Angela's chest, threatening her grip on the emotions churning inside her. "Why are you even here?"

"To find a wife."

Angela snorted. "Right. Like you'd need help with that. There's probably a line out your door."

"But I don't want the ordinary," Carlos said. "I want the extraordinary." He turned his head, fixing her with his gaze. Entire galaxies danced in his eyes. "I want you."

With a gulp, Angela searched for her voice. "You don't even know me."

His gaze returned to the portrait. "I've known you long enough to know I've found what I've been looking for."

The words hit her like a slap.

What he'd been looking for.

Just another man with another list of expectations. Angela screwed her eyes tightly shut. "I'm sorry. I can't do this."

She spun on her heel and marched out of the gallery, not stopping until she climbed into a cab. Shutting the door, Angela gave the cabbie her address. She leaned her head against the seat. There would be a price to pay for what she'd just done. She only hoped she would survive the cost.

The buzzing of her phone, sitting on her nightstand, reached Angela from under the water of her bathtub. She held her breath and waited for it to go to voicemail. The moment the sound stopped, she broke the surface and sucked air into her protesting lungs. Her eyes fell closed as she leaned her head against the tub. She was so screwed.

Putting in for a transfer would be a good idea. Maybe move to London. Julia was there…but no one else. *Crap.* Her entire life was one big, murky mess.

Belle's text alert dinged. Angela heaved herself up, wrapped a towel around her wet body, and went to check it.

Joe working late. Free for movie?

Sitting down on the edge of the bed, Angela called her back. "I'm free. But lightning may strike me anytime."

"What did you do this time?"

A groan escaped her lips. "I'll tell you later. Best not to have you breaking out in laughter the rest of the afternoon."

"That good, huh?" Angela could hear her giggling already.

"You have no idea."

Belle's chopsticks hung in the air, a dragon roll perched perilously between them.

"So then I just turned and walked out," Angela finished.

"Your parents are going to kill you," Belle said, finally dipping her sushi.

Angela slumped forward on the table, moaning. "I know."

"How good looking was this guy?"

"He makes Nicky look like a nerd," Angela answered, still face down.

"Wow! And your parents found this guy?" Belle fell silent. "Did he actually propose?"

Angela shifted back up. "No, he stated he was looking for a wife and that he wanted me."

Belle lifted another dragon roll from the conveyor belt. She dipped a slice into her soy-wasabi bowl. "Would you want him?"

"I don't even know him. And he lives in New Mexico! Out in the middle of nowhere. Can you see me living in the middle of nowhere?"

Belle flashed Angela an amused grin. "No. What would you do all day? You can't cook. What's there to garden in the desert, even if you had a green thumb? What does this guy do?"

"He's a travel guide. Takes people river rafting, fishing, that sort of thing."

Belle errupted with laughter. "Yeah. I can just see you doing adventure sports." She shook her head and dipped another piece, still giggling. "No, it was best you left him behind. It may have been a little extreme but there's no way it would have worked."

Angela managed to make it to Wednesday before her parents chewed her out. They backed off only when she threatened to stop coming to dinner. Carlos left her a voice mail apologizing for having been so forward and hoped she'd change her opinion of him in the future. Angela didn't find that promising. Round two could possibly be in the making.

The next Wednesday came and went, and the Wednesday after that. No new or previous man sat across from her at her parents' table. Angela began to relax. And Dave would soon return. With, if the photo he'd texted was to be believed, a stack of absinthe chocolate.

He called Friday morning just as she was stripping the sheets off her bed.

"And what are you up to on your day off?" he asked when she answered.

"Laundry. What are you up to?"

"I'm currently sitting at a café in Heathrow."

Angela sank onto the bed. "On a Friday afternoon? They let you out early?"

"They did indeed. I'll be back in the city about eight. Meet me for a glass of wine?"

"But you'll have been up since—"

"Six a.m. in Zurich, so twenty hours."

"And you're not going to go home and go straight to bed?" she asked, unable to keep the surprise out of her voice.

"I've been talking shop, almost continuously, for the last three weeks. So, no. I'd rather meet a pretty girl for a glass of wine. I can sleep tomorrow."

Angela chuckled. "Sure, if you think you can stay awake. Where would you like to meet?"

"The wine bar on Eighth?" Dave suggested.

"Fine. I'll see you there at eight."

She stuffed her sheets into the basket, feeling a great deal more lighthearted.

Angela arrived early to make sure they got a table and sipped a glass of cabernet while she waited. How many months had it been since they'd first met here? She counted back. Seven. So much had happened.

So much hadn't changed.

Taking a large swallow, Angela savored the burn as the wine slid down her throat. Would there ever come a time when she didn't feel like an incredible fool? All she wanted was to capture the same feeling she'd had stepping through Hewitt's doors that first time, finally gaining a normal life. Kate had bounced up to her moments later and introduced herself. Those years at Hewitt hadn't been perfect, but they had been the best. Why couldn't she have that easiness now?

The legs heading down the stairs looked familiar. Angela spotted an intense green ribbon as Dave passed by the window.

"Where's your suitcase?" she asked as he came over.

"I stopped just long enough to wheel them through my door." He slid onto his seat. "Been here long?" Dave asked, nodding at her wine.

"Half an hour? Wanted to make sure we got a table."

"I'll have a glass of whatever she has," Dave said to the waitress who appeared.

"The cabernet. And I'll take another glass as well." Their waitress nodded and left.

Dave placed the ribbon-tied stack on the table. "Replenishing your stash. Don't eat it all at once."

"Not this! I portion it out and make it last." Angela set it on the banquette beside her.

"How were the last three weeks?" Dave asked.

"Interesting."

"Interesting? Hmm. That doesn't sound good."

She shot Dave her best "you-have-no-idea" look and tilted her wine to her lips.

"Work?…Or home?" With a wide-eyed glance, Angela drank again. "Home," Dave said. "How were dinners now that Nicky's gone?"

"Interesting," Angela said again, and turned her gaze to the bar.

"Ah. I take it that there was another person warming Nicky's seat."

Angela met Dave's gaze and raised her brow in confirmation before looking away again.

"Want to talk about it?" he asked.

"No."

"Ah. That bad. Well, let's see…I did some Christmas shopping while I was away."

"Already?"

"Well, it *is* the end of October. And when you have the chance to import things directly…"

Angela laughed. "What did you get? Or would that be telling?"

"Scotch for my father. A box of those Highland chocolates for my mother, though the trick will be keeping them from melting when I go down to Florida for Christmas."

"Not very Christmassy for you."

"My mother's hosting Thanksgiving in St. Louis but she wanted to be able to walk the beach as a reward for the work, so we're all going to Tom's for Christmas."

The waitress returned with their wine. Angela polished off her first glass and handed her the empty.

"Pick anything up in your other two cities? Or just chocolate?" she asked.

"Cow bells in Zurich for my nieces and nephews. You can never have too much cow bell."

"Cow bells?"

"Jenny's kids are huge Grand Rapids Griffins fans. Hockey," Dave added when Angela wrinkled her brow. "Hockey fans ring cow bells instead of cheering and Jenny's family has season tickets. This way they'll get to ring authentic Swiss cow bells at the games."

"Your nieces and nephews in Tampa are into hockey, too?"

"Tampa Bay Lightning. The Michigan cousins have rubbed off on them."

She raised a wistful smile. "Must be nice."

"We're not talking hockey, are we?"

Her shoulders rose and fell. "Having people who share your interests."

Dave fell silent, studying her. "What are you doing for Christmas? Any traditions?"

Angela shook her head. "My family's not big into Christmas. I've worked it the last couple of years."

"Jewish?" Dave asked.

Angela laughed. "No. Nor Muslim or atheist. Just much more low key. We'll have dinner and exchange gifts sometime during the last two weeks of December. But our family tradition is that every day is a gift and magic is always possible."

"So you acknowledge that Christmas is magical?"

"Absolutely. Light shining in the darkness. The world has reached its darkest point and yet, because of Christmas, people count their blessings, acknowledge those important to them. Without it, it would be a time of sheer survival. Unless you live in the Southern hemisphere, and then it's a time to celebrate the return of summer."

"Summer." Dave shuddered. "It's just such a wrong season for Christmas."

"Says the man who'll be spending Christmas in Tampa."

"I'd much rather spend it in St. Louis but my mother wanted the beach." Dave held up his hands. "How can you say 'no' to your mother?"

"With great difficulty," Angela muttered and took a large swallow of her wine.

Dave's eyes widened, and he changed the subject. "I've not had a home-cooked meal in three weeks. Want to help me shop tomorrow?"

"What are we cooking?" Angela asked, more than willing to put aside the contemplation of her life for the comfort of Dave's kitchen.

"Italian."

At mid-afternoon they met on their usual corner in Union Square. Tomatoes, zucchini, sausage, and ricotta were soon added to their bags. Swinging by Veniero's, they picked up cannoli before walking the four blocks to Dave's apartment.

The smell of the sauce he'd left simmering on the stove peppered the air, even in the hall. Soon sausage was frying, adding its savory smell to the tang already on the air.

Dave showed Angela how to layer the lasagna—a ladle of sauce, now bumpy with chunks of meat; a layer of pasta; a layer of cheese. The process was repeated until the pan was full. Dave topped the dish with freshly grated mozzarella and popped it in the oven. Then he brought up and opened a bottle of wine and took down the game of Scrabble from its place on the shelf.

"I'm hoping jet lag will kick in soon," Angela said as Dave quickly surged a hundred points ahead of her.

"Not for a day or two," Dave said, arranging the tiles on his bar.

Angela squinted at the board then back at her tiles.

"So," Dave said. "Feel like telling me what made the last three weeks so 'interesting' for you yet?"

"No, cheater. Quit trying to distract me." She laid down L,A,X to make FLAX.

Dave added up her points. "Now it's my turn. Why were the last three weeks interesting?"

A sharp staccato filled the air as she tapped a tile on the table. "Fine! If you must know, the parade restarted while you were gone and I don't feel like reliving it."

"I'm sorry," Dave said. "Want me to go easy on you?" His hand hovered over the board, a tile pinched between his fingers.

"No." Angela sighed. "Though I will have more wine." She picked up the bottle and refilled her glass.

"Plenty more where that came from."

Angela raised her glass in silent toast before bringing it to her lips. "Bring yourself back anything?" she asked, setting it back down.

"A bottle of scotch."

"Oh! So *two* bottles of scotch. Those didn't go in your garment bag."

Dave laughed. "No. I had to check a large suitcase as well as my garment bag this time."

"And you were willing to play Russian roulette with two bottles of fifty year-old scotch?"

Dave looked up from his tiles. "How did you know they were fifty years old?"

Crap. Hopefully her face didn't betray her. "Oh…um…good guess?" Angela said, trying to put some puzzlement into her voice. "I've seen it listed on dessert menus for ridiculous prices. And," she added mischievously. "You did say one bottle was a gift."

"Ridiculous prices, yes. But for my dad for Christmas…"

"And for how hard you work. You should indulge yourself every once and awhile."

"Well, thank you." Gratitude filled his face. "It's nice to have someone other than my clients acknowledge my efforts."

Angela returned his warm smile. "Any time."

"When was the last time you had a vacation?" Dave asked the following Saturday as they strolled through the market.

"Um…" Angela racked her memory. Her face grew warm as the information clicked into place. "New Year's last year." She tamped down the mixture of embarrassment and mortification that followed. At least her answer had come out normally.

"What did you do?"

The warmth became a fire. "Stayed at Parrot Cay in the Turks and Caicos." How had her face had not yet burst into flame?

"Ah. *That* kind of vacation," Dave said. "How was the beach?" he asked nonchalantly as he linked his arm with Angela's.

"Amazing," she said with a sigh. It had been, at the time.

"What you need to do is build some new memories. Do you remember what you did on November 14th when you were in the fifth grade?"

"No. Do you?"

"No idea. But that's my point. You've done so many things since then, it simply doesn't matter. If you want Parrot Cay to fade into the past, you've got to create a reason for it to."

"What do you have in mind?" Angela asked warily.

"Come with me to Paris next week."

"Right. Like that's a good idea."

"It is," Dave insisted. "You'll get out of town, avoid the parade. I'll have someone other than business people to breakfast with."

"You'll what!"

"You know what I mean. When we *meet* for breakfast. You'd have your own room."

Angela set her hand on Dave's arm and considered his offer. "I think you're just looking for a way to make your own Parrot Cay become…not so important," she said after a moment. "Wasn't Paris the scene of your last dumping?"

"Yup."

"And you think my being there will make…"

"Lauren," Dave said.

"Fade into the background?"

"It would be a start. Every time I'm there, every time I return to an empty hotel room, that whole last blow up plays in my mind. I swear, it's almost as if she cursed me."

"Hmm. You don't really believe in curses, do you?"

Dave leaned some of his weight against Angela. "I don't know. Sometimes it seems that way. Sometimes—" He nudged Angela. "Sometimes, Miss Jinx, you do, too."

Her air rushed out in a heavy exhale. "I don't know. My family would freak out if they found out about it."

"You don't have to tell them."

"Julia would," Angela reminded him. "She'd know."

Silence fell again.

"So is that a 'no'?" Dave asked, his voice heavy.

"We're not even dating," Angela said.

"It would be nice to have a friend with me. Someone to perk me up when I get blue."

"Let me think about it."

Angela really wanted to say "no." Her parents would hit the roof, it would be taking things with Dave a step further than she was really sure she wanted to, and she wasn't even certain she could get the time off.

But knowing how much she wished she could erase Alex from her life, Angela understood Dave's suffering. She doubted Lauren had actually cursed Dave. But there were times she felt like Alex had cursed her.

She called Kate for a second opinion.

Angela explained the situation and waited as silence fell on the other end of the line.

"I guess it comes down to do *you* want to go to Paris?" Kate said.

"Not my first choice of a vacation at this time."

"So you'd basically be going just to be there with him."

"Okay," Angela said. "That sounds more—romantic? Desperate?—than it really is."

"I like Dave," said Kate. "I think he's good for you. But unless you're willing to start blurring the lines between 'friend' and 'girlfriend' then I think you need to bow out."

"Is that what I'd be doing?"

"Listen sweetie, you didn't say, 'Yay! An opportunity to visit Paris!' Which you would be doing basically alone since he'd be working all day, probably doing client dinners at night. This Lauren dumped him because he was never there. I think that says something."

Angela chewed on a nail. "You're right. We'd been talking about Parrot Cay, which makes me want to barf every time I think about it. I'd love to have someone erase that from my life. I wish I could do that for him."

Kate's heavy sigh whooshed through the phone. "You're going."

"Wait a minute. Didn't you say just moments ago that I should bow out?"

"I said you should if you don't want to blur the lines. But I know you. You're going to want to help him associate Paris with someone other than Lauren. Just, do me a favor. Find a reason to go to Paris other than that. That way Dave just happens to be in Paris and you'll be there—"

"For the shopping?" Angela suggested.

"I would have said art and architecture. But as Belle says—"

"Shoes are art," they finished together.

Angela called Dave to tell him she was going. "As a friend. To help you leave the Paris of Lauren behind."

"Thank you," Dave said with a heavy exhale. "All you'll need to do is come and shop. Or whatever."

"What makes you think I'm coming to shop?"

"You always look great. And your pursuits seem more Belle than Kate."

"Fat lot you know. I was just at the Metropolitan last—" With a rush of horror, the events washed over her. Her throat constricted, shutting off her air. *I want a wife…I want you.*

"Last…? Angela?" Dave's voice seemed to come from far away. She blinked back tears. "Say something or I'm calling 911."

Angela pushed words past lips that were heavy as stone. "I'm here." They were nothing but breath.

A whooshing sound filled her ear as Dave exhaled. "God, you scared me!"

"Sorry," she said, her voice tiny.

"I take it you relived the something you didn't want to talk about."

She sniffed. "Yup."

"So, museums will be off the list next week?"

A gentle laugh filled her lungs, easing her turmoil. "No. Kate's already provided me with a list of things I need to see."

"Hmm. So, Kate knew you were coming before I did."

"I needed a second opinion. I *am* known for doing things without thinking them through."

The sounds of Dave hemming and hawing drifted through the receiver. "I guess I should lay out my expectations and you can decide if you really want to go. I've got more frequent flyer miles that I could ever use so I'm getting you a first class ticket. I'll book us rooms on the same floor of my hotel. This time I'm staying at the Hotel du Collectionneur. I'm paying for your hotel room. You can spend the savings on shoes."

Angela laughed. "I know you'll be gone days. How about evenings?"

"I'll have business dinners one or two nights. The others, usually someone from whatever company I'm working with will take me out. I generally eat dinner alone once, just to give myself a break."

"So I'll need to find something to do evenings as well."

"Unless you want to join me for the ones that aren't working dinners. Maybe I can even find an excuse to turn down their hospitality."

"If you're really so busy, why have me join you?"

As the silence grew, Angela checked her phone. Had they been disconnected? No, the timer was still ticking. She brought it back to her ear as Dave cleared his throat. "It would be nice to have a friend in Paris," he said gruffly.

Angela's heart turned to mush.

"What time are you planning on picking me up?"

19

Paris might be known for its glorious springtimes, but not even Angela's gremlin blood was ready for the wind and cold of November. They checked into the hotel on Sunday and then hired a car to take them out to Versailles. Monday, after breakfast, Angela bundled up and rode the number 2 line down to Anvers. She trudged up Montmartre and into her favorite sweet shop. One large shopping bag later, she continued up the hill to Sacré-Coeur.

Rain beat down upon the city, which spread out before her as a study in gray. Below her, the city moved at full speed but, up on the hill, all was still except for the rain.

When tranquility had settled into every pore, Angela collapsed her umbrella, and stepped into the church. The hush of whispered voices and shuffling feet washed over her. The scent of incense and candles hung in the air.

Angela slipped onto a bench and closed her eyes. *Sanctuary.* A place of refuge. Something she'd been lacking in New York. Here she was alone, and yet she didn't feel alone.

She lingered in the quiet until her stomach begged for lunch. Angela collected her things and made her way back down the hill to catch the Metro to Notre Dame. At one of the cafés that surround the ancient cathedral, she took a table by a steamy window and watched the world go by. After lunch, she wandered Shakespeare and Company and picked up a couple of books which she took back to her hotel room. She ate dinner alone, and yet, she wasn't alone.

Her phone beeped at 10:30.

YOU STILL UP?

YES

WANT TO GET A DRINK?

SURE

Angela slipped on her shoes. Dave waited, leaning against the wall, his tie still knotted but loose around his neck.

"Have a good day?" he asked.

"I did. You?"

"Good. Want to do the executive lounge or the bar downstairs?" Dave asked.

"It's less crowded up here. Unless you want the excitement of the bar."

"Here's good," Dave said. A smile crinkled his eyes.

They each got a glass of wine and took seats side by side, gazing out at nighttime Paris and the glowing Eiffel Tower.

"Long day for you," Angela remarked.

"My Mondays usually are. Tomorrow will be like this, too. Did you find much to do in the rain? Or did you spend the whole day at the Louvre?"

Angela laughed. "I stocked up at La Cure Gourmande, went to Sacré-Coeur, spent the afternoon in the Latin Quarter. I'm saving museums for tomorrow."

"I see you have your priorities straight—chocolate first!"

Dave's right hand, so close to hers, twitched. Then he reached out and took up his wine, his arm creating a barrier that hadn't been there a moment before.

Angela turned her gaze back out window. "Did Lauren haunt you last night?"

Dave stiffened. "Just going to throw that out there, are you?"

Angela lifted a shoulder. "Thought I should see if your plan was working."

A gentle laugh jiggled Dave's chest. "Yeah. She wasn't as loud as usual, though."

"What does she say?"

Dave's head fell. He opened and closed his mouth several times. "That I'm a selfish jerk who deserves to be alone," he said quietly, fiddling with his wine.

"Ouch!…Do you believe it?"

Dave shrugged. "Do you—" He shook his head. "Never mind."

Angela finished Dave's sentence for him. "Do I believe it? No."

"That's—never mind." His shoulder brushed against hers in a gentle nudge. "Thanks."

Angela spent the next morning at the Musée Rodin, touring the exhibition of *Flesh and Marble* per Kate's instructions. After lunch, she took in the advertising posters at *Musée de la Publicité* and then wandered the Latin Quarter, examining the set menu offerings, eventually taking a table at a Greek restaurant for dinner. She was on the Metro on her way back to the hotel when Dave texted.

YOU AROUND?

ON THE METRO

MEET FOR DRINKS?

WHERE?

Dave texted her the location of a café, along with the note—AMAZING CHOCOLATE!—and met her there fifteen minutes later.

"You're done early this evening," she said as he took his seat. "Did they feed you?"

"No, just drinks. I'm starving!"

Dave ordered—tagliatelli with foie gras and Serrano ham, and a glass of Bordeaux. Angela decided on a glass of the same and the chocolate gateau.

"What did you have for dinner?" he asked Angela, after handing his menu back to the waiter.

"Greek. Little place in the Latin Quarter."

"Been there before?"

"No, just wandered around until I happened upon it."

Dave's eyes twinkled as he smiled. "The best treasures are always found that way. So, other than Greek, what did you do today?"

"Couple of museums, smaller ones. Things on Kate's list."

"And what did our art history major have you looking at?"

The waiter brought over their wine.

"Rodin's marble and the much 'under-appreciated' art form known as the advertising poster." If she was lucky, her infamous one would soon slip into obscurity.

"Still holding the Louvre in reserve, I see."

"I've been before."

"What? You've seen all of sixty-thousand meters of the Louvre?" A teasing smile quirked Dave's lips.

"No, silly." Angela nearly swatted him. "What I've wanted to see. Plus the list Kate provided for me on previous trips."

Dave tugged on the knot of his tie, loosening it. He uttered a small groan as he undid the top button of his shirt.

"I can put that in my purse if you want to take it off," Angela said.

"You do mean my tie, don't you?" Dave asked.

Angela smacked him. "Of course!"

Dave unwound the silk and gently folded it over and over before putting it in the inside pocket of his suit jacket. "That's why tailors put those there."

Giving her head a small shake, she snuck a glance at her watch. 8:30.

"Why do you do it?" she asked.

Dave's brow crinkled. "Do what? Wear ties?"

"This job. Your hours are practically that of a corporate law attorney."

Dave's shoulders lifted and fell. "It's me. I would assume the people who stick with corporate law do so because of the chase, finding the clause or the item that *makes* the deal. To them, all the long hours are worth it."

"What are you chasing?"

"Ever watch *Harvard Silk*?"

She nodded. "Sometimes."

"There's one episode where the guy in charge of the associates has been given a crappy review by them and it puts the firm's recruiting privileges in danger of being revoked. Someone reminds him that he's a good attorney now because of what he learned when he was one of those associates. The guy is then able to go out and basically rally the troops. He tells them how the position is a gift; that the hell they're going through will make them better attorneys. That not every firm offers them this chance to learn. That's what I do, help companies connect with their employees, create better working conditions. Happy employees are more productive employees."

"You help companies find a way to convince their employees to work forty-eight hours straight?"

"Not necessarily," Dave said. "Let's take a look at your job. What's important about it?"

Her brows tugged together as she thought. "Um, I check people in."

"Go on."

Angela racked her brain, trying to figure out where Dave was going with this. "I verify their identification…tag their luggage."

Dave shook his head. "I may need to give your uncle a call. You, Miss Grimalke, are the first point of contact for a customer. You set the tone for their experience. You are the first line of security. You are the person to whom they are trusting their belongings."

"Wow!" She'd never looked at it that way before.

"Every employee matters. Every employee should know why they matter. A team member who is standing out in the field simply because the team needed a warm body out there is not going to be part of a winning team."

Angela stared at Dave, wide-eyed. "Wow!" she repeated, and held out her hand. "Give me your phone."

"Why?" Dave asked, taking it from his pocket.

"I'm giving you my uncle's number. I'll call him in the morning. Tell him to expect your call."

"I wasn't angling—" Dave said before Angela cut him off.

"I know. But no one's made me feel that important before." Angela shook her head, overcome with disbelief. "If everyone felt that way…"

"Amazing things can happen."

"Did you ever explain this, what you do, to Lauren?"

Dave's eyes hardened. He brought his glass to his lips and swallowed, as if the wine could wash both his memories and her words away. "Not interested. All that mattered was that I wasn't around as much as she wanted."

"Well, I'd share you with the world." Panic flared in her chest as her words registered. "N-not that I'm—"

"It's okay." A smile tugged his mouth. "I know what you meant.

Thanks." Dave placed his index fingers on the base of his glass and began to turn it. "Would you be interested in joining us tomorrow, for dinner? You don't need to. Just didn't know if you were getting lonely, or if you liked having some quiet time."

"Sure, why not? Might be interesting to see what your dinners are like."

"Interesting, huh? Why do I get the feeling you're trying to compare my corporate 'family' dinners to your own?"

Pressing her lips into a mysterious smile, she skipped an answer and made room on the table for the chocolate cake wending its way toward her.

Dave stopped talking mid-sentence when Angela walked into the restaurant dining room. His frozen gaze caused the other heads at the table to turn.

Really! She hadn't made much more of an effort this evening than she usually did. Sure, she was the image of Paris chic with her simple black dress and new Christian Dior pumps she'd found while wandering the Avenue Montaigne after lunch, but her outfit wasn't far off from the Armani she'd worn that evening they first went bowling all those months ago.

Dave rose and attempted to close his mouth, but his smile kept drifting back down into a gape. "G-gentlemen," he said. "I'd like you to meet my friend, Angela Grimalke."

"Evening, all." Angela slid onto her chair with a sultry smile. She flashed Dave a wink as the men stretched out hands to shake hers, jostling their water glasses.

Dave's lips curled under and he gave a tiny shake of his head as he took his seat. He went around the table, providing the introductions. Angela grasped each hand in turn, smiling at their "*Enchantés*" and puzzled attempts to kiss her from the other side of the table.

"So, Miss Grimalke, what brings you to Paris this time of year?" Edouard Beaumont asked, the one man who's name she actually remembered.

"I needed a bit of a vacation so I wheedled Dave into letting me come. I knew he'd keep me from going home with an additional suitcase."

"Angela developed a fondness for beautiful clothes when she worked as a model," Dave told them.

"Runway or print?" the man in the green suit asked.

"Print," Angela said, flashing him a smile. "I proved too much of a klutz for the runway."

"*Ce n'est pas possible!*"

"Oh," Dave said. "I assure you. Things have a tendency to happen when Angela's around."

"David said 'worked.' You are not still modeling?"

"No as…David…said, things have a tendency to happen when I'm around. I'm currently working for my uncle."

"What field?" the gentleman with the pin striped suit asked.

"Transportation."

"Your uncle," Purple Tie said. "Have I heard of him?"

"Nigel Palliser." Angela waited for the onslaught of recognition.

"Windsor Airlines!" several exclaimed.

She flashed Dave a look of apology. Her arrival had ended any continuation of business. Of his, at least. But his amused smile told Angela that may have been his intention all along.

Rain pounded against the window when Angela awoke the next morning. In no mood to deal with it, she had the hotel's concierge book an appointment for her at a spa. Four hours later, after having been scrubbed and wrapped and soaked and massaged, her limbs had turned as limp as spaghetti. Angela grabbed a baguette sandwich to eat in the taxi and went back to the hotel for a nap. She spent the rest of the afternoon lost in her book.

Dave texted that he'd be late again so she ate dinner at the hotel restaurant before venturing back outside to go to the cinema. Pulling up *Pariscope* on her phone, she found a comedy playing at Le Champo and sat in the dark, trying not to snort chocolate olives out her nose when she laughed.

Dave met her later that night for drinks. They sat again at the banquette, Paris looking like a watery version of van Gough's *Starry Night*. The rain splattered windows diffused and bent the lights into objects only guessed at. Angela caught Dave leaning closer and sniffing.

"You smell different," he said. "What did you do today?"

"It's the spa."

"Ah. You pampered yourself today."

"Well, I wasn't up for another museum and I didn't want to fight the rain shopping, so I figured, why not? You didn't pamper yourself today. That one was another marathon."

"Mostly my choice," Dave said. "I tried to get as much stuff cleared up as possible so that I can take you out to dinner tomorrow, just you and me."

Just you and me. That sounded wonderful.

"Thank you," Angela said the next night at dinner.

"For what?"

"Paris," she said with a sigh. "This."

"The view?"

"Getting me out of New York. I hadn't realized how all the drama of the last few months was dragging me down. I hadn't realized how lost I felt."

"So you've found yourself in Paris," Dave said with a flirtatious wink.

"Yes, actually. I'm feeling much more like me. How about you? Lauren still voicing her accusations?"

Dave looked at the table and shook his head. "There was—is—an element of truth to what she said. But you've exorcised her. You've been amazing this week. The dinner with my clients, willing to squeeze me in late in the evening."

Angela lifted a wry smile. "Isn't that why successful men are successful? They do more than an eight-to-five."

"Sad but true. There's not time to have a 'normal' life."

"You'll just need to find someone who sees time with you as a gift."

"And you, what would the person in your life need to understand about you?" Dave asked.

What was the thing she'd been searching for?

"That different can be a good thing," Angela said. Something her family didn't understand about her. Never had.

"Ah, so something we have in common," Dave said, raising his glass in salute.

"I guess we do," Angela replied and clinked her glass against his.

By Sunday, they were back in New York and Angela was back to her normal life. Hollywood producing mogul Jay Montgomery had decided to use the flight to LA to pitch his latest "thriller" to an actor recently named as The World's Sexiest Man for his pouty smile and amazing timing. Angela wished Jay had checked his carry-on containing the script, *Leporidae Holocaust*—a thriller where genetically modified bunnies are unleashed on an unsuspecting world by a spiteful scientist. If he had, she would have been able to have Wendell lose it permanently. Instead, she wistfully watched it head for security and had to be content with sending just his suitcase to Cleveland.

A Saturday night out bowling with Dave gave Angela the only break she had before the holiday rush began. Tuesday, she saw Dave off to St. Louis and then worked a double shift on Wednesday to deal with the flood of extra travelers, which allowed her to make Thanksgiving dinner at her parents' on time.

Her heart warmed when she spied the table set for four. Nicky must have been able to make it from Dublin.

But when the doorbell rang a few minutes later, she realized the place setting wasn't for him. Angela lingered by the kitchen as her father went to answer the door.

"Carlos, welcome!" Angela's heart sank.

She hoisted a smile onto her face as they walked into the dining room. Carlos appeared elegantly relaxed in dark gray slacks and a navy shirt which made his bronzed skin seem to glow. Her fingers twitched, wanting to trace his throat. His eyes met hers, and her stomach responded with a series of enthusiastic flips, pulling her voice right down with them. Angela stood mute as he walked toward her, hand extended.

"Nice to see you again."

Angela gulped. Folding her hands safely behind her, she willed her voice back into her throat. "Carlos. What brings you to New York?"

"I did," her father answered. "Wanted him to look over a book deal I'm working on. A modern Kokopeli tale."

"Autobiographical?" Angela asked.

"No," Carlos said. His lips twitched with an amused smile.

"Angela," her mother called from the kitchen. "Could you help me get dinner on the table?" Angela jumped at the chance to excuse herself.

"Put the potatoes and green bean casserole on the table then come back for the bread," Evelyn told her. "Could you send your father in to carve the goose?"

Angela picked up the dishes and hit the kitchen door with her hip. She set them on the table without looking at its occupants and informed her father that he was wanted in the kitchen.

Damon handed Carlos the bottle of wine he'd just opened. "Excuse me. Help yourself."

She trailed after her father. Angela picked up the bread basket and sighed. Her mother was now stirring the gravy and her father had begun carving the goose. What she wouldn't give to hide out in the kitchen with them and avoid Carlos. But with her luck, her mother would shove her out the door if she tried. Reluctantly, Angela slunk out.

"Wine?" Carlos asked holding the bottle over her glass.

"Sure." Angela sank onto her seat. "So you're back."

"Um," Carlos hummed in acknowledgement and set the bottle back down.

"You know I don't want you here."

Carlos folded his hands on the table. "I think we got off on the wrong foot. I'd like to apologize for having been so forward."

"But here you are."

Carlos lifted his glass and considered her. "What are you looking for?"

Angela reared back. "Pardon?"

"You're looking for something in particular. Nicky told me—"

"Nicky!" Angela gritted her teeth. There were times she really wanted to kill her brother.

"Your brother and I have some mutual friends," Carlos continued. "Nicky said you'd been turning men down left and right."

Angela looked down, squirming in her seat. "Yes, well, I don't do well with expectations."

"Ah." A corner of his mouth lifted into a smile. "They can be rather confining."

"But you *expect* that I'd make you a good wife."

"Yes, but not for the reason that you think."

"Oh, really?" Angela couldn't help rolling her eyes. "And apart from the fact you think I'm 'extraordinary,' what makes you think I would?"

Carlos studied the table. "'She's different,' your brother told me. 'She cares. Perhaps too much so.'"

Heat filled her face. Carlos lifted his gaze from the table to meet hers. "Gremlins are usually reflections of those around them. But not you. Your purpose is different so you feel out of place. You don't belong here."

Angela picked up the knife from her place setting and toyed with it. "And what do you think my purpose is?"

"A guardian."

Whatever she had expected his answer to be, it was not that. "What makes you think I'm meant to be a guardian?"

"Your heart makes it rather obvious. To me, anyway. You're not into tricks. You're not a reflection of the person you're dealing with. You care, so much so, that you don't use your magic, and it backs up, spilling over, causing accidents. You care, Angela. And that is what I'm looking for."

Carlos's eyes filled with tenderness. His overt sexual magnetism melted away. Angela stared at him. This man truly believed her to be amazing? Could she really make a difference in people's lives?

The hinges on the kitchen door squeaked, breaking the moment, and her father backed into the room bearing the platter of roast goose.

She lost all track of the dinner conversation. Carlos sat, chatting with her parents, filling the dreaded spot across from her as no one else had. As no one else could. Something ancient and infinite emanated from him. It wrapped around her, brushing against her skin and leaving a serenity in its wake.

Her mother stood to clear the dessert plates, startling Angela out of her contemplation.

"Angela, I'll wash up. Why don't you take our guest for a walk?"

Carlos's eyes held a quiet encouragement. Her coat was in her hand before she realized she had even stepped to the closet. They rode the elevator down in silence. The cool night air hit her as the doorman held it open.

"Will you make a break for freedom this time?" Carlos asked, close enough that his breath warmed her ear.

Angela tamped down the tingling that rose. "I should apologize for that. It was rude."

Carlos opened his mouth but then snapped it shut. They had walked the length of the block and crossed to the street before he spoke.

"My fault, actually. I just presumed—"

"That I'd follow tradition?" Angela cut in.

"I should have realized, from our conversations…" Angela shrugged, brushing away the apology. "Is that what people do with you, make presumptions?"

Angela knotted her hands in her pockets. "All the time."

Carlos drew a deep breath. "How about I start again? I'm a prince in search of a princess." Angela snorted. "Which part do you find funny? Me being a prince or you being a princess?"

Her head shook as she rolled her eyes.

"There are advantages to my kingdom, fair lady. And I am looking for someone extraordinary to rule it with me."

"It's a kingdom you rule, is it?"

"An ancient one that needs protection."

Angela snuck a sideways glance at him. Carlos had wrapped his words in a joking kind of chivalry, but she got the feeling they were true. He took his ancient role seriously.

A red light slowed their progress. Carlos moved closer to her side as the shoal of people grew. They joined the throng that stepped off the curb as soon as there was a break in traffic though the light had not yet turned green.

When the crowd had thinned out and it was just the two of them, Carlos continued.

"Just give me a chance. I am old-fashioned, but you are not. Let me try it your way. Just give me an opportunity."

Angela sighed. It wasn't an unreasonable request. Unwanted, yes. But not unreasonable. As much as she didn't want to let him try, she couldn't work out a good reason why she should say "no."

"Fine. But unleash any of that Kokopeli magnetism on me and I'm done. I'm not looking for any of that."

Mirth flashed in his eyes, and Carlos's mouth curled into a smile. "Very well."

Sunday passed in a maelstrom of activity, all the Thanksgiving passengers heading back from whence they came. Somewhere in the sea of people, Dave passed through, returning from his time in St. Louis, though Angela never caught sight of him.

She fell into bed that night, exhausted, waking the next morning when her phone rang. Too tired to open her eyes, Angela curled the covers under her chin and let it go to voice mail. The text alert sounded a minute later.

Reaching a sleepy arm over, she picked her phone up off the nightstand. Dave.

How was your Thank…

Angela moaned. Her arm fell back to the bed.

Odd. My Thanksgiving was definitely odd.

She didn't bother to look at the rest of Dave's message. Couldn't, for her finger refused to press the button. She rolled onto her back, her arms splaying out like some forgotten rag doll, and stared at the ceiling. After twenty minutes, she forced herself up and into the shower. The warm water did nothing to dispel the strange heaviness that had settled over her heart.

Though she had three hours before her shift started, Angela put on her uniform and went to work.

Dave's unanswered text nagged at her as she rode the A train home. She reached into her purse and dug out her phone.

Fine. Yours?

Loud, came Dave's reply, ten minutes later.

Angela smiled. The bands encircling her heart eased their grip.

Do you still have hearing?

Ringing? Yes.

Maybe you'd better rethink those cowbells.

: P

Angela pressed her phone against her lips. Sure, it was Monday, but that meant Saturday was only four days away.

"How did Joe do in Baltimore?" Angela asked Belle at breakfast Saturday morning.

Belle moaned. "It was awful. We actually talked about moving to Azerbaijan."

"Why Azerbaijan?"

"'Cause it's halfway across the world and they don't celebrate Thanksgiving." Belle stabbed viciously at a piece of asparagus.

"I got a parade," Angela announced.

"No!" Belle and Kate chorused with matching expressions of horror.

"Yep." She speared a banana slice and dragged it though the chocolate sauce and whipped cream.

"Who did they pull out this time?" Kate asked.

"The last one."

Belle slowly raised her eyes. "Mr. Greek God?"

Angela flashed Belle a smile, full of as much irony as she could muster.

"Okay," Belle said. "Your Thanksgiving was way better than mine. At least you had something to give thanks about."

"Did he propose again?" Kate asked.

"Nope. He wanted to start over."

Their eyebrows rose like flags in the morning as Kate and Belle met each other's gaze.

"And?" Kate asked.

Angela focused on making a figure-eight pattern in the sauce on her plate and didn't answer.

"And?" Belle asked.

Angela stopped tracing and gripped her fork tighter. "I said 'fine.'"

Belle and Kate gave a nearly audible gulp.

"What about Dave?" Kate asked. Her casual tone sounded forced.

"We're just friends."

"Friends who vacation together," Belle said.

"Exactly. Friends."

Belle and Kate exchanged another look.

"So did you and…Mr. Greek God—"

"Carlos."

"Carlos," Kate continued. "Did you start over?"

"We did some stuff together."

"Stuff—" Belle started but Kate shut her down with a look.

Great. Belle thought she'd slept with him.

"And?" Kate prompted.

Angela shrugged. "It was fine. Though I did not sleep with him." She gave Belle a pointed look.

"This is the guy who lives in New Mexico, right?" Belle asked.

Angela nodded.

"What do you think about New Mexico?" Kate asked.

"It's desert. There's mountains. And rivers. Carlos gives rafting tours."

"Uh huh." Belle and Kate continued to share Oh-My-God! expressions.

"And Dave went to, where, for Thanksgiving?" Kate asked.

"St. Louis."

"Is he going to be around for New Year's? You guys are going to come to the gallery party, aren't you?" Kate's tone let her know that she really didn't have a choice in the matter.

"I'll ask him," she said, and let the conversation drift into holiday plans.

Dave stood stomping on his usual corner, his breath condensing in feathery clouds, hands tucked under his arms against the bitter cold. He broke into a grin as Angela approached.

"I don't know how you do it," he said, shaking his head. "I'm absolutely freezing but you look like you're merely on some catwalk, showing off this year's winter look."

"I didn't do the catwalk. Way too dangerous for this klutz. I'm like that guy who can get buried in snow with no hint of hypothermia or even indication that he's feeling the cold. It's just mind over matter."

"Right. So if we had some ice cream, you'd just imagine it was summer."

Angela lifted a sardonic grin and took Dave's arm. "What's on the menu for today?"

"Duck cassoulet, salad gourmande, and for dessert a pear soufflé with ginger caramel sauce."

"Duck? Not turkey?"

"Too hard to get leftovers through security so I'm using confit."

Angela's brow wrinkled. "What's confit?"

"Duck is high in fat," Dave said. "You poach it in its own fat with some salt. It not only makes the meat tender but it acts as a preservative. Keeps in the refrigerator for weeks."

"Thank you, Bobby Flay."

"Nah," Dave said. "I'm not Bobby. I'm more like Alton Brown. I like the science behind food."

"I just like your food," Angela told him as they stopped at the produce stand.

Dave selected some greens, potatoes, and pears and put them in the one bag he carried. She turned in surprise when he guided her toward the exit. "What? That's it today?"

"The confit is made, the cannellini beans are soaking, and I already have eggs."

Angela eyed the lone grocery bag, its bottom lumpy, its upper half sagging. "It's kind of sad. There's not even bread poking out."

Dave snapped his fingers. "Bread! I knew I was forgetting something. And we'll want it to soak up the sauce from the stew." He put a guiding hand on Angela's elbow and steered her back to the sea of tents.

"Are you going to be back from Tampa in time for New Year's?" she asked.

Dave gave her a sideways glance. "Yes."

"We're invited to the New Year's Eve party at Kate's gallery."

"We?"

"Unless you want to sit home and watch the ball drop on TV. I'm not going to that party alone."

Dave stopped at his favorite bread vendor and selected a loaf of Viennese. "I guess I'll just have to turn down the black tie event in the Hamptons I was invited to," he said, paying for the loaf.

Her face drained. "Black tie?"

"But, hey! Fireworks are overrated. I'd rather spend the evening with you. And you," Dave said, giving Angela a nudge. "Would rather spend it with your friends than at some black tie event where you'd feel like you were on display."

Relief flooded her. "You know me so well."

Dave chuckled. "I try."

Dave opened a bottle of wine and Angela climbed on her usual perch. Dave fried up some pancetta and then garlic chicken-sausage pennies. He removed the meats, added a scoop of duck fat, and tossed in a chopped onion.

Closing her eyes, she breathed in the tangy aroma that wafted up from the sizzling pan. "I love your kitchen."

"You love what comes out of my kitchen," Dave said. He flung a checked dish towel over his shoulder and gave the onions another stir.

"That too."

Dave glanced over his shoulder. "What's so special about my kitchen?"

Angela's shoulders rose and fell. "I don't know. It's… it's so peaceful."

"Ha! That's because you're not the one doing the cooking."

"But even when you do put me to work, sure, I'm afraid we'll end up in the ER because I'll have sliced off a fingertip, but somehow, even that would be okay. You'd bundle me off, get me bandaged up, and then bring me back and fill me with comfort food."

"You're still that scared of my knives?"

A strangled sound escaped Angela's throat. "I can't even use a vegetable peeler without taking a chunk out of a knuckle or nail."

Dave nodded. "True. Maybe I'll have to get you one of those holders they make for handicapped people."

"Yup, that's me. Handicapped by klutziness."

"Maybe there's a reason for it," Dave said. "Maybe you've got that condition Daniel Radcliffe has…dyspraxia. Can you tie your shoelaces?"

"Somehow my finger always gets stuck."

"Would it make you feel better if there was a medical reason for your clumsiness?"

Angela considered. What if the reason she was a klutz was because she didn't use her magic *and* she had dyspraxia?

"I don't think it really matters. I am who I am, no matter the reason why. Or are you saying there's treatment for it?"

"Occupational therapy. I believe they set up routines and have you practice things that are hard to do."

Practice. Yes, that would certainly remove what she suspected was the root of her problem.

"Not in public," Dave rushed to add as his gaze fell on her face. "It probably works like stuttering. The more you think about it, the worse the problem."

Angela gave a small nod of agreement.

A lopsided grin appeared on Dave's face. He slowly shook his head. "That's okay. I like you just the way you are."

After dinner, Dave and Angela sat next to each other on the floor, backs against the sofa, their legs stuck under the coffee table, wine in their hands, enjoying the gas flame flickering in the fireplace as seasonal music drifted from the speakers.

Angela leaned against Dave in a fog of food contentment and sung softly, adding her voice to the wish for it to keep snowing.

"You do realize that it's been snowing for the last half hour," Dave said.

Her head whipped toward the window. "What? Crap!" Collapsing like a marionette cut from its strings, she let her head fall back onto the sofa. "I hate working when it snows," Angela moaned to the ceiling.

"I'd think you were even more important when it snows."

"You're going to give me one of your pep talks, aren't you?" Angela said, bracing herself.

"Do you know why people can fly?" Dave asked, launching right in.

"Because engineers figured out things about lift and thrust and pressurization."

"That's the mechanics. Why can we do it? Why can we leave the ground? We're not like birds who feel safer in the air, who roost in trees so they can sleep in open space. We're ground dwellers. Yet every day millions of us get into a tiny tube and leave terra firma miles below. Why is that?"

She uncurled her fingers from the rug. Every hair on her arms had lifted. "No idea," she said a little breathlessly.

"We *feel* grounded."

"How?"

"Do you know anything about child psychology?" Dave asked. Angela shook her head. "Ever watch a toddler at a restaurant or even the airport, someplace new, away from home? The child will sit near his mother's legs, maybe even cling onto them while he or she checks out the area. When the child is sure the parent isn't going anywhere, she'll move, begin to explore. But he'll check in, make sure Mom or Dad is still there. As the child becomes confident that the thing *grounding* her is still there, her ability to explore, to spread her wings and fly, grows.

"You are that person for people who fly—the touchstone. As the world becomes chaotic due to weather conditions or other events and people begin to sense the true distance between the earth and that plane, you help provide a sense of security that allows them to let go, to leave the ground behind.

"Now you could leave that job to someone else, or even be the parent who gets irritated at the clinginess, but I know you, Miss Grimalke. You would rather give them wings."

And she did. It might go against her purpose as a gremlin, but she wanted to be the pair of gentle hands that tossed the frightened bird back into the sky with a whispered, *You can fly.*

Angela turned her gaze out the window. Large fat flakes drifted past, weighing down the world. By morning, everything would be covered in a heavy blanket. Hot chocolate in front of the fire or TV weather, not flying weather.

Yet people still needed to go. Vacations scrimped and saved for. Meetings arranged months ago. A birth or death to rush to. All of them wondering if the plane would make it out of the snow, into the air, safely.

"You're right," she said with a sigh. "It's even more important."

Dave checked his watch. "Do you want me to pour you into a taxi yet?"

Angela held her glass out to him and sang in time with the words now sounding from the speakers, "Well, maybe just a half a drink more."

"You're early and you're *cheerful!*" Jackson exclaimed when Angela showed up mid-morning for work. "What's with that?"

Angela opened her mouth to reply but he cut her off.

"No, wait. Never mind. You got a pep talk from Management Boy."

She let Jackson's derogatory comment slide. "Yes, and I figured you guys could use some help with all the cancelations."

"True. Very true. Squeeze in anywhere," Jackson said as he craned his neck and looked for the end of the queue.

Angela logged onto a computer and waved the next person forward.

"Good morning. How can I help you today?"

Filled with satisfaction, Angela kept catching herself humming on her commute home. The steamy train was loaded with weary people, at odds with how alive she felt despite the long shift overflowing with delays. Something had clicked today. For the first time in her life, she felt like she'd found her purpose.

And it was all due to Dave.

At home, Angela got out her laptop and brewed a latte while it booted up. Dave deserved something special as a thank you. Inspiration had struck when the New York skyline had come into view from the train.

Angela entered her idea into the search engine and clicked enter. One company had five different options. She scrolled through them and nearly choked on her coffee as she read the description of number four.

It couldn't be true. But there it was. In black and white. Fate.

Cringing, she clicked on it and checked out before she could change her mind. An eight hundred-dollar hit to her credit card.

But as she thought of Dave's reaction, the pain melted away. It was worth every penny.

"Friday. Lunch at the Boathouse."

"Well, hello to you, too," Angela said to Dave as she dug through her closet Wednesday night in a desperate attempt to locate the sweater she was sure she'd hung up in there.

"Come on," Dave wheedled. "I know you hate Fridays, everyone working, no one to enjoy your day off with. So, I'm taking you out. Reward for a crazy week. If you are going to have to deal with snow, it should at least be from Central Park with a glass of wine."

"And you'll be playing hooky?" Angela asked, giving up the search and grabbing the first sweater from the stack in her dresser drawer.

"Yup. Reward for all the hours I work. Besides, I need to pack for my trip to Turin next week."

"What's in Turin?" Angela asked, jumping up and down as she pulled on her jeans, her phone crushed between her shoulder and her cheek.

"Why are you breathing heavy?" Dave asked. "Have I interrupted something?"

"Only a mad dash to get dressed and out the door," Angela said, stuffing first one foot then the other into a pair of brown boots. "What's in Turin?"

"A car company. By the way," Dave added, the grin in his voice unmistakable. "That is a very sad reason for heavy breathing."

"Maybe you can help me have a better reason Saturday night," Angela replied in a sultry tone.

"W-w-what?"

"Dancing. Belle's birthday is Saturday. We're celebrating at a salsa club. She's craving paella. You're invited, of course."

There was a whoosh of air as Dave exhaled. "Dancing. Right. Sure. Of course. Yeah, I'll be there."

"I hate to rush you, but I still need to stuff myself into my sweater. When do you want to meet Friday?"

"Pick you up about eleven?"

"Great! See you then!"

Angela slammed the sweater over her head, grabbed her coat and purse and keys, and skidded out the door at a dead run.

Twenty minutes late. Her mother was going to kill her if the pork szelet had gone dry.

Angela stared out the floor to ceiling windows of The Boathouse. Dave had been right. If you had to deal with the snow, this should be the reward. Fat, white flakes drifted down, covering the trees and lake. Melting snow dripped from Dave's hair, creating little rivulets down his neck. She suppressed a laugh, thinking about how excited he'd been to see the squirrels in the park. Teasing him about his canine ADD. *Squirrel!*

"Hard to believe how different it will look six months from now when Belle gets married," she said.

"How are our bride and birthday girl's plans coming?" Dave asked.

Angela wrinkled her brow. "You really want to know?"

"Why not? Just don't go into agonizing detail on ribbon color choices or anything else really mundane."

"Okay. Uh, she and Joe are going with a nature theme."

"Huh. I would have pictured the Guggenheim or the Waldorf Astoria—either super slick or super fancy."

"I know," Angela said. "But that's my mother for you. She has this gift for steering clients into what they're really envisioning, and for Belle and Joe that turned out to be a relaxed day in the park."

"Where a hundred of their closest friends and a priest just happen to show up."

"Yeah, something like that."

Dave chuckled and shook his head. "Wow. So when do I get to meet this amazing mother of yours?"

Angela choked. At least, she wasn't mid-sip with her wine. Spraying liquids in a restaurant was one humiliation she had thus far managed to avoid. "I'm not letting you anywhere near my mother."

"I don't scare that easy," Dave said.

"Uh, maybe. But I like you better still breathing. And so do your clients."

"She can't be that bad," Dave said.

"Look, every time you and I have done something big together, she's upped her game on the parade. Come to think of it, I shouldn't worry about you. I should worry about me. I bring you home, even as a friend, and the next time I show up there'll be a priest there for *me*."

"Oh, so you're Catholic," Dave said.

"No. Never mind who'd be there. It would be an officiant and some guy that I'd leave married to."

Dave shook his head. "I just don't get your family. Or is your father really Romani? They still force arranged marriages on their kids."

"Romani, no. But something like that."

"Why, Miss Grimalke!" Dave said. "You've gone all mysterious on me."

"Are you trying to undo Paris?" Angela asked. "And the pep talk you gave me last week? Because talking about my family will do it."

Dave held his hands up. "I bow to the pressures of the parade. And I did bring you here as a treat."

The waiter arrived with their wine and took their order. As soon as their waiter departed, Dave lifted his glass in toast.

"To a grown-up snow day."

"To a grown-up snow day," Angela echoed. "I hope that means you're taking me sledding."

"We can certainly arrange that," Dave said with a twinkle.

The cold, snowy weather was nowhere to be found the next evening in the salsa club where they met for Belle's birthday. After the dinner plates had been cleared away, Joe ordered two bottles of their best champagne and raised his glass as soon as it was poured.

"To Belle," he said. "The love of my life. I am so eternally grateful—*we*," he amended, gesturing around. "Are eternally grateful to have had you in our lives for another year. Here's to many more."

"Here, here," they all said, clinking their glasses together.

Joe drained his in one fell swoop. "And now..." He stood and took Belle's hand. "I'm going to take my bride-to-be and get her in the mood for tonight."

Belle gave him a saucy look but turned and fanned her face as Joe dragged her off. Angela clamped down hard to make sure any images of the Agent Provocateur to be used tonight wouldn't be seared into her brain.

Myles stood and extended a hand to Kate with a flourish. "Shall we?"

Kate gave him the same saucy smile that Belle had just used, took his hand, and with a grace that belied her shorter frame, uncurled her limbs and followed.

"Am I missing something?" Dave asked.

"Myles and Kate have been taking salsa lessons Friday nights," Angela said.

"Did you want to dance?"

"Sure, though I don't know how to salsa. I just move to the music."

"Me, too," Dave said. "I only know how to waltz."

"Waltz?" Angela wrinkled her brow. "Where did you learn to waltz?"

"I did *Hello, Dolly!* in high school."

Angela did a double take. "Really? You don't seem like the musical theater type."

"I wasn't. But Stacy Perkins was."

"Ah." A grin crept up her face. "Did you get the girl?"

"Nope. Matt Hind was such a charming Cornelius that he got all the girls. I did, however, learn to waltz."

"Not that you can use it here," Angela said.

"Maybe New Year's Eve."

"No roulette this time," Dave said as he placed his garment bag on the scale the next day. "Send it to Turin. Not Toledo!"

"Spain?" Angela asked, raising a grin.

"Either one!"

"Why the change of heart?" Angela asked as she printed out the luggage ticket.

"New city. Don't know any tailors in Turin. Yet," he added.

"Do you want to?"

"I could do with some Italian style," Dave said, striking a model-like pose in his Northwestern sweatshirt.

She fastened the tag onto his bag. "Why do you travel in that thing?"

"Keeps people guessing. Ratty old sweatshirt, Henk roller. Did he steal it? Is he a dot-com millionaire?"

"What is the story with the Henk? It doesn't seem like you."

"Christmas gift from Martin a couple of years ago," Dave said. "I never would have bought myself one. But it certainly is handy and it helps my chaos-loving side."

Angela shook her head. "Which is just so wrong, given what you do."

"Not necessarily. A little chaos keeps us on our toes. None and we get fat and lazy and can't adapt to change."

"Yes, I guess it's better to be the mouse than the dinosaur."

"Being a mouse is always better," Dave said with a wink, and waved farewell.

Angela's mouth curled into a smile. Mouse. She could hardly wait for Christmas.

They parted for Christmas at the airport. Angela had cradled her gift in a nest of tissue paper within a small box. There was no need for Dave to guess what it was before the big day. Dave's box for her was even lighter. And smaller.

"It's just chocolate," Dave said as Angela hefted it in her hand.

Chocolate that weighs next to nothing? She resisted the urge to dip into his head. He wasn't being truthful, but it was the season for deception. Her own wrapping job was proof of that.

"Well, thank you," she said, placing it under the counter.

"You're welcome," Dave replied. "What do you think? Open them together Christmas Eve via Messenger?"

Angela squirmed. She wasn't ready to meet Dave's family, even virtually.

"I'm working that day. Christmas, too. But we can text each other," she quickly added as Dave's face fell. "Call me after I should be home, after some of the craziness has died down. Even if it's late. You're not the only one with a time-sucking job, you know."

Dave held his hands up in surrender. "Touché."

"Bastard," she said with a grin.

"I suppose it is your turn." Dave picked his claim ticket from the counter. "Try not to lose too many bags, Miss Grimalke," he said with a smirk. "And I'll talk to you soon."

The rush provided Angela with plenty of opportunity to use her magic. She sent Amy Burke's luggage to Buenos Aires. Amy was just going to have to borrow some of her mother's clothes for a day or two. Besides, she should be looking forward to spending time with her cancer-fighting mother instead of being resentful that she'd been "guilted into the trip." Spending Christmas in St. John's with her boyfriend could always happen next year.

Angela thought about her own mother on the hour-long train ride back to the city. Her family home didn't feel safe anymore. Dave's apartment felt more like home—filled with the smells of cooking, the sounds of laughter, and the chance to learn new things. Expectations and disapproval were all that her parents' apartment was filled with. And Nicky was no longer there to be a buffer.

She leaned her head against the steamy window, girding her heart. She would not be one of those pathetic people crying on a train. Maybe her family was right. Maybe she did spend too much time around humans. She was certainly wallowing in human emotion now, wanting what she couldn't have. A true gremlin wouldn't feel that way. They would find a way to take what they wanted.

Angela sighed. Dave would be in Tampa by now, welcomed by a crush of people, all glad to see him. Tonight, she'd be greeted by two people filled with concern and criticism. She was of half a mind to go to Kate's instead.

But running from her problems wouldn't make them go away. Hugging her bag to her chest, she nestled the soft, lumpy leather under her chin and let the rhythmic rumble of the train massage away some of her dread.

Angela shoved her key into the lock and froze. Voices in conversation drifted from inside her parents' apartment. They weren't alone.

With a bracing breath, she twisted the key and turned the knob. Her father's voice was familiar but not the other, muffled from its trip around the corner and down the hall. As she pushed the door closed behind her, the other man laughed and she froze again.

Carlos.

Angela sagged against the door. She'd like him more if he were on his own, no parents hovering around.

Are you a mouse or a dinosaur?

Her head bobbed. *Mouse.*

Right. Time to change things up. Her mother could freeze the leftovers.

"Carlos," Angela said, marching around the corner. "I've come to rescue you."

Carlos plucked another mussel from the bucket. "This is certainly unlike anything I'd find in the desert."

Angela breathed in the mixed aroma of beer and mussels, waffles and wine, duck and vinegar and herbs. Candles lit the faces of the diners in the darkened restaurant, so different from the usual view. "I eat here all the time. Though it's usually for breakfast."

His fork froze mid-spear. His eyes widened, raising his eyebrows toward his perfect hair. "You've let me into your inner sanctum?" With a shake of his head, he returned to the mussel in his hand. "That's a change."

Angela shrugged. "I figured it was time to take my parents out of the equation."

"Well, thank you."

Carlos's eyes sparkled in the candlelight, creating a tug of otherworldliness that brushed against her magic. Surprise filled her at the touch. Instead of making her wary, it made her curious. What would he be like in his element, in the desert?

He drew another mussel from the bucket. His hands appeared soft despite his occupation. Strong but gentle hands cradled the dark, blue-gray shell.

Angela's back tingled. She shook away the vision of those hands grasping her waist.

"How long do I get you as a tour guide this time?" Carlos asked.

"Oh, um." She shifted her gaze away and tossed her empty shell into the large white bowl. "I'm working most of this week. Volunteered for extra shifts since I don't celebrate the holiday and they always need the help."

"Any chance of you taking me to a club this time? I still haven't been." His head bent, focusing on his dinner, framing his impossibly long, dark lashes against his cheeks.

"Maybe," Angela squeaked. Her heart beat out a tempo. Perhaps if she focused on his eyes, she wouldn't be able to see what his hips were doing on a dance floor.

"What can I do to turn that 'maybe' into a 'yes'?"

Angela plucked a mussel from the bucket, holding the blossomed shell by its edge, and braced it in her bowl as she stabbed the small fork into the meat. He was different tonight. There was still a sense of the infinite about him—the past, present, and future compressed inside one being. But here, in this place, something about him reminded her of the night sky of the Moroccan desert—an endless expanse of dark and light that made one feel tiny and yet connected at the same time. At the Metropolitan, he'd been a tightly wound ball of energy. Could he be this way at a club, relaxed and open?

"You're not as intense this evening. Can you take this new level of, what? Comfort? Into a high energy place? I like you more when you're not being overwhelming."

An amused smile lit Carlos's face. "I'm more used to New York now, how to process the energy of eight million people in such a confined space. For you, for a club, I'll find a way not to be overwhelming."

The flickering candles reflected in his dark eyes like stars twinkling in a velvet night. Her heart fell into the solace they offered, the peace she'd felt in the African desert.

"I'll pick you up at eight."

22

Angela called in a favor and had her name put on the list at one of the swankier clubs that boasted amazing views of the Manhattan skyline.

She peered in the mirror, debating whether or not to glam it up. Usually, the attention it garnered made her skin crawl, but she needed to create a buffer between the trawling socialites and Carlos. She had no desire for a repeat of her last night out with Nicky.

Carlos didn't get the full effect of her silver sequined dress and four-inch rhinestone heels until he helped her out of the cab. Her tissue-thin cream cashmere wrap slid off her shoulders and draped around her arms.

"Wow!" Carlos gasped, his hand frozen around hers. "And you made me promise not to be overwhelming."

Angela slipped her hand from his and adjusted her shawl. "Had to do something to keep the piranha from attacking."

"Piranha?" Carlos's brow furrowed.

"You'll see. This—" She waved her arms, gesturing from her shoes to her shoulders. "—this is only a buffer. They'll still be hanging around, waiting to devour you."

"So you've dressed this way for my protection." Carlos grinned.

"Mine. I don't intend to spend the entire evening trying to get your attention."

"So you do want my attention!" Carlos said, giving her a triumphant look from underneath his amazing lashes.

"Normal attention. We're trying to be normal here."

Carlos merely chuckled and followed Angela into the elevator. She gave her name at the front desk and they were shown to a booth, a red "reserved" card on the table.

Carlos sat down and picked up the menu card. "What do you feel like? Something to eat? A cocktail?" He flipped it over. "Champagne?" His eyes traveled further down the menu and bugged as he neared the bottom. "A hundred-thousand dollars! For one bottle of champagne?"

"They put those on there so drunk trust fund kids can show off just how much money they have. Stick to the thirty-dollar cocktails."

Angela unwound her shawl and glanced around the club. It was fairly empty, but then it was only eight.

A waitress in a super-short stretchy black dress came over. "Anything I can get you?" She gave Carlos a once-over and leaned towards him, causing her cleavage to strain against the fabric containing it. Angela rolled her eyes.

"Um," Carlos said, flipping to the cocktail side of the menu. "A Beautiful Nightmare and the tuna tartare."

"Pomegranate martini," Angela told her.

The waitress nodded once then gave a little sigh as she turned away, her head only following her body after she bumped into the chair that completed the "U" around their low-slung table.

A low chuckle rumbled in Carlos's throat. Angela slowly shook her head. It was going to be a long night.

"I think someone is trying to get your attention," Carlos said, leaning in to be heard above the growing din. Angela was afraid to look.

"Darling!" a voice gushed.

"My, my! Isn't he yummy!" said another.

She should have known the temptation would be too great. Of course, Mikel would want to check out her out-of-town guest.

"Mikel, Evan, this is Carlos Pelli. We have Mikel to thank for the reservation," Angela told Carlos as Mikel slid onto the settee next to her. Evan lowered his lanky frame into the chair like the queen he was and swung one leg over the brown leather of the arm.

"This is quite the place," Carlos said, leaning forward and resting his arms on his knees.

"And you're quite the dish! Where've you been hiding him?" Mikel asked, giving Angela a nudge.

"New Mexico."

Mikel put one hand on Angela's arm and the other over his heart. "Truly the Land of Enchantment."

"Mikel was my favorite stylist when I was modeling," Angela told Carlos.

"And Angela was my favorite model. Something was always bound to happen on set with Angela around," Mikel said mischievously.

"Yes, well, you were the only one who found the chaos amusing."

"How goes it in the land of air travel?" Mikel asked. "Losing lots of luggage?"

Angela smiled. "Only when it deserves to be lost."

Mikel gave her a saucy grin. "That I don't doubt. Where did you find Mr. Gorgeous here? A passenger?"

"Friend of the family," Carlos said.

"Nicky," Angela added.

"And how is your breathtaking brother?"

"Fine, last I heard. He's moved to Dublin."

"Shame," Evan said, running a finger along the blue velvet back of his chair.

Mikel pouted his lips and hummed his displeasure. His eyes drifted over Carlos's head and followed the approach of two gazelle-like women.

"Hi, Mikel!" they chimed and held onto each other, promptly turning their attention to Carlos.

"Shall we?" Carlos asked, extending a hand to Angela. "Ladies," he said with a bob of his head and led Angela to the dance floor.

"That was nicely done," Angela told him as they joined the mass of people gyrating to a hypnotic beat echoed in pulsating light.

"They'd been looking for an excuse to come over," Carlos said. "But I'm here with you tonight."

Angela dipped her head and watched the flashing lights reflecting off her dress—red, blue, white; tiny sparkles cast from the diamante on her shoes. She lifted her gaze and focused on the dancers around them, lost in the music or each other. What was Carlos doing? Did she really want to know?

She forced her gaze to his face. A smile crinkled his eyes. He was one with the music, his body moving easily in tempo but without the writhing and thrusting of many around them, the motions she'd been afraid of.

Her heart swelled. She gave herself over to the music and the movement. No flirting. No need for walls. Just two people enjoying a shared energy.

Angela brought the evening to a close at ten.

"Sorry," she said as they waited for the elevator. And she was sorry. To her surprise, Carlos had been easy to be with tonight. "I volunteered to work tomorrow. When do you head back to New Mexico?"

"Tomorrow night. I'm heading up to Angelfire to do some skiing over Christmas."

"Maybe next time then."

Angela woke early on Christmas morning. At least it was a Sunday so she had a few hours to herself before work. She slipped on her robe and padded out to make her latte. After rinsing out the steamer, she brought her mug over to the sofa and stared at Dave's present sitting in the Venetian bowl.

What kind of chocolate? Chocolate silk like her New Year's dress? Though the box felt somewhat heavier than a scarf.

Angela slipped her finger under the tape to remove the paper. She lifted the lid. A small velvet box sat cushioned in a nest of tissue paper. A lump formed in her throat. Angela swallowed hard, attempting to dislodge it. Grasping the box, she slowly lifted the lid.

Chocolate diamonds. And pearls. On a bed of white velvet sat earrings—drops of chocolate pearls suspended from a swirl of chocolate and white diamonds.

Angela placed the box on the table and set her hands in her lap. The earrings would look amazing with her dress. But they were diamonds. Dave had bought her diamonds.

She launched herself off the sofa and marched into the kitchen. The box of Vegan chocolates and bottle of cabernet Belle had given her for Christmas sat on the counter. Her hand reached out for the bottle opener.

No. It was only 8 a.m.

She pulled the ribbon off the chocolates, dropped it to the floor, and began shoveling in the brightly painted bonbons as she wended back to the couch. Sinking down, she stared at the velvet box and waited for the dopamines to kick in.

Dave called about an hour later. At least, the caller ID said it was Dave. All she heard was a loud sniff.

"Thanks for the gift," Dave choked out, several heartbeats later. "How did you find it?"

"Internet."

"But signed…as if to me."

It had been a miracle find. An autographed first edition of *Stuart Little* that read:

> *To David,*
>
> *May you enjoy Stuart's adventures as much as I have.*
> *Your friend,*
> *Garth Williams*

"I figured it was fate," Angela said.

"Well, thank you. It was perfect." Dave's voice had a strange microphone-like quality to it. Not speakerphone, but more like—

"Is that an echo?" What could be causing the strange reverb? "Are you in the bathroom?"

Angela listened several seconds before Dave responded.

"Maybe."

She bit back a smile. "I take it it's kind of crowded at your brother's."

"Yeah, Jenny's family is bunking here. The kids are loving being doubled up. I'm at the beachfront hotel my folks are staying at, but all twelve of us are currently eating cookies and opening presents. What are you doing?"

"Procrastinating getting ready for work. Eating chocolate."

"Uh huh." Angela heard the grin in his voice.

"And not eating the chocolate you gave me."

"Might break a tooth."

"They were quite the surprise," she said. "I'm not sure what to say. Other than, thank you?"

"They're not that extravagant," Dave said. "Probably set me back less than your book did. Got the idea when Belle said you were wearing chocolate for New Year's. Decided this time to get you chocolate that could actually last."

"Well, thank you. They'll be perfect with my dress."

"Can't wait to see."

23

Angela tried to quiet the butterflies in her stomach as she secured Dave's diamonds to her ears. What with the beading on the halter top encircling her neck, she needed no other jewelry. Once the backs were secure, she stepped back from the mirror for a final look.

The brown silk fell in tiny pleats from her neck to her toes. Flat panels cinched in her waist, curving around and framing her bust like a corset. The dress was a masterful combination—sporty and sexy, a froth of fabric contained by smooth, sleek glamour.

She checked the contents of her black silk evening bag—cellphone, compact, lipstick, a little silver case meant for business cards but containing her driver's license and a credit card, and a tin of Godiva Mint Chocolate Pearls.

Snapping it shut with nervous hands, she debated whether there was time for a glass of wine before Dave picked her up. Best not. She was sure to have several glasses of champagne at the gallery.

The click of her high heels on the hardwood floors sounded extra loud for some reason. Angela closed the door to her bedroom and straightened the contents of the hall table as she went by. After the

Venetian bowl was perfectly centered on the coffee table, she sat down on the sofa.

How could this be the first time Dave had been inside her apartment?

Probably because her kitchen was all of four feet. Hard to even make snacks in there.

Angela caught herself worrying the edge of her dress and pulled out her phone. Maybe a game would keep both her hands and her mind occupied.

Dave buzzed about the time she cleared the tenth level.

"Come on up," she said, hitting the door release.

She checked her reflection one last time, smoothing down the wrinkles she'd caused on the hem, then took her long, black cashmere coat out of the closet and threw it over her arm just as Dave knocked.

"Whoa!" he exclaimed as she opened the door. Dave's gaze traveled over her. A smile began to spread across his face and disappeared as he bit his lips.

"What?"

He reddened and shook his head.

"Something wrong?" Angela looked over one shoulder then the other.

Good enough to—

She drew in a startled breath. Her magic careened away. That was the problem with mind reading. You often heard things you didn't want to.

They both jumped in surprise as the globe from the kitchen light shattered on the floor.

"What the?" Dave brushed by her and looked in the kitchen. "Got a dust pan?" he asked. "Don't want you forgetting and stepping on this later."

Angela sheepishly opened the closet door and handed Dave the pan and a hand broom. He gave her a smile and set about sweeping the floor and wiping down the counters. Angela leaned against the door frame and watched him—dark top coat, navy suit, white shirt, patterned blue tie—more than filling the tiny space, yet oddly at home.

Until he knocked his knee against the oven.

"I can see why you don't cook much," he said, wincing as he rubbed the sore spot.

"I'm your typical New Yorker. Heaven forbid something happens and I'm forced to fend for myself when the restaurants close."

"Or seek shelter with your mother."

Angela laughed. "These days, anyway."

"There you go." He handed the pan and broom to Angela with a flourish. "Crisis averted."

She took them with a "Thank you."

Dave stepped into the living room and looked around. "Cute space. I like it. You could shoot Pottery Barn ads in here."

Angela closed the closet door and shrugged on her coat. "Thanks. You ready?"

Dave gave a small bow and extended his arm. "After you, milady. Your chariot awaits."

Angela gave her name to the guy holding a clipboard at the door. Security flanked him, hired by the gallery to keep uninvited guests out.

Many of the display walls had been moved to make room for a series of round tables and a dance floor complete with a bank of lights and a DJ. Dave and Angela handed their coats in at the coat check, and she scanned the room, searching for her friends. She spotted Kate and Myles about fifty feet away. Myles held a glass of champagne but whatever Kate had in hers was clear. Their faces were lit with a strange excitement.

"Happy New Year!" they caroled as Dave and Angela approached.

"What are you drinking?" Angela asked, peering at the contents of Kate's glass. Tiny bubbles fizzed in the clear liquid.

"Club soda."

"Whatever for?"

Kate blushed deeply. "I'll tell you when Belle gets here." Radiance spread across her face.

Angela's heart flipped and landed in her stomach. "Well, I could use a glass of the real stuff." She turned her head in search of a waiter.

"Dave's got quite a few there," Myles said, hamming it up with a har-har.

"Is that what those are?" Kate asked, leaning in to peer at Dave's tie.

Dave flopped the end of his sapphire-blue tie and smoothed it back down. So the dots were champagne flutes adorning his tie. "Yup. Figured it was a good night for a party tie."

"Was it Rudolph or Frosty for your Christmas sweater?" Myles asked.

"Rudolph. My brother Tom wore Frosty."

Myles clapped Dave on the shoulder, and they laughed heartily. Angela shared an eye roll with Kate and renewed her quest for champagne. She spied Belle and Joe handing their coats in. Belle's gaze searched the room, and she waved excitedly when she caught Angela's gaze.

She took a breath to steel herself. But on her exhale, she found, to her horror, that her hand had been reaching for Dave's. Angela altered its track and played with the clasp of her purse, opening and closing it as she watched Belle's approach.

Belle bounced up, excited and somewhat breathless. "Happy New Year everyone!" She did a double take when she spotted Kate's glass. "What *are* you drinking?"

"Well…" Kate began, beaming. Myles put his hands on her shoulders. His face took on a glow. Angela's hand snaked out and took Dave's. He gave Angela a brief, puzzled look. "We're pregnant! I mean, I'm pregnant."

Myles slipped his arms around Kate and pulled her close, folding his arms over her stomach.

"That's great! That's…" Belle's gaze followed Myles's arms, and her face momentarily fell. Then she hoisted a smile and gushed on. "We'll need to get you a different bridesmaid dress but that's *great*! It'll be great!"

"Ang?"

Angela blinked. Her grip had become too tight, crushing Dave's fingers. She dropped his hand and reached for Kate. "It is great." Angela pulled Kate close. "You're going to be a mother," she whispered into Kate's ear.

"I know. Weird idea, huh?"

Angela stepped back and squeezed Kate's arms. "No. You'll be wonderful."

Dave gave Angela a thoughtful look then, catching sight of the elusive waiter, raised a hand to get his attention.

"Nice to see you finally have a real smile," Dave shouted in Angela's ear about an hour later on the dance floor.

Her face grew cold as the blood rushed from it. "Was I that obvious?" she shouted back.

Dave twisted his face into an apologetic expression. Angela groaned.

"Is this the way you want to start the New Year?" he shouted at her.

"What? Here?"

Dave rolled his eyes. "No, depressed. Want to tell me about it?" He gave her an encouraging smile.

Angela lowered her eyes and took a couple more half-hearted steps. She leaned in. "I'm a bitch."

"What for this time?"

"I'm jealous."

A sad smile crinkled his mouth. Dave put a hand on her arm and guided her back to their table.

"Feeling left behind?"

Angela sniffed and stared at the table. She nodded.

"It's hard to be the last man—woman in your case—standing. Life is marching on and you feel like you've been forgotten in the shuffle."

Angela turned her gaze up to Dave. He pointed a finger at himself. "Last man standing. The one who had a hotel room to himself on Christmas." He waved his hand dismissively but there was a hardness to his smile. "Surrounded by family so it wasn't as bad as that sounded. But still, the only one not married, the only one without kids. Missing out on half the conversation because you don't really have anything to contribute, because that's not what your life is like. Yeah, that part is hard," he said. "But they're still there. Kate will still be there, just not as readily as before. And if Jenny's horror stories are typical, she'll need you to help her escape from time to time."

Angela managed a weak smile. "Thanks."

"You're welcome. Now, I thought I saw them setting up a dessert buffet. Shall we go see if they've set out any chocolate mousse?"

Angela found it easier after Dave's encouraging talk; able to enjoy the dancing, able to enjoy the conversation, even if Kate and Myles's shared glances made her wistful. Midnight was approaching when the DJ put on Christina Perri's "A Thousand Years."

"They're playing a waltz," Dave said. He stood and took Angela's hand. "Time to teach you to waltz."

He gave her basic instructions as they made their way to the dance floor. "It's a one-two-three pattern. Step, together, together. Step, together, together."

Dave found a space, drew her to him, and took her right hand in his left. His right hand clasped her waist. Beads of magic gathered and pelted her heart, creating a shockwave that raced along every nerve. Dave's next instructions were lost as the buzz of energy obliterated her hearing.

"Angela."

She swallowed hard and lifted a smile to mask her panic as her gaze met Dave's.

"Back with your right, back with your left, step in place." Dave applied a gentle pressure to their clasped hands, guiding her backward, and Angela's feet followed. "Forward left, forward right, step in place."

The hand around her waist pulled her forward. Angela's heart leapt as she moved toward him. Only to have him move away as his arms held the frame.

"That's it. One, two, three. One, two, three."

Thump-two-three, thump-two-three, Angela's heart pounded, her feet moving in tempo with its beat. Faster than the couples simply rocking back and forth around them.

Dave drew her closer and picked up speed, weaving them through the other couples on the dance floor. Her heart beat faster, pumping to keep up with the movement. Something inside her burst out, taking flight.

Her chest lifted. She fought the urge to fling her arms wide like Kate Winslet on the bow of the Titanic. New bubbles of magic rippled inside her. Angela struggled to put a name to the emotion. It was…joy.

Don'tkissher don'tkissher don'tkissher

Angela lost her concentration, stepping on Dave's foot. "Sorry." She bowed her head, suddenly aware of the energy between them. Her cheeks flushed and the furnace inside her put out so much heat it was a miracle she hadn't burst into flame.

Locked in Dave's embrace, she finally understood what had been the scandal and attraction of the waltz—the close contact, the pounding hearts.

As last notes of the song faded away, Angela struggled to catch her breath.

"Time to pull someone close and count down the last seconds until the New Year!" the DJ shouted into the microphone.

Whoops, hollers, and cheers erupted around them. Angela stilled. Her joy turned to panic.

"Ten! Nine! Eight! Seven!" With supreme effort, she forced her mouth to move. In, "Four! Three!" seconds Dave was going to kiss her. Tradition, right?

"Happy New Year!"

Confetti cannons went off, showering them in sparkly paper as "Auld Lang Syne" blared from the speakers.

She could do this. No big deal, right?

"Happy New Year," Dave said as Angela lifted her face to his. He leaned towards her and brought his lips to hers. A hum of white noise buzzed inside his brain. Dave's lips were soft and tender against hers. A kiss that could have been just between friends but with a gentle pressure that wondered at more.

He wanted more.

A stinging buzz welled up inside her, slicing into her heart like tiny little knives. Tears slid down her face before she could even try to stop them. Dave's lips left hers. Angela dipped her head but not quickly enough to keep Dave from seeing.

"Oh, my God! I didn't mean to make you cry."

Angela tried to hide her face as she wiped them away. "It's fine. Can we go? As in leave?" There'd been too many surprises tonight. It was time to flee.

Her heart clenched at Dave's crestfallen face. "Sure, sure."

They made their way back to the table where the others were toasting with champagne and club soda.

"We're going to go," Angela said. "I've been fighting a headache all evening. I made it to midnight but I'm done for."

"I wondered what was up," Kate said, a worried expression on her face. "Call me tomorrow when you feel better."

Dave called Manuel to collect them and retrieved their coats. Angela didn't speak until Dave directed Manuel to take them to Angela's apartment. A tiny little voice in her head told her that was a bad idea.

"Actually, I could use a latte. Could we go to yours?"

"Okay." Dave's face knit in puzzlement and then slowly hardened to stone. The space between them widened into a chasm. Dave stared hard at the seat in front of him and didn't say anything to Angela, even after the car pulled up to his building.

She followed in Dave's silent wake, nervously latching and unlatching the clasp on her purse all the way to his door. The kitchen that had always seemed so welcoming now appeared long and cold. She hugged her coat closer and went straight through, sitting down on the sofa. As Dave pulled down a glass and frothed the milk, Angela tried to figure out why her heart felt so heavy.

He brought it over with a quiet, "Here you are," and sat down next to her, leaving a full cushion between them.

Angela blinked. Tears overflowed and rolled down her face. How had it gone so wrong? This wasn't like the gala where Alex had exposed her to be a supermassive black hole that needed to be managed but, like that night, something had happened that risked her friendship with this man. What had she done to turn him so cold?

Her head wouldn't move. She couldn't even look at him. "I don't want to lose my friend." The words caught in her throat.

Dave sighed. He leaned forward, resting his arms on his knees. "Just tell me what I did wrong."

"You haven't done anything wrong," Angela said, as the ache roiled inside her.

"Then why are you crying?"

Her teeth began to chatter. "Because I don't want to lose you."

"Why would you lose me?"

Inside her, something broke. Some wall or vault in which she'd hidden every moment of self-doubt, every taunt, every accusation, cracked open, paralyzing her voice and leaving Dave with no answer.

He reached and took her hand. A whine erupted from her throat.

"I'm not going to be scared off," he said, and squeezed her hand. "You are worthy. You are worthy of having someone love you."

The whine grew to a howl. Dave scooted closer and wrapped Angela in his arms. Her willpower collapsed. Now unhindered, years of denied emotion rushed out, trampling her heart.

And there was nothing she could do to stop it.

24

Her sobs slowly faded. Angela began to notice how nicely she fit in the crook of Dave's arm. How comforting his shoulder felt. How nice his neck smelled.

She turned her head away from the soft curve and the swooping feeling it caused and shifted back. Dave let one arm fall away but kept the other around her.

"I don't think you realize how important you've become to me." Angela grasped the edge of her coat and twisted it between her fingers. "I feel at home with you. Shopping, cooking, losing spectacularly at Scrabble." Dave smiled. "To change that, to change what you are, would mean losing what I have."

"For something more," Dave said.

"If it worked out. And it usually doesn't. No matter what choice I make, things will never be the same. I'll be the girl who turned you down and things will become awkward. Or I'll hope for something more and you'll eventually grow disappointed in me."

"I don't want to lose you, either," Dave said. "But I can't imagine you disappointing me so much that I'd cut you out of my life. You're the only woman who's ever 'got' me. You don't complain about my crazy schedule. You don't complain when I want to stay in." Dave sighed. "I guess I've messed it up, hoping there could be more. Wanting to see you in my kitchen in the morning. Hoping you'd be here at the end of a long trip or day."

Angela pulled the images out of Dave's brain, images that weren't so different from the things they'd actually done. Pictures of two people sharing a home.

Wasn't that what she'd been seeking, even tonight? Coming here for a latte, hoping that this place, this man, could work magic of their own and calm her turmoil?

Her latte sat as untouched as the man next to her. All she needed to do was reach out to it, to him.

Could she be brave? Take one step, as the lyrics of Dave's waltz had suggested. One step. One breath. One kiss?

"Okay," Angela said, collecting her courage. "Let's try a kiss. If it doesn't feel right, we chalk it up to New Year's and too much champagne and never speak of it again. We'll go back to being just Angela and Dave and continue with the dinners and Scrabble and occasional night out bowling."

"Right." Dave looked suspiciously like he was holding back a smirk. "One kiss. No big deal."

He scooted closer. Angela closed her eyes, lifted her face, and held her breath.

His lips were tender, a soft caress, almost as if he were afraid of hurting her. His hands slid up her back. Angela inhaled, giving her a lungful of Dave's cologne mixed with that certain something that was uniquely male. Her own arms went around Dave, and suddenly she wanted to breathe him in. New tears slid down her face. Dave's mouth left her lips and started kissing the salty tracks, gently erasing their traces.

Angela pressed him to her, curling her fingers into the fabric of his jacket.

Dave chuckled softly. "Is that a hint you'd like me to continue?"

"Shut up and kiss me," she breathed in his ear, and then gave herself over to the magic of the moment.

A strange rumbling noise pulled Angela from her slumber. Her pillow was vibrating.

Not vibrating. Snoring.

Dave. She'd kissed Dave.

And was now in his bed, using him as a pillow. A hot flush of horror ran through her. Dave snorted and brought an arm up, pulling her closer to him in his sleep.

In his sleep.

He'd been very tender and sweet last night. No raging passion or lust like the other men who had taken her to bed. It had definitely been making love on his part. He'd been filled with such surprise that she was really there. His utter joy had brought her to tears yet again. Dave had merely smiled, wiped them away, and gone back to caressing every inch of her, silencing the tiny voice deep inside her that whispered it was too good to be true.

In the quiet and still of the morning, the voice started up again. Angela wistfully ran her fingers through the dark hairs on Dave's chest. She could sense a proverbial shoe about to drop, but the reason why was out of reach.

Maybe Dave was right. Maybe she didn't think she was worthy of someone actually loving her.

Angela snuggled closer as if his presence could silence the voice.

"Umm?" Dave lifted a sleepy head and broke into a grin as his eyes met hers. "Morning," he said, and ran a hand through her hair, combing it back. He tucked a strand behind her ear.

"Morning."

"Feel like breakfast? I could make waffles. I have berries and yogurt. Or is that too healthy for you? I don't remember if there's any ice cream."

"Berries and yogurt are good."

Dave leaned forward and kissed her. "I'm glad you're here."

Angela took her usual spot on a stool at the counter, dressed in the spa robe Dave had added to the guest room as a present for Jenny. He padded about in flannel pajama bottoms and a T-shirt, his curly hair perfectly disheveled. It was just like that pancake ad she'd shot.

She sipped a latte and watched Dave work, attempted to shut out the nagging little voice, but it must have shown.

"You've got that look again," Dave said, one hand on his whisk, the other holding the bowl of waffle batter, a frown creeping his eyebrows together.

She lifted a shoulder but didn't meet his eyes. "You say I couldn't disappoint you…" Angela took a deep breath. Perhaps she could trust Dave with half the truth. "There's something wrong with me, you know. That's why they never stay. That's why my parents set up the parade." A lightning bolt of recognition shot through her and the shoe dropped.

Carlos. *Crap!*

The cool kitchen counter met her cheek as she fell forward. The whisk clinked as Dave let it go and set the bowl down next to her head. He stroked her hair, running his fingers through it, gently untangling the snarls that snagged his fingers. Her heart contracted. A ball of magic shot out. To where, she didn't know. Dave's fingers were untangling something tight in her chest as well as her hair.

He sighed. "I would love to track down everyone who's ever hurt you and make them pay. As for your parents…I guess they mean well, but parents don't often get their own children. I was treated to quite the lecture by my mother this Christmas on how my work habits would keep me forever single. She knew I wasn't gay since I'd already let several 'wonderful' women slip through my fingers."

Angela lifted her head. "Really?"

A wry smile twisted his face, and he gave a tight nod of confirmation. "Ouch."

"So for me, last night was kind of a minor miracle. My best friend actually wanted to be with me."

Angela bit back a smile. "That sounds so wrong."

"Hey, I could swing both ways," Dave said with a saucy grin. "But I don't. You, Angela Grimalke, are my best friend. And I'd like to keep you, always."

"Always is a long time."

"We'd need a long time, what with our work schedules. I'm perfectly happy sharing you with Windsor if you don't mind sharing me with corporations all over North America and Europe." He took her hands in his and gently caressed the backs with his thumbs.

There was a pleading look on his face that Angela wanted to reach up and smooth away. Then run her fingers through his curls. Then—

Pain curled in her stomach. Quite the opposite of the heat she was feeling further south. Angela glanced down. The edge of granite counter cut into her as she leaned across it, moving closer to Dave.

And she did want to be closer to Dave, as close as she'd been last night. Cover herself with him and let the magic tingle across her skin. Angela sighed as she savored the memory.

Dave's fingers slid up and began to caress her wrists. "So, what do you think?" His voice had turned husky. The granite bit deeper into her as she leaned even closer. His hands slid up her arms. Angela's chair inched back with a *screech* as she closed her eyes, searching out the source of the tingle, the scent of Dave's cologne filling her breaths.

She could share him.

A hiss, a crackle, and then a loud *pop!* jerked her eyes back open. Smoke and flames shot out from behind Dave. With a yelp, he whipped around and yanked the cord of the flaming waffle iron from its socket.

"Okay, okay." His chest heaved. His arms were outstretched, whether to protect her or have them ready to grab something, Angela couldn't tell.

"Baking soda works best," she said, offering her hard-won knowledge.

"Right. Right." Dave grabbed a box from the cupboard and shook it violently over the already dying fire.

Angela watched his ministrations and sighed. "I don't mind sharing you, but are you sure you can live with the minor disasters that follow me? Truly invite a jinx into your life?"

A chuckle started deep inside Dave and then bubbled up until he was bent over and wiping his eyes. "Well, New Year's certainly started with a bang. I hope you didn't have your heart set on waffles."

"Actually, I was thinking breakfast could wait. It's a sign that we shouldn't be in the kitchen."

"And where should we be?" Dave asked, his eyes beginning to smolder as much as the appliance behind him.

"Downstairs. Wait until the smoke has cleared."

"Uh huh. Wait until the smoke has cleared," Dave said and then leaned in and kissed her soundly.

It had been a wonderful beginning to the New Year but by mid-afternoon, the glow had been replaced by a familiar ache in the pit of her stomach. Carlos had texted Angela to wish her a happy New Year. She would need to reply. And he was just one of three phone calls she'd need to make.

Bars of lead added to the pit inside her as she got closer to her apartment. One bar when she stepped into the taxi. Two bars when she got out. Another when she opened the door to her building. Three bars in the elevator. Two more walking to her door.

Angela unlocked her door and dragged herself over to the sofa. She dropped onto it and tucked her cashmere coat closer.

But which of the three phone calls to make first? Kate—probably wouldn't be surprised she and Dave were now more than just friends. Carlos—disappointed considering how much she'd warmed during his last visit. Though—punch to her stomach—he wanted to marry her. Her parents—maybe she'd never tell them. Maybe she'd just move and never have to tell them. But Dave was here in New York, too. *Crap!* Definitely not telling her parents.

In the end, she made the easiest call first.

"I slept with Dave," Angela announced when Kate answered.

"Just slept with him?" Kate asked. "Or something more?"

Angela tucked the coat closer around her knees. "More."

"Good. About time you found someone who really cares for you. Assuming it was 'more' for Dave, too."

"Yup," Angela said, and blinked away a sting that rose in her eyes.

Kate gave a small sigh. "I told you months ago, Dave's good for you. It's always nice to come home to your best friend. Uh—" Kate's voice faded off. "You know what I mean."

Angela smiled. "I do. Thanks."

She held onto the glow as she dialed Carlos's number.

"Hello, beautiful. Happy New Year," he said.

Angela could hear a strange creaking. "Where are you?"

"Chair lift. The sky is a brilliant blue. The snow—drifts of sparkling powdered sugar. I'm communing with the magic of the mountain. What are you up to on this glorious first day of the new year?"

"Oh, a little of this and a little of that." Angela squirmed.

"Hopefully a little list of things we can do when I'm there in two weeks. Though I'd love to have you out here and show off my mountain. Do you ski?"

"Actually…" Angela twisted the lapel of her coat, working up her courage. "I thought I should tell you that I've met someone."

A clanging noise got louder which she could hear only too well as Carlos had fallen silent. As it receded, she could hear the crunch of snow.

"Does he know you are not human?" Carlos asked, after what seemed like forever.

"That doesn't matter."

"That would be a 'no'." Carlos made a small noise of frustration. "I like you because you're different. I want you because you are different. But humans…they kill what they do not understand. You know this. You have always felt different because of this."

"I've felt different because I'm not human!"

Carlos sighed. "I have spoken to Nicky. I know you have always hated the path you are on. But you are not human, my Angel. This will only bring you pain and frustration. You will either spend a lifetime hiding what you are or he will run from you in fear and disgust when he finds out, when he finds out you lied to him."

"It's not a lie!"

"Ah, but it is," Carlos said sadly. "We look like them but we are not them. The great design to let us move among them. There are those who remember and still look for us, but this modern man who you are seeing is not one of them and he will not understand. He thinks that you are something you are not, and to keep it from him is a lie. Will you tell him?"

Angela was unable to lift her tongue to answer.

"Call me when he does this. You belong here with me where the very air is filled with magic and the people remember who we are." Carlos gave a heavy sigh. "Until then, my Angel," he said and was gone.

Angela tucked her coat closer around her. A chill had settled into her bones. Must be the sleeveless silk dress she had on. Gremlin blood was resistant to cold but not immune, and the January air was well below freezing. A hot shower would soak a lot away. A hot shower and some soup. Dave was making soup today.

Angela pressed his number. "Is there enough for an extra spoon?" she asked when he answered. And then, to her horror, she heard herself sniff.

Dave exhaled, a quiet shush of air. "Plenty. Come on over."

A short time later, Dave handed Angela a steaming latte spiked with—

"Nutmeg?" she asked, frowning at the aroma.

"It's more subtle than cinnamon. Less cheering, more soothing." He sat down next to her. "You want to tell me what happened?"

Carlos's accusing words rang in her ears. Angela blinked back the rush of emotion and slowly shook her head.

Dave sighed and gently rubbed her back. "I can guess. So you told them?"

Told…them? *Oh, God!* Her parents. And dinner on Wednesday…

Dave took her lack of answer as confirmation. "You don't have to go on Wednesday, you know. You could have dinner with me instead. Give them some time to get used to the idea."

Angela let her head fall onto Dave's shoulder and indulged in the fantasy he offered. But what if it wasn't a fantasy? She hadn't always saved Wednesdays for her parents. And it wasn't even like they were family dinners now that Nicky was in Dublin.

Dinner with Dave.

She straightened up and blew on her latte. The scent of nutmeg rose with the steam and, as she breathed in the aroma, the knot in her heart loosened a little. Dave's fingers continued their magic traces on her back.

"Sounds wonderful."

26

Angela and Belle watched with mingled fascination and horror as Kate dug a giant glob of apricot jam from the jar she'd taken from her purse and smeared it on her waffle, the gooey mixture blending with the ice cream and chocolate sauce.

"What?" Kate asked in response to their frozen faces. "Pregnant women have cravings. I'm craving apricot jam. I even put it on my pizza last night."

"Right," Belle said with a small shake of her head, and turned her attention to her egg white omelet, her eyes still large. "Pizza. Sounds yummy."

"I don't think I've ever seen you eat waffles before," Angela said, unable to tear her eyes away as Kate cut off a large wedge and then raked ice cream and jam onto the piece before shoving it in her mouth.

"Yef I haf. I ufe to all veh time."

"So how is Dave?" Belle asked.

Angela took her time, slowly spreading her ice cream, making sure every cavity was filled before she answered. "Good. Good. We're going to London. I mean he's going to London and I'm meeting him there for business. *His* business," Angela amended as Kate and Belle's faces registered shock. An embarrassed tingle danced across her cheeks.

"You're going to work for Dave?" Belle asked.

"No, he's got a business trip and I'm meeting him there."

"Like Paris. Why didn't you just say so?" Kate asked with a smirk.

"I thought I did."

"No, you got your words and ideas all befuddled," Belle said, her lips disappearing as she tried to bite back a smile. "Someone's all befuddled."

Angela glanced between her friends as they desperately attempted, but failed, to keep from appearing like two giggling school girls. She shook her head. "What if I am? It's not like we're going away together. I'm meeting him on a business trip. And—" She raised her voice to cut off whatever Belle had opened her mouth to say. "As Dave pointed out, I've had a hell of a year and deserve a vacation."

Kate gave her a sad smile. "I take it your parents aren't happy about Dave."

Angela blinked and forcefully cut up her waffle. "No. No, they're not."

"That must make Wednesdays interesting," Belle said.

"For them maybe. I've decided to spend Dave's Wednesdays in New York with him. If Nicky gets to spend his Wednesdays with Claire then I get to spend mine with Dave."

"Nicky's in Dublin."

Angela's voice rose. "All the more reason for me to claim them. They can have the leftover ones as long as they're polite about it."

As the voices of the other diners reached her ears, she realized her own table had gone strangely quiet. Angela stopped cutting. Belle and Kate sat frozen, sharing a wide-eyed look.

"What? They've made me feel like crap this past year. Not that they intended to, I'm sure. But the whole parade thing and then getting huffy 'cause I picked Dave instead. If they won't let me live down Alex, then I'm just going to have to live without them."

Angela viciously attacked her waffle, her knife squeaking across her plate in its ferocity.

"Wow," Kate said softly. "I'd found the parade humorous. It never really occurred to me. But you're right. Where's their vote of confidence?"

"Nowhere," Angela said, blinking furiously, cutting her waffle into ever smaller pieces.

Belle reached out and put her hand on Angela's. "I'd stop there or you'll end up with soup."

"I don't know," Kate said. "Could become the newest taste sensation. Belgian waffle could replace caramel cone."

"As long as we go with hers. And not yours," Belle said, grimacing at Kate's.

Kate shoved another piece in her mouth and grinned. "Come on. You know you want to."

Angela watched Belle desperately trying to hoist up smile. "Maybe later. When I don't have a wedding dress to fit into."

Jackson had turned bright red with the effort to hide his laughter, a color Angela didn't often notice with his chai skin tone. She, on the other hand, was simply speechless.

Jimmy Heinz tugged surreptitiously at the place where his homemade edible underwear was sticking to his pants. He hadn't anticipated that the fruit leather would be likely to bond to clothing as well as skin.

Angela checked his booking. *Oh, my God.* Jimmy was headed to Miami.

"So, um…" Angela cleared her throat. "We have you booked for a window seat…" Jimmy's fingers crept back around and pulled at the seat of his pants. Angela closed her eyes and desperately tried to block out

Jimmy's broadcast wish to free several hairs that were now being held prisoner in a delicate area. "Are you sure you wouldn't like an aisle?"

"That might be handier," Jimmy said.

Angela changed the assignment and printed out his boarding pass. She took the luggage tag and looped it around the bag before heaving it, with a shudder, onto the belt behind her.

"Enjoy your flight, sir," Angela said, handing Jimmy's stack of documents to him.

Jimmy managed a half-hearted smile and limped off toward the men's room.

She jumped as Jackson clapped her soundly on the shoulder. "Buck up," he said. "Four more hours and I'll be checking you in."

Four more hours and then the club lounge where she'd toss back a pomegranate martini. Five more hours and she'd be curled up in a private pod, winging her way toward Dave and Julia. She could survive a few more hours.

"By the way, loved how you sent that last guy's bag to Anchorage. Too bad we couldn't misdirect him. By the time he gets to his hotel that underwear of his is going to be inextricable."

"Inextricable?" Angela asked with a puzzled frown.

"Best word I learned in Freshmen English. In a story by William Faulkner. Things become so blended you can't tell where one stops and the other begins."

"Let's just hope that doesn't include the seat in 29E," Angela said, watching Jimmy emerge from the men's room with a little more spring in his step.

Julia met her just outside customs and immigration. "There have to be some perks to working in an airport," she told Angela, taking her arm. "Hungry? I know a great place for breakfast. It should be quiet, all the businessmen off to their business."

"Sounds lovely," Angela said. "I ordered the continental so I could sleep awhile longer."

"Then let's take you off and fortify you."

They hopped the Heathrow Express back to Paddington Station where they picked up a cab. Julia had the cabbie swing by the hotel so Angela could drop off her luggage and have concierge take it up to her room, and then gave the cabbie the address of a small hotel not far from Portman Square.

The taxi turned down Old Quebec Street, away from the bustle of rush hour London. Birdsong greeted Angela as she exited the taxi. The inn's threshold created a portal of its own, dropping her into what felt like a country home. Wide plank floors echoed with their footsteps. A couple of retired gentlemen wearing coats with suede elbow patches lingered at a table by the window. Cheerful smiles rose on the men's faces as she and Julia entered, and they all exchanged a pleasant head bob.

"Morning, Julia," a white-aproned waiter said, and picked up two menus. "Usual table?"

"Yes, thanks, Perry."

Rustic tables filled the room. An old-fashioned cream bottle holding a few sprigs of daisies sat in the center of each. "I take it you eat here often," Angela said as she picked up her menu.

"A few times a month," her cousin answered. "They have a full English breakfast you can actually eat, and you feel like you've been on minibreak once you leave."

After perusing the farm-to-table menu, Angela ordered the buttermilk pancakes with cinnamon apples, caramel sauce, and vanilla mascarpone.

"Still not eating protein in the morning, I see," Julia said.

"They come with cheese. That's protein."

"Cream cheese. And it's a garnish."

Julia ordered the eggs Benedict and pot of English Breakfast tea for each of them.

"So, you've come to escape for a while," Julia said when they were alone again.

Angela nodded. "Mum and Dad have been impossible, and now that Nicky's in Dublin—" Julia blanched and quickly looked away. "What?"

"Nothing." Julia began to rearrange the daisies in the bottle.

Angela narrowed her eyes and then forced herself to shrug it off. She was here to relax and get away from the drama. "It was nice to get away back in November when I met Dave in Paris so when he suggested I come this time…It's been too long since I've had you to buck me up."

She had flown from Paris to London and spent two months crying on Julia's shoulder after she'd been fired from the modeling agency.

Julia stopped her rearranging. "Well, since you don't have any gremlin friends in New York, and Kate and Belle are…preoccupied…I know it's hard on you."

"What do you have planned for us?" Angela asked.

"Oh, a little of this and a little of that." Julia glanced away evasively. "Dave's given me his schedule so I know what I need to fill in."

Angela played with her teaspoon. "And what do you think of him?"

"Dave?" Julia chuckled lightly. "Dave's a kick. You could certainly do worse than Dave."

Angela was curled up reading a book when Dave finally came in. "Sorry I'm so late," he said, leaning in for a kiss.

"Didn't you tell them you had a beautiful blond waiting for you in your bed?"

Dave turned around. "You really want me to share that information?"

She raised a smile. "Might help."

"Well, I do have a make-up present for you." He reached into his coat pocket and pulled out a long envelope.

With a puzzled glance, she took it from him. Angela slid the flap open with her finger and pulled out a piece of cardstock—a voucher for the famous chocolate tea at one of London's hotels.

"You can go direct to the source this time," Dave said. "And they have special packaging for leftovers, though you will need to share. You and Julia have reservations for two o'clock tomorrow."

Dave unknotted and slid off his tie. He opened the closet door, hung it on a special tie rack he'd brought with him, and slipped off his jacket. Angela tucked the voucher back in the envelope and placed it on the nightstand. Dave had his arm twisted around, undoing the buttons on his cuffs, when she looked back up.

"Need any help with those buttons?" Angela asked, drawing up her legs and tilting her head.

A slow smile spread across Dave's face.

"Sure, if you're offering."

Angela lay in bed long after Dave had kissed her goodbye the next morning. How could he be so chipper after the time change? Even though she'd set her watch to London time as soon as she'd boarded the plane, her body still screamed it was one-thirty when the bedside clock insisted it was six-thirty.

The alarm went off at eight. She found a note from Dave stuck to it. He'd set the alarm so she'd be forced to get up and move. Angela threw clothes on and headed downstairs for breakfast. It would have been way too tempting to crawl back in bed if she'd ordered room service.

Fog still filled her brain as she exited the elevator.

Until she caught sight of the dark-haired man sitting in a chair just a few feet away. *Nicky.*

He looked up just as she took a step back into the elevator.

"Oh, no, you don't!" he said, rising. "I've been camped out here since six-thirty waiting for you. You're going to buy me breakfast."

A moan materialized despite her attempt to suppress it. She stepped out of the elevator. "Nice to see you, too," she said, without bothering to hide her insincerity. "What are you doing here?"

"What? My sister comes to my neck of the woods and I can't come say 'hello'?"

"Your neck of the woods is in a different country."

"True. But it's the first opportunity I've had in three months."

"Yes," Angela said. "But planes fly both directions."

"Oh, look at you! So wise, now that you work for an airline." He put an arm around her. "Come on, I'm starving!"

Nicky kept his hand on the small of her back as he guided her into the restaurant and didn't let go of her until he'd pushed her chair in.

Angela bit back the sarcastic comment that sprang to her lips. Best not to have her fears confirmed.

"How is Dublin?" she asked, and picked up her menu.

"Wonderful! Don't miss New York at all."

Angela looked over the menu and frowned. What the hell? There was nothing remotely normal on it. *Spiced red wine poached tamarillo with Greek yoghurt and Manuka honey.* What the heck was tamarillo? Their waffle was made with corn meal, green chili, and feta. She scanned the eggs. The fry-up came with grilled chorizo, caramelized plantain fritters, and slow-roasted, vine-ripened tomatoes.

Giving up, she ordered the pain au chocolate and a pot of coffee.

"Not being more adventurous?" Nicky commented. "I thought you were doing lots of cooking with Management Boy."

Her eyes narrowed. Apparently, Nicky had been talking to Jackson. Another conversation he'd had behind her back.

"Not for breakfast," she said, letting his use of the nickname slide. "The day should be started with dessert, otherwise what's the reason for getting out of bed?"

"Oh, there's lots of good reasons to stay in bed." Nicky smoldered at her. "I thought you would have discovered that by now. Or was your bed cold this morning?"

"You leave my bed out of this." Angela snapped her napkin open. "Going to tell me why you're here? And don't bother saying it's just brotherly love."

Nicky steepled his hands on the table and rested his chin on them. "But it is. You've turned down a very delightful chap for a human."

Carlos—very delightful? "I picked the man who wanted me."

"Carlos wanted—wants—you. He knows more about you than this Dave."

"Dave likes me the way I am."

A disbelieving bark of a laugh erupted from her brother. "Right. Until he finds out what you are."

Angela ground her teeth and then hauled up a smile as their waiter returned with their drinks.

"The thing that really irritates me—" she said, stirring her coffee a little too forcefully.

"You're going to spill," Nicky said just as it sloshed over the edge.

"Thanks," Angela said sarcastically. She wiped off the bottom of the cup with her napkin. "What gets me is that if it were you fooling around with a human, no one would say boo."

"So you are fooling around," Nicky countered.

Angela closed her eyes and counted to three. Then five more.

"Look, I get that you love me and want the best for me. I will acknowledge that you have gone above and beyond trying to make me happy."

"I knew Carlos was good," Nicky said. Angela wiped the grin off his face with one look.

"But I am a grown woman and get to make my own decisions. If I fall flat on my face, then I'm the one who has to live with it. Not you, not Mum, not Dad. Your well-intentioned interfering has made me feel like crap this year." Angela inhaled deeply. "Dave doesn't make me feel like crap. He thinks I'm wonderful. And I've made a New Year's resolution to only speak to people who make me feel wonderful," she said, making it up on the spot. Hey, it was January. New Year's resolutions weren't exclusive to the first. She sat up a bit taller. "So, I'd watch what you say or you may just finish this breakfast on your own."

Nicky's eyes had grown so wide that the little arteries normally hidden off to the side were visible. "Wow! You've grown a pair since I last saw you."

"When you know your value anything is possible," Angela said.

Nicky gave a little shiver. "Okay, that was definitely Management Boy. He's…he's…he may actually be good for you," Nicky conceded. Angela accepted the compliment with a nod of her head. "Just…be careful, okay Ang? I don't want to see you hurt again."

Angela waited that afternoon until they'd finished their sandwiches and the waitress had brought out their tea tray before confronting Julia.

"You knew Nicky was in town," she said as Julia snagged the Battenberg slice.

Julia's cheeks flushed with guilt. "Yes, he wormed the name of your hotel out of me two days ago. Why? Did he call?"

"No, he ambushed me on my way to breakfast this morning."

Julia held out the shortbread butterfly in silent question. Angela shook her head.

"I think he feels guilty," Julia said, putting it on her plate. "He left town and you were floundering a bit."

"He set me up with Kokopeli." Angela picked up the Sacher Torte and cut off a chunk with her fork.

"Really! Is he as hunky as his reputation?"

"Yep. Mr. Greek God of the Desert."

Julia helped herself to the raspberry cupcake. "So you turned down your own Prince Harry."

"Julia, Carlos makes Nicky look like a nerd."

Julia froze mid-bite. She recovered but chewed and swallowed slowly. "Okay, so the man's good looking. But you were interested in…?"

Angela finished her torte and licked the chocolate off her fork. "The family have all warned me off of Dave, of humans. But you know Dave. You told me I could do worse than him."

"Are you asking about long-term or short-term?"

"Long-term?" Angela said.

"At some point you'll need to tell him," Julia said.

"And how does that usually work out?"

"Well, it doesn't happen very often, one of our kind picking a human. Human women generally don't care. Human men…Well, it takes a remarkable man to partner with a powerful woman no matter the species. Generally, it doesn't work out very well."

The torte settled into her stomach like a lead weight. Or maybe that was her heart.

"I'm not saying it won't," Julia continued. "But at some point, you're going to come to a hard decision with the potential of an unhappy outcome. Not to mention the potential for posts that would make the "Supermassive Black Hole" dedication look like a ringing endorsement."

Angela pictured the tabloid headlines—*My Girlfriend's a Gremlin Claims Top International Businessman.* She buried her face in her hands. "Oh, God!"

"You see why they haven't been too keen. But Dave is different. And he likes you a lot. Why not just see where it goes?"

Julia buttered a chocolate chip scone with praline chocolate and handed it to Angela. At least she could drown her fears in chocolate.

London was not Paris. Nicky's visit and the new realization of just how badly the relationship could end kept it from being the celebration Angela had hoped for, but she hid it from Dave. Mostly. It was easier to block out the nagging little voices in her head when she was wrapped in Dave's arms, and he didn't comment on her mood, if it showed.

Julia had sent her off with a hug and an assurance that "all will be fine," much as she had three years before when she'd packed Angela off to New York and her new job at Windsor.

And things were fine. Until the end of March when Dave returned from Detroit with a proposal for Angela.

"Move in with me," he told her while they sat on his sofa, enjoying a cup of coffee after dinner. "I want what we had in London. I want to come home to you."

"Are you forgetting about my late nights?" Angela asked. "I don't get home 'til nearly midnight three days a week."

Dave tried to brush her fears away with a shake of his head. "So you'd come home to me. But I'd still get to wake up with you every morning I'm in town." He scooted closer and took her hand. "I don't want to miss any more moments than I have to."

It was a test, she pulled from his brain. He had a different proposal in mind but was afraid the reality of living with him would not match what he feared her expectations would be. Angela could see his point. Half the pilots at Windsor were divorced, their wives having discovered that being married to someone who was frequently gone was not the glamorous lifestyle they'd imagined.

But if she moved in, knowing that Dave intended this to be one step away from walking down an aisle, then she needed to decide if she could marry this man. Or, more importantly, if she could tell him the truth.

"I have to think about it," Angela said. "It's a big step. I haven't lived with a man before."

Dave tilted her toward him and kissed the top of her head. "Take all the time you need."

Angela decided she needed a test run of the conversation. If she was going to tell Dave what she really was, she should probably start with someone who'd be more understanding. She called Kate. Then opened a bottle of wine and drank half of it out of nerves before Kate got there, though being drunk would offer the perfect excuse for her outrageous claims.

Kate, however, wasn't surprised.

"A gremlin, huh. I just thought you were a witch." Angela's eyes boggled. "A bad one. Not evil," Kate quickly amended. "Just not a very good one. Your being a witch explained all the funny things that happen when you're around."

"When did you start to think this?"

"Oh, that first year at Hewitt. I felt like I was living in my own version of *Sabrina.*"

"But you never said anything!"

"Hey, didn't want you running off if you knew I'd discovered your secret. It was better to keep my knowledge to myself and keep you around." Kate's head shook from side to side. "Gremlin," she said. "That I never would have guessed."

"So do I tell him? Or not?" Angela asked.

Kate reached a hand out for Angela's wine glass and then stopped herself. "I miss wine," she said with a little pout. "So you think this is one step away from marriage?" Kate asked.

"I know it is. I pulled it right from his brain."

Kate's eyes bugged. "You can read minds?" she said, aghast.

"Ye-e-e-s-s," Angela said.

"How often have you read mine?"

Angela squinched up her nose as she thought.

"Not often, obviously," Kate answered for her.

"I try not to. Which is my biggest problem. All those things that happen around me happen because I don't like to use my magic."

"Why not?"

"I didn't like the way I saw it being used by kids at school. The school I went to before Hewitt."

"I thought you went to some Hungar—" Kate broke off as the penny dropped. "Oh…How many of you *are* around?"

"A few," Angela said.

"A few? There were—are—apparently enough around for a whole school in New York. So who else is a gremlin? Nicky, of course. And your parents. And your uncle!" Kate's eyes somehow managed to grow even wider. "Oh, my God! An airline run by gremlins! Are all airlines run by gremlins?"

"No." Angela bit back a smile. "Just the one. Though we do love to work with things mechanical."

Kate's facial expression changed with every thought. "So you work with mechanical things. You…you send bags to Cleveland. On purpose!"

"Got to keep my Cousin Wendell busy."

Kate's eyes bugged again. Unseeing, she reached out for the wine and had the glass halfway to her mouth before Angela took it away.

"Let's try these instead." Angela opened the large tin of chocolate olives Dave had brought back from Paris two weeks before. Kate grabbed a handful and started shoving them into her mouth, one after the other, somehow managing to chew before she swallowed. Angela hopped up and got her a glass of water to wash them down with.

After a while Kate slowed down. She shook her head. "There's a whole world out there I never knew existed. How much of those old stories is real?"

"Myths, unlike fables, are generally based in truth. Gremlins evolved as humans poured their energy into mechanical things. We're there to balance out human nature. Reflect the good and the bad. You can tell Nicky has siren genes."

"Sirens are real, too?"

If Kate's eyes grew any larger, they'd pop right out of her head. "Why do you think everyone lusts after Charlize Theron?"

"Oh. Wow." Kate chewed a couple more olives. A slow smile spread across her face. "So who else? Who else is magical?"

"Steve Jobs was a gremlin."

"Really!"

"Why do you think Apple doesn't get the Blue Screen of Death? He programmed it to be more reliable. Though the gremlins at Microsoft have lots of fun writing code that shuts the computer down if the person types too hard, hasn't saved in a while, or gets frustrated."

"There are gremlin nerds, too?"

"My parents set me up with a few. A Microsoftie who spent the whole dinner talking about the eleven dimensions of reality. There was one who taught at MIT."

Kate grabbed a few more olives out of the tin. Angela held back a sigh at how the level was dropping. This might be the last can she had for a while depending on what happened with her source.

Kate's consumption slowed down. She drank half the glass of water. "So you've got an even bigger problem than Dave. You've got your parents not wanting you to be with…a human?" Angela gave a nod of confirmation. "If Dave sticks around, you'll need to battle your parents. And if Dave leaves…"

Angela's heart clenched so tightly her breath caught in her throat. "Then they were right all along."

Angela sent Kate on her way with the remainder of the chocolate olives. She didn't want them sitting on her table as a reminder if things went badly after her revelation to Dave and, if they didn't, she had an easy import source. It was still another hour before she could pick up her phone and call him.

"Can I come talk to you?" she asked, her voice choked with nerves.

"Sure." Dave sounded funny, but then the loud whining buzz in her head was probably fiddling with her hearing.

Every foot Angela put toward the door made the other one want to pull her in the direction of her bed. Her heart kept voting for her to stay home and just bury herself under the covers, afraid this would be the last time she'd leave for Dave's. Her brain made her go. Dave deserved this.

She was sure her face was swollen and puffy by the time Dave let her in. He took one look at her and opened the door wider. Angela didn't see his expression. Her eyes refused to rise any higher than the floor. She trudged in and curled up on the sofa. Dave lowered himself into a chair across from her. The gulf between them widened.

"I need to tell you something since you want me to move in."

"Okay," Dave said cautiously.

"The stuff that happens around me…there's a reason for it." Out of the corner of her eye, Angela saw Dave bend forward and rest his arms on his legs. "It's going to sound crazy but…" Angela screwed up her eyes and her courage. "I'm not human."

Dave made a sound as though she'd punched him. He let out a huge whoosh of air and sat back. "What?"

"I'm not human. I'm…a gremlin."

Angela could hear Dave making little gasping sounds, unable to formulate a reply but trying. She looked up as he sat forward again, massaging his brow.

"Wow. That's just…" He trailed off and shook his head. "I don't get it. I don't get why you'd make up such a story…It's beyond cruel."

Angela choked back a sob and struggled to pull up magic. It kept slipping from her control, sliding back to protect the heart she felt breaking. With a lurch and a twirl of her finger, she sent it to the Nespresso frother.

Dave jumped as the machine sprang to life, grinding away with a high-pitched whine. Horror slid across the features of his face as he rose and marched across the room. With a yank, he jerked the cord from the outlet, but the frother continued spinning.

Dave slowly turned around, his mouth agape, and her world crumbled.

Her cheeks stung when Angela opened her eyes the next morning. Had Dave slapped her? She lifted a hand, gingerly touching them, flinching when her fingers found places that burned. From what?

Angela heaved herself out of bed and shuffled into the bathroom. Red eyes framed by swollen lids stared back at her from the mirror. Tears had rubbed her cheeks raw, not a hand. She stifled another sob.

How had she gotten home? She couldn't remember. She couldn't remember much of anything. Only the look Dave had given her when he'd turned back around.

The floor rushed toward her as her knees gave out. She grabbed the edge of the sink as she went down, fresh tears coursing down her face.

As the cool tile of the floor called to her, Angela let the porcelain slip past her fingers and sank onto the floor. Curling into a ball, she eased the rug out from under her and clutched it to her like a doll. This was what they'd wanted to save her from, her parents and Nicky. Their overprotectiveness had wanted to save her from this.

She lay there until her hip screamed in agony. Angela pushed herself up. A heaviness had settled into her soul. Her heart pulsed, beating in irregular thumps. She lurched her way back to the bedroom and threw herself on the bed. Death would be easier than this.

But she didn't die. Gradually, her body adjusted to the ache in her chest. Her brain began to work again. Life in New York would never be the same. How could she keep doing her job? Constantly seeing Dave, if he didn't change airlines.

It would be better to leave.

He will run from you in fear and disgust when he finds out, when he finds out you lied to him.

Carlos's prediction rang in her ears. He'd known this was going to happen.

And had left the door open for her.

A spark of hope took hold, held captive by the state of fear her body was in, but it was there, the possibility of a life with a man who wanted her.

In New Mexico. Did she want a life in New Mexico?

There was only one way to find out.

Angela left her phone on the hall table, a hastily scribbled note to Kate beneath it. Kate would come looking for her, become concerned when Angela didn't answer. She didn't say where she was going, just that she needed some time to figure things out.

She locked her door and wheeled her suitcase down and out of her building, catching a cab to the Chelsea car rental company she knew didn't have gremlins working at it. An hour later, with Albuquerque plugged into the car's GPS, Angela set off. She drove two days straight, stopping only for gas and bathroom breaks, hitting drive-through restaurants when she grew hungry, pulling up magic to ward off sleep and get her there faster.

She dropped down from the Sandias into Albuquerque just as the sun was setting behind the mesas in the west, the sky the most rich, full red she'd ever seen. She checked into a hotel, got a room with a view of Sandia Peak, and watched the stars come out, standing at the window. The hair on her arms tingled with magic as she watched the sky darken, become a deep, velvet blue. Hold its own against the lights that came on in the city.

The last of her magic finally dripped away and begged to be refilled. She closed the curtains, took her first shower in three days, and fell into bed.

There were Belgian waffles on the breakfast menu at the hotel restaurant, but Angela passed. They were only a reminder of what she'd be giving up if she moved here. Instead, she ordered the scrambled eggs with corn tortillas, cheddar and cotija cheese, and green chile. After breakfast, she browsed through the rack of flyers by the check-in counter and decided how to spend the day.

The sun was brighter than any place she'd ever been except Morocco, but it didn't beat down as harshly. She took the tram to the top of Sandia Peak. There was a spiciness to the air, a hint of creosote and pinyon pine. Angela breathed it in and turned her face to the sun. Her chest lifted and her spine straightened in a sun salutation.

The ground tingled beneath her feet. Magic danced on her fingertips. Carlos had been right—the very air was filled with enchantment. Angela breathed deep and allowed it to enter, to replenish what she'd lost on her marathon drive.

She set out on the hiking trail, throwing a nervous glance at the rattlesnake warning sign. They'd be out now, soaking up the sun, energizing themselves for the day, just like her. Hiking had never been her thing, but here it felt right. Felt necessary.

Though these trails would not be the ones she'd wander. Carlos lived further north, toward Taos.

Angela continued down the trail, moving with a grace that had eluded her on the runway. What to do next?

She spent the afternoon strolling through Old Town, had dinner at an outdoor café. She ordered blue corn enchiladas, ate sopapillas for dessert. Tomorrow she would move north, to Santa Fe, though she half-feared Carlos would feel her come. She wasn't yet ready to make a decision.

The wind picked up in the morning. Angela watched a dust storm gather, blocking out her view of the volcanic fields to the west of the highway as she followed Interstate 25 north. Magic waxed and waned as she drove. She could feel it more in the mountains, less in the flat, dusty expanses, though even those still somehow felt full.

The GPS in her car guided her to a hotel picked from one of the flyers she'd looked at the day before. Angela booked a room with a fireplace and set out to explore the old section of the city.

Galleries lined every block, filled with every kind of art imaginable. Never before had she seen so much creativity crammed into one place. The air thrummed with excitement. And yet something serene. Something, she had come to realize, that was just this Land of Enchantment.

Her heart sent out tendrils, pulling the place even closer. Small things called to her—a belt of silver and turquoise, a floaty skirt, a clay pot etched with chains of hummingbirds. Pieces that began to create a life for her outside of New York.

And she'd have Carlos, a man that made her skin sing, a man who thought she was extraordinary, in this place where life seemed simple. She would grow to love him as they built a life together. Wasn't that how it happened in arranged marriages?

She left the next day, left without calling Carlos. She'd make her final decision when she was back in New York, back where the magic wasn't filling her every pore. Back in reality.

CALL ME RIGHT AWAY!!!!!! Kate had scribbled on the note Angela had left. Angela tossed her keys into the bowl, picked up her phone, and wheeled her suitcase into her room. She plugged her phone into the charger and waited for it to turn on.

Seventeen missed calls. Twenty-three text messages. Voicemails.

Angela ignored them all and called Kate.

"I'm back."

"Thank God!" Kate took a deep breath and exhaled. "You do realize that stress is bad for pregnant people."

"Sorry." Angela wound her finger through the charger cord.

"I can guess where you went. You didn't do anything rash, did you?"

"I wanted to know if I could live there."

"And?"

"I could."

"Did you talk to Carlos?" Kate asked.

"No," Angela said. "I wanted this to be me making the decision, not his irresistible magnetism."

Kate gave a small huff of amusement. "Good thinking." There was a long pause. "It's good…because you need to talk to Dave."

Angela's heart went into fight or flight mode. Mostly flight. "What if I don't want to?"

"You sprang some big news on him. Bigger than it was for me since I already—"

"Thought I was a witch," Angela finished for her.

"Thought you were otherworldly. Dave hadn't had time to figure that out. You just sprung it on him. A necessity," Kate said, drowning out Angela's started protest. "But not something he'd been expecting to hear." Kate swallowed a couple of times then said, "He'd thought you were going to be like Lauren and the rest, dumping him. Though that's really his story to tell. Call him, sweetie. He deserves a chance to be heard."

Instead, Angela went over. Dave canceled his trip to Geneva, Kate had told her, wanting to be in town, waiting for news that Angela was okay, her disappearing act having caused many people a lot of worry.

Dave crushed her to him with an, "Oh, thank God!" before releasing her like the hot handle of one of his pans. He took several steps back and raised his hands. "Sorry, sorry!" His breathy words were said to the ground.

"Can I come in?" Angela asked.

"Sure, sure." Dave backed further into the kitchen, leaving her to close the door or keep it open.

Angela gently closed it behind her.

Dave wouldn't look at her. He stood by the island, one shaking hand on the counter. "Sorry I didn't take things very well," he said.

"It was a lot to spring on you."

He shook his head back and forth, blinking back tears. "All my life I'd so envied the Littles, wishing that if I couldn't be Stuart that I'd at least have the chance to get to know someone like him." Dave clenched his jaw. "And when I do, when I find out the best thing in my life is Stuart, that you *are* Stuart, I FREAK OUT...and then you were gone," Dave said, choking on the last word.

"Sorry," Angela said. She gasped, fighting back the rising sobs. "I didn't think you wanted me."

"Not want you?" Dave said. He was there in an instant, crushing her to him again. "When you're everything I've ever wished for?"

His warm, strong arms held her up as her legs gave way. Years of anguished sobs surged up and carried her away. But Dave kept her grounded, kept her safe as the torrent of pain raged through her.

If he hadn't been there, she would have died. But he was, kissing the top of her head and crying with her, rocking her gently. When she finally turned a tear-stained face to him, Dave looked at her with an expression of such love and longing that Angela couldn't wait a moment longer to have his lips on her. She pulled them to her and crushed him against her.

There was no need to hide who she was. Home. She was finally home.

Angela leaned her head against Dave's shoulder. Could there be a more beautiful setting? The weather had been perfect all day, and Angela had managed to not fall in when she'd stepped in and out of the gondola this afternoon.

Candles now flickered on all of the tables. Much like the bubbles of happiness that rippled inside her as she watched Joe lead Belle onto the dance floor.

Dave brought his lips close to her ear. "When are you going to tell them?"

Slowly, so as not to bop his nose, she lifted her head and met his eyes. "You don't break the news of a new engagement at a wedding."

Dave's eyes twinkled and a crooked smile lifted his mouth. "Can I help it if I want to tell the world?"

Angela wanted to tell the world, too. Though she suspected that her mother already knew, had already pulled the information right out of Dave's brain. There had been the malfunction of the photographer's camera, after all. Both Kate and Belle had looked at her when he'd had to pull out another one, surprised that the battery had suddenly drained.

She wrapped her hands around Dave's and stared at the joy on Belle's face. Her heart swelled. Angela did want to tell the world how Dave had taken her hands this morning as she had adjusted his tie, how he'd stared into her eyes, and said, "Marry me." Sure, she'd fried out all the lightbulbs in the room with her shock, but Dave hadn't cared. The quirk of his lips was all she had needed to say "yes."

Angela returned her head to Dave's shoulder. She had everything she had ever wanted. So why was there a niggling little ache in her stomach?

Carlos.

Dave rubbed Angela's hand as if he sensed the change in her mood.

With her "yes" to Dave, she was firmly turning her back on the magical life her family had wanted for her. Well, as firmly as she could since her magic would always be with her. It still caused an ache, knowing she had hurt Carlos. Had she been a better gremlin, they would have built a life together. Angela sent out a little prayer wrapped in magic. *Help him find someone who loves him as much as Dave loves me.*

The music changed, and Angela teared up as she recognized the song. The waltz from New Year's.

"Hey, my beautiful mouse," Dave said in her ear. "Would you like to dance with me?"

Angela reached out to cup his face. "Always."

www.ingramcontent.com/pod-product-compliance
Lightning Source LLC
Chambersburg PA
CBHW051634180726
48284CB00006B/1725